THE PLAYBOY BOOK OF
CRIME
AND
SUSPENSE

THE PLAYBOY BOOK OF

CRIME
AND
SUSPENSE

SELECTED BY THE EDITORS OF
PLAYBOY

A PLAYBOY PRESS BOOK

Cover Illustration: Richard Tyler

Copyright© 1966 by HMH Publishing Co. Inc. All rights reserved. From PLAYBOY® magazine: Copyright© 1955, 1956, 1957, 1958, 1959, 1960, 1961, 1962, 1963, 1964 by HMH Publishing Co. Inc.

Published simultaneously in the United States and Canada by Playboy Press, Chicago, Illinois. Printed in the United States of America.

Playboy Press hardcover edition published 1966. Playboy Press softcover edition published 1968.

CONTENTS

PREFACE

WE ARE ALL CRIMINALS, potentially. Temptation tugs at us twenty-four hours a day, awake or asleep, and the seeds of corruption lie patiently in our hearts, waiting to burst and blossom into flowers of evil. And, just as we are all potential criminals, so we are all potential victims, too.

If these home truths did not obtain, nobody would read stories of crime and suspense. But they are read, avidly, because they serve to remind us that, even in our most humdrum routines, we live on the brink of danger, we are dangled over the pit of iniquity.

Newspaper editors have always known this. Crimes are front-page news—crimes of passion, crimes for gain, crimes for kicks, and the larger crimes of war. Accounts of these crimes are good for newspaper circulation. They are good for the readers' circulation, too, for they provide healthy and legitimate catharsis, an innocent way of siphoning off our own buried hostilities and antisocial tendencies. Recently, a writer who had hitherto enjoyed only the limited rewards available to a weaver of fragile fiction made himself a cool million and became a national figure by writing a detailed, book-length report of a multiple murder: Truman Capote's *In Cold Blood*.

So it goes: "Here's to crime" is a toast so common it's banal —are we completely in jest when we say it? *Crime and Punishment* is an acknowledged masterpiece. Certainly Ernest Hemingway's most celebrated short story is *The Killers*. And, unless we are greatly mistaken, nobody ever wrote a play called *Macduff*.

Stories of crime and suspense, therefore, are by no means

vii

caviar: They are bread-and-butter—staples of television, the movies, the stage and the popular magazines, both slick and pulp, as well as being the bulwarks of the world's classic literature, mythology and grand opera. But a PLAYBOY story of this stripe is usually distinguished by an important and refreshing difference: a point of view not clouded by hypocrisy, not distorted by prefabricated moral judgments. PLAYBOY recognizes that there is a wild and nonconformist part of us all that hopes against hope that retribution isn't as inevitable as run-of-the-police-blotter detective novels and movie makers and J. Edgar Hoover say it is; a part of us that silently cheers the outlaw because he is a maverick who defies and flouts authority as we might wish to if society and our innate ethics did not prevent us. And as for The Shadow's quaint old cackle that "Crime doesn't pay," only a very naive person, surely, could deny that crime often goes undetected, unpunished, and often pays very well, indeed.

Consider, for example, the blithe and likable vigilantes of *The Morning After*, in the pages ahead; or the jolly GI avengers of *With All Due Respect*; the doomed innocent of *The Bottom of the Ocean*; the secret and profane pleasures of *Naked in Xanadu*; the evil wrought with complete impunity by *The Distributor*; the literally and figuratively chilling turning-of-tables at the end of *A Cry from the Penthouse*—to name but a few tart tales that would be tolerated at your neighborhood bijou only after thorough emasculation.

In this book, some of the master storytellers of our time have assembled to make you pleasantly uneasy. Ian Fleming, Fredric Brown, Charles Beaumont, Steve Allen, Herbert Gold, Ken W. Purdy, Richard Matheson, Ray Russell, Gerald Kersh—these and many others will tell you no one is immune, no place is safe, nothing is above suspicion. Some of their stories may make you say, with a sigh of relief, there-but-for-the-grace-of-God-go-I. Others may remind you of your friends. Still others may remind you of your enemies (you have no

viii

enemies? don't be so sure). Above all, these stories will excite and entertain you as they artfully drive home their inescapable point:

At home, at the office, in a bar, on a street, on a business trip, on vacation—it could happen to you.

—the editors of PLAYBOY

THE HILDEBRAND RARITY

BY IAN FLEMING

The moderately popular adventures of 007 suddenly zoomed to feverish fame when John F. Kennedy, in his first year as President, publicly expressed a liking for them. PLAYBOY had expressed a liking for them some time before that— by publishing, early in 1960, the James Bond novelette that opens this volume, as well as by playing host to Mr. Fleming when he visited Chicago to gather research for his non-fiction book, "Thrilling Cities" (in which PLAYBOY, PLAYBOY's pretty secretaries, PLAYBOY's editors and Contributing Editor Charles Beaumont are all prominently mentioned.) "The Hildebrand Rarity" was the first Fleming story to appear in PLAYBOY, but a far cry from the last. PLAYBOY also published, before and after his untimely death, the novels and novelettes "On Her Majesty's Secret Service," "You Only Live Twice," "The Man with the Golden Gun," "The Property of a Lady" and (in 1966) "Octopussy." In the following story, James Bond takes a trip to Chagrin with a blonde, a brute and death.

THE STING RAY was about six feet from wing tip to wing tip and perhaps ten feet long from the blunt wedge of its nose to the end of its deadly tail. It was dark gray with that violet tinge that is so often a danger signal in the underwater world. When it rose up from the pale, golden sand and swam a little distance, it was as if a black towel were being waved through the water.

James Bond, his hands along his flanks and swimming with only a soft trudge of his fins, followed the black shadow across the wide, palm-fringed lagoon, waiting for a shot. He rarely killed fish except to eat, but there were exceptions: big moray eels and all the members of the scorpion fish family. Now he proposed to kill the sting ray because it looked so extraordinarily evil.

It was ten o'clock in the morning of a day in April and the lagoon, Belle Anse near the southernmost tip of Mahé, the largest island in the Seychelles group, was glassy calm. The northwest monsoon had blown itself out months before and it would be May before the southeast monsoon brought refreshment. Now the temperature was eighty in the shade and the humidity ninety, and the enclosed water of the lagoon was near blood heat. Even the fish seemed to be sluggish. A ten-pound green parrot fish, nibbling algae from a lump of coral, paused only to roll its eyes as Bond passed overhead, and then went back to its meal. A school of fat gray chub, swimming busily, broke courteously in half to let Bond's shadow by, and then joined up and continued on their opposite course. A chorus line of six small squids, normally as shy as birds, did not even bother to change their camouflage at his passage.

Bond trudged lazily on, keeping the sting ray just in sight. Soon it would get tired or else be reassured when Bond, the big fish on the surface, did not attack. Then it would settle onto a patch of flat sand, change its camouflage down to the palest, almost translucent gray and, with soft undulations of its wing tips, bury itself in the sand.

The reef was coming nearer and now there were outcrops of coral niggerheads and meadows of sea grass. It was like arriving in a town from open country. Everywhere the jeweled reef fish twinkled and glowed and the giant anemones of the Indian Ocean burned like flames in the shadows. Colonies of spined sea eggs made sepia splashes as if someone had thrown ink against the rock, and the brilliant blue and yellow feelers of langoustes quested and waved from their crevices like small dragons. Now and then, among the seaweed on the brilliant floor, there was the speckled glitter of a cowrie bigger than a golf ball—the leopard cowrie—and once Bond saw the beautiful splayed fingers of a Venus' harp. But all these things were now commonplace to him and he drove steadily on, interested in the reef only as cover through which he could get to seaward of the ray and then pursue it back toward the shore. The tactic worked and soon the black shadow and its pursuing brown torpedo were moving back across the great blue mirror. In about 12 feet of water the ray stopped for the hundredth time. Bond stopped also, treading water softly. Cautiously he lifted his head and emptied water out of his goggles. By the time he looked again the ray had disappeared.

Bond had a Champion harpoon gun with double rubbers. The harpoon was tipped with a needle-sharp trident—a short-range weapon but the best for reef work. Bond pushed up the safety and moved slowly forward, his fins pulsing softly just below the surface so as to make no sound. He looked around him, trying to pierce the misty horizons of the great hall of the lagoon. He was looking for any big lurking shape. It would not do to have a shark or a large barracuda as witness to the kill. Fish sometimes scream when they are hurt, and even when they do not the turbulence and blood caused by a sharp struggle bring the scavengers. But there was not a living thing in sight and the sand stretched away into the smoky wings like the bare boards of a stage. Now Bond could see the faint outline on the bottom. He swam directly over it and lay motionless on the surface looking down. There was a tiny movement in the sand. Two minute fountains of sand were dancing above the nostril-like holes of the spiracles. Behind the holes was the slight swelling of the thing's body. That was the target. An inch behind the holes. Bond estimated the possible upward lash of the tail and slowly reached his gun down and pulled the trigger.

Below him the sand erupted and for an anxious moment Bond could see nothing. Then the harpoon line came taut and the ray showed, pulling away from him while its tail, in reflex aggression, lashed again and again over the body. At the base of the tail Bond could see the jagged poison spines standing up from the trunk. These were the spines that were supposed to have killed Ulysses, that Pliny said would destroy a tree. In the Indian Ocean, where the sea poisons are at their most virulent, one scratch from the ray's sting would mean certain death. Cautiously, keeping the ray on a taut line, Bond trudged after the furiously wrestling fish. He swam to one side to keep the line away from the lashing tail which could easily sever it. This tail was the old slave-drivers' whip of the Indian Ocean. Today it is illegal even to possess one in the Seychelles, but they are handed down in the families for use on faithless wives and if the word goes round that this or that woman "*a cu la crapule,*" the Provençal name for the sting ray, it is as good as saying that that woman will not be about again for at least a week. Now the lashes of the tail were getting weaker and Bond swam round and ahead of the ray, pulling it after him toward the shore. In the shallows the ray went limp and Bond pulled it out of the water and well up on the beach. But he still kept away from it. It was as well he did so. Suddenly, at some move from Bond and perhaps in the hope of catching its enemy unawares, the giant ray leaped clean into the air. Bond sprang aside and the ray fell on its back and lay with its white underbelly to the sun and the great ugly sickle of the mouth sucking and panting.

Bond stood and looked at the sting ray and wondered what to do next.

A short, fat white man in khaki shirt and trousers came out from under the palm trees and walked toward Bond through the scattering of sea grape and sun-dried wrack above high-water mark. When he was near enough he called out in a laughing voice, "The Old Man and the Sea! Who caught who?"

Bond turned. "It *would* be the only man on the island who doesn't carry a machete. Fidele, be a good chap and call one of your men. This animal won't die and he's got my spear stuck in him."

Fidele Barbey, the youngest of the innumerable Barbeys who own nearly everything in the Seychelles, came up and stood looking down at the ray. "That's a good one. Lucky you hit the right spot or he'd have towed you over the reef and you'd have had to let go your gun. They take a hell of a time to die. But come on. I've got to get you back to Victoria. Something's come up. Something good. I'll send one of my men for the gun. Do you want the tail?"

Bond smiled. "No. But what about some *raie au beurre noir* tonight?"

"Not tonight, my friend. Come. Where are your clothes?"

On their way down the coast road in the station wagon Fidele said, "Ever hear of an American called Milton Krest? Well, apparently he owns the Krest hotels and a thing called the Krest Foundation. One thing I can tell you for sure. He owns the finest damned yacht in the Indian Ocean. Put in yesterday. The Wavekrest. Nearly two hundred tons. Hundred feet long. Everything in her from a beautiful wife down to a big transistor gramophone on gimbals so the waves won't jerk the needle. Wall-to-wall carpeting an inch deep. Air conditioned throughout. The only dry cigarettes this side of the African continent and the best after-breakfast bottle of champagne since the last time I saw Paris." Fidele Barbey laughed delightedly. "My friend, that is one hell of a bloody fine ship and if Mr. Krest is a grand slam doubled in bastards, who the hell cares?"

"Who cares anyway? What's it got to do with you—or me for that matter?"

"Just this, my friend. We are going to spend a few days sailing with Mr. Krest—and Mrs. Krest, the beautiful Mrs. Krest. I have agreed to take the ship to Chagrin—the island I have spoken to you about. It is bloody miles from here—off the African Banks, and my family have never found any use for it except for collecting boobies' eggs. It's only about three feet above sea level. I haven't been to the damned place for five years. Anyway, this man Krest wants to go there. He's collecting marine specimens, something to do with his Foundation, and there's some blasted little fish that's supposed to exist only around Chagrin island. At least Krest says the only specimen in the world came from there."

"Sounds rather fun. Where do I come in?"

"I knew you were bored and that you'd got a week before you sail, so I said that you were the local underwater ace and that you'd soon find the fish if it was there and anyway that I wouldn't go without you. Mr. Krest was willing. And that's that. I knew you'd be fooling around somewhere down the coast so I just drove along until one of the fishermen told me there was a crazy white man trying to commit suicide alone at Belle Anse and I knew that would be you."

Bond laughed. "Extraordinary the way these island people are afraid of the sea. You'd think they'd have got on terms with it by now. Damned few of the Seychellois can even swim."

"Missionaries. Don't like them taking their clothes off. And as for being afraid, don't forget you've only been here for a month. Shark, barracuda—you just haven't met a hungry one. And stone fish. Ever see a man that's stepped on a stone fish? His body bends backwards like a bow with the pain. Sometimes it's so frightful his eyes literally fall out of their sockets. They very seldom live."

Bond said unsympathetically, "They ought to wear shoes or bind their feet up when they go on the reef. They've got these fish in the Pacific and the giant clam in the bargain. It's damned silly. Everybody moans about how poor they are here although the sea's absolutely paved with fish. And there are fifty varieties of cowrie under those rocks. They could make another good living selling those round the world."

Fidele Barbey laughed boisterously. "Bond for Governor! That's the ticket. Next meeting of LegCo I'll put the idea up. You're just the man for the job—far-sighted, full of ideas, plenty of drive. Cowries! That's splendid. They'll balance the budget for the first time since the patchouli boom after the war. 'We sell sea shells from the Seychelles.' That'll be our slogan. I'll see you get the credit. You'll be Sir James in no time."

"Make more money that way than trying to grow vanilla at a loss." They continued to wrangle with lighthearted violence until the palm groves gave way to the giant sangdragon trees on the outskirts of the ramshackle capital of Mahé.

It had been nearly a month before when M. had told Bond he was sending him to the Seychelles. "Admiralty are having trouble with their new fleet base in the Maldives. Communists creeping in from Ceylon. Strikes, sabotage—the usual picture. May have to cut their losses and fall back on the Seychelles. A thousand miles farther south, but at least they look pretty secure. But they don't want to be caught again. Colonial Office says it's safe as houses. All the same I've agreed to send someone to give an independent view. When Makarios was locked up there a few years ago there were quite a few security scares. Japanese fishing boats hanging about, one or two refugee crooks from England, strong ties with France. Just go and have a good look." M. glanced out of the window at the driving March sleet. "Don't get sunstroke."

Bond's report, which concluded that the only conceivable security hazard in the Seychelles lay in the beauty and ready availability of the Seychellois, had been finished a week before and then he had nothing to do but wait for the S.S. Kampala to take him to Mombasa. He was thoroughly sick of the heat and the drooping palm trees and the plaintive crying of the terns and the interminable conversations about copra. The prospect of a change delighted him.

Bond was spending his last week in the Barbey house and after calling there to pick up their bags they drove out to the end of Long Pier and left the car in the Customs shed. The gleaming white yacht lay half a mile out in the roadstead. They took a pirogue with an outboard motor across the glassy bay and through the opening in the reef. The Wavekrest was not beautiful—the breadth of beam and cluttered super-structure stunted her lines—but Bond could see at once that she was a real ship, built to cruise the world and not just the Florida Keys. She seemed deserted, but as they came along-side, two smart-looking sailors in white shorts and singlets appeared and stood by the ladder with boathooks ready to fend the shabby pirogue off the yacht's gleaming paint. They took the two bags and one of them slid back an aluminum hatch and gestured for them to go down. A breath of what seemed to Bond to be almost freezing air struck him as he went down the few steps into the lounge.

The lounge was empty. It was not a cabin. It was a room of solid richness and comfort with nothing to associate it with the interior of a ship. The windows behind the half-closed Vene-tian blinds were full size as were the deep armchairs round the low central table. The carpet was the deepest pile in pale blue. The walls were paneled in a silvery wood and the ceiling was off-white. There was a desk with the usual writing materials and a telephone. Next to the big gramophone was a sideboard laden with drinks. Above the sideboard was what looked like an extremely good Renoir—the head and shoulders of a pretty, dark-haired girl in a black-and-white-striped blouse. The impression of a luxurious living room in a town house was completed by a large bowl of white and blue hyacinths on the central table and by the tidy range of magazines to one side of the desk.

"What did I tell you, James?"

Bond shook his head admiringly. "This is certainly the way to treat the sea—as if it damned well didn't exist." He breathed in deeply. "What a relief to get a mouthful of fresh air. I'd almost forgotten what it tastes like."

"It's the stuff outside that's fresh, feller. This is canned." Mr. Milton Krest had come quietly into the room and was standing looking at them. He was a tough, leathery man in his early 50s. He looked hard and fit and the faded blue jeans, military-cut shirt and wide leather belt suggested that he made a fetish of doing so—looking tough. The pale brown eyes in the weather-beaten face were slightly hooded and their gaze was sleepy and contemptuous. The mouth had a downward twist that might be humorous or disdainful, probably the latter, and the words he had tossed into the room, innocuous in themselves except for the patronizing "feller," had been tossed like small change to a couple of coolies. To Bond the oddest thing about Mr. Krest was his voice. It was a soft, most attractive lisping through the teeth. It was exactly the voice of the late Humphrey Bogart. Bond ran his eyes down the man from the sparse close-cropped black and gray hair, like iron filings sprinkled over the bullet head, to the tattooed eagle above a fouled anchor on the right forearm and then down to the naked leathery feet that stood nautically square on the carpet. He thought: this man likes to be thought a Hemingway hero. I'm not going to like him.

Mr. Krest came across the carpet and held out his hand. "You Bond? Glad to have you aboard, sir."

Bond was expecting the bone-crushing grip and parried it with stiffened muscles.

"Free-diving or aqualung?"

"Free, and I don't go deep. It's only a hobby."

"Whaddaya do the rest of the time?"

"Civil Servant."

Mr. Krest gave a short, barking laugh. "Civility and Servitude. You English make the best goddam butlers and valets in the world. Civil Servant you say? I reckon we're likely to get along fine. Civil Servants are just what I like to have around me."

The click of the deck hatch sliding back saved Bond's temper. Mr. Krest was swept from his mind as a naked, sunburned girl came down the steps into the saloon. No, she wasn't quite naked after all, but the pale brown satin scraps of bikini were designed to make one think she was.

" 'Lo, treasure. Where have you been hiding? Long time no see. Meet Mr. Barbey and Mr. Bond, the fellers who are coming along." Mr. Krest raised a hand in the direction of the girl. "Fellers, this is Mrs. Krest. The fifth Mrs. Krest. And just in case anybody should get any ideas, she loves Mr. Krest. Don't you, treasure?"

"Oh don't be silly, Milt, you know I do," Mrs. Krest smiled prettily. "How do you do Mr. Barbey. And Mr. Bond. It's nice to have you with us. What about a drink?"

"Now just a minute, treas. Suppose you let me fix things aboard my own ship, eh?" Mr. Krest's voice was soft and pleasant.

The woman blushed. "Oh yes, Milt, of course."

"OK then, just so we know who's skipper aboard the good ship Wavekrest." The amused smile embraced them all. "Now then, Mr. Barbey. What's your first name, by the way? Fidele, eh? That's quite a name. Old Faithful," Mr. Krest chuckled bonhomously. "Well now Fido, how's about you and me go up on the bridge and get this little old skiff moving, eh? Mebbe you better take her out into the open sea and then you can set a course and hand over to Fritz. I'm the captain. He's the mate, and there are two for the engine room and pantry. All three Germans. Only darned sailors left in Europe. And Mr. Bond. First name? James, eh. Well Jim, what say you practice a bit of that civility and servitude on Mrs. Krest. Call her Liz, by the way. Help her fix the canapes and so on for drinks before lunch. She was once a Limey too. You can swap yarns about Piccadilly Circus. OK? Move, Fido." He sprang boyishly up the steps. "Let's get the hell outa here."

When the hatch closed, Bond let out a deep breath. Mrs. Krest said apologetically, "Please don't mind his jokes. It's just his sense of humor. And he's a bit contrary. He likes to see if he can rile people. It's very naughty of him. But it's really all in fun."

Bond smiled reassuringly. How often did she have to make this speech to people, try and calm the tempers of the people Mr. Krest had practiced his "sense of humor" on? He said, "I expect your husband needs a bit of knowing. Does he go on the same way back in America?"

She said without bitterness, "Only with me. He loves Americans. It's when he's abroad. You see his father was a German, a Prussian really. He's got that silly German thing of thinking Europeans and so on are decadent, that they aren't any good any more. It's no use arguing with him. It's just a thing he's got."

So that was it! The old Hun again. Always at your feet or at your throat. Sense of humor indeed! And what must this woman have to put up with, this beautiful girl he had got hold of to be his slave—his English slave? Bond said, "How long have you been married?"

"Two years. I was working as a receptionist in one of his hotels. He owns the Krest group, you know. It was wonderful. Like a fairy story. I still have to pinch myself sometimes to make sure I'm not dreaming. This for instance," she waved a hand at the luxurious room, "and he's terribly good to me. Always giving me presents. He's a very important man in

America, you know. It's fun being treated like royalty wherever you go."

"It must be. He likes that sort of thing, I suppose?"

"Oh yes," there was resignation in the laugh. "There's a lot of the sultan in him. He gets quite impatient if he doesn't get proper service. He says that when one's worked very hard to get to the top of the tree one has a right to the best fruit that grows there." Mrs. Krest found she was talking too freely. She said quickly, "But really, what am I saying? Anyone would think we had known each other for years." She smiled shyly. "I suppose it's meeting someone from England. But I really must go and get some more clothes on. I was sunbathing on deck." There came a deep rumble from below deck amidships. "There. We're off. Why don't you watch us leave harbor from the afterdeck and I'll come and join you in a minute. There's so much I want to hear about London. This way." She moved past him and slid open a door. "As a matter of fact, if you're sensible, you'll stake a claim to this for the nights. There are plenty of cushions and the cabins are apt to get a bit stuffy in spite of the air conditioning."

Bond thanked her and walked out and shut the door behind him. It was a big well deck with hemp flooring and a cream-colored semicircular foam-rubber settee in the stern. Rattan chairs were scattered about and there was a serving bar in one corner. It crossed Bond's mind that Mr. Krest might be a heavy drinker. Was it his imagination, or was Mrs. Krest terrified of him? There was something painfully slavish in her attitude toward him. No doubt she had to pay heavily for her "fairy story." Bond watched the green flanks of Mahé slowly slip away astern. He guessed that their speed was about ten knots. They would soon be at North Point and heading for the open sea. Bond listened to the glutinous bubble of the exhaust and idly thought about the beautiful Mrs. Elizabeth Krest.

She could have been a model—probably had been before she became a hotel receptionist—that respectable female calling that yet has a whiff of the high demimonde about it—and she still moved her beautiful body with the unself-consciousness of someone who is used to going about with nothing, or practically nothing on. But there was none of the chill of the model about her—it was a warm body and a friendly, confiding face. She might be 30, certainly not more, and her prettiness, for it was not more than that, was still immature. Her best feature was the ash-blonde hair that hung heavily to the base of her neck, but she seemed pleasantly lacking in vanity about it. She didn't toss it about or fiddle with it and it occurred to Bond that she didn't in fact show any signs of coquetry. She had stood quietly, almost docilely, with her large, clear blue eyes fixed almost the whole time on her husband. There was no lipstick on her mouth and no lacquer on her fingernails or toenails and her eyebrows were natural. Did Mr. Krest perhaps order that it should be so—that she should be a Germanic child of nature? Probably. Bond shrugged his shoulders. They were certainly a curiously assorted couple—the middle-aged Hemingway character with the Bogart voice and the pretty, artless girl. And there was tension in the air—in the way she had cringed as he brought her to heel when she had offered them drinks, in the forced maleness of the man. Bond toyed idly with the notion that the man was impotent and that all the tough, rude act was nothing more than exaggerated virility-play. It certainly wasn't going to be easy to live with for four or five days. Bond watched the beautiful Silhouette Island slip away to starboard and made a vow not to lose his temper. What was that American expression? "Eating crow." It would be an interesting mental exercise for him. He would eat crow for five days and not let this damnable man interfere with what should be a good trip.

"Well, feller. Taking it easy?" Mr. Krest was standing on the boat deck looking down into the well. "What have you done with that woman I live with? Left her to do all the work, I guess. Well, and why not? That's what they're for, ain't it?

Care to look over the ship? Fido's doin' a spell at the wheel and I've got time on my hands." Without waiting for an answer, Mr. Krest bent and lowered himself down into the well deck, dropping the last four feet.

"Mrs. Krest's putting on some clothes. Yes, I'd like to look over the ship."

Mr. Krest fixed Bond with his hard, disdainful stare. " 'K. Well now, facts first. It's built by the Bronson Shipbuilding Corporation. I happen to own ninety percent of the stock so I got what I wanted. Designed by Rosenblatts—the top naval architects. Hundred feet long, twenty-one broad, and draws six. Two five-hundred-horsepower Superior diesels. Top speed, fourteen knots. Cruises two thousand five hundred miles at eight. Air conditioned throughout. Carrier Corporation designed two special five-ton units. Carries enough frozen food and liquor for a month. All we need is fresh water for the baths and showers. Right? Now let's go up front and you can see the crew's quarters and we'll work back. And one thing, Jim," Mr. Krest stamped on the deck, "this is the floor, see? And the head's the can. And if I want someone to stop doing whatever they're doing I don't shout 'belay' I shout 'hold it.' Get me, Jim?"

Bond nodded amiably. "I've got no objection. She's your ship."

"*It's* my ship," corrected Mr. Krest. "That's another bit of damned nonsense, making a hunk of steel and wood a female. Anyway, let's go. You don't need to mind your head. Everything's a six-foot-two clearance."

Bond followed Mr. Krest down the narrow passage that ran the length of the ship and for half an hour made appropriate comments on what was certainly the finest and most luxuriously designed yacht he had ever seen. In every detail, the margin was for extra comfort. Even the crew's bath and shower was full size and the stainless-steel galley, or kitchen as Mr. Krest called it, was as big as the Krest stateroom. Mr.

Krest opened the door of the latter without knocking. Liz Krest was at the dressing table. "Why, treasure," said Mr. Krest in his soft voice, "I reckoned you'd be out there fixing up the drink tray. You've sure been one heck of a time dressing up. Puttin' on a little extra ritz for Jim, eh?"

"I'm sorry, Milt. I was just coming. A zipper got stuck." The girl hurriedly picked up a compact and made for the door. She gave them both a nervous half-smile and went out.

"Vermont birch paneling, Corning glass lamps, Mexican tuft rugs. That sailing ship picture's a genuine Montague Dawson, by the way. . . ." Mr. Krest's catalog ran smoothly on. But Bond was looking at something that hung down almost out of sight by the bedside table on what was obviously Mr. Krest's side of the huge double bed. It was a thin whip about three feet long with a leather thonged handle. It was the tail of a sting ray.

Casually Bond walked over to the side of the bed and picked it up. He ran a finger down its spiny gristle. It hurt his fingers even to do that. He said, "Where did you pick that up? I was hunting one of these animals this morning."

"Bahrein. The Arabs use them on their wives." Mr. Krest chuckled easily. "Haven't had to use more than one stroke at a time on Liz so far. Wonderful results. We call it my 'Corrector.' "

Bond put the thing back. He looked hard at Mr. Krest and said, "Is that so? In the Seychelles where the creoles are pretty tough it's illegal even to own one of those, let alone use it."

Mr. Krest moved toward the door. He said indifferently, "Feller, this happens to be United States territory. Let's go get ourselves something to drink."

Mr. Krest drank three double bullshots before luncheon and beer with the meal. The pale eyes darkened a little and acquired a watery glitter, but the sibilant voice remained soft and unemphatic as, with a complete monopoly of the conversation, he explained the object of the voyage. "Ya see, fellers, it's like this. In the States we have this Foundation system for the lucky guys that got plenty of dough and don't happen to want to pay it into Uncle Sam's Treasury. You make a Foundation —like this one, the Krest Foundation—for charitable purposes —charitable to anyone, to kids, sick folk, old folk, the causes of science—you just give the money away to anyone or anything except yourself or your dependents and you escape tax on it. So I put a matter of ten million dollars into the Krest Foundation and since I happen to like yachting and seeing the world I built this yacht with two million of the money and told the Smithsonian, that's our big natural history institution, that I would go to any part of the world and collect specimens for them. So that makes me a scientific expedition, see? For three months of every year I have a fine holiday that costs me next to nothing!" Mr. Krest looked to his guests for applause. "Get me?"

Fidele Barbey shook his head doubtfully. "That sounds fine, Mr. Krest. But these rare specimens. They are easy to find? The Smithsonian it wants a giant panda, a sea shell. You can get hold of these things where they have failed?"

Mr. Krest slowly shook his head. He said sorrowfully, "Feller, you sure were born yesterday. Money, that's all it takes. You want a panda? You buy it from some goddam zoo that can't afford central heating for its reptile house or wants to build a new block for its tigers or something. The sea shell? You find a man that's got one and you offer him so much goddam money that even if he cries for a week he sells it to you. Sometimes you have a little trouble with governments. Some goddam animal is protected or something. All right. Give you an example. I arrive at your island yesterday. I want a black parrot from Praslin Island. I want a giant tortoise from Aldabra. I want the complete range of your local cowries and I want this fish we're after. The first two are protected by law. Last evening I pay a call on your Governor after making certain inquiries in the town. Excellency, I says, I understand you want to build a public swimming pool to teach the local kids to swim. OK. The Krest Foundation will put up the money. How much? Five thousand, ten thousand? OK so it's ten thousand. Here's my check. And I write it out there and then. Just one little thing, Excellency, I says, holding onto the check. It happens I want a specimen of this black parrot you have here and one of these Aldabra tortoises. I understand they're protected by law. Mind if I take one of each back to America for the Smithsonian? Well there's a bit of a palaver, but seeing it's the Smithsonian and seeing I've still got hold of the check, in the end we shake hands on the deal and everyone's happy. Right? Well on the way back I stop in the town to arrange with your nice Mr. Abendana, the merchant feller, to have the parrot and tortoise collected and held for me and I get to talking about the cowries. Well it so happens that this Mr. Abendana has been collecting the damn things since he was a child. He shows them to me. Beautifully kept— each one in its bit of cotton wool. Fine condition and several of those Isabella and Mappa ones I was asked particularly to watch out for. Sorry, he couldn't think of selling. They meant so much to him and so on. Crap! I just look at Mr. Abendana and I say, how much? No no. He couldn't think of it. Crap again! I take out my checkbook and write out a check for five thousand dollars and push it under his nose. He looks at it. Five thousand dollars! He can't stand it. He folds the check and puts it in his pocket and then the damn sissy breaks down and weeps! Would you believe it?" Mr. Krest opened his palms in disbelief. "Over a few goddam sea shells. So I just tell him to take it easy and I pick up the trays of sea shells and get the hell out of there before the crazy so-and-so shoots himself from remorse."

Mr. Krest sat back, well pleased with himself. "Well, whaddaya say to that fellers? Twenty-four hours in the island

and I've already knocked off three-quarters of my list. Pretty smart, eh Jim?"

Bond said, "You'll probably get a medal when you get home. What about this fish?"

Mr. Krest got up from the table and rummaged in a drawer of his desk. He brought back a typewritten sheet. "Here you are." He read out: " 'Hildebrand Rarity. Caught by Professor Hildebrand of the University of the Witwatersrand in a net off Chagrin Island in the Seychelles group, April 1925.' " Mr. Krest looked up. "And then there's a lot of scientific crap. I got them to put it into plain English and here's the translation." He turned back to the paper. " 'This appears to be a unique member of the squirrel fish family. The only specimen known, named the "Hildebrand Rarity" after its discoverer, is six inches long. The color is a bright pink with black transverse stripes. The anal, ventral and dorsal fins are pink. The tail fin is black. Eyes, large and dark blue. If found, care should be taken in handling this fish because all fins are even more sharply spiked than is usual with the rest of this family. Professor Hildebrand records that he found the specimen in three feet of water on the edge of the southwestern reef.' " Mr. Krest threw the paper down on the table. "Well, there you are, fellers. We're traveling about a thousand miles at a cost of several thousand dollars to try and find a goddam six-inch fish. And two years ago the Revenue people had the gall to suggest that my Foundation was a phony!"

Liz Krest broke in eagerly, "But that's just it Milt, isn't it? It's really rather important to bring back plenty of specimens and things this time. Weren't those horrible tax people talking about disallowing the yacht and the expenses and so on for the last five years if we didn't show an outstanding scientific achievement? Wasn't that the way they put it?"

"Treasure," Mr. Krest's voice was soft as velvet. "Just supposin' you keep that flippin' trap shut about my personal affairs. Yes?" The voice was amiable, nonchalant. "You know what you just done, treas? You just earned yourself a little meeting with the Corrector this evening. That's what you've gone and done."

The girl's hand flew to her mouth. Her eyes widened. She said in a whisper, "Oh no, Milt. Oh no, please."

. . .

On the second day out, at dawn, they came up with Chagrin Island. It was first picked up by the radar—a small bump in the dead-level line on the scanner—and then a minute blur on the great curved horizon grew with infinite slowness into half a mile of green fringed with white. It was extraordinary to come upon land after two days in which the yacht had seemed to be the only moving, the only living thing in an empty world. Bond had never seen or even clearly imagined the doldrums before. Now he realized what a terrible hazard they must have been in the days of sail—the sea of glass under a brazen sun, the foul, heavy air, the trail of small clouds along the rim of the world that never came closer, never brought wind or blessed rain. How must centuries of mariners have blessed this tiny dot in the Indian Ocean as they bent to the oars that moved the heavy ship perhaps a mile a day! Bond stood in the bows and watched the flying fish squirt from beneath the hull as the blue-black of the sea slowly mottled into the brown and white and green of deep shoal. How wonderful that he would soon be walking and swimming again instead of just sitting and lying down. How wonderful to have a few hours' solitude—a few hours away from Mr. Milton Krest!

They anchored outside the reef in ten fathoms and Fidele Barbey took them through the opening in the speedboat. In every detail Chagrin was the prototype coral island. It was about twenty acres of sand and dead coral and low scrub surrounded, after fifty yards of shallow lagoon, by a necklace of reef on which the quiet, long swell broke with a soft hiss.

Clouds of birds rose when they landed—terns, boobies, men-of-war, frigates—but quickly settled again. There was a strong ammoniac smell of guano, and the scrub was white with it. The only other living things were the land crabs that scuttled and scraped among the *liane sans fin* and the fiddler crabs that lived in the sand.

The glare from the white sand was dazzling and there was no shade. Mr. Krest ordered a tent to be erected and sat in it smoking a cigar while gear of various kinds was ferried ashore. Mrs. Krest swam and picked up sea shells while Bond and Fidele Barbey put on masks and, swimming in opposing directions, began systematically to comb the reef all the way round the island.

When you are looking for one particular species underwater —shell or fish or seaweed or coral formation—you have to keep your brain and your eyes focused for that one individual pattern. The riot of color and movement and the endless variety of light and shadow fight your concentration all the time. Bond trudged slowly along through the wonderland with only one picture in his mind—a six-inch pink fish with black stripes and big eyes—the second such fish man had ever seen. "If you see it," Mr. Krest had enjoined, "just you let out a yell and stay with it. I'll do the rest. I got a little something in the tent that's just the dandiest thing for catching fish you ever saw."

Bond paused to rest his eyes. The water was so buoyant that he could lie face downward on the surface without moving. Idly he broke up a sea egg with the tip of his spear and watched the horde of glittering reef fish darting for the shreds of yellow flesh among the needle-sharp black spines. How infernal that if he did find the Rarity it would benefit only Mr. Krest! Should he say nothing if he found it? Rather childish, and anyway he was under contract, so to speak. Bond moved slowly on, his eyes automatically taking up the search again while his mind turned to considering the girl. She had spent the previous day in bed. Mr. Krest had said it was a headache. Would she one day turn on him? Would she get herself a knife or a gun and one night, when he reached for that damnable whip, would she kill him? No. She was too soft, too malleable. Mr. Krest had chosen well. She was the stuff of slaves. And the trappings of her "fairy tale" were too precious. Didn't she realize that a jury would certainly acquit her if the sting ray whip were produced in court? She could have the trappings without this dreadful, damnable man. Should Bond tell her that? Don't be ridiculous! How would he put it? "Oh Liz, if you want to murder your husband, it'll be quite all right." Bond smiled inside his mask. To hell with it! Don't interfere with other people's lives. She probably likes it— masochist. But Bond knew that that was too easy an answer. This was a girl who lived in fear. Perhaps she also lived in loathing. One couldn't read much in those soft blue eyes, but the windows had opened once or twice and a flash of something like a childish hate had shown through. Had it been hate? It had probably been indigestion. Bond put the Krests out of his mind and looked up to see how far round the island he had got. Fidele Barbey's snorkel was only a hundred yards away. They had nearly completed the circuit.

They came up with each other and swam to the shore and lay on the hot sand. Fidele Barbey said, "Nothing on my side of the property except every fish in the world bar one. But I've had a stroke of luck. Ran into a big colony of green snail. That's the pearl shell as big as a small football. Worth quite a lot of money. I'll send one of my boats after them one of these days. Saw a blue parrot fish that must have been a good thirty pounds. Tame as a dog like all the fish round here. Hadn't got the heart to kill it. And if I had, there might have been trouble. Saw two or three leopard sharks cruising around over the reef. Blood in the water might have brought them through. Now I'm ready for a drink and something to eat. After that we can swap sides and have another go."

They got up and walked along the beach to the tent. Mr. Krest heard their voices and came out to meet them. "No dice, eh?" He scratched angrily at an armpit. "Goddam sandfly bit me. This is one hell of a godawful island. Liz couldn't stand the smell. Gone back to the ship. Guess we'd better give it one more going over and then get the hell out of here. Help yourselves to some chow and you'll find cold beer in the icepack. Here, gimme one of those masks. How do you use the damn things? I guess I might as well take a peek at the sea's bottom while I'm about it."

They sat in the hot tent and ate the chicken salad and drank beer and moodily watched Mr. Krest poking and peering about in the shallows. Fidele Barbey said, "He's right, of course. These little islands are bloody awful places. Nothing but crabs and bird dung surrounded by too damn much sea. It's only the poor bloody frozen Europeans that dream of coral islands. East of Suez you won't find any sane man who gives a damn for them. My family owns about ten of them, decent-sized ones too, with small villages on them and a good income from copra and turtle. Well, you can have the whole bloody lot in exchange for a flat in London or Paris."

Bond laughed. He began, "Put an advertisement in the *Times* and you'd get sackloads——" when, fifty yards away, Mr. Krest began to make frantic signals. Bond said, "Either the bastard's found it or he's trodden on a guitar fish," and picked up his mask and ran down to the sea.

Mr. Krest was standing up to his waist among the shallow beginnings of the reef. He jabbed his finger excitedly at the surface. Bond swam softly forward. A carpet of sea grass ended in broken coral and an occasional niggerhead. A dozen varieties of butterfly and other reef fish flirted among the rocks and a small langouste quested toward Bond with its feelers. The head of a large green moray protruded from a hole, its half-open jaws showing the rows of needle teeth. Its golden eyes watched Bond carefully. Bond was amused to note that Mr. Krest's hairy legs, magnified into pale tree trunks by the glass, were not more than a foot away from the moray's jaws. He gave an encouraging poke at the moray with his spear, but the eel only snapped at the metal points and slid back out of sight. Bond stopped and floated, his eyes scanning the brilliant jungle. A red blur materialized through the far mist and came toward him. It circled closely beneath him as if showing itself off. The dark-blue eyes examined him without fear. The small fish busied itself rather self-consciously with some algae on the underside of a niggerhead, made a dart at a speck of something suspended in the water and then, as if leaving the stage after showing its paces, swam languidly off back into the mist.

Bond backed away from the moray's hole and put his feet to the ground. He took off his mask. He said to Mr. Krest, who was standing gazing impatiently at him through his goggles, "Yes, that's it all right. Better move quietly away from here. He won't go away unless he's frightened. These reef fish stick pretty well to the same pastures."

Mr. Krest pulled off his mask. "Goddam, I found it!" he said reverently. "Well, goddam I did." He slowly followed Bond to the shore.

Fidele Barbey was waiting for them. Mr. Krest said boisterously, "Fido, I found that goddam fish. Me—Milton Krest. Whaddaya know about that? After you two goddam experts had been at it all morning. I just took that mask of yours—first time I ever put one on, mark you—and I walked out and found the goddam fish in fifteen minutes flat. Whaddaya say to that eh, Fido?"

"That's good, Mr. Krest. That's fine. Now how do we catch it?"

"Aha," Mr. Krest winked slowly. "I got just the ticket for that. Got it from a chemist friend of mine. Stuff called rotenone. Made from derris root. What the natives fish with in Brazil. Just pour it in the water where it'll float over what you're after and it'll get him as sure as eggs is eggs. Sort of poison. Constricts the blood vessels in their gills. Suffocates them. No effect on humans because no gills, see?" Mr. Krest turned to Bond. "Here Jim. You go on out and keep watch. See the darned fish don't vamoose. Fido and I'll bring the stuff out there," he pointed upcurrent from the vital area. "I'll let go the rotenone when you say the word. It'll drift down toward you. Right? But for land's sakes get the timing right. I've only got a five-gallon tin of this stuff. 'K?"

Bond said "All right" and walked slowly down and into the water. He swam lazily out to where he had stood before. Yes, everyone was still there, going about his business. The moray's pointed head was back again at the edge of its hole, the langouste again queried him. In a minute, as if it had a rendezvous with Bond, the Hildebrand Rarity appeared. This time it swam up quite close to his face. It looked through the glass at his eyes and then, as if disturbed by what it had seen there, darted out of range. It played around among the rocks for a while and then went off into the mist.

Slowly the little underwater world within Bond's vision began to take him for granted. A small octopus that had been camouflaged as a piece of coral revealed its presence and groped carefully down toward the sand. The blue and yellow langouste came a few steps out from under the rock, wondering about him. Some very small fish like minnows nibbled at his legs and toes, tickling. Bond broke a sea egg for them and they darted to the better meal. Bond lifted his head. Mr. Krest, holding the flat can, was twenty yards away to Bond's right. He would soon begin pouring, when Bond gave the sign, so that the liquid would get a good wide spread over the surface.

"OK?" called Mr. Krest.

Bond shook his head. "I'll raise my thumb when he's back here. Then you'll have to pour fast."

"OK, Jim. You're at the bombsight."

Bond put his head down. There was the little community, everyone busied with his affairs. Soon, to get one fish that someone vaguely wanted in a museum five thousand miles away, a hundred, perhaps a thousand small people were going to die. When Bond gave the signal, the shadow of death would come down on the stream. How long would the poison last? How far would it travel on down the reef? Perhaps it would not be thousands but tens of thousands that would die.

A small trunk fish appeared, its tiny fins whirring like propellers. A rock beauty, gorgeous in gold and red and black, pecked at the sand, and a pair of the inevitable black-and-yellow-striped sergeant majors materialized from nowhere, attracted by the scent of the broken sea egg.

Inside the reef, who was the predator in the world of small fishes? Who did they fear? Small barracuda? An occasional billfish? Now, a big, a fully grown predator, a man called Krest, was standing in the wings, waiting. And this one wasn't even hungry. He was just going to kill—almost for fun.

Two brown legs appeared in Bond's vision. He looked up. It was Fidele Barbey with a long-handled landing net and a big creel strapped to his chest.

Bond lifted his mask. "I feel like the bomb-aimer at Nagasaki."

"Fish are cold-blooded. They don't feel anything."

"How do you know? I've heard them scream when they're hurt."

Barbey said indifferently, "They won't be able to scream with this stuff. It strangles them. What's eating you? They're only fish."

"I know, I know." Fidele Barbey had spent his life killing animals and fish. While he, Bond, had sometimes not hesitated to kill men. What was he fussing about? He hadn't minded killing the sting ray. Yes, but that was an enemy fish. These down here were friendly people. People? The pathetic fallacy!

"Hey," came the voice of Mr. Krest. "What's goin' on over there? This ain't no time for chewing the fat. Get that head down, Jim."

Bond pulled down his mask and lay again on the surface. At once he saw the beautiful red shadow coming out of the far mists. The fish swam fast up to him as if it now took him for granted. It lay below him, looking up. Bond said into his mask, "Get away from here, damn you." He gave a sharp jab at the fish with his harpoon. The fish fled back into the mist. Bond lifted his head and angrily raised his thumb. It was a ridiculous and petty act of sabotage of which he was already ashamed. The dark-brown oily liquid was pouring out onto the surface of the lagoon. There was time to stop Mr. Krest before it was all gone—time to give him another chance at the Hildebrand Rarity. Bond stood and watched until the last drop was tilted out. To hell with Mr. Krest!

Now the stuff was creeping slowly down on the current—a shiny, spreading stain which reflected the blue sky with a metallic glint. Mr. Krest, the giant reaper, was wading down with it. "Get set, fellers," he called cheerfully. "It's right up with you now."

Bond put his head back under the surface. Everything was as before in the little community. And then, with stupefying suddenness, everyone went mad. It was as if they had all been seized with St. Vitus' dance. Several fish looped the loop crazily and then fell like heavy leaves to the sand. The moray eel came slowly out of the hole in the coral, its jaws wide. It stood carefully upright on its tail and gently toppled sideways. The small langouste gave three kicks of its tail and turned over on its back, and the octopus let go its hold of the coral and drifted to the bottom upside down. And then, into the arena drifted the corpses from upstream—white-bellied fish, shrimps, worms, hermit crabs, spotted and green morays, langoustes of all sizes. As if blown by some light breeze of death, the clumsy bodies, their colors already fading, swept slowly past. A five-pound billfish struggled by with snapping beak, fighting death. Down-reef there were splashes on the surface as still bigger fish tried to make for safety. One by one, before Bond's eyes, the sea urchins dropped off the rocks to make black ink-blots on the sand.

Bond felt a touch on his shoulder. Mr. Krest's eyes were

bloodshot with the sun and glare. He had put white sunburn paste on his lips. He shouted impatiently at Bond's mask, "Where in hell's our goddam fish?"

Bond lifted his mask. "Looks as if it managed to get away just before the stuff came down. I'm still watching for it."

He didn't wait to hear Mr. Krest's reply but got his head quickly under water again. Still more carnage, still more dead bodies. But surely the stuff had passed by now. Surely the area was safe just in case the fish, his fish because he had saved it, came back again! He stiffened. In the far mists there was a pink flash. It had gone. Now it was back again. Idly the Hildebrand Rarity swam toward him through the maze of channels between the broken outposts of the reef.

Not caring about Mr. Krest, Bond raised his free hand out of the water and brought it down with a sharp slap. Still the fish came. Bond shifted the safe on his harpoon gun and fired it in the direction of the fish. No effect. Bond put his feet down and began to walk toward the fish through the scattering of corpses. The beautiful red and black fish seemed to pause and quiver. Then it shot straight through the water toward Bond and dived down to the sand at his feet and lay still. Bond only had to bend to pick it up. There was not even a last flap from the tail. It just filled Bond's hand, lightly pricking the palm with the spiny black dorsal fin. Bond carried it back under water so as to preserve its colors. When he got to Mr. Krest he said "here" and handed him the small fish. Then he swam away toward the shore.

.   .   .

That evening, with the Wavekrest heading for home down the path of a huge yellow moon, Mr. Krest gave orders for what he called a "wingding." "Gotta celebrate, Liz. This is terrific, a terrific day. Cleaned up the last target and we can get the hell out of these goddam Seychelles and get on back to civilization. What say we make it to Mombasa when we've taken on board the tortoise and that goddam parrot? Fly to

Nairobi and pick up a big plane for Rome, Venice, Paris—anywheres you care for. What say, treasure?" He squeezed her chin and cheeks in his big hand and made the pale lips pout. He kissed them wetly. Bond watched the girl's eyes. They had shut tight. Mr. Krest let go. The girl massaged her face. It was still white with his finger marks.

"Gee, Milt," she said half-laughing, "you nearly squashed me. You don't know your strength. But do let's celebrate. I think that would be lots of fun. And that Paris idea sounds grand. Let's do that, shall we? What shall I order for dinner?"

"Hell, caviar of course." Mr. Krest held his hands apart. "One of those two-pound tins—the grade ten shot size, and all the trimmings. And that pink champagne." He turned to Bond. "That suit you, feller?"

"Sounds like a square meal." Bond changed the subject. "What have you done with the prize?"

"Formalin. Up on the boat deck with some other jars of stuff we've picked up here and there—fish, shells. All safe in our home morgue. That's how we were told to keep the specimens. We'll airmail that damned fish when we get back to civilization. Give a press conference first. Should make a big play in the papers back home. I've already radioed the Smithsonian and the news agencies. My accountants'll sure be glad of some press cuttings to show those darned Revenue boys."

Mr. Krest got very drunk that night. It did not show greatly. The soft, Bogart voice became softer and slower. The round, hard head turned more deliberately on the shoulders. The lighter's flame took increasingly long to relight the cigar and one glass was swept off the table. But it showed in the things Mr. Krest said. There was a violent cruelty, a pathological desire to wound quite near the surface in the man. That night, after dinner, the first target was James Bond. He was treated to a soft-spoken explanation as to why Europe, with England and France in the vanguard, was a rapidly diminishing asset to the world. Nowadays, said Mr. Krest, there were only three powers—America, Russia and China. That was the big poker game and no other country had either the money or the cards to come into it. Occasionally some pleasant little country—and he admitted they'd been pretty big league in the past—like England would be lent some money so that they could take a hand with the grown-ups. But that was just being polite like one sometimes had to be—to a chum in one's club who'd gone broke. No. England—nice people, mind you, good sports—was a place to see the old buildings and the Queen and so on. France? They only counted for good food and easy women. Italy? Sunshine and spaghetti. Sanatorium, sort of. Germany? Well they still had some spunk, but two lost wars had knocked the heart out of them. Mr. Krest dismissed the rest of the world with a few similar tags and then asked Bond for his comments.

Bond was thoroughly tired of Mr. Krest. He said he found Mr. Krest's point of view oversimplified—he might even say naive. He said, "Your argument reminds me of a rather sharp aphorism I once heard about America. Care to hear it?"

"Sure, sure."

"It's to the effect that America has progressed from infancy to senility without ever having passed through a period of maturity."

Mr. Krest looked thoughtfully at Bond. Finally he said, "Why, say, Jim, that's pretty neat." His eyes hooded slightly as they turned toward his wife. "Guess you'd kinda go along with that remark of Jim's, eh treasure? I recall you saying once you reckoned there was something pretty childish about the Americans. Remember?"

"Oh Milt," Liz Krest's eyes were anxious. She had read the signs. "How can you bring that up? You know it was only something casual I said about the comic sections of the papers. Of course I don't agree with what James says. Anyway it was only a joke, wasn't it, James?"

"That's right," said Bond. "Like when Mr. Krest said England had nothing but ruins and a queen."

Mr. Krest's eyes were still on the girl. He said softly, "Shucks, treasure. Why are you looking so nervous? Course it was a joke." He paused. "And one I'll remember, treasure. One I'll sure remember."

Bond estimated that by now Mr. Krest had just about one whole bottle of various alcohols, mostly whiskey, inside him. It looked to Bond as if, unless Mr. Krest passed out, the time was not far off when Bond would have to hit Mr. Krest just once, very hard on the jaw. Fidele Barbey was now being given the treatment. "These islands of yours, Fido. When I first looked them up on the map, I thought it was just some specks of fly dirt on the page." Mr. Krest chuckled. "Even tried to brush them off with the back of my hand. Then I read a bit about them and it seemed to me my first thoughts had just about hit the nail on the head. Not much good for anything, are they, Fido? I wonder an intelligent guy like you doesn't get the hell out of there. Beachcombing ain't any kind of a life. Though I did hear one of your family had logged over a hundred illegitimate children. Mebbe that's the attraction, eh feller?" Mr. Krest grinned knowingly.

Fidele Barbey said equably, "That's my uncle, Gaston. The rest of the family doesn't approve. It's made quite a hole in the family fortune."

"Family fortune, eh?" Mr. Krest winked at Bond. "What's it in? Cowrie shells?"

"Not exactly." Fidele Barbey was not used to Mr. Krest's brand of rudeness. He looked mildly embarrassed. "Though we made quite a lot out of tortoise shell and mother-of-pearl about a hundred years ago when there was a rage for these things. Copra's always been our main business."

"Using the family bastards as labor I guess. Good idea. Wish I could fix something like that in my home circle." He looked across at his wife. The rubbery lips turned still further down. Before the next jibe could be uttered, Bond had pushed his chair back and had gone out into the well deck and pulled the door shut behind him.

Ten minutes later Bond heard feet coming softly down the ladder from the boat deck. He turned. It was Liz Krest. She came over to where he was standing in the stern. She said in a strained voice, "I said I'd go to bed. But then I thought I'd come back here and see if you'd got everything you want. I'm not a very good hostess, I'm afraid. Are you sure you don't mind sleeping out here?"

"I like it. I like this kind of air better than the canned stuff inside. And it's rather wonderful to have all those stars to look at. I've never seen so many before."

She said eagerly, grasping at a friendly topic, "I like Orion's Belt and the Southern Cross the best. You know, when I was young, I used to think the stars were really holes in the sky. I thought the world was surrounded by a great big black sort of envelope and that outside it the universe was full of bright light. The stars were just holes in the envelope that let little sparks of light through. One gets terribly silly ideas when one's young." She looked up at him, wanting him not to snub her.

Bond said, "You're probably quite right. One shouldn't believe all the scientists say. They want to make everything dull. Where did you live then?"

"At Ringwood in the New Forest. It was a good place to be brought up. A good place for children. I'd like to go there again one day."

Bond said, "You've certainly come a long way since then. You'd probably find it pretty dull."

She reached out and touched his sleeve. "Please don't say that. You don't understand." There was an edge of desperation in the soft voice. "I can't bear to go on missing what other people have—ordinary people. I mean," she laughed nervously, "you won't believe me, but just to talk like this for a few minutes, to have someone like you to talk to, is something I'd almost forgotten." She suddenly reached for his hand and held it hard. "I'm sorry. I just wanted to do that. Now I'll go to bed."

The soft voice came from behind them. The sibilants had slurred, but each word was carefully separated from the next. "Well, well. Whaddaya know? Necking with the underwater help!"

Mr. Krest stood framed in the hatch to the saloon. He stood with his legs apart and his arms upstretched to the lintel above his head. With the light behind him he had the silhouette of a baboon. The cold, imprisoned breath of the saloon rushed out past him and for a moment chilled the warm night air in the well deck. Mr. Krest stepped out and softly pulled the door to behind him.

Bond took a step toward him, his hands held loosely at his sides. He measured the distance to Mr. Krest's solar plexus. He said, "Don't jump to conclusions, Mr. Krest. And watch your tongue. You're lucky not to have got hurt so far tonight. Don't press your luck. You're drunk. Go to bed."

"Oho! Listen to the little feller." Mr. Krest's moon-burned face turned slowly from Bond to his wife. He made a contemptuous, Hapsburg lip grimace. He took a silver whistle out of his pocket and whirled it round on its string. "He sure don't get the picture, does he, treasure? You ain't told him that those Heinies up front ain't just for ornament?" He turned back to Bond, "Feller, you move any closer and I blow this—just once. And you know what? It'll be the old heave-ho for Mr. goddam Bond," he made a gesture toward the sea, "over the side. Man overboard. Too bad. We back up to make a search and you know what, feller? Just by chance we back up into you with those twin screws. Would you believe it! What lousy bad luck for that nice feller Jim we were all getting so fond of!" Mr. Krest swayed on his feet. "D'ya get the photo, Jim? OK, so let's all be friends again and get some shut-eye." He reached for the lintel of the hatch and turned to his wife. He lifted his free hand and slowly crooked a finger, "Move, treasure. Time for bed."

"Yes, Milt." The wide, frightened eyes turned sideways. "Good night, James." Without waiting for an answer she ducked under Mr. Krest's arm and almost ran through the saloon.

Mr. Krest lifted a hand. "Take it easy, feller. No hard feelings, eh?"

Bond said nothing. He went on looking hard at Mr. Krest. Mr. Krest laughed uncertainly. He said, "OK then." He stepped into the saloon and slid the door shut. Through the window, Bond watched him walk unsteadily across the saloon and turn out the lights. He went into the corridor and there was a momentary gleam from the stateroom door and then that too went dark.

Bond shrugged his shoulders. God, what a man! He leaned against the stern rail and watched the stars and the flashes of phosphorescence in the creaming wake and set about washing his mind clear and relaxing the coiled tensions in his body.

Half an hour later, after taking a shower in the crew's bathroom forward, Bond was making a bed for himself among the piled foam-rubber cushions when he heard a single, heart-rending scream. It tore briefly into the night and was smothered. It was the girl. Bond ran through the saloon and down the passage. With his hand on the stateroom door, he stopped. He could hear her sobs and, above them, the soft, even drone of Mr. Krest's voice. He took his hand away from the latch. Hell! What was it to do with him? They were man and wife. If she was prepared to stand this sort of thing and not kill her husband or leave him it was no good Bond playing Sir Galahad. Bond walked slowly back down the passage. As he was crossing the saloon, the scream, this time less piercing, rang out again. Bond cursed fluently and went out and lay down on his bed and tried to focus his mind on the soft thud of the diesels. How could a girl have so little guts? Or was it that women could take almost anything from a man? Anything except indifference? Bond's mind refused to unwind. Sleep got further and further away.

An hour later Bond had reached the edge of unconsciousness when, up above him on the boat deck, Mr. Krest began to snore. On the second night out from Port Victoria Mr. Krest had left his cabin in the middle of the night and had gone up to the hammock that was kept slung for him between the speedboat and the dinghy, but that night he had not snored. Now he was snoring with those deep, rattling, utterly lost snores that come from big blue sleeping pills on top of too much alcohol.

This was too damned much. Bond looked at his watch. One-thirty. If the snoring didn't stop in ten minutes Bond would go down to Fidele Barbey's cabin and sleep on the floor even if he did wake up stiff and frozen in the morning.

Bond watched the gleaming minute hand slowly creep round the dial. Now! He had got to his feet and was gathering up his shirt and shorts when, from up on the boat deck, there came a heavy crash. The crash was immediately followed by scrabbling sounds and a dreadful choking and gurgling. Had Mr. Krest fallen out of his hammock? Reluctantly Bond dropped his things back on the deck and walked over and climbed the ladder. As his eyes came level with the boat deck, the choking stopped. Instead there was another, a more dreadful sound—the quick drumming of heels. Bond knew that sound. He leaped up the last steps and ran toward the figure lying spread-eagled on its back in the bright moonlight. He stopped and knelt slowly down, aghast. The horror of the strangled face was bad enough, but it was not Mr. Krest's tongue that protruded from his gaping mouth. It was the tail of a fish. The colors were pink and black. It was the Hildebrand Rarity!

The man was dead—horribly dead. When the fish had been crammed into his mouth he must have reached up and desperately tried to tug it out. But the spines of the dorsal and anal fins had caught inside the cheeks and some of the spiny tips now protruded through the blood-flecked skin round the obscene mouth. Bond shuddered. Death must have come inside a minute. But what a minute!

Bond slowly got to his feet. He walked over to the racks of glass specimen jars and peered under the protective awning. The plastic cover of the end jar lay on the deck beside it. Bond wiped it carefully on the tarpaulin and then, holding it by the tips of his fingernails, laid it loosely back over the mouth of the jar.

He went back and stood over the corpse. Which of the two had done this? There was a touch of fiendish spite in using the treasured prize as a weapon. That suggested the woman. She certainly had her reasons. But Fidele Barbey, with his creole blood, would have had the cruelty and at the same time the macabre humor. *"Je lui ai foutu son sacré poisson dans la gueule."* Bond could hear him say the words. If, after Bond had left the saloon, Mr. Krest had needled the Seychellois just a little bit further—particularly about his family or his beloved islands—Fidele Barbey would not have hit him then and there, or used a knife, he would have waited and plotted. On the other hand, it could even have been one of the German helots. . . .

Bond looked round the deck. The snoring of the man could have been a signal for any potential murderer. There were ladders to the boat deck from both sides of the cabin deck amidships. The man at the wheel in the pilot house forward would have heard nothing above the noise from the engine room. To pick the small fish out of its formalin bath and slip it into Mr. Krest's gaping mouth would have needed only seconds. Bond shrugged. Whoever had done it had not thought of the consequences—of the inevitable inquest, perhaps of a trial in which he, Bond, would be an additional suspect. They were certainly all going to be in one hell of a mess unless he could tidy things up.

Bond glanced over the edge of the boat deck. Below was the three-foot-wide strip of deck that ran the length of the ship. Between this and the sea there was a two-foot-high rail. Supposing the hammock had broken and Mr. Krest had fallen and rolled under the speedboat and over the edge of the upper deck, could he have reached the sea? Hardly, in this dead calm, but that was what he was going to have done.

Bond got moving. With a table knife from the saloon he carefully frayed and then broke one of the main cords of the hammock so that the hammock trailed realistically on the deck. Next, with a damp cloth, he cleaned up the specks of blood on the woodwork and the drops of formalin that led from the specimen jar. Then came the hardest part—handling the corpse. Carefully Bond pulled it to the very edge of the deck and himself went down the ladder and, bracing himself, reached up. The corpse came down on top of him in a heavy, drunken embrace. Bond staggered under it to the low rail and eased it over. There was a last hideous glimpse of the obscenely bulging face and the protruding fish tail, a sickening fume of stale whiskey, a heavy splash and it was gone and rolling sluggishly away in the small waves of the wake. Bond flattened himself back against the saloon hatchway, ready to slip through if the helmsman came aft to investigate. But there was no movement forward and the iron tramp of the diesels held steady.

Bond sighed deeply. It would be a very troublesome coroner who brought in anything but misadventure. He went back to the boat deck, gave it a final look over, disposed of the knife and the wet cloth, and went down the ladder to his bed in the well. It was two-fifteen. Bond was asleep inside ten minutes.

. . .

By pushing the speed up to twelve knots they made North Point by six o'clock that evening. Behind them the sky was ablaze with red and gold streaked across aquamarine. The two men, with the woman between them, stood at the rail of the well deck and watched the brilliant shore slip by across the mother-of-pearl mirror of the sea. Liz Krest was wearing a white linen frock with a black belt and a black-and-white handkerchief round her neck. The mourning colors went well with the golden skin. The three people stood stiffly and rather self-consciously, each one nursing his own piece of secret knowledge, each one anxious to convey to the other two that their particular secrets were safe with him.

That morning there had seemed to be a conspiracy among the three to sleep late. Even Bond had not been awakened by the sun until ten o'clock. He showered in the crew's quarters and chatted with the helmsman before going below to see what had happened to Fidele Barbey. He was still in bed. He said he had a hangover. Had he been very rude to Mr. Krest? He couldn't remember much about it except that he seemed to recall Mr. Krest being very rude to him. "You remember what I said about him from the beginning, James? A grand slam redoubled in bastards. Now do you agree with me? One of these days, someone's going to shut that soft ugly mouth of his forever."

Inconclusive. Bond had fixed himself some breakfast in the galley and was eating it there when Liz Krest had come in to do the same. She was dressed in a pale blue shantung kimono to her knees. There were dark rings under her eyes and she ate her breakfast standing. But she seemed perfectly calm and at ease. She whispered conspiratorially, "I do apologize about last night. I suppose I'd had a bit too much to drink too. But do forgive Milt. He's really awfully nice. It's only when he's had a bit too much that he gets sort of difficult. He's always sorry the next morning. You'll see."

When eleven o'clock came and neither of the other two showed any signs of, so to speak, blowing the gaff, Bond decided to force the pace. He looked very hard at Liz Krest who was curled up in the well deck reading a magazine. He said, "By the way, where's your husband? Still sleeping it off?"

She frowned. "I suppose so. He went up to his hammock on the boat deck. I've no idea what time. I took a sleeping pill and went straight off."

Fidele Barbey had a line out for amberjack. Without looking round he said, "He's probably in the pilot house."

Bond said, "If he's still asleep on the boat deck he'll be getting a hell of a sunburn."

Liz Krest said, "Oh, poor Milt! I hadn't thought of that. I'll go and see."

She climbed the ladder. When her head was above the level of the boat deck she stopped. She called down, anxiously, "James. He's not here. And the hammock's broken."

Bond said, "Fidele's probably right. I'll have a look forward."

He went to the pilot house. Fritz, the mate, and the engineer were there. Bond said, "Anyone seen Mr. Krest?"

Fritz looked puzzled: "No, sir. Why? Is anything wrong?"

Bond flooded his face with anxiety. "He's not aft. Here, come on! Look round everywhere. He was sleeping on the boat deck. He's not there and his hammock's broken. He was rather the worse for wear last night. Come on! Get cracking!"

When the inevitable conclusion had been reached, Liz Krest had a short but credible fit of hysterics. Bond took her to her cabin and left her there in tears. "It's all right, Liz," he said. "You stay out of this. I'll look after everything. We'll have to radio Port Victoria and so on. I'll tell Fritz to put on speed.

I'm afraid it's hopeless turning back to look. There've been six hours of daylight when he couldn't have fallen overboard without being heard or seen. It must have been in the night. I'm afraid anything like six hours in these seas is just not on."

She stared at him, her eyes wide. "You mean—you mean sharks and things?"

Bond nodded.

"Oh Milt! Poor darling Milt! Oh, why did this have to happen?"

Bond went out and softly shut the door.

. . .

The yacht rounded Cannon Point and reduced speed. Keeping well away from the broken reef it slid quietly across the broad bay, now lemon and gun metal in the last light, toward the anchorage. The small township beneath the mountains was already dark with indigo shadow in which a sprinkling of yellow lights showed. Bond saw the Customs and Immigration launch move off from Long Pier to meet them. The little community would already be buzzing with news that would have quickly leaked from the radio station to the Seychelles Club and then, through the members' chauffeurs and staffs, into the town.

Liz Krest turned to him. "I'm beginning to get nervous. Will you help me through the rest of this—these awful formalities and things?"

"Of course."

Fidele Barbey said, "Don't worry too much. All these people are my friends. And the Chief Justice is my uncle. We shall all have to make a statement. They'll probably have the inquest tomorrow. You'll be able to leave the day after."

"You really think so?" A dew of sweat had sprung below her eyes. "The trouble is I don't really know where to leave for or what to do next. I suppose," she hesitated, not looking at Bond, "I suppose, James, you wouldn't like to come on to Mombasa? I mean, you're going there anyway and I'd be able to get you there a day earlier than this ship of yours, this Camp something."

"Kampala." Bond lit a cigarette to cover his hesitation. Four days in a beautiful yacht with this girl! But the tail of that fish sticking out of the mouth! Had she done it? Or had Fidele, who would know that his uncles and cousins on Mahé would somehow see that he came to no harm? If only one of them would make a slip. Bond said easily, "That's terribly nice of you, Liz. Of course I'd love to come."

Fidele Barbey chuckled. "Bravo, my friend. And I would love to be in your shoes, but for one thing. That damned fish. It is a great responsibility. I like to think of you both being deluged with cables from the Smithsonian about it. Don't forget that you are now both trustees of a scientific Koh-i-noor. And you know what these Americans are. They'll worry the life out of you until they've got their hands on it."

Bond's eyes were hard as flint as he watched the girl. Did that put the finger on *her*?

But the beautiful, candid blue eyes did not flicker. She looked up into Fidele Barbey's face and said, easily, charmingly, "That won't be a problem. I've decided to give it to the British Museum."

James Bond noticed that the sweat dew had now gathered at her temples but, after all, it was a desperately hot evening . . .

The thud of the engines stopped and the anchor chain roared down into the quiet bay.

EVERYBODY HATES DAVID STARBUCK

BY STEVE ALLEN

Comedian, musician, composer, lyricist, poet, novelist, essayist, short-story writer, dabbler in politics—in an age of specialization, Steve Allen dares to be a jack-of-all-trades, a true Renaissance man. He is also a committed man: when his involvement in crusades and reform brings down upon him the epithets Bleeding Heart and Do-Gooder, he says, "That's a lot better than being a Dry Heart and a Do-Nothin'." "Everybody Hates David Starbuck" is his story of an ingenious retribution meted out to a deserving heel.

THE POLICE are not surprised when, in connection with a highly publicized murder that has gone unsolved, a number of people come forth to confess to the crime.

It is, on the other hand, unusual if not unknown for a man to confess to having committed a murder when beyond the shadow of a doubt a suicide rather than a killing was involved. That is why nobody paid any attention to Walt Swanson when he said he had murdered David Starbuck. Starbuck killed himself in the bathroom of his palatial Palm Springs home on the night of September 14th. There were at least 30 people who knew that Swanson had spent that night at the bar of the Villa Loma, a spaghetti-and-rendezvous joint on the Sunset Strip.

The door of Starbuck's toilet was locked from the inside. He had slashed his wrists, stretched out on the pink tile floor with a folded rug-mat under his head, and died almost peacefully. As one wag said when Swanson first confessed that *he* had cut Starbuck's wrists, although it was clearly established that he had been in Beverly Hills on the night in question, "Must have had a mighty long razor."

The police spent a little time checking Swanson's story, marked him as a psycho, and told him to get lost. I guess I'm the only one who knows that he was telling the truth after all, because I listened to the *whole* story.

To say that Starbuck was not widely admired is to win the understatement championship of any year. The movie business is never short of phonies but Dave was the champ. He came out here in the late Thirties with a reputation as a hot-shot salesman and there was always the vague idea that he had *had* to come West, that something he had been involved in in the East had not been strictly kosher. The idea was founded on bedrock. Dave had gotten into the habit of selling things he didn't own. In Hollywood he soon found that this trick could be valuable. First he palmed himself off as a writer, sold a book he hadn't written, stole half the profits from the poor bum who did write it, wangled a share of the production arrangement and found himself with a smash on his hands. From there on in there was no stopping him.

By 1945 he was second in command at World-American, living in Bel Air with his fourth wife, and climbing fast by reason of his shrewd and ruthless ability to manipulate men with big talent and small guts.

But I am getting ahead of myself, as they say. Let's go back a wife or two. We never knew just who Dave was married to back East. She never made the trip. He stole his second woman from Walt Swanson. Nobody but the old-timers remember much about Walt now, but in his time he was the greatest cameraman of them all. Some of the old stars wouldn't make a picture without him. Eventually he started directing and he would have made a fine director except that he began belting the bottle. Charming as he was sober, he was a mean drunk. They put up with his bats for a couple of years but eventually the word got around that hiring him for a picture meant added costs in lost shooting time. He never had a prayer after that. Well, no, he did have one chance. Dave Starbuck hired him for a picture and made a rather peculiar deal with him.

"Walt," Dave said, "here's the arrangement. Nobody else in town will hire you because you're a stewbum, right? Here's my offer. I'll give you your regular price for this picture and you get it the day we're through shooting, in one lump. Unless you start drinking. The first day you're drunk on the set the money drops to 50 percent. If you pull it a second time you get 25 percent. Take it or leave it."

Walt took it. You have to eat.

The third week of shooting Starbuck hired an out-of-work writer to take Walt to lunch and get him loaded. Then he came around to the set after lunch, walked up to Swanson, smiled broadly, smelled Walt's breath and said, "Cheer up, baby. At 50 percent you're still being overpaid." Walt's ego being what it was, he went on a week's bender. Starbuck threatened to throw him off the picture. Eventually he paid him peanuts and kicked him out. In desperation Walt sent his wife around to plead for a break.

"Listen, sweetie," Dave said, "what do you want from me? We made a deal."

"But Dave," Swanson's wife said, "Walt's having a rough time. He did a good job for you, didn't he?"

Dave looked at Swanson's wife. She had good legs and was years younger than Walt.

"Listen, Myrna," he said, "doesn't it make you feel sorta cheap to have to go around town begging for handouts for a has-been like Walt? You deserve better than that. You're a looker. I happen to know you have talent. You should be acting again. Whadda ya say we forget about the deal Walt and I made? It's all over. He made his bed. Let him lie in it. But let's say you have a small part in my next picture, at pretty good money. Now how's that?"

Well, when you're a former callgirl, when you'd love to do a little picture work, when you're married to a man 20 years your senior, and when you married him in the first place just because you were tired and he offered someplace to rest, a pitch like Starbuck's is pretty hard to resist. To spare the painful details, within six months Myrna had left Walt and moved in with Dave.

That did it for the poor bastard. He was no good after that. Never directed another picture. It must have been about that time that he first thought of killing Starbuck. He wasn't the first, of course, nor the only one, but he must have been head of the club.

The philosophers tell us that when you lust after a woman in your heart, or long to commit a murder, you're already on record, even if you never get to realize your amibition. On that basis I guess quite a few of us around town are guilty of the murder of David Starbuck. But here's how Walt Swanson did it.

By 1955 he was all washed up as a director, although Alcoholics Anonymous had put him back in one physical piece for the time being. To pay for the booze he had sold everything he had and now to keep eating he had to take any odd job he could get. An old friend eventually landed him a spot with Consolidated Film Service, a subsidiary of the Consolidated Studio, that did film exchange work. For example, when a wealthy producer wanted to go to the movies, well, it didn't work out that way. The movies went to him. His secretary just called the film exchange, ordered a certain picture, or maybe a double feature, and the films were shipped to the producer's home, to be shown in his private projection room, for his private pleasure. Walt Swanson thought it was a pretty grim joke the first time he got an order to ship a can of film to Starbuck's Bel Air pleasure-dome.

Then one day he learned that Starbuck had an ulcer. A snatch of conversation overheard at a restaurant and Walt's own stomach tingled in a momentary frenzy of vengeful glee. So the bastard could be hurt after all, if only by his conscience, his own fears. At the time that Walt noted this fact he did not file it away in any sort of conscious realization that eventually he would be able to call it out, to employ it. It was just something he heard about and was glad about and that was that.

The catalyst was dropped into the seething caldron of his mind a year later when he read a story in the *Hollywood Reporter* about subliminal advertising. A theatre in New Jersey had cut into a motion picture film commercial announcements that flashed on the screen too quickly to be seen consciously but, according to the theory, not too quickly to transmit to the eye and the subconscious mind an impression which subsequently would suggest action to the individual. In the test case the action suggested was the purchase of a particular soft drink. Sales of the drink increased markedly on the night of the test.

It was after reading that story that Walt Swanson began to

get even with David Starbuck. At first the idea of murder was not actually in his mind. He only wanted to hurt, to lash out, to avenge himself. The first thing he did was to print up two small cards, using white ink on black paper. One card said "Dave Starbuck, you stink." The other one said "Everybody hates David Starbuck." Then he borrowed a hand-operated movie camera from a friend, shot stills of the two cards, clipped out the film frames, put them into his wallet and waited.

Within a week Starbuck's secretary called to order a picture. When Walt received the shipping slip he got the film out of the vault, set it up on spools, scissored a line and inserted one of the still frames he had shot at home. Twenty minutes farther along on the reel he slipped in the second insert.

The picture was a comedy but that night after running it Dave Starbuck didn't feel amused. A certain insensitivity had always been part of his make-up, but faced even if subconsciously with the knowledge that he was actively disliked, and being at the same time unable to erect any of his customary defenses, he became vaguely depressed.

Swanson at first, and for a long time afterward, had no sure way of knowing how effective his attack was, but eventually he began to pick up stray bits of information that convinced him that he was striking telling blows. Column items about suddenly planned vacations, rumors about physical check-ups, stories about angry blowups in conference rooms. And only Swanson knew the reason. Once a week for a whole year he sent his invisible arrows into Starbuck's hide. "Starbuck, you're no good." "Dave, you're a heel." "Starbuck, you're sick."

And every Monday when the film would come back to the exchange, Walt would scissor out his inserts and patch up the reel, leaving no evidence.

"Starbuck, your wife despises you!"

"David Starbuck is a jerk!"

"Starbuck, you are the lowest of the low."

Starbuck's irritation increased to the point where he became careless about his attitude toward his superiors, and in Hollywood no matter how high up you are you have to answer to somebody: chairmen of the board, stockholders' groups. One night at a party he told the head of his studio's New York office to go to hell. From that moment he started to slide downhill, although at first his speed was so slow nobody was quite sure he was moving.

It was about that time that Swanson aimed his *coup de grâce*. The next time Starbuck had a picture run off he received this message: "Dave, why don't you kill yourself?"

The following week it was "Kill yourself, Dave. It's the only way out."

Starbuck put up with eight weeks of it. He began to fall apart. Having no friends to sympathize with him, he went from bad to worse fast. Then one day he went to Palm Springs, spent all afternoon lying in the sun by his swimming pool, got drunk, went into the bathroom, locked the door, lay down on the pink tile floor, folded the fluffy lamb's-wool bath mat under his head, slashed his wrists with a single-edge razor and bled to death, slowly, lying still.

After it happened Walt began drinking again. I wouldn't be telling the story now except that, as some of you may know, poor Walt got careless with a cigarette one night in the lab and burned himself up along with a hell of a lot of film. A few weeks before the end he told me the story one night at the Villa Loma bar.

Good thing Walt didn't work in a TV film lab.

THE HUSTLER

BY WALTER S. TEVIS

Proficiency in pocket billiards is often called the sign of a misspent youth ("That game with the fifteen numbered balls is the Devil's tool!" sang Robert Preston in "The Music Man"). Walter S. Tevis, during his college years, supported himself by working in a poolroom—"misspent" time that not only made possible his higher education but also gave birth to his short story, "The Hustler"; which gave birth to his best-selling novel, "The Hustler"; which gave birth to the powerful and acclaimed film, "The Hustler," which starred Paul Newman, Jackie Gleason and George C. Scott. Mr. Tevis, who now teaches English at Ohio University, informs us that his second novel, "The Man Who Fell to Earth," has also been purchased for filming. We wish it the same success as "The Hustler."

THEY TOOK SAM out of the office, through the long passageway, and up to the big metal doors. The doors opened, slowly, and they stepped out.

The sunlight was exquisite; warm on Sam's face. The air was clear and still. A few birds were circling in the sky. There was a gravel path, a road, and then, grass. Sam drew a deep breath. He could see as far as the horizon.

A guard drove up in a gray station wagon. He opened the door and Sam got in, whistling softly to himself. They drove off, down the gravel path. Sam did not turn around to look at the prison walls; he kept his eyes on the grass that stretched ahead of them, and on the road through the grass.

When the guard stopped to let him off in Richmond he said, "A word of advice, Willis."

"Advice?" Sam smiled at the guard.

"That's right. You got a habit of getting in trouble, Willis. That's why they didn't parole you, made you serve full time, because of that habit."

"That's what the man told me," Sam said. "So?"

"So stay out of pool rooms. You're smart. You can earn a living."

Sam started climbing out of the station wagon. "Sure," he said. He got out, slammed the door, and the guard drove away.

It was still early and the town was nearly empty. Sam walked around, up and down different streets, for about an hour, looking at houses and stores, smiling at the people he saw, whistling or humming little tunes to himself.

In his right hand he was carrying his little round tubular leather case, carrying it by the brass handle on the side. It was about 30 inches long, the case, and about as big around as a man's forearm.

At ten o'clock he went to the bank and drew out the 600 dollars he had deposited there under the name of George Graves. Only it was 680; it had gathered that much interest.

Then he went to a clothing store and bought a sporty tan coat, a pair of brown slacks, brown suede shoes and a bright green sport shirt. In the store's dressing room he put the new outfit on, leaving the prison-issued suit and shoes on the floor. Then he bought two extra sets of underwear and socks, paid, and left.

About a block up the street there was a clean-looking beauty parlor. He walked in and told the lady who seemed to be in charge, "I'm an actor. I have to play a part in Chicago tonight that requires red hair." He smiled at her. "Can you fix me up?"

The lady was all efficiency. "Certainly," she said. "If you'll just step back to a booth we'll pick out a shade."

A half hour later he was a redhead. In two hours he was on board a plane for Chicago, with a little less than 600 dollars in his pocket and one piece of luggage. He still had the underwear and socks in a paper sack.

In Chicago he took a 14-dollar-a-night room in the best hotel he could find. The room was big, and pleasant. It looked and smelled clean.

He sat down on the side of the bed and opened his little leather case at the top. The two piece billiard cue inside was intact. He took it out and screwed the brass joint together, pleased that it still fit perfectly. Then he checked the butt for tightness. The weight was still firm and solid. The tip was good, its shape had held up; and the cue's balance and stroke seemed easy, familiar; almost as though he still played with it every day.

He checked himself in the mirror. They had done a perfect job on his hair; and its brightness against the green and brown of his new clothes gave him the sporty, racetrack sort of look he had always avoided before. His once ruddy complexion was very pale. Not a pool player in town should be able to recognize him: he could hardly recognize himself.

If all went well he would be out of Chicago for good in a

few days; and no one would know for a long time that Big Sam Willis had even played there. Six years on a manslaughter charge could have its advantages.

In the morning he had to walk around town for a while before he found a pool room of the kind he wanted. It was a few blocks off the Loop, small; and from the outside it seemed to be fairly clean and quiet.

Inside, there was a short order and beer counter up front. In back there were four tables; Sam could see them through the door in the partition that separated the lunch room from the pool room proper. There was no one in the place except for the tall, blond boy behind the counter.

Sam asked the boy if he could practice.

"Sure." The boy's voice was friendly. "But it'll cost you a dollar an hour."

"Fair enough." He gave the boy a five dollar bill. "Let me know when this is used up."

The boy raised his eyebrows and took the money.

In the back room Sam selected the best 20-ounce cue he could find in the wall rack, one with an ivory point and a tight butt, chalked the tip, and broke the rack of balls on what seemed to be the best of the four tables.

He tried to break safe, a straight pool break, where you drive the two bottom corner balls to the cushions and back into the stack where they came from, making the cue ball go two rails and return to the top of the table, killing itself on the cushion. The break didn't work, however; the rack of balls spread wide, five of them came out into the table, and the cue ball stopped in the middle. It would have left an opponent wide open for a big run. Sam shuddered.

He pocketed the 15 balls, missing only once—a long shot that had to be cut thin into a far corner—and he felt better, making balls. He had little confidence on the hard ones, he was awkward; but he still knew the game, he knew how to break up little clusters of balls on one shot so that he could pocket them on the next. He knew how to play position with very little English on the cue, by shooting "natural" shots, and letting the speed of the cue ball do the work. He could still figure the spread, plan out his shots in advance from the positions of the balls on the table, and he knew what to shoot at first.

He kept shooting for about three hours. Several times other players came in and played for a while, but none of them paid any attention to him, and none of them stayed long.

The place was empty again and Sam was practicing cutting balls down the rail, working on his cue ball and on his speed, when he looked up and saw the boy who ran the place coming back. He was carrying a plate with a hamburger in one hand and two bottles of beer in the other.

"Hungry?" He set the sandwich down on the arm of a chair. "Or thirsty, maybe?"

Sam looked at his watch. It was 1:30. "Come to think of it," he said, "I am." He went to the chair, picked up the hamburger, and sat down.

"Have a beer," the boy said, affably. Sam took it and drank from the bottle. It tasted delicious.

"What do I owe you?" he said, and took a bite out of the hamburger.

"The burger's 30 cents," the boy said. "The beer's on the house."

"Thanks," Sam said, chewing. "How do I rate?"

"You're a good customer," the boy said. "Easy on the equipment, cash in advance, and I don't even have to rack the balls for you."

"Thanks." Sam was silent for a minute, eating.

The boy was drinking the other beer. Abruptly, he set the bottle down. "You on the hustle?" he said.

"Do I look like a hustler?"

"You practice like one."

Sam sipped his beer quietly for a minute, looking over the top of the bottle, once, at the boy. Then he said, "I might be looking around." He set the empty bottle down on the wooden chair arm. "I'll be back tomorrow; we can talk about it then. There might be something in it for you, if you help me out."

"Sure, mister," the boy said. "You pretty good?"

"I think so," Sam said. Then when the boy got up to leave he added, "Don't try to finger me for anybody. It won't do you any good."

"I won't." The boy went back up front.

Sam practiced, working mainly on his stroke and his position, for three more hours. When he finished his arm was sore and his feet were tired; but he felt better. His stroke was beginning to work for him, he was getting smooth, making balls regularly, playing good position. Once, when he was running balls continuously, racking 14 and 1, he ran 47 without missing.

The next morning, after a long night's rest, he was even better. He ran more than 90 balls one time, missing, finally, on a difficult rail shot.

The boy came back at 1:00 o'clock, bringing a ham sandwich this time and two beers. "Here you go," he said. "Time to make a break."

Sam thanked him, laid his cue stick on the table, and sat down.

"My name's Barney," the boy said.

"George Graves." Sam held out his hand, and the boy shook it. "Just," he smiled inwardly at the thought, "call me Red."

"You *are* good," Barney said. "I watched you a couple of times."

"I know." Sam took a drink from the beer bottle. "I'm looking for a straight pool game."

"I figured that, Mister Graves. You won't find one here, though. Up at Bennington's they play straight pool."

Sam had heard of Bennington's. They said it was a hustler's room, a big money place.

"You know who plays pool there, Barney?" he said.

"Sure. Bill Peyton, he plays there. And Shufala Kid, Louisville Fats, Johnny Vargas, Henry Keller, a little guy they call 'The Policeman' . . ."

Henry Keller was the only familiar name; Sam had played him once, in Atlantic City, maybe 14 years ago. But that had been even before the big days of Sam's reputation, before he had got so good that he had to trick hustlers into playing him. That was a long time ago. And then there was the red hair; he ought to be able to get by.

"Which one's got money," he asked, "and plays straight pool?"

"Well," Barney looked doubtful, "I think Louisville Fats carries a big roll. He's one of the old Prohibition boys; they say he keeps an army of hoods working for him. He plays straights. But he's good. And he doesn't like being hustled."

It looked good; but dangerous. Hustlers didn't take it very well to find out a man was using a phony name so he could get a game. Sam remembered the time someone had told Bernie James who he had been playing and Bernie had got pretty rough about it. But this time it was different; he had been out of circulation six years, and he had never played in Chicago before.

"This Fats. Does he bet big?"

"Yes, he bets big. Big as you want." Barney smiled. "But I tell you he's mighty good."

"Rack the balls," Sam said, and smiled back. "I'll show you something."

Barney racked. Sam broke them wide open and started running. He went through the rack, then another, another, and another. Barney was counting the balls, racking them for him each time. When he got to 80 Sam said, "Now I'll bank a few." He banked seven, knocking them off the rails, across, and into the pockets. When he missed the eighth he said, "What do you think?"

"You'll do," Barney said. He laughed. "Fats is good: but you might take him."

"I'll take him," Sam said. "You lead me to him. Tomorrow night you get somebody to work for you. We're going up to Bennington's."

"Fair enough, Mister Graves," Barney said. He was grinning. "We'll have a beer on that."

At Bennington's you took an elevator to the floor you wanted: billiards on the first, pocket pool on the second, snooker and private games on the third. It was an old-fashioned set-up, high ceilings, big, shaded incandescent lights, overstuffed leather chairs.

Sam spent the morning on the second floor, trying to get the feel of the tables. They were different from Barneys, with softer cushions and tighter cloths, and it was a little hard to get used to them; but after about two hours he felt as though he had them pretty well, and he left. No one had paid any attention to him.

After lunch he inspected his hair in the restaurant's bathroom mirror; it was still as red as ever and hadn't yet begun to grow out. He felt good. Just a little nervous, but good.

Barney was waiting for him at the little pool room. They took a cab up to Bennington's.

Louisville Fats must have weighed 300 pounds. His face seemed to be bloated around the eyes like the face of an Eskimo, so that he was always squinting. His arms, hanging from the short sleeves of his white silk shirt, were pink and dough-like. Sam noticed his hands; they were soft looking, white and delicate. He wore three rings, one with a diamond. He had on dark green, wide suspenders.

When Barney introduced him, Fats said, "How are you, George?" but didn't offer his hand. Sam noticed that his eyes, almost buried beneath the face, seemed to shift from side to side, so that he seemed not really to be looking at anything.

"I'm fine," Sam said. Then, after a pause, "I've heard a lot about you."

"I got a reputation?" Fats' voice was flat, disinterested. "Then I must be pretty good maybe?"

"I suppose so," Sam said, trying to watch the eyes.

"You a good pool player, George?" The eyes flickered, scanning Sam's face.

"Fair. I like playing. Straight pool."

"Oh." Fats grinned, abruptly, coldly. "That's my game too, George." He slapped Barney on the back. The boy pulled away, slightly, from him. "You pick good, Barney. He plays my game. You can finger for me, sometime, if you want."

"Sure," Barney said. He looked nervous.

"One thing." Fats was still grinning. "You play for money, George? I mean, you gamble?"

"When the bet's right."

"What you think is a right bet, George?"

"50 dollars."

Fats grinned even more broadly; but his eyes still kept shifting. "Now that's close, George," he said. "You play for a hundred and we play a few."

"Fair enough," Sam said, as calmly as he could.

"Let's go upstairs. It's quieter."

"Fine. I'll take my boy if you don't mind. He can rack the balls."

Fats looked at Barney. "You level with that rack, Barney? I mean, you rack the balls tight for Fats?"

"Sure," Barney said, "I wouldn't try to cross you up."

"You know better than that, Barney. OK."

They walked up the back stairs to the third floor. There was a small, bare-walled room, well lighted, with chairs lined up against the walls. The chairs were high ones, the type used for watching pool games. There was no one else in the room.

They uncovered the table, and Barney racked the balls. Sam lost the toss and broke, making it safe, but not too safe. He undershot, purposely, and left the cue ball almost a foot away from the end rail.

They played around, shooting safe, for a while. Then Fats pulled a hard one off the edge of the rack, ran 35, and played him safe. Sam jockeyed with him, figuring to lose for a while, only wanting the money to hold out until he had the table down pat, until he had the other man's game figured, until he was ready to raise the bet.

He lost three in a row before he won one. He wasn't playing his best game; but that meant little, since Fats was probably pulling his punches too, trying to take him for as much as possible. After he won his first game he let himself go a little and made a few tricky ones. Once he knifed a ball thin into the side pocket and went two cushions for a break up; but Fats didn't even seem to notice.

Neither of them tried to run more than 40 at a turn. It would have looked like a game between only fair players, except that neither of them missed very often. In a tight spot they didn't try anything fancy, just shot a safe and let the other man figure it out. Sam played safe on some shots that he was sure he could make; he didn't want to show his hand. Not yet. They kept playing and, after a while, Sam started winning more often.

After about three hours he was five games ahead, and shooting better all the time. Then, when he won still another game, Sam said, "You're losing money, Fats. Maybe we should quit." He looked at Barney and winked. Barney gave him a puzzled, worried look.

"Quit? You think we should quit?" Fats took a big silk handkerchief from his side pocket and wiped his face. "How much money you won, George?" he said.

"That last makes 600." He felt, suddenly, a little tense. It was coming. The big push.

"Suppose we play for 600, George." He put the handkerchief back in his pocket. "Then we see who quits."

"Fine." He felt really nervous now, but he knew he would

get over it. Nervousness didn't count. At 600 a game he would be in clover and in San Francisco in two days. If he didn't lose.

Barney racked the balls and Sam broke. He took the break slowly, putting to use his practice of three days, and his experience of 27 years. The balls broke perfectly, reracking the original triangle, and the cue ball skidded to a stop right on the end cushion.

"You shoot pretty good," Fats said, looking at the safe table that Sam had left him. But he played safe, barely tipping the cue ball off one of the balls down at the foot of the table and returning back to the end rail.

Sam tried to return the safe by repeating the same thing; but the cue ball caught the object ball too thick and he brought out a shot, a long one, for Fats. Fats stepped up, shot the ball in, played position, and ran out the rest of the rack. Then he ran out another rack and Sam sat down to watch; there was nothing he could do now. Fats ran 78 points and then, seeing a difficult shot, played him safe.

He had been afraid that something like that might happen. He tried to fight his way out of the game, but couldn't seem to get into the clear long enough for a good run. Fats beat him badly—125 to 30—and he had to give back the 600 dollars from his pocket. It hurt.

What hurt even worse was that he knew he had less than 600 left of his own money.

"Now we see who quits." Fats stuffed the money in his hip pocket. "You want to play for another 600?"

"I'm still holding my stick," Sam said. He tried not to think about that "army of hoods" that Barney had told him about.

He stepped up to the table and broke. His hand shook a little; but the break was a perfect one.

In the middle of the game Fats missed an easy shot, leaving Sam a dead set-up. Sam ran 53 and out. He won. It was as easy as that. He was 600 ahead again, and feeling better.

Then something unlucky happened. Downstairs they must have closed up because six men came up during the next game and sat around the table. Five of them Sam had never seen, but one of them was Henry Keller. Henry was drunk now, evidently, and he didn't seem to be paying much attention to what was going on; but Sam didn't like it. He didn't like Keller, and he didn't like having a man who knew who he was around him. It was too much like that other time. That time in Richmond when Bernie James had come after him with a bottle. That fight had cost him six years. He didn't like it. It was getting time to wind things up here, time to be cutting out. If he could win two more games quick, he would have enough to set him up hustling on the West Coast. And on the West Coast there weren't any Henry Kellers who knew that Big Sam Willis was once the best straight-pool shot in the game.

After Sam had won the game by a close score Fats looked at his fingernails and said, "George, you're a hustler. You shoot better straights than anybody in Chicago shoots. Except me."

This was the time, the time to make it quick and neat, the time to push as hard as he could. He caught his breath, held steady, and said, "You've got it wrong, Fats. I'm better than you are. I'll play you for all of it. The whole 1200."

It was very quiet in the room. Then Fats said, "George, I like that kind of talk." He started chalking his cue. "We play 1200."

Barney racked the balls and Fats broke them. They both played safe, very safe, back and forth, keeping the cue ball on the rail, not leaving a shot for the other man. It was nerve-wracking. Over and over.

Then he missed. Missed the edge of the rack, coming at it from an outside angle. His cue ball bounced off the rail and into the rack of balls, spreading them wide, leaving Fats at least five shots. Sam didn't sit down. He just stood and watched Fats come up and start his run. He ran the balls, broke on the 15th, and ran another rack. 28 points. And he was just getting started. He had his rack break set up perfectly for the next shot.

Then, as Fats began chalking up, preparing to shoot, Henry

Keller stood up from his seat and pointed his finger at Sam.

He was drunk; but he spoke clearly, and loudly. "You're Big Sam Willis," he said. "You're the World's Champion." He sat back in his chair, heavily. "You got red hair, but you're Big Sam." He sat silent, half slumped in the big chair, for a moment, his eyes glassy, and red at the corners. Then he closed his eyes and said, "There's nobody beats Big Sam, Fats. Nobody *never*."

The room was quiet for what seemed to be a very long while. Sam noticed how thick the tobacco smoke had become in the air; motionless, it was like a heavy brown mist, and over the table it was like a cloud. The faces of the men in the chairs were impassive; all of them, except Henry, watching him.

Fats turned to him. For once his eyes were not shifting from side to side. He looked Sam in the face and said, in a voice that was flat and almost a whisper, "You Big Sam Willis, George?"

"That's right, Fats."

"You must be pretty smart, Sam," Fats said, "to play a trick like that. To make a sucker out of me."

"Maybe." His chest and stomach felt very tight. It was like when Bernie James had caught him at the same game, except without the red hair. Bernie hadn't said anything, though; he had just picked up a bottle.

But, then, Bernie James was dead now. Sam wondered, momentarily, if Fats had ever heard about that.

Suddenly Fats split the silence, laughing. The sound of his laughing filled the room, he threw his head back and laughed; and the men in the chairs looked at him, astonished, hearing the laughter. "Big Sam," he said, "you're a hustler. You put on a great act; and fool me good. A great act." He slapped Sam on the back. "I think the joke's on me."

It was hard to believe. But Fats could afford the money, and Sam knew that Fats knew who would be the best if it came to muscle. And there was no certainty whose side the other men were on.

Fats shot, ran a few more balls, and then missed.

When Sam stepped up to shoot he said, "Go ahead, Big Sam, and shoot your best. You don't have to act now. I'm quitting you anyway after this one."

The funny thing was that Sam had been shooting his best for the past five or six games—or thought he had—but when he stepped up to the table this time he was different. Maybe it was Fats or Keller, something made him feel as he hadn't felt for a long time. It was like being the old Big Sam, back before he had quit playing the tournaments and exhibitions, the Big Sam who could run 125 when he was hot and the money was up. His stroke was smooth, steady, accurate, like a balanced, precision instrument moving on well-oiled bearings. He shot easily, calmly, clicking the shots off in his mind and then pocketing them on the table, watching everything on the green, forgetting himself, forgetting even the money, just dropping the balls into the pockets, one after another.

He did it. He ran the game. 125 points, 125 shots without missing. When he finished Fats took 1200 from his still-big roll and counted it out, slowly, to him. He said, "You're the best I've ever seen, Big Sam." Then he covered the table with the oilcloth cover.

After Sam had dropped Barney off he had the cab take him by his hotel and let him off at a little all-night lunch room. He ordered bacon and eggs, over light, and talked with the waitress while she fried them. The place seemed strange, gay almost; his nerves felt electric, and there was a pleasant fuzziness in his head, a dim, insistent ringing sound coming from far off. He tried to think for a moment; tried to think whether he should go to the airport now without even going back to the hotel, now that he had made out so well, had made out better, even, than he had planned to be able to do in a week. But there was the waitress and then the food; and when he put a quarter in the juke box he couldn't hear the ringing in his ears any more. This was no time for plane trips; it was a time for talk and music, time for the sense of triumph, the sense of being alive and having money again, and then time for sleep. He was in a chromium and plastic booth in the lunch room and he leaned back against the padded plastic backrest and felt an abrupt, deep, gratifying sense of fatigue, loosening his muscles and killing, finally, the tension that had ridden him like a fury for the past three days. There would be plane flights enough tomorrow. Now, he needed rest. It was a long way to San Francisco.

The bed at his hotel was impeccably made; the pale blue spread seemed drum-tight, but soft and round at the edges and corners. He didn't even take off his shoes.

When he awoke, he awoke suddenly. The skin at the back of his neck was itching, sticky with sweat from where the collar of his shirt had been pressed, tight, against it. His mouth was dry and his feet felt swollen, stuffed, in his shoes. The room was as quiet as death. Outside the window a car's tires groaned gently, rounding a corner, then were still.

He pulled the chain on the lamp by the bed and the light came on. Squinting, he stood up, and realized that his legs were aching. The room seemed too big, too bright. He stumbled into the bathroom and threw handfuls of cold water on his face and neck. Then he dried off with a towel and looked in the mirror. Startled, he let go the towel momentarily; the red hair had caught him off guard; and with the eyes now swollen, the lips pale, it was not his face at all. He finished drying quickly, ran his comb through his hair, straightened out his shirt and slacks hurriedly. The startling strangeness of his own face had crystallized the dim, half-conscious feeling that had awakened him, the feeling that something was wrong. The hotel room, himself, Chicago; they were all wrong. He should not be here, not now; he should be on the West Coast, in San Francisco.

He looked at his watch. 4:00 o'clock. He had slept three hours. He did not feel tired, not now, although his bones ached and there was sand under his eyelids. He could sleep, if he had to, on the plane. But the important thing, now, was getting on the plane, clearing out, moving West. He had slept with his cue, in its case, on the bed. He took it and left the room.

The lobby, too, seemed too bright and too empty. But when he had paid his bill and gone out to the street the relative darkness seemed worse. He began to walk down the street hastily, looking for a cab stand. His own footsteps echoed around him as he walked. There seemed to be no cabs anywhere on the street. He began walking faster. The back of his neck was sweating again. It was a very hot night; the air felt heavy against his skin. There were no cabs.

And then, when he heard the slow, dense hum of a heavy car moving down the street in his direction, heard it from several blocks away and turned his head to see it and to see that there was no cablight on it, he knew—abruptly and lucidly, as some men at some certain times know these things— what was happening.

He began to run; but he did not know where to run. He turned a corner while he was still two blocks ahead of the car and when he could feel its lights, palpably, on the back of his neck, and tried to hide in the doorway, flattening himself out against the door. Then, when he saw the lights of the car as it began its turn around the corner he realized that the doorway was too shallow, that the lights would pick him out. Something in him wanted to scream. He pushed himself from his place, stumbled down the street, visualizing in his mind a place, some sort of a place between buildings where he could hide completely and where the car could never follow him. But the buildings were all together, with no space at all between them; and when he saw that this was so he also saw at the same instant that the carlights were flooding him. And then he heard the car stop. There was nothing more to do. He turned around and looked at the car, blinking.

Two men had got out of the back seat; there were two more in front. He could see none of their faces; but was relieved that he could not, could not see the one face that would be bloated like an Eskimo's and with eyes like slits.

The men were holding the door open for him.

"Well," he said. "Hello, boys," and climbed into the back seat. His little leather case was still in his right hand. He gripped it tightly. It was all he had.

WALK TO THE STATION

BY STANLEY COOPERMAN

"The pity of death," says a character in this story, "decreases in direct ratio to the progression of its mass." All of us can testify to the regrettable truth of that callous formula: the passing of a single child can move us to tears, but the destruction of a city is too vast for us to comprehend. In this very short, very quiet, very good story, Stanley Cooperman warns us that doomsday can come in a little black bag.

"THOSE ARE NOT PEOPLE," the fat man said. "They are not people at all. If you think of them as people, you lose everything."

Peter struck a match and watched the small flame blink in the wind. He took the unlit cigarette from his mouth and tossed it away.

"How easy it is," he said, "for you to decide what to think."

The fat man shifted the black suitcase to his other hand and grimaced. "It isn't easy at all," he said, grunting with the effort and the late afternoon heat. "But too many thoughts are unnecessary. During the war . . ."

"There wasn't time to think."

The two men turned off Fifth Avenue and walked east along 42nd Street. They were carrying black overnight cases with tennis racquets strapped to them. The offices had started to empty, and they made their way awkwardly through the rush of bodies. Exhaust piled up from the taxis and buses inching forward in cross-town traffic.

"The eyes are most of it," Peter said, "I find myself looking at a single pair of eyes, and very often the eyes look back."

"Yes," the fat man said. "I had that trouble at first." He hesitated. "Thirteen years ago. It doesn't seem that long."

"Of course," Peter said with heavy irony. "In your case, however, they stopped looking back soon enough."

"The trick," the fat man continued, ignoring the interruption, "is to look at them as a group, so that there are no complications. Once—when we were first putting them in the cars—an old man tripped and sprained his ankle. I rushed to help him before I knew what I was doing. I knew at the time that it was quite ridiculous, an obsolete impulse." The fat man paused and smiled. "If he had been shot I wouldn't have bothered. As it was, it nearly cost me my job."

They entered Grand Central Station and stood on the marble-surfaced steps, resting the black suitcases. There was no hurry. Peter looked down into the busy space before them. "A goldfish bowl," he said.

"That's right. You see? It becomes easier when you think like that."

They picked up the suitcases and went down the steps, becoming part of the station's movement. Peter stopped before a poster of a famous, smiling face. Beneath the face, printed in large letters, was a request for civilian defense volunteers. Peter turned away from the picture. "Do you think they really expect a warning from the sky?" he asked.

The fat man grinned thickly at him, and wiped his forehead with a white handkerchief. "Would you like some ice cream?" he said. "There are still a few minutes, and this heat . . ."

"By all means," Peter said. "The ice cream here is very good." He added, with a glance at the fat man's waistline, "And very rich."

"Like the rest of the country," the fat man said, unperturbed. "Very rich indeed."

They entered a drug store featuring a large soda fountain, and sat at the chrome-trimmed counter. A young waitress came toward them. She was blonde and quick. Peter stared at the waitress while the fat man gave their order. A single drop of sweat glistened from her upper lip. For some reason the drop fascinated Peter, and he stared at it so that the waitress blushed nervously as she turned away.

"Do you like them that thin?"

Peter ignored the question. He glanced down at the black suitcase resting against his leg. "You are quite right," he said to the fat man.

"About what?"

"During the war," Peter continued, "we were on strafing assignment. The roads were full, so that from the air the roads themselves seemed to be alive. They were moving. Our job was to kill the roads, to stop the movement. It was like shooting at a black snake, and there was nothing to think about."

"Exactly," the fat man said, drumming his fingers on the counter. He could almost taste the coolness of the ice cream, and waited impatiently.

"Did you know Novak?" Peter asked suddenly.

The fat man thought for a moment. "No. Who was he?"

"A mathematician. Killed in 1944. He put it into a formula."

The waitress returned with the ice cream, and the fat man began eating quickly, smacking his lips. Peter looked at him.

"I said he put it into a formula."

The fat man stopped eating. "All right," he said. "What was it?"

"He said this: 'The pity of death decreases in direct ratio to the progression of its mass.' "

"Very impressive, but I have been telling you the same thing, and without the big words." The fat man wiped his forehead again. "Eat your ice cream."

When they left the drug store the fat man stopped, his features warped into sudden panic. "What is it?" Peter demanded, enjoying the tension. This job had been too easy. There was no danger, nothing to act against. Even when he had been strafing the roads there had been the exhilaration of flying recklessly. Now he was simply a messenger, an errand boy. He welcomed the fat man's fear.

"The lockers! I am unfamiliar with their location! We must call Headquarters . . ."

"Idiot!" Peter said sharply. "We will do nothing of the sort." He looked around for a guard or policeman. "Come with me and keep your mouth shut."

They approached a tall, middle-aged policeman who was standing next to a newsstand. "Pardon me," Peter said. "Can you direct us to the nearest locker? We wish to check our bags there for a while."

"Certainly," the policeman said, and gave them instructions. "Going away for a trip?" he added, eyeing the tennis racquets strapped to the cases.

"Yes," Peter said. "The city is so uncomfortable this time of year . . ."

"Don't I know it! New York is hot enough to scorch asbestos. I was raised in a small town myself." The policeman grinned ruefully at them.

Peter began to tremble. He knew that he was talking to a dead man, and as he looked at the policeman's eyes he saw them turning into steam, bubbling out of their sockets. "Thank you," he said quickly.

When they were safely away, the fat man looked at Peter with approval. "Congratulations," he said. "You did that very neatly."

"Yes," Peter said. "Neatly."

They arrived at the lockers, and the fat man fumbled in his pocket. He finally produced two dimes, and inserted them into the two slots. Peter opened the doors, and placed the black suitcases in the lockers. He stepped back and looked at them, while the fat man breathed heavily beside him.

"Look at the clocks," the fat man said, motioning to a display in the window of a jewelry shop across the arcade. The clocks gave the time at Moscow, Paris, London, Chicago, Los Angeles and other cities. "Look at them," the fat man repeated. "Each hour they show is different, yet each is the same. Agent One in Moscow, Two in Paris, Three in London." He touched the locker gently, while his words marched in parade. "The soldiers have quietly begun the battle . . ."

"What battle?" Peter looked at the fat man with distaste. "What soldiers?" He stared at the fat man's double-breasted business suit, and looked down at his own conservative suit, his black shoes and respectable tie. "The time for soldiers has passed. There are no more soldiers."

The fat man shrugged and closed the doors. They walked rapidly away from the lockers. As they went to the exit, a small girl eating a large candy looked at Peter. She held her mother's dress while the woman spoke to a porter. The little girl looked solemnly at Peter, as though she had seen him somewhere before. Peter felt himself drowning in the little girl's eyes.

The fat man tugged at Peter impatiently. "Let's go," he said. "There is still a long drive." Peter turned away from the little girl, and they went to the exit. "I've never seen a 'jackpot' before," the fat man said lightly. "It should be something to remember—providing," he added, winking at Peter, "we drive carefully."

They hailed a taxi, and gave the address of the parking lot where they had left their car. In the station a loudspeaker announced the schedule to waiting travelers. At a newsstand, an old man argued about his change. And in the street, exhaust piled up from crosstown traffic.

NAKED IN XANADU

BY RAY RUSSELL

Ray Russell's books include three collections—"Sardonicus and Other Stories," "The Little Lexicon of Love," "Unholy Trinity"—and a novel, "The Case Against Satan." A literary critic, in reviewing the novel, said: "There is an unusual stamp of authority about Ray Russell's writing, a disturbing sense of authenticity." It is a comment that is also applicable to the following story by PLAYBOY's *former Executive Editor. As one reads this artfully structured tale, one feels that Sonny Gray's invisible empire might actually exist, at this very moment, in any city, and that one's self or one's intimates might unknowingly be part of the insidious web. This peculiar You-Are-There feeling, this "disturbing sense of authenticity," is partially attributable to the author's almost documentary use of his adopted town, Hollywood, as a backdrop, and to his painstaking research into certain psychological techniques; but the story's reality is more directly due to what Russell calls "my absolute conviction that I could do everything Sonny does in the story, if I had the time, and the nerve, and the need."*

WITH A FLUTTERING whimper that burst into a yell, Sonny Gray battled his way out of sleep, blinking and gasping, greeting the day in the abrupt style that had, of late, become usual with him.

The nightmare, as always, had been distressing, but the act of waking up invariably sponged it from his memory, bringing the customary morning smile to his face.

It was a small smile, but then it was a small face, small and undistinguished and not what you would call attractive. The smile was one of secret knowledge, private joy, the smile of a cat who has swallowed a large number of the fattest, juiciest canaries.

He sat up in bed and, rubbing sleep-clogged eyes, looked out the window. From his quiet home on St. Ives Drive, just above Sunset Strip, he could see a great section of the city, laid out at his feet like an Oriental rug. Here, near, was Hollywood, pungent and vulgar; over there, the beginnings of Beverly Hills, elegant and sedate. The morning was clear; no smog; he could see far. Sonny liked to see far. It made him inordinately happy.

He had not always been happy. As he got out of bed, padded downstairs, and made himself an enormous breakfast, he remembered other, hapless days. Days when time had pressed heavily upon him, crushing him like iron weights; days when boredom and misery had been corrosive acids blackening and diminishing his spirit; days when life had edged him closer and closer to the brink of suicide. Those had been bad days, and worse nights, nights of drinking and desperate tears. Now, after zealously cramming his skinny carcass with scrambled eggs, sausages, buttered toast, jam, milk and coffee (plenty of protein: he had to keep up his strength), he patted his lips with his napkin and sighed contentedly.

In the bathroom, he sang as he showered, hummed as he shaved. By singing and humming, he managed to get through half the bubbly first act of *La Traviata*. He looked at his face in the mirror, and laughed. "You monkey," he said, affectionately, "you ugly little monkey."

Sonny did, in fact, resemble a monkey. For most of his life, that uncomely face and, later, that balding skull had caused him considerable melancholy. Currently, he didn't give a good god damn *what* he looked like. Sonny was 43. He felt like a kid. He stood five-five in elevator shoes. He felt like a giant. Switching from Verdi to Rodgers, "Oh what a beautiful morning," he sang, "oh what a beautiful day."

He did not dress, exactly, but put on fresh pajamas and a crisp robe. Then he walked downstairs to his study, unlocked a drawer in his desk and flipped the pages of a fat appointment book, bound in Florentine leather of a tan so light it was almost ivory and of a texture as smooth and sleek as a girl's belly. His fingertips lingered on the leather (he had always liked nice things) as he looked down at the open book. Long-time bachelors frequently talk to themselves: "Saturday," Sonny murmured, "a full schedule."

He replaced the appointment book, locked the drawer, and warmly contemplated the word *simplicity*. There were other words that came to mind, like *flawless* and *foolproof*, but he faithfully returned to the thought that pleased him most—that the single most remarkable aspect of his life, these days, was its simplicity. Its sinewy, spare, sublime simplicity.

He sauntered into the living room and sat down, patiently waiting. He looked at the clock on the fireplace; it was almost ten. He heard a car approach and stop; the slam of its door; then a soft discreet knocking on his front door. It was now exactly ten.

Smiling, Sonny rose to answer the knock. "Right on cue," he observed, somewhat smugly.

His day had begun.

Late that afternoon, his phone rang. "Hello?" he said.

He recognized the voice. "This is Millie Van Bustenhalter. I have a friend named Sandra Sharnoe who would like to speak to you."

"All right, put her on."

After a pause, an unfamiliar voice said, "Hello? Mr.—uh——"

"Did I understand Millie to say your name is Sandra Sharnoe? I gather you have some kind of problem and you'd like my help?"

"Well, yes, she said you get *wild* results, and I'm just desperate——"

"I'll tell you what, Miss Sharnoe. There's a delicatessen on the Strip, just west of Doheny. Can you be there in, oh, an hour?"

She was hesitant. "I . . . guess so. Sunset and Doheny?"

"North side of the street. I'll be sitting in there, drinking a glass of buttermilk. I'll be wearing a charcoal suit, with a red necktie, and there will be a white carnation in my buttonhole."

Wavering, Sandra Sharnoe said, "I don't really know . . ."

"It's entirely up to you. I'll be there in any case. If we happen to run into each other, fine. If not, I couldn't care less. Charcoal suit, red tie, white buttonhole."

"All right, Mr.—wait a minute, what's your——"

"See you soon, then."

He hung up and got dressed for the first time that day, putting on his charcoal suit and a tie of scarlet silk, which he skewered with a garnet stickpin. He remembered, then, that the florist had been all out of white carnations and had apologetically sent white roses instead. Snipping one from the group in the vase on the piano, he inserted it neatly into his lapel. It would serve.

The winding downhill walk to the deli was short and pleasant, taking him past Stravinsky's house, the sight of which always afforded him a glow of moderate wattage, seeming almost to link him, Sonny Gray, with the brilliant distant Paris of Picasso and Nijinsky, of the furor over *Le Sacre*, of the famous promenade through the Place de la Concorde that night when Diaghilev, adjusting his monocle, said to Cocteau: "*Étonne-moi.*" (Ah, *cher* Diaghilev, smiled Sonny as he strolled, how *I* would have astonished you, if I had been there to tell you my secret!)

A long-legged thoroughbred with chocolate eyes and sable hair entered the deli as Sonny was enjoying his buttermilk. She glanced about nervously, took note of his suit, his tie and his boutonniere, and click-clacked over to his table, her lustrous dark coif bouncing. Her face was drawn tight by tension, the brown eyes dulled, probably by pain or lack of sleep or both, and she had not bothered with cosmetics; she was, nonetheless, a knockout.

Before she could open her mouth, Sonny said, "Miss Sharnoe?"

"Yes."

"I'm Halsted Gray. Please sit down. Would you like a cup of coffee? No? Nothing? Well, then. Let's get two things straight right away. First, I am not a doctor nor do I pretend to be one. Second, I do not accept money. What I do, I do only as a favor for my friends, like Millie. Or friends of my friends, like you. Understood?" Sandra Sharnoe nodded. "Fine. Then let's get to it." He drained his glass. "Is your car outside?"

She drove the short trip to Sonny's house, following his directions. To make conversation, she asked, "If you don't take money for this, Mr. Gray, what *do* you do for a living?"

"Nothing at all," he said promptly. "Which does not mean I'm idle, however. I'm kept extremely busy by my avocations. No, my father—Halsted Gray, Senior—was the worker in our family. He was kind enough to set up a small trust for me. It's not an awful lot, as those things go, but it keeps me comfortable and free from financial worry." It was a set piece; he knew it by heart. It had the advantage of being perfectly true.

As they entered his living room, he offered her a comfortable chair and suggested she remove her shoes, which she did. He slipped a Delius recording on the phonograph. "Now," he said, drawing a chair up close to her. "The trouble is?"

She pressed long, lacquer-tipped fingers to her temples. "These headaches," she said. "Like an ax in my skull. And I have an audition tomorrow. I *always* get them before an audition."

"You're an actress, Sandra?"

"A dancer. I have a chance at this *wild* TV spot, and——"

"I see. You've been to doctors, of course."

She sighed. "Of course. They tell me it's nerves, tension. I *know* that! They give me pills. The pills either do me no good or make me woozy."

Sonny nodded. "All right. We'll give it a try. How old are you, by the way?"

"Twenty."

"You don't know my method?"

Sandra shook her head. "No, Millie just said you were great . . ."

"It's hypnosis," he explained. "Nothing more than that. I can take away this headache and you'll feel fine tomorrow, for your audition. I can't—*I won't*—do anything permanent for you, because that can be dangerous. I can only remove the symptom, I can't remove the cause. I'm saying all this because I want to be completely open and aboveboard."

Sandra nodded. Sonny went on: "I need your complete cooperation, that goes without saying. Don't resist. Are you comfortable? Good. Just relax now and listen to the music. I find it very restful music. Very drifting, floating music. Do you see this stickpin I'm wearing in my tie? The stone is a garnet; a beautiful garnet, I think, soothing to look at, limpid, liquid, with depths beyond depths, and beyond those, more depths. Look at it. As you look at the garnet, you are going deep, deep asleep." He paused. "Your body is relaxing, deeply relaxing." He paused. "Your legs are growing heavy, very, very heavy."

He paused. "Your arms are growing heavy, very, very heavy . . ." Before long, he was saying, "Your eyes are growing very heavy. Your eyes are growing very tired. Your eyes are beginning to close. Your eyes are closing, closing, closing, closing, closing, closing . . . Close your eyes and sleep."

She did just that, her breathing becoming slow and even.

He induced depth: "With each and every breath you take, your sleep is growing deeper . . . deeper . . . and deeper."

He established control: "Nothing will awaken you, until *I* awaken you. Nothing will disturb you. You will hear no sound except my voice."

He tested: "Your eyes are closed tight, so tight you cannot open them. The harder you try, the tighter they stick. Try to open them." Her eyes remained shut. "Try! But you can't!" Her eyes did not open. "Now stop trying. You can't do it."

He made a few other tests. Her response to them all was satisfactory. With a light step, he trotted into his study, and returned in a moment with the appointment book and a pencil. Flipping its pages, he said, "What is your name?"

Her voice came from a great distance: "Sandra . . . Sartelli . . ."

"And you are how old?"

"Twenty . . . two . . ."

"That's right, Sandra, you must always tell me the truth. Remember that. Always the truth. Are you married?"

"No . . ."

"Do you usually have . . . let me see . . . Thursday afternoons free?"

"No . . ."

"Why not?"

"Dancing class . . ."

"Ah. Then Friday morning between ten and eleven, are you ordinarily free at that time?"

"Yes . . ."

He made a notation in the book. "Listen carefully. Next Friday morning, the tenth of this month, you will make every reasonable effort to be here in this house at ten o'clock. Every reasonable effort. That means you will try to keep Friday morning free—to the best of your ability—of routine commitments. However, if anything urgent stands in the way of your being here, you will not feel compelled to come. Instead, you will simply postpone the visit until the following Friday morning at ten o'clock. Repeat those instructions."

"Next Friday morning, the tenth of this month . . ." As she droned on, Sonny congratulated himself on this particular refinement. Planting a compulsive posthypnotic suggestion could be disastrous. The subject, delayed by snarled traffic, might have a serious accident if under a compulsion to reach the destination by a designated time. Or be on a hospital bed, convalescing from surgery, or in another city, where the impossibility of getting to his house would bring on hysteria. Therefore, he had hit upon the idea of the qualified, conditional suggestion. ". . . . simply postpone the visit until the following Friday morning at ten o'clock," Sandra concluded. On Friday morning, Sonny would plant the suggestion for the Friday to come, and so on, each week setting up the following week's visit.

"When you leave here," said Sonny, "you will drive directly home. At the first green traffic light you see, you will forget my address. At the second green traffic light you see, you will forget my telephone number. At the third green traffic light you see, you will forget my name. As you get into your bed tonight, you will forget what I look like, you will forget what this house looks like, and you will forget you were here. *You will completely forget you were ever here*. Repeat those instructions."

She did. If she were to bump into Sonny on the street the next day, she would not recognize him.

"You will suddenly remember the location of this house on Friday morning, the tenth of this month. You will remember the location and you will be able to find it, but you will not remember the actual address, or the phone number, or my name. Repeat those instructions."

She did.

"If anyone wants to know where you're going, you will not tell them. You will not tell them because you will not know. You will, however, make up a story, the most logical, most believable story for the particular person who happens to ask you. Repeat those instructions."

She did. In a couple of months, Sonny would change the day and time of her weekly visits, to avoid their falling into an attention-drawing pattern.

"You will take note of a word. The word is *Xanadu*. It will mean nothing out of the ordinary to you when most people say it, or when you read it in print. But when I say *Xanadu* to you, you will immediately sink into deep trance. Deep, deep trance, of the kind you are in now. When I, and only I, say *Xanadu*. Repeat those instructions."

She did. On Friday morning, when she would return, a long, slow induction would not be necessary. He would open the door for her, and she would enter, with a bemused smile, somewhat apologetic, groping for his forgotten name, not quite knowing why she was here, and he would casually ask her to sit down, and then, just as casually, he would ask her if she happened to know the Coleridge lines that began "In Xanadu did Kubla Khan/A stately pleasure dome decree," and even before "pleasure dome" was out of his mouth, her eyes would be closed and her head fallen forward. "Xanadu," he would repeat, and her mind would slip deeper into the trance; "Xanadu, Xanadu, Xanadu," and each repetition of the signal would push her more profoundly and more surely under his control.

"Stand up, Sandra."

She did, and he took her hand. "Just come with me," he said, and led her upstairs.

They sat side by side on his bed. "Sandra," he said, "you

must be very honest and answer my next question truthfully. It is extremely important that you be completely honest with *yourself*, as well as with me . . ." He allowed that directive to sink in, then went on. "I want you to remember. I want you to remember all the men you have ever known in the past, shall we say, six years? All the men, let me add, that you have known with more than a nodding acquaintance, *and* all the men you have thought a great deal about, dreamed about, even if you have not known them personally. Search your memory, Sandra. Let them pass in parade through your mind."

As the parade filed by, Sonny got up and lit a cigarette. It had all been such a stroke of dumb luck, he marveled for by no means the first time; such a beautiful screwy accident. It so easily might never have happened at all, and he felt eternally in debt to Fortune that it had. If he had not been sitting idly at home that evening six months before, watching some awful thing on television, bored to petrifaction; and if that writer fellow, Clayton Horne, had not phoned and invited him to an impromptu party; and if Horne, as the evening wore on, had not allowed himself to be coaxed into demonstrating his rumored powers of hypnotism—but, Sonny smiled into the cigarette smoke, all this *had* happened . . .

"Oh, all right, all right," Horne said, "but no wisecracks or catcalls from the audience. And no promises, either. I make no promises. I'm not a wizard. Sometimes it works, sometimes it doesn't. There's no mystery in this—just a simple scientific technique."

"Twenty dollars says you can't do it at all," said Sonny.

"No bet. I only bet on sure things, and, like I said, sometimes it works, sometimes it doesn't. Who's going to volunteer? You, Sonny?"

"I'd rather watch."

Horne turned to a tall, willowy model. "Mavis, what about you? Girls make good subjects, for some reason."

"Don't do it, dear," Mavis' escort, Rudy, said, only half

joking. "Once he gets you under, he'll make you perform all sorts of nastiness."

Mavis laughed and retorted, "That's not true, Rudy. I read someplace that a hypnotist can't force a person to do anything against the person's moral code. Isn't that right, Clay?"

Horne smiled. "Actually, there are ways of getting around that . . ."

"And besides," said Rudy, "I've yet to discover anything that *is* against your moral code, old love."

That got a laugh, perhaps too much of a laugh for Mavis' taste, because she balked. Horne turned to a quiet, rather plain girl who'd said practically nothing the whole evening. "Doris? Come on, be a sport."

She hesitated. "I wouldn't mind, except that I feel awful. I really should be home. I have this damn toothache."

"Perfect. Dr. Horne will charm it away. Sit over here . . ."

Doris moved to an armchair, saying, "You're bluffing."

"Sit down. Take off your shoes. That's it. Comfortable? No, no, don't cross your legs—that interferes with the circulation and might wake you up in the middle of the whole thing. You say I'm bluffing. Not at all. I've done it before, very successfully. I've also failed. When you come right down to it, nobody hypnotizes anybody—people hypnotize themselves. The so-called hypnotist just helps them do it. I can't do it unless you want me to, understand, dear? If you're afraid——"

"I'm not afraid," said Doris, "it just seems a little silly."

"That's perfectly all right. I don't mind your thinking it silly. Natural reaction. Very healthy, as a matter of fact. Helps you relax. Think of it as a game, a silly little game, and you're just playing along, being a good sport, humoring me, all right? Attagirl."

Sonny watched with total fascination, his skepticism peeling away in layers as he saw Doris close her eyes, then go deeper and deeper into trance. Horne trotted out all the tricks: told her she was a cat, and she obediently meowed and licked her paws; told her she was watching the funniest comedy ever filmed, and she laughed uproariously; told her she was watching the saddest play ever penned, and she copiously wept. Then, winking at Doris' escort, a man named Joe, he told her it was getting terribly hot in the room—eighty, ninety, ninety-five degrees—and she was all alone, and her clothes were so oppressively uncomfortable . . . sure enough, she began to unbutton her blouse.

Joe said, "Wait a *minute*, Clay!"

"The mercury," Horne told Doris, "is going down now. Eighty, seventy, sixty-five . . ." She buttoned up her blouse again. Turning to Mavis, he said, "See what I mean about that moral code stuff? If I hadn't stopped her, she'd have stripped to the buff. And yet if I'd simply ordered her to take her clothes off, she wouldn't have done it."

Addressing Doris again, Horne said, "When you awaken, you will not remember any of this. And your toothache will be completely gone. Sometime after you awaken, Joe will offer you a cigarette. As you take it from the package, you will sing one chorus of *The Star-Spangled Banner*. I am going to count to five. At the count of five, you will open your eyes and be completely awake. One, two, three, four, *five*."

The first thing she noticed was the missing toothache. Horne carefully explained that he had removed the symptom, not the cause, and made her promise to call her dentist first thing in the morning. Half an hour later, behind her back, Horne pantomimed the act of smoking to Joe, and Joe offered Doris a cigarette. She took one, and casually began to sing, in a bland, tuneless voice:

> *"Oh, say can you see*
> *by the dawn's early light . . ."*

Sonny was the last guest to leave. He stayed behind, after all the others had dribbled away, expressing his admiration for Horne's great mesmeric powers. "Powers, schmowers," said

Horne, "I wasn't kidding when I said I was no wizard. The amazing thing, the *appalling* thing about hypnotism is that it's so incredibly easy. A few phrases and rituals that are a cinch to learn, a certain amount of confidence, a certain amount of susceptibility on the part of the subject, and wham, you're a hypnotist. Remember when you were a kid, those ten-cent books on *How to Hypnotize?* We always figured they were fakes? The fantastic thing is that they're *not*. You actually *can* learn to hypnotize from a ten-cent book. Anyone can. You can."

You can. With those two words, Horne had, unknowingly, changed the whole direction and color of Sonny's life. He'd thoroughly grasped the fundamentals in a few days, had his first small mesmeric success a week later at another party of Horne's, then gone on to a few failures from which he learned much, discovered how to pretest a subject for susceptibility, and then, one day, saw and grabbed a quite unpremeditated opportunity to use his new talent to his own distinct advantage.

Crushing out his cigarette in an ashtray, Sonny returned to Sandra Sharnoe and sat next to her again on the bed. "Those men, Sandra," he said, "which one, among all of them, would you want most to make love to you?"

After a moment, she said, "Bob . . ."

"Who is Bob?"

"Bob . . . Ritchie . . ."

"And who is Bob Ritchie?"

"High school . . . basketball . . . champion . . ."

Sonny smiled. A nobody. How remarkably often it was a nobody. How surprisingly seldom it was a fantasy object like Rock Hudson, John Glenn, Robert Kennedy. So be it: Bob Ritchie.

"How long has it been," he asked, "since you've seen him?"

"Not since . . . high school . . ."

A long, slow-burning torch. "Bob was—Bob *is* a very handsome boy, very popular?"

"Yes . . ."

"You've dated him?"

"A . . . few times . . ."

"Has he ever made love to you?"

"Not . . . really . . ."

"But you want him to?"

"Yes . . ."

"Very much?"

"Yes . . ."

"Then you love Bob with all your heart?"

"Yes . . ."

"And you will do anything at all for him, anything he wishes, because you love him so much and want to make him happy?"

"Yes . . ."

"Does Bob have a little nickname for you, a pet name?"

"Brownie . . ."

"Because of your eyes?"

"Yes . . ."

Sonny released a long breath and stood up. Without hurrying, he made himself comfortable by removing his tie, coat and shoes. He sat next to Sandra again, and this time put his arm around her waist, saying, "Hi, Brownie. It's me. Bob."

. . .

Sonny lay in the dark, next to Sandra, thinking.

Many, he realized, would call him an evil man, luring unsuspecting damsels to his lair, tricking them into helplessness by black arts, to ruthlessly cleave them on the sacrificial *fascinum* of his lust.

If it were evil to magically change himself from a wretched, lonely, unfulfilled creature to a man who awoke eagerly to each new day and sang *La Traviata* in the shower, then, Sonny reasoned, he was evil.

He turned to Sandra. Even in the dark, he could see the serenity and contentment on her face. If it were evil to make a woman's deepest wish come true, then he was evil. For years, Sandra had harbored a buried, nagging, unrequited love for Bob Ritchie, and today that love had been, in a manner of speaking, returned.

Nothing degenerate had taken place, no vile depravities, no abominations, no foul De Sadean horrors. Where, then, was the evil? Who had been hurt? Sandra? Sonny? Ritchie? None of them had been hurt, and two had brightly benefited.

(Is this what they call rationalization? he wondered. Under all the "logic," mightn't there lurk something infinitely corrupt, something perverted, unnatural, inhuman, something stinking with decay, in the transformation of a girl—even temporarily—into a windup toy, a zombie without will or choice, a corpse in which the blood still flowed? No: sentimentality, puritan cant, romantic rubbish!)

Perhaps, Sonny mused, if he had more pride, if he had not lived so many desperate years of longing and shyness, he would feel shame about being loved not "for himself" but only for the masks of the Bob Ritchies. Sonny was too content to be bothered by such fastidious distinctions. Beggars can't be choosers. Besides, he asked, what man is loved for himself? What does that mean, "himself"? A man is loved for many things: for his good looks, or his charm, or his noble character, or his money, or his power. Sonny felt he had been shortchanged by Fate, since he possessed none of these. So he was loved for being Bob Ritchie, and he didn't see much of anything wrong in that.

He reached out and turned on a lamp. It cast a soft, low light over the bed. Tenderly, he pulled away the bedclothes from the girl, pulled them all the way down to her lacquered toetips, uncovering her completely. For several moments he admired her beauty, the art of every swelling hill and shadowed dale, the placid rhythm of her breathing, the buttery smoothness of her skin, the almost unendurable piercing sweetness of the great and gleaming masterpiece she was.

He felt grateful, awed, appreciative and good, as he always did at such times.

Then he got up and dressed. Still in the persona of Bob, he gently advised her to put on her clothes. He watched her fondly as she did so, then said, "Brownie, I'll see you again real soon, but right now I'm going to turn you over to Mr. Gray." He took her hand and led her downstairs to the living room.

Her shoes still stood in front of the armchair, her purse was still on the coffee table where she'd left it. "Take your comb from your purse," he said, "and comb your hair." She did. "Sit down." She sat down. "Do you remember my instructions about my address and telephone number? Repeat them."

"When I leave here . . . I will drive directly home. At the first green traffic light I see . . . I will forget your address. At the second green traffic light I see . . . I will forget your telephone number . . ."

"Very good. Now, listen carefully. Under certain conditions, you will remember my telephone number, which is CR 2-3041. Repeat it."

"C . . . R . . . two . . . three oh four one . . ."

"You will remember that number only under the following circumstances. From time to time, friends of yours may need my help. They will be troubled by headaches, or insomnia, or fits of depression, or anxiety, or they may just want to give up smoking. At such a time, you will tell your friend about a wonderful man you happen to know about. You will not mention his name—because you will not remember it—and for the same reason you will not mention his phone number or his address. You will go to the nearest telephone. By the act of picking it up, you will remember my number. You will dial it. If you hear a busy signal, you will hang up and try again exactly five minutes later. If there is no answer, you will hang up and take care of it some other time. If I answer, you will say: 'This is Sandra Sharnoe. I have a friend named (and you will tell me your friend's name) who would like to speak to you.' Then you will call your friend to the phone. As you hand the phone to your friend, you will forget my number again. Repeat those instructions."

She did. "Pay close attention now, Sandra," said Sonny, coming to the crucial part of the command. "These friends of yours, the ones who will need my help, they must not ever be men. They must be unmarried ladies." The unmarried requirement was another refinement of which Sonny felt proud. It was not motivated by morality. Married women had less freedom of movement, as well as husbands who could make life hideous for Sonny. "Unmarried ladies," he repeated, "*young* unmarried ladies, young and pretty, with pretty young faces and pretty young bodies, as pretty and as young as yours. No others. No others at all. Repeat those instructions."

She did. Sonny checked Sandra's clothes, and his own, made sure her purse was in precisely the same place it had been when she went into the trance, and said, "I am going to count to five. At the count of five, you will awaken. You will remember nothing that happened during your trance. Your headache will be gone and will remain gone all day tomorrow. At your audition, you will feel alert and refreshed. One, two, three, four, *five*."

"Oh!" Sandra said. "It's gone. I feel marvelous!"

Sonny modestly smiled. "I'm glad I was able to help."

"It's just *wild*, Mr. Gray." She put on her shoes. "I don't know how to thank you."

"There's no need," he assured her. Then, rising, he said, "And now, I'm afraid I must rush you off, because I have a great deal to do." He gallantly ushered her toward the door.

As they passed the telephone, she said, "Do you mind if I write down your number?" and began to reach into her purse for pencil and paper.

"I'll do it," said Sonny, swiftly picking up a note pad and ballpoint pen. He made a quick scribbling motion, tore off the sheet, folded it, and then, with a playful elfin gesture, shoved the piece of paper into her purse, deep among the feminine paraphernalia, and snapped the purse shut again. "There you are," he said. The piece of paper was, of course, blank.

At the door, just before she left, Sandra said, "Thank you again, Mr. Gray."

With a straight face, he replied, "The pleasure was mine."

"There she goes," thought Sonny, as the door closed, "another little talent scout, geared to carefully select only the choicest morsels for my private stock." Each morsel, in turn, would be geared to select other morsels, and every morsel would return once a week at her allotted time. After a while, if it should threaten to become too much of a good thing (his appointment book was rapidly becoming jammed), he could easily weed out the morsels of lesser magnitude, eliminating from their minds the command to return the following week. It was an autoerotic fantasy come true: the morsels came to *him*, on a platter, obedient to his will, requiring no effort or courtship on his part. Yes, Sonny thought with a sigh as he went upstairs and gazed luxuriously out his picture window, the most remarkable part of it all was, indeed, the simplicity.

Night had fallen. The city was a tangle of luminous necklaces on black velvet. The invigorative sting of power buzzed through him, along his veins, quickening his blood. They were all out there, somewhere among those lights, his little puppets, attached to his whims by long, invisible strings. Steadily, their numbers grew with awesome and easy momentum, burgeoning by inexorable mathematic laws. Sonny laughed, softly. It was killingly funny. They were his, ugly little Sonny Gray's. They were all his, the whole city was his, as far as the eye could see it ranged: his select and secret harem; his corps of dancers to a private piping; his limitless warm acres of lushness; his lovely legions; his empire; his Xanadu.

And nobody had a clue. Not even the puppets themselves

suspected. There wasn't a soul in all the world who knew.

He was quite tired. Tomorrow was another big day. He yawned, undressed again, fell into bed and was soon asleep. As he began to spiral down toward the waiting shock of the dream, however, he was spared by the faraway buzz of his doorbell. He groaned into wakefulness, got slowly up, and shuffled downstairs, pulling on his robe. The doorbell continued buzzing, with patient, insistent regularity. The living-room clock said 12:40.

"Who is it?" Sonny asked through the door.

"Los Angeles Police, Mr. Gray."

Sonny's heart jumped, jabbed by fear's calloused finger. Then, collecting himself, he opened the door a crack.

"You're not the police," he said when he saw who stood there: a pock-marked vulgarian wearing bad-taste mufti and an indifferently trimmed mustache.

"No," said the night visitor, "but I think we better have a talk, Mr. Gray."

"Go away or I'll call the police."

"No you won't."

"Who the devil do you think you are?"

"Let's say my name is," and he smiled, showing odious olive-drab teeth, "Mr. Xanadu. How'll that do for openers?"

The earth slid away under Sonny's slippered feet, but only for a moment. "What do you want?"

"Like I said, a talk. Come on, let me in, I won't bite." The o.d. smile again.

Apprehensively, Sonny let him in. Was he a husband, boyfriend, father? He was a big man and beefy: would he beat him up? How had he found out? Sonny breathed deeply and took himself in hand. Perhaps it had nothing to do with the girls. But if not, then . . . ?

The visitor looked about the living room. "Nice," he said, "nice." He sat down, and pulled from a pocket a package of Black Jack chewing gum, which he offered to Sonny, who declined with a shake of his head. The visitor unwrapped two sticks and inserted them in his mouth like letters into a mail slot. Methodically chewing, he said, "I give up cigarettes."

After several dismal moments, Sonny said, "What do you want to talk about, Mr.——"

"Mr. X will do. I'll come right to the point. I'm a private investigator, specializing in divorce work—don't get panicky, nobody's naming you as a corespondent—but a couple of weeks ago, I got a slightly different kind of assignment. From an *ex*-husband, very jealous, a bit of a nut, who's still hooked on his blonde ex-wife and wants to know where she goes every Tuesday afternoon at three-thirty and who she sees and what she does. Chick's name is Betty Sanderson: ring a bell? I thought it would. Well, it was no sweat to slip a bug into her purse one Tuesday and tail her. She came here, to your place. I parked on the road outside, a few houses down, and listened in (it's a fifty-to-hundred-megacycle bug, a beaut, can send a signal damn near half a mile). I'm sitting there, parked, and as I tune in my receiver I hear a man's voice. Figures. But what doesn't figure is what he's saying. Not the usual stuff—Baby, Sugar, How About A Little Drink—no. Xanadu, Xanadu, Xanadu. What the hell is *this*, I say to myself. I keep listening. Pretty soon, of course, I'm hip. Well, my client, I told him she went to a headshrinker every Tuesday: what he don't know won't hurt him. But me, I had a hunch about you, so I came back that night while you were out and pounded a spike mike into your front door. I don't like spike mikes, they pull in a lot of garbage, but once in a while you gotta settle for 'em. And, brother, did I pick up a tapeful of stuff from that spike the next day! And the day after that, and the day after *that*."

The visitor paused for a breath, while the sickening feeling of *this can't be happening but it is* crawled over Sonny.

"Yeah, I heard plenty," Mr. X went on. "Enough to be absolutely certain. Before I make a deal, I like to be certain."

"A deal," said Sonny.

"That's right, Mr. Gray. A little deal."

Sonny said, "I see." Then he said, "Look here. Somehow, you seem to have the impression that I'm a rich man. You're wrong. I live a quiet life, I'm comfortably situated, but I don't have a lot of money."

"Did I ask you for money?"

Sonny said, "Let us not be coy, Mr. X. Do you deny that you are here in my house for purposes of blackmail? And please," he added quickly, "don't use that hackneyed old line about blackmail being an ugly word. You're a little too much like something out of the late show as it is."

Mr. X laughed. "Sure, I'm blackmailing you," he said. "But there's blackmail and blackmail."

Sonny sighed. "At least twenty minutes ago you said you were coming right to the point. I still don't see . . ."

"Keep your money," said Mr. X. "I want *in.*"

"You want what?"

"I want a slice of the cake. All them lovely cakes. Betty Sanderson, Sandra Sharnoe, Millie Van Bustenhalter. All the others. I just want you to share the wealth a little, that's all. With me."

"Are you suggesting . . ." Sonny's voice trailed off.

"You know what I'm suggesting, Mr. Gray." The visitor stood up. "Sorry to get you out of bed. I'll go now, it's late. But I'll give you a buzz tomorrow and we'll set up the first cake-slicing."

Mr. X moved out of the living room, toward the door. A blemishing leer twisted his face. "You know that Monday-night one of yours, that redhead, Carolyn?"

Sonny said nothing.

"I got a particular yen for that one, Mr. Gray. We'll start with her. Know what I'd like to do with her? First . . ." The gloating wealth of pathological detail, the Hieronymus Bosch landscape he painted with a few lurid strokes, caused Sonny's stomach to tighten into a knot and his face to be bleached by disgust and fear.

Sonny's voice shook with anger. "You filth. You rotten ugly swine. *Get out of here!* If you seriously think I'm going to be a party to——"

"Oh, you'll be a party, all right," Mr. X assured him. "You'll be a party or else there won't *be* any more parties, for anyone. You don't want your sweet little setup knocked over. You don't want the wrong people to know what's going on here. You don't want me to pull the plug on you and watch you go down the drain, glug-glug-glug. Not you, Mr. Gray. You'll play ball. You won't like it, but you'll play ball."

Yes I will, thought Sonny, after the visitor left and he walked heavily upstairs again, the spring gone from his step, a decade of age suddenly added to him: *I'll play ball, in his ball park, according to his rules.*

Right there, on the stairs, he remembered the dream. He had never recalled it when awake, but now it flooded over him in a rush. He was stripped, he was standing stark naked in his pleasure palace and it was made of glass, all glass, and there was a crowd of people outside, looking in and pointing and smirking at his nakedness. All the people he knew were out there, grinning cruelly at his humiliation; all the world seemed to know his secrets; there was nothing they didn't know about him. And then the glass cracked and splintered into bright cold cutting shards, and Xanadu crashed loudly in a million shining pieces to the ground.

Just as it was crashing now.

But no, no, Sonny groaned piteously. He deserved his little private pleasures. He had paid dearly for them, with 43 years of loneliness. He couldn't let this happen to Xanadu, and to himself, and especially he couldn't let it happen to all those lovely, helpless darlings. Could he?

. . .

"Where's the broad?" asked Mr. X, lighting a cigarette.

"Carolyn? She'll be here," said Sonny.

"She better be. Y'know, I've been thinking. Sometime, maybe later this week, you oughta arrange for two or three of them to be here all at the same time. Know what I mean? Could get real interesting."

Sonny smiled. "Would you believe it—I never thought of that?"

"I got a lot more ideas."

"I'll have to be candid with you," Sonny said. "At first, I didn't look forward to this at *all*. But now I must admit I'm rather, I don't know, stimulated." Sonny leaned toward his guest, his monkey eyes bright. "You see, there's always been something missing. And do you know what that something was? Sharing the experience. Telling somebody. I've always had to keep it a secret, and that secret kept building up inside me like steam until I sometimes felt I had to tell someone or burst. It even gave me nightmares! But now all that's changed, you see. The two of us are . . . partners, so to speak."

"Right. Partners."

"We can talk about it, laugh about it, plan things together. Yes, that's something else—I tend to be a fairly conservative person; I *never* would have thought to bring several of the girls together all at once, for instance; while you, on the other hand, have a very lively imagination . . ."

"You know it."

"So, in a sense, I feel you are opening new doors for me, just as I'm doing for you. We each have something to contribute. It's a reciprocal arrangement."

"Reciprocal, yeah."

"Incidentally, I thought you said you'd given up smoking."

"What?" Mr. X looked at his cigarette. "Oh. Damn it." He crushed it out. "Habit. Didn't even know I lit up. Can't seem to kick the damn things."

"I know," Sonny said sympathetically. "I had the same problem at one time. Smoked two packs a day."

"And you just quit? Like that?"

"Oh yes. No trouble. Self-hypnosis. The same way I remove the girls' headaches and so on. Speaking of the girls, there *is* a little thing I've been longing to try with one of them, but I guess I just haven't been adventurous enough. It's——"

"Wait a minute," Mr. X interrupted, "tell me about the smoking. You mean you can just . . . hypnotize it away?"

Sonny shrugged modestly. "You might say that. It's ridiculously simple. The hypnotist simply plants the suggestion that cigarettes will have a decidedly unpleasant, even nauseating, flavor to the subject. That's all there is to it, really. You have no idea what can be done. For example, the very act of love can be made immeasurably better by self-hypnosis. The right kind of suggestion can actually—how can I say it without sounding gross?—improve a man's prowess, prolong certain things, do you understand?"

Mr. X understood very well. "Listen, Sonny," he said. "It's all right I call you Sonny, isn't it? This with the smoking, and this other what you call prowess . . . could you do the same thing, like, for me?"

"It all depends," said Sonny. "If you're a receptive subject, I think I could. Of course, if you resisted me, even a little, if you weren't completely willing, I couldn't do a thing . . ."

"Sure, sure . . ."

"But if you helped me . . . cooperated . . . it wouldn't be difficult at all."

"How would you do it?"

"*We*. We would do it. Together, co-operating, partners. First, I might just ask you to look at this stickpin I'm wearing in my tie. The stone is a garnet; a beautiful garnet, I think, soothing to look at, limpid, liquid, with depths beyond depths, and beyond those, more depths . . ."

Not much later, and bare moments before redheaded Carolyn arrived, Sonny cordially escorted Mr. X to the door, waved goodbye, and watched him drive away.

Mr. X drove directly home. At the first green traffic light

he saw, he forgot Sonny's address. At the second green traffic light, he forgot Sonny's telephone number. At the third green traffic light, he forgot Sonny's name. At the first red light, while he sat in the idling car, a girl crossed the street, walking directly in front of him. She was no older than 20, honey-haired, pert-nosed, high-breasted, round-butted, and as she walked quickly on her long, tapering legs, all of her flowed and rippled like the skin of a fine lithe leopard.

The sight of her almost turned his stomach.

THE BOTTOM
OF THE OCEAN

BY KEN W. PURDY

Prior to becoming PLAYBOY'*s most prolific Contributing Editor, Ken W. Purdy held the highest editorial posts at* True *and* Argosy. *He is a respected authority on the men and machines of the automotive world (his books on the subject include "Bright Wheels Rolling," "Kings of the Road," "Wonderful World of the Automobile," "All But My Life" and "The New Matadors," which has been bought for filming), and he is a three-time winner of* PLAYBOY *writing awards— once for fiction, twice for non-fiction (he excels in both). He has a special feeling for the cadences of contemporary urban speech and a suitably acerbic insight into the minds of coppers and conmen, bimbos and bindlestiffs, the artists of the back-stab and the double-cross. "The Bottom of the Ocean" is a typically Purdean tale of Virtue Untriumphant.*

DEAR CHARLIE,

It's ten o'clock, on what day, or what night, I don't have to tell you, and I suppose you are marveling that I have anything left to say. It would be a marvel if I had anything new to say, Counselor, after the time we've spent together in the last seven months. I don't have anything new to say. I just want to put everything down in one place for somebody to have, for you to have, and do with what you can. I want my story, at least, to stay alive. And look, Charlie, someday, if you watch and wait, a chance to get that monster will come. *A chance will come!*

The girl's name was Patty Felston. Or Patty Barnes Felston. (I know you know all this, Charlie. I'm just trying to make a record.) Her husband's name was James Felston. He's an architect and he and Patty were of the same age, as it happened, 32. I met her in February or March of 1958. She was working for a decorator outfit on Hellmer Street, Interiors Unlimited. I took her to lunch a couple of days after I met her, an entirely legitimate thing to do, since after all I did have the responsibility for getting the whole four floors of offices done over.

I saw her now and again while the work was being done. That was finished in July 1958, and I kept right on seeing her, usually for lunch, very occasionally for a drink after work. Once or twice we had dinner. By the fall I was working on her very hard, and I admit it. I never denied that. I was working very hard on two other girls as well, and I never denied that, either. Look, Charlie, nobody ever accused me of making a secret of the fact that I like girls. During the late unpleasantness, you remember, there was a big fuss made over the fact that nobody could find a girl I'd ever asked to marry me. There's a simple enough reason: I never had such a notion. I like to go out with girls, and I like to sleep with girls, and after a while I like to do the same thing all over again with other girls, and what about it? I used to like to, rather, to state things strictly accurately. No, I still *like* to, but I used to *do* it. Ugh. Gackles.

You never knew Patty, and that's a shame. There were prettier girls, but not many, Counselor, not many. Patty was brown all over. Brown-blonde hair, brown eyes damned near black, gold-brown skin. She wasn't frantic. She didn't bounce. She moved slowly, almost as if she wasn't sure which way to turn, but she was sure, all right. She was bright. But this slow, soft air of hers was wild. It always seemed to me that she was winding up, winding, winding, winding up some great big goddamned ever-loving blue steel spring in there and God help us all when the ratchet slipped and the spinning started.

I got nowhere with Patty for a long time. Oh, for a good long time. I'm telling you the truth, Charlie, I never knew anything like it. In the whole business, I think the one thing that you never believed was my telling you that before that night in the Bellanca we'd gone to bed those other times and two of them just to hold hands and talk and nothing else but that's the way it was. We did. Twice. I had to, with her. It had to be that slow. I always believed and I still do that more women are talked out of bed than are talked into it, and I think that if you're going to make out, a minimum of conversation about it is what you need, but there are exceptions to every rule and Patty certainly was an exception. We must have had twenty hours of talking before we did even the bundling bit. It wasn't that she didn't want to. She did, of course. Well, I say of course and it doesn't necessarily follow. I mean, I'm not trying to suggest that because I asked her, she couldn't say no. She said no for a long time, and she said maybe for a long time, but she did like me. You know that. I knew it early. She more than liked me, she was in love with me, and that was the first of the three mistakes I made: not running like a thief the first minute she said she loved me. Love, I don't need. That was *not* a good break, when Foster came up with that letter of Patty's to the Dorrance girl.

(What has caused more grief than women blabbing to their girlfriends?) If she'd said only that she loved me, OK, but when she said that she'd *told* me she loved me, and put down what I said—that was poor. Well, there's no point in going over all that, is there. Hardly. Not now.

Of course I was stupid. If I hadn't been stupid I wouldn't be here, and man, I'm *here*, and when you're *here*, I just don't know how to say it, this is the *here*-est place there is, this is the *only* place there is, right here, one foul, square, dirty-gray chunk of space, and how you know you're *here* is it's just as if the room was at the bottom of the ocean and all that weight was pressing down on you from every direction, to be sure you can't get out. This is really the big squeeze, and I wish I could get it across to you what it means to be here.

Hell, what's it matter, it's not a problem that's going to bother me for a lot longer.

But I was stupid to stand still for the love bit, and I was stupider when I knew she was talking. After all, it's poor form for any girl to talk, and it's really seriously bad when she's married. When Pete Timken phoned me, I should have left for Hong Kong. I must have been out of my mind.

"This is Dr. Peter Timken," he said. The slob! The fat-headed, stinking, brassed, mothering son of a bitch. Die, you dog, you pig's, you camel's, die, goddamn you, that's the message he's going to get from me. I'll see him tonight, Charlie. I mean right down the hall, I'll see him. I'm *sure* the bastard will be there. Look, he's a doctor, he can get in, he'll be there. And why not? Isn't he doing the job? He sure is. He's the one who fixed it all up for me.

"I'm Dr. Timken," he said to me that day in his office. It was all very mysterious. I didn't know what the hell I was doing in his damned office. I even shook his hand.

"I'll get right to the point," he said. "Mrs. James Felston is a patient of mine. She gave me your name and your telephone number. I asked her to after we had spent a considerable amount of time in conversation about you. She told me, in detail, about her relationship with you. I've advised her to break it off, to stop seeing you, and that's the same advice I'm going to give you."

"Well, thanks a lot," I told him. "It's big of you. I have the same delight in unsolicited advice that most people do, the same gratitude for it, and the same likelihood of paying any attention to it. Tell me, you say Patty's your patient: are you a psychiatrist?"

"I," this monster from forty fathoms says, "am a cardiologist. I'm also a very old friend of Mrs. Felston's."

I admit this shook me a little. "Does Patty have some difficulty with her heart?" I asked him.

"I told you she was my patient," he said. "You may draw from that any conclusion you wish."

I didn't say anything, so he started in again. He was Patty's friend. He had her best interests in view. He knew her husband. He had *his* best interests in view. He didn't know me, but he had *my* best interests in view. He was a real missionary, out to take care of everybody. I was doing an enormously cruel thing, he said, scheming and plotting to make Patty fall in love with me, intent on nothing but getting her into bed, no matter if it loused up her marriage—and it would, he was sure of that. I could agree with him there. Could be. That's a chance a girl has to take.

Timken raved on. Words like "evil" and "fraudulent" and "fake" came pretty easily to him. I finally asked him a question. I said, "How long have you been in love with Patty, Doc?"

It got rough, then. I told him what I thought of him, butting into other people's affairs, and he told me what he thought of me as a home-wrecker, and if I wouldn't have been giving him fifteen or twenty pounds I'd have taken a shot at him, but he was too big. And too rugged. You know the type: he probably played lacrosse all the time he was at Johns Hopkins and now he plays squash twice a week at the Harvard

Club. Anyway, I said goodbye to him. In a way. What I actually said was, "I'll bet you a couple of guineas, Doc: I'll lay her before you do."

Naturally I never saw him again until that night. The strange thing was, it wasn't the first time, or the second or the third, that night in the Bellanca. If it had happened the first time, I'd be able to understand it better. But maybe that's not reasonable. Maybe, for her, the importance and the excitement of it grew each time, instead of declining each time as it did with me.

If it hadn't been for Timken's big-brother attitude, I would never have bothered to make it with Patty. I'd have quit, like a bright boy, the minute I knew she was talking, and the minute I knew she had a heart thing, or any suspicion of one. But Timken really roused the beast in me. And you know, a funny thing? I don't believe he *wanted* to go to bed with Patty. All right, I know he was in love with her, but it was some weird kind of high-level thing, in his mind, where he took care of her, and watched out for her, and loved her madly from a distance, one of those deals. I know that's what it was. I could tell from the way he acted, and of course I went round and round with Patty about him, and I could tell from what she said. Hell, they'd known each other for 11 years, and he'd never even tried, she said.

I don't count calling him that night a mistake. I thought then and I think now that it was the only thing to do. I had to have a doctor for her, he was near, and she was his case. Well, maybe it wasn't the *smart* thing to do. I suppose the smart thing to do would have been to get her dressed and get her out of the hotel some way. That's hard, but it's been done. At least with men it's been done. In our own time, and only with famous people, I know for sure of three: a millionaire businessman, an actor, a composer. They all died in somebody's arms, the wrong somebody's arms, and they were all walked out. But you can't do it alone, it takes at least two people. In the back of my head, maybe I thought Timken would help me do just that, if he couldn't bring her back, but actually I think I called him because I knew she'd had a heart attack, and because I thought he might be able to bring her back.

Well, as I guess everybody in this country who can read must know, he couldn't. He tried. He gave her a big injection of adrenaline right into the heart. No good. He tried everything he could, short of opening her chest and massaging her heart, and he even thought of that, he had a scalpel in his hand, but he said he knew it wouldn't work. Maybe he was right, maybe he was wrong. I doubt his judgment was at its best. He was coming unstuck around the edges. He was crying, you know. He was standing there, looking down at her, crying, crying, you wouldn't have thought he was a doctor.

I made the third mistake then. He said that he'd have to call the police, and he said that since it was a hotel, it would look better for me if I wasn't in the suite. He told me to go downstairs and wait. And like a moron, I did. I left him alone with her. For some fat-headed reason, I thought that Patty's death had softened him up, and too I remember thinking that of course he would want to help keep down the scandal as much as possible, since he was a friend of her husband's, and the longer I could be kept out of the picture, the better. So I went. I went. Great Christ in his pain, what a monster, what a thing, what a crawling, slime-soaked slug, God roast the bastard and don't oil him, I went. And that was the third mistake. I don't count going into the bar. I don't think it mattered, then, that the cops found me there. It looked bad in the papers, but I don't think it really mattered, the lobby or the bar, people could understand that at a time like that the thing you'd want most would be a drink. The big thing was that I wasn't in the room where Patty was. Of course Timken knew that, and planned it, but that was only the side effect. He had a better reason for wanting to get me out of the room.

Hell, Charlie, I was so fat, dumb and happy that even when they hustled me into the station house I wasn't worried. Look, people die that way every night. All right, they're mostly men and they're mostly old but they die that way all the time. I knew there was going to be some trouble, some publicity, some questions, I knew I was going to have maybe a little nuisance with her husband, but I wasn't really scared. I even remember I said to myself that at any rate she'd died happy, in ecstasy and believing that somebody loved her. It should happen to me tonight.

Well. They walked me into the station house and there was this old sergeant on the desk. One of the cops said, "This is the fella from the Bellanca."

"Is it now?" the sergeant said. He stared at me for a while, then he turned to some joker up there with him, a civilian, and he said, "You know, there's two things I hate, and that's a man that will steal from the poor and a man that will beat a woman naked. Mind, now, I'm not sayin' there's not times when it does a woman good to feel the flat of your hand, and good and hard, too, but that's just in the ordinary way of things, across the table, you might say. But a man that beats a woman naked is an evil thing, and nothing too bad can happen to him."

I didn't know what the hell the old goat was talking about. I thought he was finishing off some conversation that he'd had going before I came in. Then he said to one of the cops, "What do you want to book him for right away? Take him out in the back and let him talk for a while, until he gets it straight in his mind what really happened. And mind the stairs."

That was when they hustled me into the squad room, and through that into another room and then one of them opened a third door and the other shoved me and the next thing I knew I was flying down the cellar steps on my head. And that was why I looked the way I did when you saw me the first time. It was quick, I'll say that for them. They had me back out in the front room ten minutes later, and I must have looked like I'd jumped off a building.

"The poor man fell down the stairs, didn't he," the sergeant said.

"Afraid so, Sarge," one of the cops told him.

"And after I told you to watch out for that," the sergeant said. "You're a careless fella, the both of you. As for you," he said to me, "we're about to book you for murder in the first degree, unless you have some outstanding objection."

"I don't know what's going on here," I said. "All I know is that you've got me mixed up with somebody else. All right, a girl died in my bedroom, but that's not murder in *any* degree, that's not even manslaughter, that's just an accident, for God's sake, and . . ."

"You shut your dirty mouth," the sergeant said, "or I'll come down there to you myself. An accident, was it? And the girl lying over there one mass of bruises from head to toe, her nose broke, an ear on her half off, a bruise over her heart as big as your two hands. An accident, you call it?"

Charlie, that's the way I found out what he'd done. That was how I got the message, and where and when. Why did he do it? In the first place, how could he bring himself to do it? He'd known her for 11 years. For 11 years he claimed he'd loved her. She told me that. So how could he? Well, all right, he's a monster, he's no part of anything human, he's a creeper, a crawler, you lean on him and your arm will slide into him up to the shoulder, all right, all right, but what did I do to him that would let him do it to *me*, I went to bed with a girl he didn't want and he's going to hang me for it, an hour from now he's going to hang me for it, they're not going to do it, he is, and he's going to get away with it just like he got away with what he did in that room in the Bellanca, like he got away with being at the autopsy and faking that up about the blow killing her, not the excitement, and the whole rest of it.

Charlie, the thing is, for God's sake keep this letter, and let people read it. Let them know, Charlie, let them know.

BERTRAND L. JELLINOE

A CRY
FROM THE PENTHOUSE

BY HENRY SLESAR

Although president of his own advertising agency and, before that, vice-president of three other agencies, Henry Slesar has authored about 400 stories. His books include "Enter Murderers," "Clean Crimes and Neat Murders," "A Crime for Mothers and Others" and "The Grey Flannel Shroud," a novel for which he won the Mystery Writers of America Award. He also has several dozen television plays to his credit. In the following story (which, after its PLAYBOY *appearance, was dramatically televised with Oscar-winner Ray Milland in the starring role) Slesar creates an atmosphere of direst peril and excruciating suspense in an ordinary metropolitan apartment building.*

THAT WAS COOMBS FOR YOU; he had to pick a night like this to settle his affairs. Chet Brander tightened the muffler around his throat and dug his gloved hands into his overcoat pockets, but there was no way of barricading his body from the subzero cold. The city streets seemed glazed with ice, and the taxis rumbled past the corner with clouds of frost billowing from their exhaust pipes. The wind carried knives; Chet winced at every thrust, and was almost tempted to forget the whole thing. But he couldn't afford it. Tonight was payoff night, and he longed to get his hands on the money that had lingered so long in Frank Coombs' pocket.

Then he got lucky. A cab pulled up and a redcheeked matron got out, he almost knocked her down in his haste to occupy the back seat. He gave the hackie the address of Coombs' apartment house on the river, and stepped out ten minutes later into a night that had grown even more insufferable. He fought the arctic river breeze all the way to the entrance, and was grateful when the glass doors closed behind him.

There was something eerie about the apartment house, an unearthly quiet that was a combination of overcarpeting and underoccupancy. The building had been opened for rentals only two months before, with plenty of fanfare and slick newspaper ads. But the stampede of renters had never really gotten underway, the hundred-dollar-a-room apartments remained largely untenanted. Nevertheless, Frank Coombs had been impressed. Frank Coombs had been one of the first to sign a lease, and for nothing less than the building penthouse. In the operatorless elevator, Chet Brander's mouth twisted in a frown as he rode past eight unoccupied floors to reach the plush apartment that Coombs' borrowed money had bought.

At the door of the penthouse, he stabbed the bell and muttered: "Big shot!"

Warmth flooded out of the doorway when Coombs answered. Pleasant steamheat-and-fireplace warmth, whiskey warmth, the warmth of geniality. That was Coombs for you: the perennial host, always ready to smile and clap you on the back and make you welcome, and all so smoothly that you hardly even noticed the hand dipping into your pocket to count the contents of your wallet. "Chester!" Coombs chortled. "Damn nice of you to come out on a lousy night like this. Come on in, fella!"

Brander went in, shedding his coat as he followed Coombs into the lavish front room. It was a room rich in textures: furry carpets and nubby upholstery, satiny drapes and grainy wood paneling. Coombs had many textures himself: waxen smooth hair, silken cheeks, velvety smoking jacket, roughcut briar. He gestured with the pipe, and said:

"Well, what do you think, Chet? Does this place beat the pants off that old dump of mine or not? Minute I heard about this building I jumped for it——"

Brander grunted. "Nobody's killing themselves to get in. Half the apartments are empty."

"Only the top-floor apartments; they're the ones that cost real dough, you know." He gathered up his visitor's outer clothing. "Let me hang this stuff up. Maybe you want that jacket off? I keep it warm in here." He put his hand on Brander, and was shaken off.

"I'll hold on to it," he said, looking around. "Yeah, it's quite a place, Frank. Sure you can afford it?"

Coombs laughed. "Don't you worry about old Frankie. When I told you I knew my investments, I knew what I was talking about. You won't regret lending me that dough, Chet, take my word for it."

"Then the deal worked out?"

Coombs coughed. "Let's have a drink, pal. I'm ten fingers ahead of you."

"We can have the drink later. Look, Frank, I came out on a hell of a night for this. You made a lot of big promises about that dough, and now I have to know. Is it a payoff, or a stall?"

Coombs started to make himself a highball, and then ignored the soda. He downed the drink in three large gulps, and said: "It's a payoff, Chet, like I told you. Before you leave, I'll give you a check for every nickel you loaned me. Plus."

"Plus what?"

Coombs laughed again, and took a step forward, swaying slightly. "You'll see, Chet, you'll see. But come on, don't be so mercenary. We used to be pals, remember. I want you to see the place——"

"I saw it."

"You didn't see the best part." He swept his hand around the room, encompassing the wide, heavily draped windows. "I got three hundred feet of terrace out there, and it's all mine. Greatest view of the city you ever saw——" He strode over to the double doors and flung them open, admitting an inquisitive cloud of cold air.

"Hey," Chet Brander said.

"Come on, you won't freeze. Just take a look at this, will ya? You never saw anything like it in your life——"

Brander stood up. Through the open doors, the lights of Manhattan blinked and glowed. It was a hard sight to resist; city lights, like earthbound stars, had always compelled and excited him. Then, as if to tempt him further, Coombs gleefully pulled back the drapes from the window, enlarging the view.

"How about that, huh? Gets you right here, don't it?" Coombs touched the monogram on his velvet jacket.

"What are all the bars for?" Brander said.

"The window bars?" Coombs tittered. "You know me, Chet. Never trusted anybody. Burglars are always bustin' into penthouses, so I had the building bar all the windows. Even the door is made of steel; I don't take any chances. But come on, fella!"

Brander went forward, out onto the terrace, no longer

feeling the cold or hearing the wind. Manhattan, obliterated in contours, was etched before him only in golden lights. He caught his breath.

"What do you say, Chet?" Coombs chuckled. "Is this living, Chet? Is this the life?"

"Yeah," he breathed.

"You feast your eyes, boy. I'm going to make us a drink. You just look at that, Chet," Coombs said, going back into the room.

Chet Brander looked, and felt strange and restless and exalted. As if in a dream, he looked, until he realized that he was coatless and hatless in the worst cold that had descended upon the city in seven years. Shivering, he turned back to the doorway of the warm apartment, just in time to see Coombs' grinning face, in time to see Coombs, calmly and without hurry, closing the terrace doors.

"Hey," he said, shaking the knob. "Open up, Frank."

Misty behind the small diamond-patch of glass set into the metal door, Coombs' face stopped grinning and became a silken mask. He lifted the drink in his hand, as if in salute, and took a long swallow. Then he moved away.

"Hey!" Chet Brander shouted, shaking the door harder but not causing a single rattle in its hinges. "Let me in, Frank! It's goddam cold out here!" He couldn't see Coombs any more, but he knew he must be there, enjoying his little prank. Brander thudded on the small pane of glass with his fist, and felt the solidity of it, saw the tiny octagonal wire mesh that made it unbreakable. He shoved against the door, and remembered that it was steel. "Frank! Goddam it, cut out the clowning, Frank! Let me in, will ya?"

Then the lights went out in the penthouse apartment.

It was only then that Chet Brander knew that Coombs had planned more than an impulsive prank. He wasn't going to reopen the sturdy door that led back into the warmth, not in the next minute, or the next hour. Maybe even——

"Frank!" Brander screamed, and realized that he could barely hear his own voice as the wind came by and swallowed the syllables greedily. *"Let me in!"* Brander yelled soundlessly, hammering and pounding and kicking at the door.

There was no telling how long he stood there, denying the fact that the entrance was closed to him. Finally, he moved away, toward the windows; one touch of his hand recalled that they had been barred against intruders, against the entry of strangers or friends. He was neatly sealed out of Coombs' penthouse, where the warmth was. He was alone, outside, with the cold.

Cold! So heated had been his exertions that Brander hadn't even been aware of the temperature. But he felt it now—a cold that gripped his flesh as if there hadn't been an ounce of clothing on him. Cold, and a howling, vicious wind that whirled the frost like an icy shroud around his body. Cold so terrible and so inescapable that Chet Brander had thoughts of death and the grave.

It was no prank. He knew that now. It was no coincidence that Coombs had chosen this night for his rendezvous. It was cold that Coombs had been waiting for, cold and the freezing wind and dark night, and the chance to leave his creditor shivering and alone outside the steel door of his penthouse apartment, to end his debt forever in death.

But how would Coombs explain it? What would he say when they found Chet Brander's body, a victim of exposure in the middle of the city? . . .

Brander stopped thinking about it, and went to the terrace wall, to peer down at the terrifying distance between himself and the street.

"Help!" Chet Brander shrieked: *"Help me!"*

The wind took his words. He cried out again, but the lights were dark in the untenanted floors beneath him, and no one heard.

"They'll never hear me," he said aloud, the sobs beginning in his throat. "They'll never know I'm here. . . ."

. . .

He made a circuit of the terrace, round and round and round the penthouse, searching for some weakness in the fortress of Coombs' apartment. There was none. Already, his feet had become numb; he could barely feel his own footsteps. He clapped his hands together, and then pounded them over his body in an effort to keep the blood circulating.

"Got to keep moving," he muttered. "Keep moving. . . ."

He began to run. He ran wildly, staggering around the terrace, until his breath left him, and he fell, panting, to the frigid stone floor.

"Got to get help," he said to himself.

He began a frantic search of his pockets. His hands first touched the bulk of his wallet, but his fingers barely felt the leather. He looked at it stupidly for a moment, and then took it to the edge of the wall.

"Write a note," he said. But even as he said it, hopefully, he knew that he had discovered no solution. He carried no pen, no pencil, no tool that would help him tell the indifferent world below that he was a prisoner of cold 20 stories above the street.

He looked at his wallet, and then flung it over the wall. He lost sight of it at once, and there was no hope in his heart for rescue.

In his breast pocket, he found cigarettes and matches. He tossed the cigarettes aside, and then tried to light a match in his cupped hands, eager for even one pinpoint of warmth. The wind, capricious, wouldn't permit the luxury; in disgust, he hurled the matches over the wall.

In his right-hand jacket pocket, he found a key. He looked at it blankly for a moment, not recognizing it. It wasn't *his* key; he'd never seen it before. He almost threw it away, but then stopped when he realized what it was. It was a key to Coombs' apartment. Coombs must have slipped it into his pocket. But why?

Then he knew. If Coombs had given him a key, then Coombs could explain Chet Brander's mysterious death. If he were found with a key on his frozen body, then anyone would believe that he had used it to enter Coombs' apartment, and then had been locked out on the terrace by his own foolishness or misfortune. . . .

Clever! Brander wanted to laugh, but his features were like stone. Not so clever, he thought, getting ready to hurl the key out into the night. But then he stopped, clutching it in his hand, knowing that, though useless to him here on the terrace, it was a key to the warmth only a few tantalizing inches away. He couldn't part with it. . . .

He put the key into his trouser pocket, and went back to the penthouse door. He hammered on it until the skin of his hands cracked and bled. Then he fell in a heap and sobbed.

When he got to his feet again, he was in a delirium. For a moment, he thought that the cold had gone, that the weather had suddenly turned deliciously balmy. But it was only the delirium and a moment's surcease of wind. When the freezing wind came again, it was a kind of blessing: it woke him to his situation, filled him once more with the desire to help himself.

He leaned over the waist-high wall and shouted helplessly into the night.

"I'm here," he moaned. "Oh, my God! Don't you know I'm *here?*"

Then he thought of the roof.

The penthouse had a roof. If he could find access to it, he might find a door leading below, into the other floors of the building!

He took a handkerchief from his trouser pocket and wrapped it about his painful, bleeding right hand. Then he felt his way carefully along the wall.

A wire brushed his face.

At first, he didn't do more than touch it lightly. Then he gripped the wire between his numb hands and yanked. The wire held; it was thick, stout cable. If he could climb it . . .

He tensed every muscle in his body, and held on. Then he leaped off the ground and swung his feet to the penthouse wall.

For a second, he was frozen in the posture, unable to move, willing to give up and die rather than force his aching, frozen body into action once more.

Then he thought of Coombs' silken smile, and the hate gave him strength. He inched upwards, slowly, the smooth wire cutting like a razor's edge into his palms.

It was an agony. He went upwards another inch, and then turned his eyes into the darkness. He saw the lights of the city, and now they seemed like the distant fires of hell.

Another inch. Another. He wanted to let go, and enjoy the luxury of falling, the tranquillity of death, but he kept on.

He saw the edge of the roof.

With a last, gasping effort, he clambered up the wire, scraping his knees against the side of the masonry walls until the rough stone shredded cloth and skin. Then he flung himself over the side, to safety.

It was only some ten feet above the terrace, but the wind and the cold seemed more terrible here. Along the rim, ghostly jutting shapes surrounded him. Television antennas. He blinked at them, as if they were curious spectators.

He staggered about in the darkness until he found the roof door. His hand touched a doorknob, and he cried out in relief. Then the cry became a moan.

The door was locked.

He screamed and raged at it in fury, but not for long. He put his hand in his trouser pocket, and felt the key to the penthouse. "You win, Frank," he tried to say aloud, but his lips couldn't move to form the words.

He moved back toward the edge, knowing no sensation in his limbs. He leaned against a tall antenna, limply.

"They say don't fall asleep," he thought, chuckling in his throat.

He began to slip to the roof floor, and held on to a trailing wire for support.

The wire!

The flat, broad, light wire lay in his numbed hand, and he remembered what this wire could do.

He tugged at it. He tugged harder. He tugged frantically, desperately, insanely. He found other broad, flat wires depending from the antennas of the roof, and tugged at them. One of them came loose in his hand, but he wasn't satisfied. He went to them all, tugging and yanking until he felt sure that the effects of his work had been seen or noticed somewhere below, that he had ripped or torn the metal ribbons from the bright, glowing instruments of the warm, unaware people in the fancy apartment house by the river. . . .

He began to laugh, through unmoving lips, as he went about his destructive labors. And then, when he was too exhausted to go on, he fell to his hands and knees and tried to remember how prayer went.

Minutes later, a light exploded on the rooftop.

"Hey, will you look at this?" he heard a voice say. "Must be some kind of nut. . . ."

"I thought my picture was acting funny, but I thought it was just the wind. . . ."

"I haven't been getting *any* picture . . . and right in the middle of the show. . . ."

Hands touched him. Warm hands.

"Hey, this guy's in bad shape. . . ."

"Wouldn't be surprised if he froze to death out here. . . ."

"Better get him inside. . . ."

"Thanks," Chet Brander tried to say, but it was only an unspoken thought. When he felt the first touch of the warmth on the other side of the roof's door, he let himself enjoy the luxury of unconsciousness.

. . .

He was on a sofa. His mouth held a bitter, molten taste, and there was a furnace roaring in his stomach. His hands and feet were burning, and he began to squirm to avoid the tongues of the flames.

He opened his eyes, and saw the broad, fleshy face of an anxious, elderly man.

"You OK, son? What the hell were you doing out there, anyway?"

He couldn't answer.

"That's all right, don't try to talk. I'm Mr. Collyer, from Apartment 12-D. I found you up on the roof. Those other people wanted me to call the police, but I said, what for, all he needs is to get warm. That's why I brought you here, to my place."

Brander looked about him, and studied the new textures of the strange apartment. He forced himself to sit up, and recognized the alcohol taste in his mouth.

"I thought a little brandy'd help," the man said, watching him. "I guess you got locked out, eh? You live in the building?"

"No," Brander said, in a voice he didn't recognize. "I—I was just looking at the apartments upstairs. Thinking about renting, maybe. Then I remembered hearing something about a sundeck on the roof, and I went to have a look——"

"Hell of a night for sightseeing," the man grunted.

"Yes. But I went, just to see. The next thing I knew, the door slammed behind me."

"Quite a wind up there, all right. We all thought it was the wind that knocked the antennas out, until we found you." He chuckled. "Lot of people in the building sore at you, son. 'Specially since they can't get a repair man til late tomorrow morning."

"I'm sorry."

"Never mind that; you did the smart thing. Hey, where're you going?"

Brander was on his feet, tightening the knot in his tie, moving unsteadily toward the doorway.

"You can't go out like that, mister——"

"It's OK, I'll get a cab. Got to be going."

"Let me lend you something. Coat or something——"

"No, I'll be all right," Brander said, turning the doorknob.

"Maybe you ought to see a doctor. . . ."

"I will, I will!" Brander said, and went out into the quiet, overcarpeted hallway.

He pressed the button that would bring the automatic elevator to the 12th floor, and then dug into his trouser pocket. It was still there, icy to his touch. The key to Coombs' penthouse.

When the elevator arrived, he stepped inside the car and punched P.

. . .

He didn't turn on the lights as he entered. He went to the closet and found his overcoat, his hat and his muffler.

He put them on, but felt no warmer.

Then he went to the double doors of the terrace, unlatched them, and opened them a scant two inches.

He returned to Coombs' sofa, and sat down in the dark to wait.

At 1:30, he heard the key in the lock. He rose unhurriedly, and went toward the doorway of Coombs' bedroom, concealing himself behind it.

The front door opened. Coombs, muttering, stepped inside. He stumbled about the darkened room, dropping his overcoat on the carpet before his hand found the light switch. Then, still mumbling, he looked blearily toward the terrace, and chuckled drunkenly. He went to the liquor cabinet, and poured himself something from a bottle, no ice. He downed it, still looking at the terrace.

Chet watched as the glass came down slowly, and heard Coombs say, thickly:

"What the hell?"

Coombs went to the doors. When he found them unlatched, he opened them wide and stepped out onto the terrace.

"*Brander!*" he heard him shout, in chorus with the wind.

But Brander wasn't there. Brander was racing across the carpet of the penthouse living room, racing to reach the terrace doors before Coombs could return. He won the contest easily, slamming the steel portals shut even before Coombs was close enough to see his triumphant face. But he waited behind the wire-meshed diamond pane of glass, waiting for Coombs to get near enough to know, to understand.

"*Brander!*" he heard Coombs cry, his voice muffled and thin. "For God's sake, Brander, let me in!"

Chet smiled, and moved away. "Don't try messing with the antennas," he said, although he knew Coombs could not hear him. "Nobody's watching TV tonight. . . ."

"Chet! Chet, for the love of God! *Chet!*"

Outside, in the hallway, he could no longer hear the faintest sound of Coombs' pleas. He took the elevator to the ground floor and nodded pleasantly at the doorman, who was looking skyward with a frown.

"Bad night," Chet said, conversationally.

"And gettin' worse," the doorman answered, holding out a broad, flat palm. "See what's comin' now?"

"What?" Chet asked, looking at the sky.

"Snow," the doorman said.

Chet corrected him: "Sleet."

THE SIGN
OF SCORPIO

BY CHARLES MERGENDAHL

In a short but productive lifetime, Charles Mergendahl contributed fiction to most of the leading magazines and wrote nine novels (among them, "The Bramble Bush," "The Drums of April," "The Next Best Thing"), in addition to being a lecturer in mathematics at Bowdoin College in Brunswick, Maine, where he died suddenly, at the age of 40, in 1959, the year after this story was published. "The Sign of Scorpio" tells of a voluptuous wife whose strict fidelity to her marriage vows takes a surprisingly literal turn.

AT FIRST she was startled by the ringing phone. But then, moving into the hallway, humming a little nursery rhyme, she thought that even a ringing telephone was *something* on this hot, dreary afternoon.

"Helen? . . . Maury Coates. I'm in town for a few days, and just wanted to make sure you were home before I drove over."

"Maury," she said, and the phone became slippery between her fingers. "Listen, Maury——"

But he'd hung up before she finished.

She put down the receiver and sat twisting her wedding band in an old nervous habit, then rose and moved slowly to the bedroom. She drew a well-read book, *Life by the Stars*, from her own "secret" drawer, and looked up today's date under SCORPIO. Her horoscope warned her to be wary of strangers. Maury was not exactly a stranger. But even so . . .

She stared at her blonde hair, her pouting red lips, her baby-blue eyes in the bedroom mirror. "It's been seven years," she told the eyes, "and he's *not* a stranger, so what are you afraid of now?" Then she turned away and slipped into a cool, ice-blue afternoon dress. It was too tight across her full breasts, but it was cut very conservatively at the neck and shoulders, and she thought, accordingly, that it would do.

Maury arrived at ten minutes after three. He was dark and lean, wearing slacks and a gay sport shirt that displayed the chocolate tan on his corded arms. "I'd have come before," he said, "but didn't know where you lived until today." He looked at her with those black, knowing eyes, then moved slowly about the room inspecting the furniture, the drapes, her prized collection of tiny dolls along the mantel.

"Would you like a drink?" she asked.

"You *still* haven't grown up."

"Maury?"

"The little girl playing house." Then, "I'd love one, if you'll have one with me."

She tried to control her naturally sensuous movements as she walked to the bar and pulled open the doors. Inside there were two decanters, one marked NED'S and one marked OTHERS. She drew out the OTHERS and poured them both a drink.

"I'm one of the OTHERS?" he said, amused.

"Ned—he doesn't like anything but this very special—very expensive Scotch."

"I remember," he said. "Ned always lived on schedule—liked everything just so." He raised his glass, smiled, said, "Well, sometime I'll have a taste of Ned's." Then he sat on the sofa watching her as she stood motionless, twisting the ring on her finger. He was dangerous, she thought in the long silence. Attractive and charming and very dangerous, as other young girls had discovered too late—as she had nearly discovered too late herself, until a gypsy fortuneteller had warned her barely in time, and she'd rushed wildly to the safety of Ned's big steadiness.

"How is Ned?" he said finally.

"Fine."

"I always liked him, you know. Steady, hard-working. Maybe a little dull——"

"Stop it, Maury!"

"But OK by the sign of Scorpio."

"Now that isn't funny."

"I'm sorry," he said.

"After all, it doesn't hurt to believe in the stars and omens and things like that."

"No . . . And what's your *future*?" he said with his eyes looking into her, through her, undressing her, so she dropped her own eyes to the gold band, twisted constantly between her fingers. She took it off, put it on again, took it off again and stared at the inscription inside the ring. *Till Death Do Us Part.* It had been her own idea, that inscription. *Her* idea, and after the ring had come back from the jewelers, she'd actually taken an oath on it, as she'd taken oaths as a child, kneeling in the grass of the back yard under the light of a full moon:

> "I swear, I swear,
> By the bright full moon,
> To keep this vow,
> Or I die too soon."

"Something written in there?" said Maury.

"Something private," she said. "You'd think it was silly." And she was not so frightened now. "He can't touch me now," she whispered to the row of little dolls. "I have a wonderful husband, and I made my vow, 'Till death do us part,' and Maury can't possibly touch me now."

Maury left at 4:30, and she felt an overwhelming relief when he'd gone. She fixed Ned his favorite dinner of corned beef hash, and when he finally arrived home exactly at 5:30 as always, she threw her soft curved self against him, then sat watching him with a touch of wifely irritation while he went through his nightly routine, a routine that never varied, she knew, even on those few occasions when she had been shopping and had not been there to greet him when he arrived home. He hung up his hat; he took off his coat; he said, "There's a ball game on TV." Then he opened the cupboard and made himself his routine drink from his own personal decanter.

"See you had company," he said, lifting the OTHERS.

"Yes, some of the girls." And she wondered why she lied, and thought that it didn't matter because Maury had come and gone and it was all over now.

That night, passionate, she tried to coax Ned to bed at 9:30. But he preferred watching the ball game, and never went to bed until exactly 10:15 in any case.

The next day was even hotter. She worked lethargically in the morning, dressed in halter and shorts. Then, after lunch, she studied her horoscope. It told her to have confidence. "I have confidence," she told her dolls, and sipped iced tea until the doorbell rang and Maury stepped into the hall before she could protest.

He strode to the bar and made himself a drink. "Someday," he said, tapping Ned's decanter. "Someday." Then he turned and smiled and appraised her body beneath the shorts and halter. "It just doesn't make sense," he said. "A beautiful face —luscious face—and yet you don't even seem to realize it yourself. A little girl collecting dolls."

"Maury," she said firmly. "I don't want you to come here again."

"I'll be leaving town in a couple of days. Maybe tomorrow."

"I don't *want* you here," she repeated, remembering to have confidence.

"We're old friends," he said, "so where's the harm?" His eyes moved over her bare legs and bare midriff and sun-tanned shoulders. "A waste," he said. "A terrible waste."

She started to protest, then finally sat wearily on the sofa and twisted her ring and stared at the row of little dolls.

"Seven years ago," Maury said, "I asked you to run off with me. At the last minute you went to some crazy gypsy, who told you to beware of a tall fellow with black hair. Now wasn't that kind of silly?" Then seriously, after a moment: "I still love you, Helen."

"Till death do us part," she murmured.

"I'm leaving town tomorrow. If you could only understand how I feel—if you could still feel the way you used to—well we could pick everything up where we left off."

"I swore by the full moon."

"Please think about it," he said. "You're a real woman, Helen, and you need adventure in your life. So stop suffocating yourself because of horoscopes and gypsies." He touched her bare shoulder, and she pulled sharply away. He said, "I'm sorry," really meaning it, she thought. "I'm leaving tomorrow," he said. "But I'll come by here first, and if you still don't want me, well—I know where you live, so I'll come by again and again, because I won't be able to help myself."

"No," she said. "No, *no!*"

"Tomorrow," he said gently, and left.

That night Ned brought her a wooden doll, carved and painted in Mongolia. She named it Sin-Sin and told Ned she loved him and at 10:15 she showed him a passion that profoundly shocked him. "I made you a vow," she whispered, "and nothing—*nothing* will ever make me break it. You'll see," she said. "*He'll* see."

"Who?" Ned asked.

"Never you mind."

"Lord, it's after *eleven*," he said, and went promptly to sleep, while she lay awake, restless, brooding in the dark.

The next morning, after Ned had gone off to work, she opened her secret drawer and checked her horoscope. "Express your feelings," it read, "but keep your promises." She laughed aloud. It was perfect. She drove to the next town and bought a small bottle of powder with a skull and crossbones on it. She took it home, opened the bar, made sure she had the right decanter, and emptied the powder into the brown liquid. She shook it well and placed it back in the bar. Then she put on a white low-necked linen dress that showed the curve of her breasts, and sat waiting near the little dolls.

The doorbell rang at precisely 20 after three. She held her breath as Maury's eyes found her moist, pouting mouth and then the smooth flesh that hinted at her body beneath the dress.

He said, "You're dressed for traveling," with a touch of disbelief in his voice.

"Yes, I read my horoscope, and it tells me to *express* myself today. And, after all—if you're going to keep coming back— keep wearing me down—why should I fight it any longer? I mean if you still love me—you still want me——"

He strode toward her eagerly, but she slipped provocatively away. "Later," she teased. "Later."

"Shall we get going then?"

"No, I—I've got to pack a bag, you see, and—I'll meet you at the corner of Main and Harvard at five o'clock."

"I'll pick you up here."

"No, it's safer for me to meet you."

"Well—all right then," and he started for the door. But he turned back and said, "How about a little drink? Just one—to celebrate? I always wanted to taste that stuff of Ned's."

Her heart beat faster. "No," she said hastily. "He'd notice right away, you see, and he'd know something was wrong and it might spoil everything." She carefully selected the bottle marked OTHERS and poured him a large double drink. "Anybody know you're here?" she asked casually.

"Not a soul."

"Anybody know where we're going? I mean so Ned can't follow?"

"I'm a gay wanderer," he said. "He'll never find us."

"Fine." She smiled and gave him the drink. "It'll take about five minutes," she said.

"What?"

"Nothing, nothing."

"Aren't you drinking?"

"No, I—I don't care for one."

"Well, then—here's to 'later.'" She stood back, twisting the ring on her slippery finger as he downed the whiskey at a gulp.

"Good," he said, "but I hate to do this to Ned. The way he'll feel."

"Now don't worry about Ned."

He started to sit, but she told him to hurry and go now. She'd meet him at five—the corner of Main and Harvard. He said, "All right," and "Boy, that drink really gave me a jolt. The heat, I guess." And then, looking at her with great contentment, he said, "We'll just have to make up for all that wasted time."

"Yes," she agreed softly. She led him to the door, then went to the window and watched his car move up the street. It swerved slightly as he rounded the corner.

At a quarter of five she kissed all her dolls good-by. He was waiting for her. They drove fast out of town, and on the first stretch of open road, he pulled to a stop and tried to kiss her.

"Later," she said. "I'll never break my vow, you see. Till death do us part."

He drove on. But at exactly 5:35, after she knew for certain that Ned had come home and had his single special drink, then she laughed and said "Now" and he stopped the car again, and she threw the ring out the open window into a little patch of weeds.

THE MAN IN
THE WELL

BY BERKELY MATHER

Berkely Mather is the nom de plume of a well-born Australian who rebelled against the respectable vocation his family had planned for him. Preferring to combine a writing career with the adventurous life of a British officer in India and the Far East, he has authored the novels "The Achilles Affair," "The Pass Beyond Kashmir," "The Road and the Star," and innumerable short stories and screenplays (including one of the James Bonds). He told PLAYBOY: *"I have made a lot of money in a comparatively short time. I intend to make a lot more—but my real ambition is to write two good, taut thrillers a year, keeping an oblique eye cocked on their film possibilities. I personally find more satisfaction and sheer enjoyment in writing than anything else I have ever done." He also says, "I never set a story in a country of which I have no personal knowledge." His personal knowledge of Upper Burma—and his great gifts as a storyteller—are evident in this story of "The Man in the Well," who, when the moon is full, struggles and screams of a treasure forever lost.*

THERE WERE SIX of them in the waiting room when Sefton arrived, so he ran a cursory eye over them and went out again and hung about in the doorway of a haberdasher on the other side of the Strand.

He had not been frightened by what he saw but let there be a dignity about all things—even applying for a job. There were two young men in duffel coats, one of them with a beard, a hard-bitten elderly character who might have been an ex-bosun from the Irrawaddy Flotilla, two one-time sahibs who looked absurdly alike in their yellowing bloodlessness and a woman who looked as if she had just crossed the Gobi on a camel. If this was the short list he was willing to bet on his chances.

He had lit his sixth cigarette by the time the last of them emerged, so he nipped it economically and crossed through the midmorning traffic and went up the narrow stairs again. A clerk took his name in and after a brief wait led him through to an inner office. A lanky, elderly man rose from behind a littered desk and held out his hand.

"Mr. Sefton?" he inquired. "Sorry if I've kept you waiting. Please sit down. You must excuse this mess—my agent has lent me his office for these interviews."

Sefton bowed, sat, balanced his hat on his knees and waited. The other man gazed at a spot on the wall over Sefton's head, screwed up his eyes and pursed his lips.

"As phony as the papers say he is," Sefton thought, and added savagely, "silly old goat."

Minutes ticked by, traffic rumbled outside and from nearby Charing Cross an engine whistled shrilly. At last the old man broke the silence.

"There have been many other applicants, Mr. Sefton," he said softly.

"Which you short-listed down to seven—none of whom so far have suited," Sefton answered. "I hope I will. I am very keen on joining you."

The other looked slightly nettled.

"May I ask where you gathered that information?"

"Counted heads in the waiting room when I arrived and then timed their exits from across the street. None of them stayed long." His grin robbed the statement of offense. "I think I'm your man, Professor Neave."

"That remains to be seen," Neave answered stiffly. He shuffled through a file of letters in front of him and selected one that Sefton recognized as his own. "Would you care to elaborate on this a little?"

"Sure," answered Sefton promptly. "Eight years as assistant engineer with the Sontal Gem Mining Corporation in Mogok, Upper Burma. I speak good Burmese and can get along in most of the dialects—Shan, Chin and Karen. I know the country well and was an M.T. officer in the Royal Indian Army Service Corps during the war. I get along with people, can take and carry out orders—" he paused very slightly, "and I can keep my mouth shut."

"Why did you leave the Sontal Corporation, Mr. Sefton?" the professor asked.

"For the same reason as the rest of the staff," Sefton told him. "The Japs were ten miles up the track and traveling fast. We sent the married men and their families to Rangoon before the railroad from Mandalay was cut off, and we ourselves set fire to the whole shebang and got out in the last vehicle to leave. We only got to Yeu—that's just north of Bhame—when our petrol gave out. We walked the rest of the way to the Chindwin, right through the dry belt. I say 'we'—but only I made it. Dysentery, malaria and starvation did for the rest. It was a bad year and the monsoon was late."

"How long did the journey take you?"

"Just over three months. Our speed was that of the sickest man."

"And then?"

Sefton shrugged. "Nothing much more to it. I crossed into

Assam by the Tiddim Track and fell in with our forces in Imphal. I was a long time in the hospital and then I joined up. I fought my war with the Fourteenth Army and finished as a major."

"What have you been doing since?"

"I put my gratuity and savings into a small engineering shop in Lancashire in the first place—and lost the lot. Since then I've had a variety of jobs in my own line of country—deep drilling in Brazil, and I've been up the Gulf with an oil concern among other things——"

"Are you married?"

"No—and I haven't a soul in the world dependent upon me."

"What remuneration would you expect?"

"I don't want anything—except to go with you."

The professor brightened visibly for a moment and then covered up. "I don't understand, Mr. Sefton," he said.

Sefton leaned forward.

"I told you I'd had a series of jobs, professor," he said earnestly. "All of them have been reasonably well paid and I left each one of them of my own accord—often in the face of strong persuasion to stay on. Restlessness—inability to find a niche in this postwar world—call it what you like, but I know I'll never be able to settle down until I get it out of my system."

"Get what out of your system?"

Sefton paused and gazed out of the window for a full minute before answering. "It's hard to say," he said at length. "Put it this way. I was a reasonably settled young man with a career ahead of me with Sontal. The war finished all that. The corporation never started up again. I had seen my friends die on that trek and I'd been unable to help them. I'm not neurotic, but—but—" he spread his hands. "Oh, hell, I don't know—I've just got a yen to go out there again, to see the places we walked through—to feel the sun beating down on me and to get the stink of the jungle back into my nostrils. I want to face up to something I've been running away from all these years and to realize how little it all means in retrospect." He stopped suddenly. He had rehearsed this speech carefully but now he wondered if he had not overdramatized it. *Hell, that wouldn't have deceived a kid*, he thought ruefully, and added aloud, "This must all sound very silly, professor."

But the professor smiled sympathetically, "Not at all. I think I understand. I was part of a lost generation myself in 1918. All right, Mr. Sefton—you've been very frank with me. Let me tell you something about myself and *my* reason for going out there." He pushed a box of cigarettes across the table and Sefton, noting the virgin ash tray, realized that he was the first who had been thus favored and felt his confidence rise accordingly. "I take it that you know a little about me— my one-man expeditions—my modest reputation as an author and popular lecturer——?"

Sefton looked suitably shocked. "Who doesn't, professor?"

"None of the previous applicants, apparently," answered the professor with more than a touch of sourness. "One young man had heard, without particular interest, a 15-minute talk of mine on television. The woman confused me with Professor Lever, the ornithologist, while most of the others were far more interested in what I could pay them than in the journey and its objects. Still, be that as it may—I want a man who knows Upper Burma, who is prepared to rough it, who can drive one jeep and maintain two and who, in short, is prepared to accompany me on a trip over the old Burma Road from Calcutta to as far as we can get toward the China border. A man who can relieve me of the chores of the trip while I collect material and take pictures for my next lecture tour, but who at the same time can be rather more—er—intellectually congenial than the average paid employee." He rose and held out his hand. "I think you might well be that man, Mr. Sefton."

In Sefton's heart was a paean of joy and relief.

. . .

He halted the jeep at the top of the last rise before Kohima. Down the winding road that led back toward Manipur he could see the second jeep snaking round the hairpin bends that multiplied the crow-flight distance tenfold. The road had all but gone back to the jungle since he had last seen it in the closing days of the war. Then it had been a tarmaced miracle of engineering that had carried four lines of heavy military traffic all round the clock. The teak-built culverts and Irish bridges had now for the most part rotted through and Sefton, breaking trail, had had to stop many times since they had crossed the Brahmaputra at Gauhati to allow the professor to catch up.

He lit a cigarette and tried for the 50th time to fight down the feverish impatience that bedeviled him. Left to himself he could have pressed on through to the dry belt in a week, but with this old fool's insistence on stopping to take photographs, plus his maddening refusal to travel in the heat of the afternoon, it looked as if the time might well be quadrupled. And now it seemed more than probable that they would be held up in Imphal. The Indian government was engaged in sporadic jungle fighting with the Naga tribes who, promised their autonomy when the British left, were demanding it in terms that bordered on small-scale warfare. Politics! Politics had stopped his getting into Upper Burma twice before. What the hell had it to do with him? All he wanted was a couple of hours in a pagoda near Yeu . . ."

The professor had arrived now. He pulled up triumphantly in just the very spot he should have avoided, and Sefton bellowed wrathfully.

"For God's sake—how many times have I told you not to stop in mud?" He strode over and pushed the old man roughly out of the driver's seat and jabbed furiously at the starter. The engine roared but the wheels spun impotently. He cursed and got the towrope out of his own jeep and for the 20th time yanked the professor onto firm ground.

"There are certain fundamental rules for good manners, too," answered the professor tartly. "Things are getting a little out of hand, Sefton. I would remind you that although you are not drawing a salary, *I* am in charge of this expedition."

"You want to get across Upper Burma to the Chinese border, don't you?" snarled Sefton. "OK then, suppose you leave it to someone who knows, and do as you're damned well told."

"I'm not a child and this is not my first experience of the jungle." Neave was thoroughly angry now. "If things are to go on like this I would much prefer to take a paid driver on from Imphal and to pay your passage back to Calcutta by lorry."

Sefton recognized danger signs and temporized.

"I'm sorry, professor," he said and drew his hand wearily over his brow. "All this rather brings things back—and I think I have a touch of fever coming on." He smiled bravely. "You were quite right to slap me down. I'll behave from now on."

The professor accepted his apology with a slight inclination of his head and turned stiffly back to his jeep.

"Once over the Chindwin, you old bum," thought Sefton as they started off again, "and you can go to blazes. I'll have to watch my step till then, though—I don't want to be left stranded when I'm this close."

The old man's Delhi-endorsed papers took them through the check point at Imphal without question and even with an offer, which Sefton politely declined, of an escort as far as the border. They camped that night at the top of the Tiddim Track where rusting Japanese tanks made green hillocks under the creeping undergrowth which still, after 12 years, could not altogether cover the scars of that last fierce battle.

Sefton lay under his mosquito net and watched the pre-monsoon clouds gathering over the pass and blotting out the stars. They had been gathering that night he crossed. He stretched out on his camp bed and listened to the jungle night sounds and the professor's gentle snores the other side of the fire. His thoughts went back over the years.

There had been six of them at first in that crazy truck. Findlay, the Scotch manager—tall, grim, ascetic—who was a Sanskrit scholar and who some said was a secret convert to Buddhism; Muirson the Eurasian clerk; the two Karen coolies; and Ngu Pah, the pretty little Burmese nurse who had insisted on standing by her tiny hospital until the last moment; and himself. The Karens had deserted early and Muirson, opium-besotted and malarial, had died at the end of the third week. That left the three of them. Three oddly assorted people on foot in the middle of the freakish dry belt after the truck had finally petered out. There was a well in the pagoda to which they had struggled before Findlay collapsed, and Ngu Pah, the lightest of them, had climbed down the rotten rope to see if any dribble remained in the sand at the bottom. But it had been bone dry. The rope had broken as she struggled back and had left her clinging to the masonry a few feet from the top and they had been hard put to it to rescue her.

It was that night that he made his decision. Findlay could obviously go no farther and Ngu Pah was showing signs of failing too. Her tiny frame had borne the brunt of that hellish journey as she had carried her full share of the water and rations and finally the heavy wash-leather bag that Findlay would entrust to nobody but her.

He knew what that bag contained because he had seen Findlay making his selection from the trays of pigeon-blood rubies before they had dynamited the strong room and set fire to the rest. They had been unable to send their usual shipments out to Rangoon for some months, so there had been a lot of stuff to choose from. That bag must have weighed seven pounds if it weighed an ounce. My God—seven pounds of uncut rubies. She had not let the bag out of her possession for an instant after Findlay had handed it to her. She had even slung it round her neck when she climbed into the well. Sefton wondered when she had first begun to suspect his intentions. He had tried for years to justify to himself that final act of treachery. He no longer bothered now. In Sefton's world it was every man for himself. He had stolen the bag that night while she slept and Findlay raved in his delirium—and with it he had also stolen their last half gallon of water and the pitiful remains of their rations, and he had set out on the last desperate stage to the Chindwin and safety.

She had cheated him though—the little devil. He made the discovery the night before he crossed the border. He had opened the bag to make a careful selection of just what he could carry on his person with safety, meaning to cache the rest where, if the war went the right way, he could come back and collect it later. He remembered the feel of the rough sand and gravel that poured over his hands as he untied the thong. He had screamed and groveled in his rage out there in the jungle and then, when sanity returned, he thought about going back— but the Japs were closing in fast and he could see the smoke from burning villages a scant five miles behind him. That's where the stuff had gone—down the bloody well—and that's where it was now. Obviously they couldn't have survived long. Findlay was almost a goner when he left them, and Ngu Pah couldn't have gone down the well again to recover the stones because the rope had snapped. He had often tortured himself with the possibility of the girl surviving the war and going back for them, but he had brushed that aside. Without food and water she could not have lasted another week. No—the rubies were still there, at the bottom of the well—of that he was convinced.

Twice he had raised the necessary money and gone out to Rangoon on the pretext of starting up in engineering, but try as he would he had been unable to get permission to go through to Upper Burma. There had been constant internecine warfare along the line of the Irrawaddy since the British had left, and both sides regarded visitors with suspicion. He had tried it without permission and had narrowly missed being shot for his pains. The third time he had attempted to go out they had refused him a visa, as had the India government when he applied for a mining license in the Shan hills. The professor's advertisement had been a heaven-sent final chance. He would *get* there this time—by God he would.

His plan of action was made. Their road lay through Yeu— there was no other way in. He would come down with a simulated attack of malaria there. The way to Mandalay was easy so he would persuade the professor to go on alone, promising to catch up with him in a few days. They weren't on such friendly terms that the old man would boggle much at that. He *would* catch up too—but then he'd quit. He had enough ready cash to pay his way back to England—and more than enough wit to get the stones in with him.

He grunted, flicked his cigarette out into the damp under-growth, swatted a mosquito and dropped quietly to sleep.

They reached Yeu four days later without incident except for a few further bog-downs on the professor's part. Sefton had suffered from malaria often enough to be able to simulate the symptoms with a degree of realism that frightened the other man. He had even had the forethought to break the ther-mometer in the medicine chest so that his temperature would not give the lie to his agonized shaking each evening.

He had no difficulty in recognizing the turn off to the pagoda as they drove past it that last afternoon. It was a few miles east of a tiny village that had been deserted in those panic-stricken days, but which was now repopulated. There was a well there which might have saved the other two had they known about it. A yellow-robed priest sat under a spreading peepul tree at the junction of road and track with a brass begging bowl before him for the offerings of the faithful. He was the first they had seen since crossing the Chindwin and the professor was delighted in spite of his preoccupation with Sefton's fever. He leaped out of his jeep, camera ready, but the priest dropped his eyes to the ground and covered his shaven head with a fold of his robe.

"The camera is a form of evil eye," Sefton explained. "These poonghies don't like 'em. Come on—plenty more of the idle devils where we are going. There's a whole monastery full of them in Yeu. By God, I'll be glad to get there—I'm feeling lousy."

They put up at the monastery rest house, and the professor wandered happily about with his camera for a couple of days while Sefton realistically recuperated. The old man was mildly indignant at Sefton's suggestion that he should go on alone but the latter worked on him skillfully. The Buddhist Feast of the Tooth would just about be starting in Meikhtila—the faithful came from all parts of Asia for this—opportunities for photography that it would be a crime to miss. Just catch the first rafts of teak coming down the Irrawaddy with the break of the monsoon. He'd be all right here—the monks were pretty decent to travelers. Catch him up in Mandalay in a week—as fit as a flea again. The old man at last capitulated and with many a guilty backward glance, went on up the road.

Sefton gave him half a day for safety, and then set off back along the road they had come. He had no fear of the pagoda being occupied. They built these things on the top of practically every hill in Upper Burma, put a statue of the Buddha inside, a couple of dragonlike chhinthes outside to guard him against evil spirits, dug a well for his refreshment and thereafter avoided the place like the plague.

It was just as he had last seen it. Perhaps the purple bougainvillea over the archway that spanned the entrance to the small courtyard was a little more luxuriant, and the monsoon rains, short-lived but fierce in these parts, had washed some more of the white plaster from the pinnacled roof, but the Buddha was unaged, sitting, feet crossed beneath him, soles upward, forefinger and thumb of the right hand grasping the little finger of the other, jeweled lotus on his brow, as serenely as he had sat and watched 15 years before.

He drove on a hundred yards or so and hid the jeep in a bamboo thicket. It was not necessary—nobody had seen him come this way, and anyhow no Burmese would dream of walking a mile or so uphill to investigate. It was the secretiveness of his nature that made him do it—just as the beasts of the jungle are at pains to conceal their tracks even when no danger threatens. He took a coil of rope and an electric torch from the toolbox and hurried back. He was sweating now in spite of the evening cool. His heart was hammering and his breath was coming in short, sharp gasps that almost choked him.

There was a carpet of dead leaves inside the pagoda that rustled and crackled under his feet as he skirted the image and hurried round to the well at the back. The shaft dropped sheer and black and the beam of his torch hardly reached the bottom of it. He dropped a stone over the edge and heard with satisfaction a slight thud as it landed on dry sand. There probably never had been water in the damned thing at all. There were some, Findlay among them, who said that these shafts had never been intended as wells at all but were relics of some older and darker religion in which they had figured in other and more sinister roles—human sacrifices or something.

He knotted the rope round a projecting stone cornice and paid it out into the darkness until its slackness told him it had reached the bottom; then he swung his legs over and commenced his descent. It was easy at first as the masonry was rough and offered some purchase to his feet. It had only been that which had saved Ngu Pah. Lower down, however, the sides became marble smooth and he was glad that he had the forethought to wear rope-soled *espadrilles*.

The ease with which he found the rubies came as an anticlimax that was almost a disappointment. He felt like a child who had been set too simple a task in a party game. He saw them in the first beam of his torch even as his feet touched the sand. They lay on a ledge in the masonry, wrapped in the rotting remains of a once-bright-blue silk scarf—a heap of dull pebbles which even in their uncut and unpolished state threw back the light of the torch in a reddish effulgence.

He wanted to shout and to sing—to throw them in fistfuls over his head like confetti. Instead, he sat down in the sand and lit a cigarette with trembling hands and then trained the beam of the torch on the rubies and just gazed.

It was a good ten minutes before he was steady enough to remove his sweat-soaked shirt and scoop the rubies into it—and a further agonizing ten before he was satisfied with the security of the bag he made of it. He finally fastened it under his belt; then, belaying the rope twice round his waist, he commenced the hard climb up.

He had gone a good 15 feet before it happened—his body bowed stiffly outward from the side of the well—feet pressed firmly against the stones. He was not aware of falling. The first realization came to him as he lay flat on his back in the sand with the rope coiled loosely about him and the chunk of masonry which had missed his head by inches beside him. He started to scream then—shrilly and horribly—and he was still screaming and tearing at the sides of the well when the moonlight at the top of the shaft was blotted out by the head and shoulders of a man—a man with a shaven poll and a swathe of yellow cotton across his chest. He could not make out his face but he knew it was the priest from the track junction and he stopped screaming and started to babble in Burmese.

The priest answered in English with a strong Edinburgh accent.

"I knew you'd be back for them, Sefton, in the fullness of time."

Sefton tried to speak but his throat muscles refused to function. The voice went on.

"Aye, vultures always return to their carrion—and that is

what those stones are. I intended to steal them from my employers in the first place. I had already broken faith by intent. It was that knowledge that brought me to the samadhi of the Middle Way. These robes are not a disguise, Sefton—they are my atonement."

"*Mad*," thought Sefton and fought down another wave of hysteria. "Findlay!" he called shakily. "Findlay—I came back to see if I could find any trace of you. I haven't rested, Findlay, in all these years——"

"That I can well believe," answered Findlay. "A man cannot escape his karma. Well, you have the chance to make your peace now—as I have."

"Findlay—you can't do this to me—you can't—don't murder me——" He was babbling now.

"I have done nothing. In your greed you tied your rope to an unsafe stone. Do you not see the symbolism of it?"

"Findlay—Findlay—listen to me—I know what you must have thought at the time, but I went off to find food, water, for all of us. I couldn't return, Findlay—before God I couldn't —I got lost and then I fell ill myself—I wandered for weeks before I was picked up and then I'd lost my memory. You've got to believe me, Findlay—you've *got* to——"

Findlay appeared not to hear him. His voice droned on dreamily, "Aye—the divine symbolism of it all—the sacrifice of little Ngu Pah—three times she made that five-mile journey for water and food for me after you had stolen our reserve. She died on her return from the last one and I made shift to bury her under the bougainvillea at the gate. Did ye no sense something as you entered, or had your greed blinded you to everything except those scraps of crystallized alumina?"

"I don't want your damned rubies——"

"They're not mine—nor yours," Findlay answered. "They've returned to the earth that formed them. Down there they can do no more harm."

"All right then—let them stay here," Sefton sank to his

knees in the sand, "but you've got to help me out, Findlay——"

"I can neither help you nor hinder you, Sefton. That is your karma—as *this* is mine." And Findlay held his hands over the opening to the shaft. Against the patch of light Sefton saw with a turning of his stomach that the fingers had degenerated into formless stubs. "Leprosy, Sefton—a curse turned blessing because it was only that which held me back from taking the jewels out myself—and thereby gave me my chance of atonement and peace."

"You can't leave me here—that's murder. You're a Buddhist, you say—Buddhists can't kill—not even animals. Get another rope, Findlay—get another rope!" His voice had dropped to a pleading whisper.

"I shall not kill you, Sefton," said Findlay, "not even by negation. You must make your own choice, though. If I get another rope I cannot tie it securely myself with these fingers. I must therefore get help from the village. You will have to come up empty-handed in that case—I should insist on that and ask the villagers' assistance if you broke faith."

"The—the other choice——?" Sefton croaked.

"I shall drop food and water to you for as long as you need it."

Sefton screamed again. "Listen, Findlay! There's money down here—millions! Be sensible. They've got cures for leprosy in Europe now—and you can get a pair of artificial hands that'll do everything your own could. There's enough here and to spare for both of us. Get a rope long enough to loop round the statue and drop both ends to me—you needn't try to tie it. Just let me come up so we can talk it over. If you don't agree to anything I say I'll go away peacefully and never come back—I swear it——"

"If you came up and I were alone, Sefton, you'd kill me," Findlay said. "You know that is in your heart already. I couldn't prevent you—nor would I try—but if that happened I would be robbing you of any chance you may still have of finding peace. That would be against the course of the Middle Way. We are all involved in the destiny of others and a man may not stand by and watch another destroy himself."

Sefton broke then. He fell forward on his face and pounded on the sand with his fists and howled like an animal in torment.

The villagers hauled him up at midnight and the monks at Yeu tended him carefully until the professor, worried at his non-arrival in Mandalay, came back to look for him. Then they shipped him home to a large house set behind high walls in the quietness of the English countryside, where he has found peace—except when the moon is full and he struggles in his canvas jacket and screams about rubies and ropes and a priest who is fed by the faithful at the roadside.

THE NEW DEAL

BY CHARLES EINSTEIN

Charles Einstein's books include "Wiretap," "No Time at All," and "Only Game in Town." While still in college, he became Midwest Sports Editor for International News Service; and continued with INS in New York until 1958, when he resigned to free lance. His sports background led naturally to his editorship of the Simon and Schuster "Fireside Books of Baseball." He has written innumerable short stories and has specialized in the short-short form, having written the introduction to a representative anthology of such stories. In this, he warns against an over-dependence on the snap ending (which he calls "the curse of O. Henry") and says, "The Grimm and Anderson fairy tales are short-shorts of which we know the ending before we even start to read them. Yet they're still fun to read. Why? Because the story ahead of the ending compels interest." We feel this is particularly true of the Las Vegas-set Einstein short-short that follows.

RAFFERTY WAS NOT the only one losing at the blackjack table, but he had been there the longest. He had been sitting there since ten in the morning; now it was after three, and the waitresses of the Wanderlust, Las Vegas' fanciest and newest hotel, had offered him drinks on the house half-a-dozen times at least. The hotel could well afford buying him a drink to keep him where he was.

But he was not drinking; he was only losing. Losers are, by profession, doubters. This was Las Vegas and the Wanderlust was a brand-new hotel and the dealers' faces were not familiar.

The dealer gave Rafferty two fives. He himself had a six showing. Rafferty had bet $40. He put eight more five-dollar chips on the line to double his bet and took one card face down. He sneaked a look under the corner: a queen. Rafferty had 20 going for him.

The dealer turned up his down card: a seven. Now he had 13. Then, an ace. Fourteen. He hit himself again: a two. Sixteen. He hit himself for the last time. A five. Twenty-one. His practiced side-hand motion swept away all of Rafferty's chips.

"I want a new deck," Rafferty said.

"What's that?"

"I said I want a new deck."

"We just broke this one ten minutes ago."

"And it's breaking me. I want a new deck." Rafferty moistened his lips. "And a new dealer."

The two other men who were playing at the table shifted uneasily. They were losing, too, and perhaps secretly they shared Rafferty's spoken sentiments, but they did not want to be drawn in on this.

They were drawn in on it. The dealer drew them in: "Either of you gentlemen want to complain?"

The two men looked down at the green of the table, studying the pattern and the arc inscription: DEALER MUST HIT 16 & STAND ON ALL 17S.

"Don't drag anybody else into it," Rafferty said coldly to the dealer. "It only takes one man to make a complaint. I'm making it."

Out of nowhere, the pit boss appeared. That is not a definitive statement; all pit bosses appear from nowhere. This one was small, cushion-footed, leathery-faced, black-haired. He said to the dealer: "And?"

The dealer nodded toward Rafferty.

"Yes, Mr. Rafferty?" the pit boss said. They knew his name. He had cashed three checks so far today.

"I don't like the cards."

The dealer said, "New deck ten minutes ago."

"Spread 'em," the pit boss said to him.

The dealer spread the deck face up.

"No," Rafferty said. "You're wasting your time. If I knew what to look for I'd be on your side of the table."

"All right," the pit boss said. "New deck."

"Ah, what for?" Rafferty said. He sighed. "They all come out of the same box, don't they?"

"Well, then," the pit boss said, "what can we do?"

Rafferty sighed again. "You know," he said, "it'd be terrible for a new place like this to get into trouble. Take away your gambling license, you're dead. You know that, don't you?"

"He asked for a new deck," the dealer said defensively to the pit boss. "You offer him one and now he says 'no.' Maybe he's got a little case of loser's fatigue."

"Oh, I want a new deck," Rafferty said. "But not out of the box backstage. Suppose I told you I had a deck upstairs in my room. Would you play with my cards?"

The pit boss laughed. Then he looked at Rafferty's face and stopped laughing. He said, "You know better than that, Mr. Rafferty. The house supplies the cards."

"I bought them at the cigar counter over there," Rafferty said. "They're the same brand the house uses, aren't they?"

"We didn't see you buy them," the dealer said. "We don't know what you did upstairs."

"Shut up," the pit boss said to him.

"And I don't know what you do downstairs," Rafferty said to the dealer. "All I know is, there's a lot of fives in your deck."

"Nobody's making you play," the dealer said to him. "You don't like the game, nobody's making you sit there."

"I told you, shut up," the pit boss said to him. Four or five people had gathered behind Rafferty and the other players to listen. "Mr. Rafferty, can I talk to you for a minute?"

"We can talk here," Rafferty said. But there was something in the way the pit boss looked at him. He shrugged and stood up. "All right." He moved away from the playing area and the pit boss ducked under the rope and joined him.

"How much are you out?" the pit boss said in a low voice.

"I don't know exactly," Rafferty said. "Couple of thousand, maybe. Does it make any difference?"

"Look," the pit boss said, "on the one hand, we run an honest game. On the other hand, we don't want any trouble. We'll do anything reasonable to prove we're on the level."

"You won't play with my cards, will you?"

"I said anything reasonable," the pit boss said.

"But they're the same cards you use. I bought them right over there."

The pit boss shook his head patiently. "Nobody would call that reasonable, Mr. Rafferty. The dealer had it right. Nobody knows you bought them here. And nobody knows how long ago it was. If you were to buy a deck right now and we played them fresh, that would be another thing."

"All right," Rafferty said.

"I beg your pardon?"

"I said all right. They're your terms. I accept."

"I don't understand."

"I will walk with you this minute to the cigar counter," Rafferty said, "and I will buy a deck of cards, and then we will walk back to the table and play blackjack with those cards."

"Ah, Mr. Rafferty," the pit boss said. "Don't be ridiculous."

"Ridiculous?" Rafferty's voice went up and the other man looked uncertainly around. "All I've just done is agree to something you yourself proposed."

"But it isn't worked that way," the pit boss said. "Suppose everybody came in wanting to play with his own cards or his own dice. We'd have to make a career out of checking up on people."

"I'm not everybody," Rafferty said. "You proposed something and the minute I agree, you change your mind. You say the cards over here are the same as the cards over there. So I'm not playing with my cards. I'm playing with your cards."

"Then what difference does it make?"

"The difference is that you said they were the same cards; I didn't. I'd like to see if the cards you sell over the counter to the public are the same as the ones you play with. Call it an experiment."

Rafferty grinned coldly, then suddenly turned and walked the few steps to the cigar counter. The pit boss followed him. He said, "What are you going to do?"

"Just buy a deck of cards," Rafferty said. He nodded at the girl behind the counter. "Cards?"

"A dollar, sir," the girl said and slid a deck across the glass top of the counter.

Rafferty set a silver dollar on the counter. He turned and held out the deck to the pit boss. "Here," he said. "You hold them. Just to make sure I'm not cheating."

The pit boss took the deck and stared at him. "You figure we're sensitive, so you're trying to make trouble, aren't you?"

"No," Rafferty said. "You're the one who's looking for

trouble. All I'm looking for is an even shake. To repeat, all I'm doing is taking up your offer."

The pit boss swallowed. "Suppose you have a run of luck."

"Then I have a run of luck."

"Then you can go around saying this proves we're crooked."

"If you're not, you don't have anything to worry about."

"And if you keep on losing? What then? Do you hang it on the dealer?"

"There'll be people watching," Rafferty said. "I'm not worried about card tricks. Not this time around."

"You could still sit there and complain and cause us more trouble."

"Not really," Rafferty said. "A deck lasts about an hour in play, doesn't it? And if I went back to the counter for another deck, that *would* be unreasonable, wouldn't it? No, I've made my play. I'm truly interested in whether you think it's asking too much."

The pit boss looked down at his shoes. "This doesn't prove a thing, you know. If we were dishonest, the easiest thing in the world now would be to rig it so you win."

"I'd be delighted," Rafferty said. "Except that doing that would make you look really bad."

"Then what do you want?"

"A fresh start with a new deck of cards."

"Mr. Rafferty," the pit boss said, "I . . ." He paused. "All right. You've got an hour."

"Thank you," Rafferty said, and they went back to the table. A new dealer was called over. The pit boss himself broke the seal and spread the cards.

Rafferty played for an hour, while the pit boss and an ever-growing crowd of onlookers watched.

At the end of the hour, Rafferty stood up. He had won $18,000.

"Are you satisfied?" the pit boss said to him.

"Not quite," Rafferty said smoothly. "I'm out a dollar."

"You're out a . . . ?"

"For the cards."

"I see," the pit boss said. His voice struggled for control. "But that's not a dollar, Mr. Rafferty, because the cards at this point aren't worth a dollar anymore. They're used. So here are the cards, Mr. Rafferty, and you sell them for what you can get for them. And I'm not supposed to say this, but I'm going to say it anyway—don't come back here, Mr. Rafferty. It costs us too much to prove to you we're honest, and I'm not talking just about money. We like people who take our word for it, because we *are* honest, and we have their good will and the only way we can stay in business is to stay honest and settle for the house edge. You understand, Mr. Rafferty?"

"Perfectly," Rafferty said. "You don't have to worry about me coming back. It's unlikely I'd ever have another run like this one."

He nodded, fended his way through the group of onlookers and went to the elevators and up to his room. When he got there, he found there was a young woman seated at the writing table. She had an extremely thin artist's pen in her hand and she was marking the backs of a new deck of cards. The package the cards came in had been opened so that the seal was left unbroken.

"Hi," she said to Rafferty. "How'd you do?" She was the girl who had been behind the cigar counter downstairs.

"Fifteen net," Rafferty said, "and I told you not to be seen up here. And lay off the cards for now. Wait till we get to Reno."

THE HUNGER

BY CHARLES BEAUMONT

Charles Beaumont died early in 1967, at the age of 38. He was among PLAYBOY's *most popular contributors for over a decade. "The Hunger" became the title story of Charles Beaumont's first collection. Its immediate success generated other collections: "Yonder," "Night Ride and Other Journeys" and "Remember? Remember?" (his* PLAYBOY *nostalgic essays); as well as a novel about racial integration, "The Intruder," which he adapted for the screen and in which he played a featured role when it was filmed on location in the incendiary Deep South. "The Hunger" explores, with poetry and understanding, the dark psychology of rape—that of the victim as well as the rapist, or perhaps we should say: of both victims.*

NOW, WITH THE SUN almost gone, the sky looked wounded—as if a gigantic razor had been drawn across it, slicing deep. It bled richly. And the wind, which came down from High Mountain, cool as rain, sounded a little like children crying: a soft, unhappy kind of sound, rising and falling.

Afraid, somehow, it seemed to Julia. Terribly afraid.

She quickened her step. I'm an idiot, she thought, looking away from the sky. A complete idiot. That's why I'm frightened now; and if anything happens—which it won't, and can't —then I'll have no one to blame but myself.

She shifted the bag of groceries to her other arm and turned, slightly. There was no one in sight, except old Mr. Hannaford, pulling in his newspaper stands, preparing to close up the drugstore, and Jake Spiker, barely moving across to the Blue Haven for a glass of beer: no one else. The rippling redbrick streets were silent.

But even if she got nearly all the way home, she could scream and someone would hear her. Who would be fool enough to try anything right out in the open? Not even a lunatic. Besides, it wasn't dark yet, not technically, anyway.

Still, as she passed the vacant lots, all shoulder-high in wild grass, Julia could not help thinking, He might be hiding there, right now. It was possible. Hiding there, all crouched up, waiting. And he'd only have to grab her, and—she wouldn't scream. She knew that suddenly, and the thought terrified her. Sometimes you *can't* scream . . .

If only she'd not bothered to get that spool of yellow thread over at Younger's, it would be bright daylight now, bright clear daylight. And——

Nonsense! This was the middle of the town. She was surrounded by houses full of people. People all around. Everywhere.

(*He was a hunger; a need; a force. Dark emptiness filled him. He moved, when he moved, like a leaf caught in some dark and secret river, rushing. But mostly he slept now, like an animal, always ready to wake and leap and be gone . . .)*

The shadows came to life, dancing where Julia walked. Now the sky was ugly and festered, and the wind had become stronger, colder. She clicked along the sidewalk, looking straight ahead, wondering, why, why am I so infernally stupid? What's the matter with me?

Then she was home, and it was all over. The trip had not taken more than an hour. And here was Maud, running. Julia felt her sister's arm fly around her, hugging. "My God."

And Louise's voice: "We were just about to call Mick to go after you."

Julia pulled free and went into the kitchen and put down the bag of groceries.

"Where in the world have you been?" Maud demanded.

"I had to get something at Younger's." Julia took off her coat. "They had to go look for it, and—I didn't keep track of the time."

Maud shook her head. "Well, I don't know," she said, wearily. "You're just lucky you're alive, that's all."

"How——"

"You listen! He's out there somewhere. Don't you understand that? It's a fact. They haven't even come close to catching him yet."

"They will," Julia said, not knowing why: she wasn't entirely convinced of it.

"Of course they will. Meantime, how many more is he going to murder? Can you answer me that?"

"I'm going to put my coat away." Julia brushed past her sister. Then she turned and said, "I'm sorry you were worried. It won't happen again." She went to the closet, feeling strangely upset. They would talk about it tonight. All night. Analyzing, hinting, questioning. They would talk of nothing else, as from the very first. And they would not be able to conceal their delight.

"Wasn't it awful about poor Eva Schillings!"

No, Julia had thought: from her sisters' point of view it was not awful at all. It was wonderful. It was priceless.

It was news.

Julia's sisters . . . Sometimes she thought of them as mice. Giant gray mice, in high white collars: groaning a little, panting a little, working about the house. Endlessly, untiringly: they would squint at pictures, knock them crooked, then straighten them again; they swept invisible dust from clean carpets and took the invisible dust outside in shining pans and dumped it carefully into spotless apple-baskets; they stood by beds whose sheets shone gleaming white and tight, and clucked in soft disgust, and replaced the sheets with others. All day, every day, from six in the morning until most definite dusk. Never questioning, never doubting the work had to be done.

They ran like arteries through the old house, keeping it alive. For it had become now a part of them, and they part of it—like the handcrank mahogany Victrola in the hall, or the lion-pelted sofa, or the Boutelle piano (ten years silent, its keys yellowed, decayed and ferocious, like teeth of an aged mule).

Nights, they spoke of sin. Also of other times and better days: Maud and Louise—sitting there in the bellying heat of the obsolete but steadfast stove, hooking rugs, crocheting doilies, sewing linen, chatting, chatting.

Occasionally Julia listened, because she was there and there was nothing else to do; but mostly she didn't. It had become a simple thing to rock and nod and think of nothing at all, while *they* traded dreams of dead husbands, constantly relishing their mutual widowhood—relishing it!—pitching these fragile ghosts into moral combat. "Ernie, God rest him, was an honorable man." (So were they all, Julia would think, all honorable men; but we are here to praise Caesar, not to bury him . . .) "Jack would be alive today if it hadn't been for that trunk-lid slamming down on his head: that's what started it all." Poor Ernie! Poor Jack!

(He walked along the railroad tracks, blending with the night. He could have been young, or old: an age-hiding beard dirtied his face and throat. He wore a blue sweater, ripped in a dozen places. On the front of the sweater was sewn a large felt letter E. Also sewn there was a small design showing a football and callipers. His gray trousers were dark with stain where he had fouled them. He walked along the tracks, seeing and not seeing the pulse of light far ahead; thinking and not thinking. Perhaps I'll find it there; Perhaps they won't catch me; Perhaps I won't be hungry any more . . .)

"You forgot the margarine," Louise said, holding the large sack upside down.

"Did I? I'm sorry." Julia took her place at the table. The food immediately began to make her ill: the sight of it, the smell of it. Great bowls of beans, crisp-skinned chunks of turkey, mashed potatoes. She put some on her plate, and watched her sisters. They ate earnestly; and now, for no reason, this, too, was upsetting.

She looked away. What was it? What was wrong?

"Mick says that fellow didn't die," Maud announced. "Julia——"

"What fellow?"

"At the asylum, that got choked. He's all right."

"That's good."

Louise broke a square of toast. She addressed Maud: "What else did he say, when you talked to him? Are they making any progress?"

"Some. I understand there's a bunch of police coming down from Seattle—you can imagine how much Mick likes *that!*"

"Well, it's his own fault. If he was any kind of a sheriff, he'd of caught that fellow a long time before this. I mean, after all, Burlington just isn't that big." Louise dismembered a turkey leg, ripped little shreds of the meat off, put them into her mouth.

Maud shook her head. "I don't know. Mick claims it isn't

like catching an ordinary criminal. With this one, you never can guess what he's going to do, or where he'll be. Nobody has figured out how he stays alive, for instance."

"Probably," Louise said, "he eats bugs and things."

Julia folded her napkin and pressed it onto the table.

Maud said, "No. Most likely he finds stray dogs and cats."

They finished the meal in silence. Not, Julia knew, because there was any lull in thought: merely so the rest could be savored in the livingroom, next to the fire. A proper place for everything.

They moved out of the kitchen. Louise insisted on doing the dishes, while Maud settled at the radio and tried to find a local news broadcast. Finally she snapped the radio off, angrily. "You'd think they'd at least keep us informed! Isn't that the least they could do?"

Louise materialized in her favorite chair. The kitchen was dark. The stove warmed noisily, its thin metal sides undulating.

And it was time.

"Where do you suppose he is right now?" Maud said.

Louise shrugged. "Out there somewhere. If they'd got him, Mick would of called us. He's out there somewhere."

"Yes. Laughing at all of us, too, I'll wager. Trying to figure out who'll be next."

Julia sat in the rocker and tried not to listen. Outside, there was the wind. A cold wind, biting; the kind that slips right through window-putty, that you can feel on the glass. Was there ever such a cold wind? she wondered.

Then Louise's words started to echo. "He's out there somewhere . . ."

Julia looked away from the window, and attempted to take an interest in the lacework in her lap.

Louise was talking. Her fingers flashed along silver needles. ". . . spoke to Mrs. Schillings today."

"I don't want to hear about it." Maud's eyes flashed like the needles.

"God love her heart, she's about crazy. Could barely talk."

"God, God."

"I tried to comfort her, of course, but it didn't do any good."

Julia was glad she had been spared that conversation. It sent a shudder across her even to think about it. Mrs. Schillings was Eva's mother, and Eva—only 17 . . . The thoughts she vowed not to think, came back. She remembered Mick's description of the body, and his words: " . . . she'd got through with work over at the telephone office around about nine. Carl Jasperson offered to see her home, but he says she said not to bother, it was only a few blocks. Our boy must have been hiding around the other side of the cannery. Just as Eva passed, he jumped. Raped her and then strangled her. I figure he's a pretty man-sized bugger. Thumbs like to went clean through the throat . . ."

In two weeks, three women had died. First, Charlotte Adams, the librarian. She had been taking her usual shortcut across the school playground, about 9:15 P.M. They found her by the slide, her clothes ripped from her body, her throat raw and bruised.

Julia tried very hard not to think of it, but when her mind would clear, there were her sisters' voices, droning, pulling her back, deeper.

She remembered how the town had reacted. It was the first murder Burlington had had in 15 years. It was the very first mystery. Who was the sex-crazed killer? Who could have done this terrible thing to Charlotte Adams? One of her gentlemen friends, perhaps. Or a hobo, from one of the near-by jungles. Or . . .

Mick Daniels and his tiny force of deputies had swung into action immediately. Everyone in town took up the topic, chewed it, talked it, chewed it, until it lost its shape completely. The air became electrically charged. And a grim gaiety swept Burlington, reminding Julia of a circus where everyone is forbidden to smile.

Days passed, uneventfully. Vagrants were pulled in and released. People were questioned. A few were booked, temporarily.

Then, when the hum of it had begun to die, it happened again. Mrs. Dovie Samuelson, member of the local P.T.A., mother of two, moderately attractive and moderately young, was found in her garden, sprawled across a rhododendron bush, quite dead. She was naked, and it was established that she had been attacked. Of the killer, once again, there was no trace.

Then the State Hospital for the Criminally Insane released the information that one of its inmates—a Robert Oakes—had escaped. Mick, and many others, had known this all along. Oakes had originally been placed in the asylum on a charge of raping and murdering his cousin, a girl named Patsy Blair.

Now he was loose. After he had broken into his former home and stolen some old school clothes, he had disappeared, totally.

Burlington, population 3,000, went into a state of ecstasy: delicious fear gripped the town. The men foraged out at night with torches and weapons; the women squeaked and looked under their beds and . . . chatted.

But still no progress was made. The maniac eluded hundreds of searchers. They knew he was near, perhaps at times only a few feet away, hidden; but always they returned home, defeated.

They looked in the forests and in the fields and along the river banks. They covered High Mountain—a miniature hill at the south end of town—like ants, poking at every clump of brush, investigating every abandoned tunnel and water tank. They broke into deserted houses, searched barns, silos, haystacks, tree tops. They looked everywhere, everywhere. And found nothing.

When they decided for sure that their killer had gone far away, that he couldn't conceivably be within 50 miles of Burlington, a third crime was committed. Young Eva Schillings' body had been found, less than a hundred yards from her home.

And that was three days ago . . .

". . . they get him," Louise was saying, "they ought to kill him by little pieces, for what he's done."

Maud nodded. "Yes; but they won't."

"Of course they——"

"No! You wait. They'll shake his hand and lead him back to the bughouse and wait on him hand and foot—till he gets a notion to bust out again."

"Well, I'm of a mind the people will have something to say about that."

"Anyway," Maud continued, never lifting her eyes from her knitting, "what makes you so sure they *will* catch him? Supposing he just drops out of sight for six months, and——"

"You stop that! They'll get him. Even if he is a maniac, he's still human."

"I really doubt that. I doubt that a human would have done these awful things." Maud sniffed. Suddenly, like small rivers, tears began to course down her snowbound cheeks, cutting and melting the hard white-packed powder, revealing flesh beneath even paler. Her hair was shot with gray, and her dress was the color of rocks and moths; yet, she did not succeed in looking either old or frail. There was nothing whatever frail about Maud.

"He's a man," she said. Her lips seemed to curl at the word. Louise nodded, and they were quiet.

(*His ragged tennis shoes padded softly on the gravel bed. Now his heart was trying to tear loose from his chest. The men, the men . . . They had almost stepped on him, they were that close. But he had been silent. They had gone past him, and away. He could see their flares back in the distance. And far ahead, the pulsing light. Also a square building: the depot, yes. He must be careful. He must walk in the shadows. He must be very quiet.*

The fury burned him, and he fought it.

Soon.

It would be all right, soon . . .)

". . . think about it, this here maniac is only doing what every man would *like* to do but can't."

"Maud!"

"I mean it. It's a man's natural instinct—it's all they ever think about." Maud smiled. She looked up. "Julia, you're feeling sick. Don't tell me you're not."

"I'm all right," Julia said tightening her grip on the chair arms slightly. She thought, they've been married! They talk this way about men, as they always have, and yet soft words have been spoken to them, and strong arms placed around their shoulders . . .

Maud made tiny circles with her fingers. "Well, I can't force you to take care of yourself. Except, when you land in the hospital again, I suppose you know who'll be doing the worrying and staying up nights—as per usual."

"I'll . . . go on to bed in a minute." But, why was she hesitating? Didn't she want to be alone?

Why didn't she want to be alone?

Louise was testing the door. She rattled the knob vigorously, and returned to her chair.

"What would he want anyway," Maud said, "with two old biddies like us?"

"We're not so old," Louise said, saying, actually: "That's true; we're old."

But it wasn't true, not at all. Looking at them, studying them, it suddenly occurred to Julia that her sisters were ashamed of their essential attractiveness. Beneath the 'twenties hair-dos, the ill-used cosmetics, the ancient dresses (which did not quite succeed in concealing their still voluptuous physiques),

Maud and Louise were youthfully full and pretty. They were. Not even the birch-twig toothbrushes and traditional snuff could hide it.

Yet, Julia thought, they envy me.

They envy my plainness.

"What kind of a man would do such heinous things?" Louise said, mispronouncing the word, carefully, heenious.

And Julia, without calling or forming the thought, discovered an answer grown in her mind: an impression, a feeling.

What kind of a man?

A lonely man.

It came upon her like a chill. She rose from the pillowed chair, lightly. "I think," she said, "I'll go on to my room."

"Are your windows good and locked?"

"Yes."

"You'd better make sure. All he'd have to do is climb up the drainpipe." Maud's expression was peculiar. Was she really saying, "This is only to comfort you, dear. Of the three of us it's unlikely he'd pick on you . . ."

"I'll make sure." Julia walked to the hallway. "Goodnight."

"Try to get some sleep," Louise smiled. "And don't think about him, hear? We're perfectly safe. He couldn't possibly get in, even if he tried. Besides," she added, "I'll be awake."

(*He stopped and leaned against a pole and looked up at the deaf and swollen sky. It was a moment of dark shapes, a hurrying, a running.*

He closed his eyes.

> *"The moon is the shepherd,*
> *The clouds are his sheep . . ."*

He tried to hold the words, tried very hard, but they scattered and were gone.

"No. No."

He pushed away from the pole, turned and walked back to the gravel bed.

The hunger grew: with every step it grew. He thought that it had died, that he had killed it at last and now he could rest, but it had not died. It sat inside him, inside his mind, gnawing, calling, howling to be released. Stronger than before. Stronger than ever before.

"The moon is the shepherd . . ."

A cold wind raced across the surrounding fields of wild grass, turning the land into a heaving dark green ocean. It sighed up through the branches of cherry trees and rattled the thick leaves. Sometimes a cherry would break loose, tumble in the gale, fall and split, filling the night with its fragrance. The air was iron and loam and growth.

He walked and tried to pull these things into his lungs, the silence and coolness of them.

But someone was screaming, deep inside him. Someone was talking.

"What are you going to do——"

He balled his fingers into fists.

"Get away from me! Get away!"

"Don't——"

The scream faded.

The girl's face remained. Her lips and her smooth white skin and her eyes, her eyes . . .

He shook the vision away.

The hunger continued to grow. It wrapped his body in sheets of living fire. It got inside his mind and bubbled in hot acids, filling and filling him.

He stumbled, fell, plunged his hands deep into the gravel, withdrew fists full of the grit and sharp stones and squeezed them until blood trailed down his wrists.

He groaned, softly.

Ahead, the light glowed and pulsed and whispered, Here, Here, Here, Here, Here.

He dropped the stones and opened his mouth to the wind and walked on.)

Julia closed the door and slipped the lock noiselessly. She could no longer hear the drone of voices: it was quiet, still, but for the sighing breeze.

What kind of a man . . .

She did not move, waiting for her heart to stop throbbing. But it would not stop.

She went to the bed and sat down. Her eyes traveled to the window, held there.

"He's out there somewhere . . ."

Julia felt her hands move along her dress. It was an old dress, once purple, now gray with faded gray flowers. The cloth was tissue-thin. Her fingers touched it and moved upward to the throat. They undid the top button.

For some reason her body trembled. The chill had turned to heat, tiny needles of heat, puncturing her all over.

She threw the dress over a chair and removed her underclothing. Then she walked to the bureau and took from the top drawer a flannel nightdress, and turned.

What she saw in the tall mirror caused her to stop and make a small sound.

Julia Landon stared back at her from the polished glass.

Julia Landon, 38, neither young nor old, attractive nor unattractive, a woman so plain she was almost invisible. All angles and sharpness, and flesh that would once have been called "milky" but was now only white, dead white. A little too tall. A little too thin. And faded.

Only the eyes had softness. Only the eyes burned with life and youth and—

Julia moved away from the mirror. She snapped off the light. She touched the window shade, pulled it slightly, guided it soundlessly upward.

Then she unfastened the window latch.

Night came into the room and filled it. Outside, great clouds roved across the moon, obscuring it, revealing it, obscuring it again.

It was cold. Soon there would be rain.

Julia looked out beyond the yard, in the direction of the depot, dark and silent now, and the tracks and the jungles beyond the tracks where lost people lived.

"I wonder if he can see me."

She thought of the man who had brought terror and excitement to the town. She thought of him openly, for the first time, trying to imagine his features.

He was probably miles away.

Or, perhaps he was nearby. Behind the tree, there, or under the hedge . . .

"I'm afraid of you, Robert Oakes," she whispered to the night. "You're insane, and a killer. You would frighten the wits out of me."

The fresh smell swept into Julia's mind. She wished she were surrounded by it, in it, just for a little while.

A walk. A short walk in the evening. She felt the urge strengthening.

"You're dirty, young man. And heartless—ask Mick, if you don't believe me. You want love so badly you must kill for it—but nevertheless, you're heartless. Understand? And you're not terribly bright, either, they say. Have you read Shakespeare's sonnets? Herrick? How about Shelley, then? There, you see! I'd detest you on sight. Just look at your fingernails!"

She said these things silently, but as she said them she moved toward her clothes.

She paused, went to the closet.

The green dress. It was warmer.

A warm dress and a short walk—that will clear my head. Then I'll come back and sleep.

It's perfectly safe.

She started for the door, stopped, returned to the window. Maud and Louise would still be up, talking.

She slid one leg over the sill; then the other leg.

Softly she dropped to the frosted lawn.

The gate did not creak.

She walked into the darkness.

Better. So much better! Good clean air that you can breathe!

The town was a silence. A few lights gleamed in distant houses, up ahead; behind, there was only blackness. And the wind.

In the heavy green frock, which was still too light to keep out the cold—though she felt no cold: only the needled heat— she walked away from the house and toward the depot.

It was a small structure, unchanged by passing years, like the Landon home and most of the homes in Burlington. There were tracks on either side of it.

Now it was deserted. Perhaps Mr. Gaffey was inside, making insect sounds on the wireless. Perhaps he was not.

Julia stepped over the first track, and stood, wondering what had happened and why she was here. Vaguely she understood something. Something about the yellow thread that had made her late and forced her to return home through the gathering dusk. And this dress—had she chosen it because it was warmer than the gray one . . . or because it was prettier?

Beyond this point there was wilderness. Marshes and fields, overgrown with weeds and thick foliage. The hobo jungles: some tents, dead campfires, empty tins of canned-heat.

She stepped over the second rail, and began to follow the gravel bed. Heat consumed her. She could not keep her hands still.

In a dim sort of way, she realized—with a tiny part of her— why she had come out tonight.

She was looking for someone.

The words formed in her mind, unwilled: "Robert Oakes,

listen, listen to me. You're not the only one who is lonely. But you can't steal what we're lonely for, you can't take it by force. Don't you know that? Haven't you learned that yet?"

I'll talk to him, she thought, and he'll go along with me and give himself up . . .

No.

That isn't why you're out tonight. You don't care whether he gives himself up or not. You only want him to know that you understand—isn't that it?

You couldn't have any other reason.

It isn't possible that you're seeking out a lunatic for any other reason.

Certainly you don't want him to touch you.

Assuredly you don't want him to put his arms around you and kiss you, because no man has ever done that—assuredly, assuredly.

It isn't you he wants. It isn't love. He wouldn't be taking Julia Landon . . .

"But what if he doesn't!" The words spilled out in a small choked cry. "What if he sees me and runs away! Or I don't find him. Others have been looking. What makes me think I'll——"

Now the air swelled with the sounds of life: frogs and birds and locusts, moving; and the wind, running across the trees and reeds and foliage at immense speed, whining, sighing.

Everywhere there was this loudness, and a dark like none Julia had ever known. The moon was gone entirely. Shadowless, the surrounding fields were great pools of liquid black, stretching infinitely, without horizon.

Fear came up in her chest, clutching.

She tried to scream.

She stood paralyzed, moveless, a pale terror drying into her throat and into her heart.

Then, from far away, indistinctly, there came a sound. A sound like footsteps on gravel.

Julia listened, and tried to pierce the darkness. The sounds grew louder. And louder. Someone was on the tracks. Coming closer.

She waited. Years passed, slowly. Her breath turned into a ball of expanding ice in her lungs.

Now she could see, just a bit.

It was a man. A black man-form. Perhaps—the thought increased her fear—a hobo. It mustn't be one of the hobos.

No. It was a younger man. Mick! Mick, come to tell her, "Well, we got him!" and to ask narrowly, "What the devil you doing out here, Julie?" Was it Mick?

She saw the sweater. The ball of ice in her lungs began to melt. A sweater. And shoes that seemed almost white.

Not a hobo. Not Mick. Not anyone she knew.

She waited an instant longer. Then, at once, she knew without question who the young man was.

And she knew that he had seen her.

The fear went away. She moved to the center of the tracks.

"I've been looking for you," she said, soundlessly. "Every night I've thought of you. I have." She walked toward him. "Don't be afraid, Mr. Oakes. Please don't be afraid. I'm not."

The young man stopped. He seemed to freeze, like an animal prepared for flight.

He did not move, for several seconds.

Then he began to walk toward Julia, lightly, hesitantly, rubbing his hands along his trousers.

When Julia was close enough to see his eyes, she relaxed, and smiled.

Perhaps, she thought, feeling the first drop of rain upon her face, perhaps if I don't scream he'll let me live.

That would be nice.

THE
SUPERMEN

BY WILLIAM M. CLARK

"Maine Is in My Heart" is not only the title of one of Mr. Clark's books, it is also an accurate expression of his love for his home state. A "regional" writer in the same good sense that Faulkner and Marquand were regional writers, most of his fiction is set in Maine and has been collected in the volumes "Tales of Cedar River" and "More Tales of Cedar River." In "The Supermen," Clark sketches an invasion of his quiet hinterlands by callous young savages of the big city—and the daring resistance of a single man.

GEORGE SUMMERS was late in closing up. The Friday-night footfalls of the trading farmers had died away while he wiped the counter in his small lunchroom. It was a soft night with a small mist and his motion was not hurried as he started for the door to snap the latch before his final act of cashing up.

There was a light shudder of brakes and the slam of a car door. He checked his movement toward the front, in anticipation of possible further business.

When the three young men strode in, he regretted his lateness and his waiting. They were of a type for whom he desired to do no favors, a breed that he feared because they were not of his age and he had given up trying to understand whatever he had read about them.

It was only through reading that he knew them for what they were. Center Brayton had never nurtured any such people. Center Brayton was too old in its fear of God and its stable employment. It had never felt the impact of the bursting of the disciplinary dam.

The three young men had an air of matured evil. They looked past the point of return. There was no boyishness in their manner, no joy in their walk. They were not excited about the misty lateness in which they were abroad. They were not excited about anything.

Two of them walked in step toward the far corner by the register. One, tall and pimpled, flung a coarse-voiced summons at George.

"Cigarettes," he said.

George had a momentary ray of hope and then he saw the third youngster reach over and snap the catch on the night latch and take up an indolent position where he could watch the street. After that, there was no more hope, and his spine tingled a little as he faced the two.

He stood and waited for them to declare themselves. That was all he could do. The telephone was too slow to be of use.

The blows would be quicker. He never doubted the coming of the blows. He felt very tired.

The old wall clock ticked solidly and the boy at the door shuffled his feet, grating the introdden sand.

George wondered what paralysis had gripped humanity that humanity had not been able to wipe out this creeping menace before it became a threat to the hinterlands around the city cradle from which it had sprung.

George knew how vulnerable the hinterlands were. Center Brayton had never known hoodlums or crime even in the days of Dutch Schultz. It had been too small for even minor gangsters.

It was not too small for this new breed, these cold-faced, old-young spawn of neglected schools of vice. Nothing was too small for them because the rewards of vice were not the reason for their acts. They sought only pain and savagery and once they had discovered the weakness of the small towns, they would be back, again and again, menacing the streets even in their absence.

They were beginning to discover the small towns. An old man with an empty cash register and a ravished store had been found dead at Turner Corners just last week. The scouts were out from the cities and it was going to take a strong shock to hold the evil to its old locale.

George noted the earmarks of the age, the long haircuts and the pseudo-Mexican sideburns, the black jacket on the one and the combat coat on the other. They showed no weapons even when they made their move. Their stance and their sneers seemed weapon enough. Their presence alone was a promise of violence.

"All right, man, this is it," suddenly said the tall invader. "You stand back against the wall and stay nice and still. You got things we want."

George backed up. He backed up tight against the shelves that lined the wall, the shelves packed with the familiar merchandise that had been his life since he had come home to find peace after the guns had gone quiet in Europe in 1945. He had gone a long way and seen much death to keep America from such as this. The thrust from abroad had been stopped but the creed had seeped silently in.

He backed up tight to the shelves and he said nothing, but his soul cried out because he did not like what was coming. He resented the need and he felt that, somewhere, there was much to be blamed.

"Hit the register, Joe," said the tall one.

The companion eased past George with a heedless push that seemed to have measured the actions to be expected from the merchant and to have found them wanting in hazard or even in bother. He punched the "No Sale" key and the drawer opened wide. He scooped bills and change into his hand and so to his pockets.

"Sixty bucks, maybe," he stated.

The tall one spat on the floor. "Big Deal," he said.

Joe brushed past George again, carelessly, as he had done before. He almost seemed to be inviting challenge and George wondered if, somewhere in the twists of his mind, he needed some kind of justification for his already planned acts, some childish symbol like the knocking of a chip from a shoulder. George would have liked to have explored the thought but there was no longer time. Things seemed to be moving faster. The clock ticked again.

Joe had reached the end of the counter when the tall leader spoke once more.

"Wait a minute, Joe," he said. He turned his voice to George. "Where's the rest of it?"

"That's all there is," said George.

"Nuts."

He turned to the watcher at the door. "How's the street?" he asked.

"Quiet," said the watcher. "The whole town's asleep.

Christ, what a burg."

"Tear the telephone, Joe," said the tall one.

Wires were snapped from the wall. The instrument was hurled across the room. The leader took a piece of lead pipe from his pocket.

"Hit him a couple, Joe," he said, unemotionally. "He's got more dough than that."

Joe put his hand into his pocket and brought out a similar, unimaginative weapon. He slapped it into his other palm. He licked his lips and took a step along the counter toward where George stood, still backed against the shelves, one hand in front of him, the other resting in back, for support.

George sighed. There was just so much in living that was so hard to explain. There were so many sides to this thing that he wished he had time to consider them all, to weigh them, to moderate his needs, to offer mercy or opportunity or a guide to other paths. There wasn't time. These things had been tried by wiser men than he. These boys had probably been lectured to and prayed over and paroled and pleaded with.

He only wished that he was sure that they were the same probers who had done the brutal job at Turner Corners.

Joe took another step.

"Why don't you just take what you have and leave?" asked George, his voice rising despite his weariness and his reluctant acceptance of their denial.

Again the clock was loud.

"Hurry up, Joe," said the tall one. "Do you need some help with the man?" He laughed and, in the stillness, the laugh rang clear and brutal and cold.

That was when George, hating the need and the waste and the recrimination that he would launch tomorrow on the lacks that had forced this ugly end, brought up the hand that had rested behind him. It was typical of the stupid arrogance of the three hoodlums that they had not noticed this hand. It showed a lack in their education, a flaw in their quick course in crime, because in that hand was their undoing. The hand held a blue-steel Luger, and their overlooking it was an error that it was now too late to remedy, and yet a natural error because they had never before encountered any semblance of resistance in their pitiful victims.

It was a fitting weapon to confront them because it was a relic of the days when hoodlumism in the black uniforms of the crooked cross had threatened the peace of the entire world. George had picked it up from the dead hand of a disillusioned superman.

For a moment, as Joe paused in mid-stride, as the tall one raised his arm for a savage throw, George thought idly of mere threats or words, but the hopelessness of any appeal save force was so clear to his inner being that he was discarding the thought even as he thumbed off the safety and ducked the flying pipe and squeezed the trigger. The Luger bucked once and he swung it to the other near target and squeezed again. There was a gurgled something from Joe as he clutched at his belly and went down, but there was no sound from the tall one as he, in turn, collapsed.

The watcher at the door was yelling in full volume as he loosed the latch, but the gun spoke once more and he grabbed his shoulder and raised the other arm aloft in surrender.

"Was it you boys at Turner Corners?" asked George, probing for the last remnant of defense, reaching for the denial that would serve to turn him from his task.

The boy nodded. He nodded twice and then his face contorted and he opened his mouth to scream, and George set his lips and shot again and the scream was cut off and the boy spun around and fell, face down, arms spread out like a fallen scarecrow, the fiery dragon on his coat stretched taut and strangely still.

Then the store was quiet except for the tick of the clock and the long drawn sigh for the terrible need.

SPEAK TO ME OF IMMORTALITY

BY KEN W. PURDY

Much of Mr. Purdy's fiction is an affirmation of the Actonian axiom, "Power tends to corrupt and absolute power corrupts absolutely." But pomposity and righteous tongue-clucking are not among his arsenal of weapons. He merely lifts the curtain, shows us the corruption at work, stands there silently with us as we watch the bloated giants eaten by their own viciousness and vice. In "Speak to Me of Immortality," we watch a deposed dictator's cleverness bring about his ultimate destruction.

JORGE O'BRIAN GOMEZ spoke softly into the telephone. It was a spidery handset, but for all its grace it was heavy. It was gold.

"Sí, sí," Gomez said. "Claro. No, nada. Finito."

He let the instrument slip through his fingers into its cradle. He walked to the door. He looked like a big clockwork toy, staring ahead, his heels driving into the soft carpet. Under the carved archway he turned and looked back at the room that had been the center of his world. It had cost a quarter of a million dollars to furnish this office to the taste of Jorge O'Brian Gomez. It was a shame to leave it to the barbarians from the south country, mountain men most of them, horsemen from the vast savannas, miners, scum of every kind, but it was not as if he were giving it up forever. He had gone away before, and come back, and he would again.

The infantryman on post at the map room snapped an arm across his chest in salute. Gomez wondered where the fellow would be in 24 hours. He was quite sure he knew where the head would be: it would decorate one of the wrought-iron posts of the fence around the Palacio. The body? Hard to say.

The map room was soundproofed, and so when the door was opened the racket came as a blow in the face: bedlam, hysteria, madness. Gomez let it slam and the shouting tailed off in a single gurgling choked-down oath. A teletype machine rattled in the sudden silence.

"Tomas," the little man said, "what is the situation?"

A colonel answered him. "It is distressing, sir," he said. "An armored column, twenty-five vehicles, has appeared just north of Casefiento. We did not even know of its existence. Here, below Mireflore, there is heavy infiltration, the first units of Jiminez' outfit; the garrison at Columbo has defected, and the rebels reached the shore, here at Nagua, over an hour ago. Further . . ."

Gomez waved him into silence. "You will see all this change

soon," he said. "I have ordered an armored attack across the entire peninsula. Keep up your spirits. There is nothing to fear. Nothing whatever! Tomas, come with me."

Their heels banged on the marble floor; they walked quickly.

"All that information is an hour old," Gomez said. He had a hard, rasping voice. "Hopeless! They are within ten miles of the city this minute, and coming like the wind. What is worse, an underground squad hit the blue airfield fifteen minutes ago. We are nailed."

"Ah!" Tomas said. "The blue one? That happened?"

"It happened," Gomez said. "We waited twenty-four hours too long. Within ninety minutes they got the yacht, the white airfield and then the blue one. We are nailed down."

"You will go to Hadrian?" the colonel asked.

"No," Gomez said. "Two people know about Hadrian's, and that is two too many. I have a different idea." He stopped before a small door, brass and mahogany. He offered his hand to Tomas. "Best luck!" he said. He smiled and nodded and opened the door. Best luck, indeed. The man was six feet four. In a crowd he stood out like a lighthouse in a dark night. He'd be ripped into dog meat before he had made two city blocks from the Palacio. Pity.

Gomez drove his thumb into a button and cedar doors at one end of the room slid open to reveal an enormous closet. There were fifty-odd uniforms at one end, more than a hundred suits at the other. Gomez thrust himself into the clothes like a weasel down a burrow. He backed out with a package in his hand. It was dusty. He shook it open: a cheap straw hat, thong shoes, pants, white cotton shirt.

Ten minutes later, his face and hands blackened, he was on the street. Within the hour, and having walked every foot of the way, he was breathing the winy air of Haraguato. The houses were nearly all dark, squared off under the ancient, crouching trees; from the shore, a mile away, the sea wind brought the rolling boom of the surf, sifting it through the ine woods. In the city behind him he could hear bursts of mall-arms fire, snapping in strings like baby firecrackers.

When he came to Delgado's house he passed it, went around he block and entered from the rear. One room was lighted. He found a door and knocked. Silence. An overhead light came on. In a narrow window, a curtain moved. Gomez took off his hat, ran a handkerchief hard across his forehead. It came away black with greasepaint. He turned in profile to the window. Then he clapped his hat on his head and gestured rudely toward the door. Within a count of 20 it had swung softly open and he was inside.

They stood in the dark, he and Tonio Delgado.

"I hardly knew you, Jorge."

"They knocked off my emergency airfields, both of them," Gomez said. "I find myself, as it were, nailed."

"No boats?"

"Would I be here?"

"Give me your hand."

They moved through the house on the cool tiles. A door closed behind them and a light snapped on.

"There is no window in this room," Delgado said. The walls were white plaster, and it was small. There were two rattan chairs, a leather couch, a rosewood cupboard.

"Brandy?" Delgado asked.

Gomez shook his head impatiently. "They'll have the city by dawn," he said. "Then the ropes will be cut. It would be idiotic to move, and I am no idiot. I made one mistake: I waited twenty-four hours too long. I will correct that mistake by waiting another month, or two months, or three. You understand me, Delgado?"

"Yes," Delgado said. "Certainly. But where? Wait where?"

Gomez smiled. "Here, my friend," he said. "Here with you."

Delgado poured brandy, and the neck of the carafe jangled on the glass' edge.

"It will be no problem for you," Gomez said. "It is well

known that we quarreled four years ago. It is well known that I have not seen you since. You have behaved yourself. You have been hedging your bets. You have friends in the mountains."

Delgado said nothing. He was looking into his second glass of brandy, his thin hand curled tightly around it. The belt of his white silk dressing gown had come untied, and one end of it dangled limply to the floor.

"I notice you do not say, 'But where with me?' " Gomez said. "That is good. I would think that unkind of you. Because you told me six, maybe seven years ago, and I have not forgotten. I rarely forget. You know that. I will stay in the nice little hide-out that opens off your wine cellar. You remember telling me?"

Delgado remembered. In that time, he and the general had been friends. It had been a fruitful collaboration. Delgado was still well off. Had the general not felt that his happiness required Carola to spend four days with him in Maraguey, they would still be friends; Delgado would be really a rich man, and he would now be running for his life and wondering if the mob would choose to burn his house or raze it flat. Seen in that obscure and twisted fashion, he owed Gomez something. Still he cursed himself. I need not have told him, he cried silently, I need not have told him! He had lived in the big house in Haraguato for five years and more before he had stumbled into the secret room. It had been beautifully and elaborately made: it lay behind a set of stone shelves in the wine cellar, dug out under the lawn. It measured ten feet by twelve by eight feet high. It held a toilet and a washbowl, a cot, chair, desk; an electric light hung from the low ceiling and a fan and a hand bellows ventilated it. With someone to feed him, a man could live for years behind the wine cellar.

"We are wasting time with this nonsense," Gomez said. "Let's go. Carola is in the house?"

Delgado nodded.

"You must tell her, naturally. And no one else. And this is what is important: There is to be no change in your pattern of living. You hear me? *No* change!"

"I'll get some blankets," Delgado said.

"Yes, and some bread, some meat," Gomez said. "We'll take wine from the cellar. Nothing else. Nothing you have to explain. Understand?"

"I understand," Delgado said.

The cell door was latched in three hidden places, one for each hand, one for a foot. The wall swung open.

Gomez stood in the doorway and peered in. "On the one hand," he said, "I am happy to see this hole. On the other, I am horrified." He turned to Delgado. "The fruit of a single error, my friend," he said, "is sometimes terrible to contemplate. You, I am sure, will make no error?"

"None," Delgado said.

"Good. Until tomorrow night, then. Is there any way to communicate with you before then?"

"No, Jorge," Delgado said. "None. That is one of the indications of intelligence in the man who planned this room. Undoubtedly he considered the circumstances that a searching party might be in the house, and just at the wrong time . . . For the same reason, there is no means of opening the door from within."

"Clever," Gomez said. "I bid you good-night, and many thanks."

"Good-night," Delgado said.

He found Carola awake. "What have you been doing?" she said grumpily.

He slipped a hand under her neck. "Get up," he said. He drew the covers down and lifted her. "Come," he said. "Up." She said no more, and he steered her into the bathroom. He opened the cold-water tap in the basin.

"Splash some on your face, my dear," he said. "Wake up." Sleepily, she did as he asked. A handsome woman, he thought, at any hour of the day or night. Her hair hung in two long plaits down her back. Her bare feet curling on the warm rough bathroom rug, her head came barely to his chest, and the fabric of her nightgown, almost light enough to float, gave her the look of a nude seen through a warm morning mist at the sea's edge. He pulled her to him and bent to her ear.

"Jorge O'B is in the cellar," he whispered. "In the hide-out. He came half an hour ago, dressed like a peon. Naturally, he was set to run, but the Serronistas moved faster than he expected. He is far too clever to try to run now, with a million people hoping for a chance to tear him limb from limb. He will wait. Here."

He moved away, to look at her. She stared at him, her eyes wide.

"How long do you think?" she said.

"No idea," Delgado said. "He will want to go as soon as he can, but remember, this is a shrewd, cold man. He will not go too soon. He wants to live to spend the money, be sure of that."

"Much?" Carola said.

Delgado laughed shortly. "Say fifty million in Switzerland, in number accounts. Say twenty-five in Spain, twenty-five in the States, and odds and ends scattered around in other places."

"*That* much?" she asked.

"More, maybe," he said. "He was wearing a money belt when he came in, I imagine it's full of thousand-dollar bills."

"Tonio, what can we do?"

"Nothing. Nothing. We must pretend to ourselves that he is not there, that there is nobody in the cellar. That's our only hope. They will not come here to look for him for a long time, if ever. If we keep our heads, we are safe enough, for now!" He spun the faucet shut and led his wife back to bed. They lay quietly in the cool darkness. He found himself straining to hear a sound from the cellar. Idiot! he told himself. The man could beat a drum and scream like a tiger down there, and not a sound would be heard. Carola turned to him.

"Tonio, I am very frightened," she said.

"So am I, pigeon," he said. "So am I."

"I keep thinking *he* will hear us," she said.

"He can hear nothing," Delgado said.

"Ah, I know, I know," she said.

. . .

The search for Jorge O'Brian Gomez had no precedent in the tumultuous history of the country. Since the rebels were certain that his presence in Havana or Miami or New York or Paris could not have escaped notice, and since they had seized his means of escape, they were convinced he had gone underground. To think that they might lay hands upon him excited them; his mere existence was a danger, and a reward of $25,000 gold had been posted. The search was unremitting and vigorous.

Serrano himself shouted to the crowds, "We will find The Monster no matter what the cost—in time, in money, in blood. We will find him! We will hang him in chains! He will rot!"

Gomistas who were known to have been close to the general fared poorly during that first month. A good many of them died under the urgent curiosity of the rebels, and many more recorded, at the tops of their voices—those of them who had voices left—their wish to do so, and promptly. Delgado told Gomez some of this, every night when he opened the door at twelve o'clock.

"They killed Pedro Marti yesterday," he said. "They had tortured him for thirty-seven hours straight. Grinde shot himself: they made him watch while his daughter was raped and then turned him loose to think it over. So far, we know of over fifty they have killed in the belief they knew where you were."

Gomez shrugged. "An omelet requires broken eggs. As for

you, relax. Have you noticed anything? Are you being followed, or anything like that?"

"No, I'm sure not," Delgado said. He watched Gomez trot up and down the cellar, exercising himself. He was white as a mushroom. He had lost ten or fifteen pounds. He was edgy but he was in command of himself. The obsessive attention to detail that had marked him all his life was fully evident. He thought of everything. There was the matter of the shower, for example. Every other night he bathed. The ritual was precise. Every door and window in the house was locked and curtained. Carola was posted at a window to watch. Then Gomez and Delgado, both undressed, went to the bathroom, Gomez to bathe, Delgado to stand guard at the door.

"Of course you must undress when I do," Gomez had said impatiently. "Where are your brains? Supposing a search party comes when I'm in the shower? Very well, I run for my hole. But how do you explain the wet shower if you are not undressed? Tell me that, idiot?"

In the fifth week he said it would be better if Delgado watched, and Carola stood guard.

"It would not do," Delgado said. "I have no night vision. I can't see around the corner at night. I never even drive a car after sunset."

Gomez grinned at him. "That's better," he said. "You can think fast when you have to, can't you?" He padded down stairs, chuckling to himself.

The next night he stated the matter more clearly.

"I am managing this very well," he said. "I am even reasonably content. But one thing is beginning to bother me: I want a woman. Since I was fifteen, I have not gone this long without a woman."

"I thought of the same thing," Delgado said. "I have an idea: we could have a small party. Among the guests would be . . ."

"Stop right there," Gomez said. "Any plan you have

hought of has a fatal flaw: it involves letting someone outside now where I am. So? Save your breath. I am not interested."

Delgado was silent.

"Tomorrow night let me have Carola for a couple of ours," Gomez said.

"Jorge," Delgado said. "You are in my house. We are isking our lives to keep you here. It is enough."

"No, my friend," Gomez said. "It is not enough. I want a voman, and of all the women in the world—think of that—of ll the women in the world only one is available to me: Carola. Therefore I will have Carola. Tomorrow."

"No."

"Tonio, listen to me. I will some day leave this house. Then, I can reward you or I can punish you as I please. You ave no alternative. You don't believe that? You can turn me n? How will you explain that I am as pale as a shark's belly, h? As for me, I will be forced to tell them you have held me risoner here hoping for a bigger reward. They will cut you nto very thin slices, my friend! And if not their people, mine. Those who know where I am."

"I should kill you," Delgado said. "Now."

"Of course you should," Gomez said. "But, alas, you annot." He smiled his little smile. "So, you will do the other hing." He walked into the hole. "Lock my door, like a nice nan," he said. "And tomorrow night, have Carola at the athroom door. I will take a chance on your night vision! I'm brave man. I will take that little chance."

"I will not do it," Delgado said.

"You will," Gomez said. "And, goddamn you, stop acting as f you were giving me your life. After all, what is another slice ff a cut loaf? I have had the girl before, you know. When I ook her to Maraguey you lived through it, didn't you? You an live through this, too. Now lock me up, and go away. You ct like a wet-nosed boy."

Delgado locked the door and went upstairs.

Carola was asleep. She woke quickly.

"I have been in the cellar," he said.

"What's wrong?" she said.

"Everything. What I've been expecting. He wants woman."

A little puff of breath whistled through her lips. "Ah, ah," she said. He lay staring at the ceiling, ice blue in th moonlight. The curtains rustled sadly, and the harsh cry of tolero bird floated in on the night wind.

"The thing to do," he said, "is run. Pull out. Run for th States."

"Run for the rest of our lives, you mean," Carola said. "I if we could run at all. How can we get out of the country Impossible now, you know that."

"I told him we could bring him a girl, somehow," Toni said. "And we could! It could be done. But he won't hear of it.

"It could only be someone we know and trust," Carola said "It could only be a good friend. We have no right to burde anybody with that, with knowing where he is. It's out of th question."

"So is the alternative," Tonio said. "My God, I can't eve think of it! That blood-soaked son of a bitch."

Carola sat up. "Look, Tonio," she said, "that, that tim before, the other time, if we had said no, he'd have killed yo Wouldn't he?"

Delgado nodded dumbly.

"This time," she went on, "he will kill you too. Only late Then, he would have done it the next day. Now, in six month in a year, who knows? And after you, me. No." She threw th covers back. "For me, I can stand it. I am only sorry for yo Please don't hate me, that's all. Just don't hate me."

"I cannot even kill myself," Tonio said. "I can't even d that."

"It is not a lifetime," she said. "In another month surely h will want to go." She leaned over and kissed him. She got ou of bed.

"Tomorrow night, he said," Tonio told her. "Not tonight! Tomorrow!"

She shook her head. "Dreading it is worse," she said. "I'll go down now. Go tell him. I'll be down in a minute."

When he had put a pot of coffee on the back of the stove and laid a place on the table, Delgado led his wife down the stairs. He swung the stone door open. Gomez stood there, smiling. "You are very kind people," he said. "And very sensible. Come in, my dear, come in." He held out his hand. "You may open the door at three, Delgado," he said. "Just at three."

. . .

"Ah, my friend," Gomez said when he saw Delgado the next night. "You have lived through it, as I thought you would! It was not so bad, eh? Anything is bearable, isn't that true?" He began his interminable jog across the cellar, and his voice rose and fell as he ran away and came back. "I am very grateful to you; never mind that I had to force you to do it, I am grateful anyway. What a dear girl, Carola! I had forgotten how lovely she was, to my shame. And another thing—she might have been bitter, she might have been cold and resisting, but she was not, she was not!" He trotted toward Delgado, his little brown eyes glistening in the half-light. "But I am being indelicate now. I must not offend you. You are my host, after all. Isn't that right?"

"Yes," Delgado said. "I am your host, all right. The complete host, that's me."

"Exactly." Gomez was puffing a little. "Exactly. And when I get out . . . and get my hands on some serious money . . . you, my friend, are a millionaire!"

"Big of you," Delgado said.

"Be as bitter as you like . . . I don't care about that . . . I'll give it to you anyway. I can spare it! As soon as I get out of here."

"And when will that be?"

"In another month, I think." He jerked himself to a halt in the middle of the room. "These pigs have killed a lot of people, but they have not killed the ones I need. The ones I need they have never thought of: like you. Hah! They make me laugh. They will never get near me. I'm an immortal. I will live forever. And I will be remembered when Serrano is not even a footnote."

"You still have to get away safely," Delgado said.

"Simple," Gomez said. "In a little while now you'll mail a letter for me, one letter. Two weeks after that I'll be in New York. With warm and happy memories, thanks to you and dear little Carola." He stretched himself. "Well, back into the cave," he said. "By the way, I didn't tell Carola. You tell her. Tomorrow night. I look forward to it. Believe me, I do."

Delgado stared at him and the blood pounded in his head. Gomez lifted one hand.

"Please," he said. "You aren't going to start another silly argument, are you? We have discussed this matter, remember? Tomorrow night, I said."

.   .   .

It is possible, I suppose, Delgado told himself, for a man to get used to anything. He sat on a three-legged stool in the wine cellar and drank brandy. Every 15 or 20 minutes he went upstairs to look around. At three he opened the door and took his wife upstairs. He ran a bath for her. He waited for her to come to bed, waited for her to go to sleep. After the first two or three times she was never awake for long, and usually by the time full dawn lay softly bright in the room he was asleep too. The alternate nights were somehow worse. He had felt at first that he should take her in his arms, somehow to show her that they were still one, that nothing could happen that would part them, but after the first week she would not accept him.

"I can't," she said. "I just can't. I cannot go from him to you and from you to him, I can't and I won't!" She rolled away from him, and huddled on the other side of the bed, her knees under her chin.

He reached out for her. "Carola," he said. "Let me go down

and shoot him. Anything is better than this. My God, the man is destroying us, he's tearing us to pieces."

"Be sensible," she said. "What would be the point of that? His friends would kill us both, in good time. Besides, don't you see, if you killed him now, the whole thing would be pointless? Everything I have done I would have done for nothing! The time to kill him was before, if at all. Now, it makes no sense." She pulled the covers to her chin. "I'm going to sleep," she said.

Two or three times a week, in the first month or so, there had been police raids in Haraguato, once only two houses away, but no one knocked on Tonio Delgado's door. He went to the city every day, to his office, and while there was little work for a lawyer during the reorganization of the courts, still no one molested him. In the evening Carola and Tonio would have dinner and watch the television, and wait until it was time for him to go to the cellar, or for both of them to go to the cellar. The pattern was so unvarying that he became absurdly sensitive to its rhythm. The only ungoverned factor lay with the servants, the housekeeper, the maid, the cook, and the gardeners, but Carola watched them carefully.

"Are you sure none of the servants was in the wine cellar today?" Delgado said one night.

She looked up slowly. "Yes, I'm sure," she said. "Why?"

"Look," he said. "Listen to me. This is very important. Tonight, when I went down, a wine bottle had been moved."

Carola laughed. "*One* wine bottle in all those hundreds?" she said. "How could you know? You're getting jumpy. You imagined it."

"Nothing of the sort!" he said. "It wasn't just one bottle out of hundreds, it was the one next to the right-hand latch, a dusty one. I've always been careful not to touch it, so that it would look as if it had never been moved. Tonight, it was a good inch away from where I'd left it. *Somebody* had touched it, I tell you!"

"But who?" Carola said. "The wine cellar is locked and I never let anyone unlock it, you know that."

"It's very strange," Tonio said. "Maybe I did imagine it, but I don't think so."

"I marvel we haven't both been seeing things under the bed," she said. "After all, darling, this is the ninth week he's been here, do you know that?"

"Yes," he said. "I know that. It's the ninth week, the fourth day, and, exactly, the twentieth hour."

"They haven't even mentioned his name on a television program for a week now," she said.

"Oh, it's cooling off," he said. "I'm sure he'll go soon."

"And you'll be a millionaire," she said gaily.

He stared at her. "How do you know that?" he asked.

"Oh, Jorge told me what he'd promised you," she said.

"When did he tell you that?" Delgado asked.

"Night before last," she said. "That or the time before, I forget. He mentioned it casually."

"You like the idea?" Tonio said.

"I don't hate it," she said slowly.

"Well, *I* hate it," he said. "I won't take a thin *peso* from that son of a bitch, and neither will you. We'll get him the hell out of here and we'll forget him, we'll never mention the bastard's name again, never, never, goddamn it, never!"

"Don't lose your temper, pet," Carola said. "A million dollars is after all a lot of money. If you don't want it, perhaps I do."

Delgado stood up. The brandy glass was shaking in his hand. Rage flowed over him, he was sick with hatred of Gomez, hatred of himself, most of all himself. He fought to hold his tongue, while the words were screaming in his brain—"Why shouldn't you want it? You have after all earned it!"—but he stood, his eyes bulging in their sockets, until he felt the cold wetness of the brandy on his hand. He mopped at himself with a handkerchief, he walked across the room and dropped into a chair.

An old French clock worked away busily on the mantel, chopping up the hours into minutes.

"I had better get undressed," Carola said. "It's five of twelve." She walked past him, trailed her hand across his shoulder. "Give yourself another drink, Tonio," she said.

When he closed the stone door at two that morning Delgado quickly sprinkled a pinch of dust on the left-hand latch and laid a sliver of dirty gray wood firmly in a crack against the door itself. Then he followed Carola upstairs and drew her bath. They went to sleep without speaking.

Once before dinner, the next night, and once afterward he started for the cellar. Both times he stopped himself. He waited until the stroke of midnight.

The dust was streaked through, the little peg of wood lay on the floor two feet from the door. The door had been opened during the day.

He held Carola's arm carefully the next night as they went down the cellar stairs. He unlocked the wine-cellar door, moved the three latches of the other one and swung it wide.

"Ah, you are so punctual," Gomez said. "Come in, my dear Carola, come in." Delgado watched his wife move quickly through the doorway, and as he closed the wall he saw her shrug easily out of her robe. He checked the latches. He turned out the light and locked the wine cellar.

He drank a cup of coffee in the kitchen. He half filled the cup again and poured brandy in it. He carried the cup through the house, from room to room and back again. He went upstairs and sat for a long time in the bedroom. He waited. He listened. There was not a sound from the cellar.

At five o'clock, just before dawn, he turned the key in the Cadillac. A big engine is a good thing, he told himself, as exhaust smoke began to fill the garage. For everything, a big engine is best. He listened to it, running smoothly at a fast idle. A headache comes first, he told himself. I know that. I expect that. He waited.

He dreamed, woke, dreamed again. He tried to put himself into the hole with Gomez and Carola. At first, he supposed, they would console each other; then they would concert on attempts to spring the latches, or to burrow through the granite walls; inevitably, finally, they would quarrel, and hate each other. He thought of Gomez' friends, their chieftain dead and no one left on whom to cry vengeance. How funny! I am spitting on you, Jorge, he said. He wondered who they might have been, these friends. Whom might Jorge have told? What had he said, about the girl, when he had been so angry? "It involves letting someone outside know where I am." An odd thing to say, if someone outside already knew where he was. Or had he meant, someone outside his circle, outside his group of confidants? No, it would not have been that. It had been a slip of the tongue. No one had known where he was: naturally not! Better than most people, Jorge O'B knew that what one man called a secret another man could make him tell. There was no one! Gomez would have trusted no one with his life unnecessarily. He had trusted only Delgado, Delgado's stupidity, he had trusted that he could bluff Delgado, surely that was it, there had been no one at all. Delgado felt a savage, sickening shock run slowly through his body. There had been no one! He could have shot The Monster when he pleased, with impunity. He could not hear the engine now, but he could hear the sound of the sea, roaring and crashing, very near. He was sobbing. He could see Gomez' white and foxlike face, laughing, laughing. He reached for the ignition key, he knew where it was, he could see it if he tried, tried as hard as a man pulling himself drowning from the sea, he could almost touch it, almost . . . he did touch it, his fingers would not obey him, he seized it in his whole fist and turned it. He fell out of the car, he crawled on his belly to the door, he butted it open and sucked in the good air, wet with the dew on the grass, tasting of the grass and the earth. When he could stand he went into the house. He went to bed but did not sleep.

The housekeeper, the first of the three servants to come, found him in the kitchen, sitting over strong coffee and stale croissants.

"The Señora," he told her, "left at six for Persouave. It's her aunt. Dying, I'm afraid."

The housekeeper made the sign of the cross.

"The Señora took almost nothing with her," he said. "No time. If you would be so good as to pack her suitcase, then I will have it sent to her this morning."

"Think of it as done," the good woman told him.

A week later he dismissed her. The Señora's aunt was so desperately ill, he said, that her return would be indefinitely delayed; he felt it his duty to join her in Persouave. He would close the house. He made a generous settlement on her, and upon the others, and bade them farewell. He told a few of Carola's friends the same story.

On the morning of the 21st day he entered the hide-out. It was bad, but not as bad as he had thought it might be. He could not guess how long it had been since Jorge O'B and Carola had died, but clearly they had not died the day before. They were on opposite sides of the room, as he had expected them to be. The money belt came quickly to hand: Jorge O'B had tossed it to a shelf. The letter was harder to find. It was interesting.

It was addressed to Paul Guivarra, an enormously wealthy plantation-owner who had spent years building a reputation as a raving anti-Gomista. Reading it, Delgado marveled at The Monster's cunning. "My dear Paul, I am tucked up in a perfectly safe place. Two people and only two, a man and a woman, know where I am, and both are safe: the man in fear (he thinks my friends have their eyes on him), the woman out of love. So. Time enough has passed, and I am ready. Go to your safe and take out the envelope I gave you in May. Open it. You will find the entire plan, and I think you will agree that it is flawless, or as nearly flawless as these things can be. (One modification: I shall not be alone. I am bringing the woman with me.) When you are ready, place the little advertisement in *La Tribuna*. Two days later you will know where I am, you will send the truck, and away we go. In the meantime, enjoy yourself. I see you had Serrano to dinner last week. Good. And very funny. I hope you have already begun to bleed him . . ."

There were 50 American thousand-dollar bills in The Monster's money belt, with 68 tissue-wrapped stones, diamonds for the most part. One was a good inch and a quarter in diameter. The others were smaller, of sizes handier for conversion into cash. There were ten 50-peso gold pieces, 5000 in paper pesos and $5000 in small bills. O'B had thought of all this as nothing, of course, mere getaway money. Delgado went through the soft chamois belt very carefully. Within one of the pockets there was another and it held a sheet of tissue paper: a list of banks and account numbers, banks in Miami, New York, London, Paris, Madrid, Zurich and Berne. The paper rattled in Delgado's hand as he read. The American and the British banks, the French, the Spanish—never mind those. But the Swiss! With these now, with their anonymous numbers, and a little ingenuity, a little audacity . . . the important thing would be not to take too much. Five million, perhaps, or ten. That would be quite enough, more than enough.

He had surprisingly little trouble getting an exit permit. He had valid business in Miami. He was not searched when he left, and the American customs people were easy. His business took him three days, as he had said it would, and then he returned. He waited a week and applied for another permit. It came through promptly. He packed his little bag, he strapped The Monster's money belt under his shirt, and he left for good. Within 24 hours he was in New York, a rich and happy man. He made the necessary inquiries, he paid the necessary monies, he visited a consulate and swore perfunctory allegiance to another country, the representatives of which rewarded him with a crisp new passport. It was all simple and businesslike.

He lived in Paris for some time, and then moved to Zurich. He stayed a year and two months in Zurich. He liked Switzerland, but the people bored him. He made little trips about Europe. Italy appealed to him for a time. He tried Sweden. But he liked the Côte d'Azur best, and he settled on a little piece of land above Nice. He had the house torn down and a new one built to his taste. It was small but pretty, full of conveniences and comforts. He found that he liked living alone. He did not want to marry again. Sometimes he told himself that he still loved Carola, and must be faithful to her memory. Sometimes he felt that he could never again trust any woman. In any case, he was an attractive man in the early autumn of his life, he was a millionaire and it was not necessary to marry anyone. He was content. He was satisfied with his life. As time passed, he began to take pride in the skill with which he conceived that he had extricated himself from hideous treachery and grave danger. Really, how neatly it had been done. It had been the perfect crime, except for one thing: no one knew a crime had been committed. Still, wasn't that the essence of the perfect crime? He supposed so, but it flawed his satisfaction, nevertheless. After all, he had brought off a great act of heroism, as well as a crime. It had been more heroism than crime. To kill a faithless wife was hardly a crime. It had been he, Tonio Delgado, who had run The Monster to ground, and killed him in his burrow. He deserved the credit.

Swimming from the stony shore one bright morning, Delgado was annoyed by a little cramp in the calf of his left leg. He rolled over and reached under to rub it out, and it occurred to him that some such stupidity might kill a man. Just two days before, he recalled unhappily, his friend M. Delacourt, of the Credit Lyonnaise, had fallen dead, flat on his face, just as he reached out his hand for the first aperitif of the morning. It could happen to anyone, but if it happened to Tonio Delgado, a secret of history would go with him. It was unthinkable that this should be so. He rolled over and swam for shore, stroking vigorously but conservatively. He was bemused with the brilliance of his new idea, and he truly could not understand why he had not thought of it before.

Writing steadily for three or four hours a day, Delgado took four months at his task. He might have done it sooner, of course, had he confined himself to the events beginning with The Monster's arrival at the house in Haraguato. He thought it better to begin with his own birth and The Monster's, sketching them in parallel until the two life lines crossed for the second time at the threshold of the back door of the house in Haraguato. That, of course, was the title of the work: *The House in Haraguato*. Finished, it amounted to 169 pages in small script. Delgado read it over three times in as many days. Really, it read rather well, he felt. It was concise and to the point, like a legal brief, and yet it held drama and excitement, too. Most importantly, it was history. It was something that mattered, and the world had very nearly gone on without knowing about it. That would have been tragic. Delgado was happy to think that he had prevented this occurrence. He was annoyed, however, when he realized that the book would contribute to the world's recollection of The Monster. Then he laughed, thinking of the quotation he had read: "I am an immortal. I will live forever." Also, to look at it another way, Delgado had assured *himself* of immortality. He could not feel that it was undeserved. Had he not been, like Churchill, both an actor in the great drama of history and a recorder of it? He had had more directly to do with the death of Jorge O'Brian Gomez, Monster, than Churchill had had to do with the death of Adolf Hitler, Monster. And who was to say that Gomez, living, might not have surpassed the crimes of Hitler? It was well known that Gomez had been spending millions, before the Revolution, in an attempt to make an atomic bomb. Hitler, mark you, never had an atomic bomb. Think of that for a moment.

Delgado could only with difficulty contemplate allowing the manuscript to leave his hands, but he knew that he must, if it was to serve its purpose. He wrote a covering letter of instructions, he wrapped the manuscript carefully and set out for Monaco and his attorney's office.

He drove carefully but with enterprise. He had a *gran turismo* Lancia, a lithe, lively automobile. The day was a marvel of warmth, of color, of scent. He was sliding down the hills into the streets of Monaco by 11:30. He parked the car and phoned Lyautey, who had no prior engagement for lunch, at least so he said, and they met at The Golden Horse. They ordered carefully and ate slowly and with gusto. With the calvados, Delgado gave his friend the package of manuscript, bright in red sealing wax.

"This is a simple matter," he said. "I just want you to keep this envelope until my death. Open it then. You will find a letter of instruction. It's a book, and I want it published."

"Very well," Lyautey said. "But why not publish it now, while you can enjoy your fame? Eh?"

Delgado laughed. "I might *not* enjoy it," he said. "Besides, it is going to make me happy, very happy, just to think about its being published. You have no idea."

Lyautey shrugged. "D'accord," he said.

It was true. The idea did make Delgado happy. He grew out of himself, and seemed to reblossom, to take a second wind in his life. He had lived as a hedonist for years. He had made no major effort since he had taken The Monster's money from the Swiss banks. That had required thought and courage, but ever since he had drifted, purposelessly, but telling himself that his purpose was to enjoy life. It seemed a thin endeavor now.

The day after his 58th birthday, Delgado married one

Therese Marbonne. She was 36, a divorcee. She was kind and sincere and loving and if she was not as intelligent as Carola had been, she was a good deal prettier. She knew that life had given Tonio Delgado most of what he wanted except children. She was pregnant in the second month of their marriage, and thus a son was born to Delgado in his 59th year. A daughter came in his 60th. He was proud of his children, and kind to them. His gratitude toward Therese was profound, and she in turn succeeded in convincing him that no other man in the world could arouse so much as a flicker of interest in her. He lived with enormous gusto and deep serenity until he was 66, when he died easily and quickly of a cerebral hemorrhage. His last conscious thought was of his manuscript, secure in Lyautey's great safe, a vision in brown paper and red wax. He knew that he was dying, and he felt a pang of conscience for allowing thought of anything but Therese and the children to occupy him, but the manuscript meant more to him in that moment, and he dwelt lovingly upon it until the dark little flood of blood, seeping over his brain, put an end to him.

Promptly at nine next morning Pierre Lyautey went to the office strongbox and broke the seals on the brown envelope. He was sad. He had been fond of Tonio Delgado. He was stunned by what he read when he came to page 117 of the manuscript. When he put it down he was horrified. He was so shaken that he locked it into the safe again and hurried out to a bar for a whiskey, and then another. Halfway through the second one, sitting at a little stone-topped table under a plane tree in the warm sun, he saw things more clearly. By the time he had finished the drink he knew what he must do. Clearly it would be an absurdity to allow an obvious *crime passionel*, committed in heat and fury and hatred, to sully the memory of so good a man and to embarrass a family so devoted. Quite out of the question. In this case, the weight of friendship must overbalance professional obligation. Lyautey took a long walk, from the railroad station to the gasometer, because he wanted to be sure that perfect sobriety would confirm his present judgment. After his walk he drank a large cup of coffee. Then he returned to his office and burned the manuscript in his little fireplace, complete with letter of instruction, envelope and wax. When he had seen to the burning of every sheet, he stirred the ashes into powder and turned to other concerns.

. . .

A matter of a few weeks later, in Haraguato, a bulldozer ripped off a corner of the hide-out. In the years that had passed since Tonio and Carola Delgado had lived there, Haraguato had changed a good deal. It had run down. The well-to-do had moved out to the East, into the hills. A new road had been cut through the old pine woods and this had given the current Liberator a whim: flatten eight square blocks of Haraguato and make it a park surrounded by low-rent apartment developments. The idea was enthusiastically received by everyone consulted, and the work was put in train.

It was about two in the afternoon, of a Friday, when the big 'dozer blade bit into the stone roof of the hide-out. The man on the seat, whose name was Gavilon, thought at first he had hit another boulder. The man on the ground, Reynosa, thought so too, and gestured for Gavilon to make another pass. The second pass showed stones laid in courses. The men looked at each other and shrugged. So? An extension of the cellar, beyond doubt. Reynosa languidly waved and Gavilon's brown hands tugged at the levers again. This time, he took a four-foot slab of the roof away. Reynosa held up a warning hand and dropped to his knees in the hole. He looked up at Gavilon, then quickly around and over his shoulder, and beckoned him down. They looked together. They could see well enough.

Gavilon said, "We had better get the police."

"Do you want my advice?" Reynosa said.

"Tell me."

"Many rich used to live here," Reynosa said. "Many important ones. Sometimes, when a thing like this is found, two skeletons in a hole, people think it wise to pretend it never happened. The best method is to do away with the people who have found things, do you understand me?"

"I understand you, I think," Gavilon said. "Yes, it is clear."

"We have ten minutes or so before the truck comes back for another load."

Gavilon pulled himself to the seat. The big diesel roared and the rain cap on the exhaust pipe stood straight up. Standing beside the hole, Reynosa made a stirring motion with his hand, his index finger pointed downward. Gavilon lowered the blade and hit the near wall. In five passes he had flattened everything. He ground the rubble under the caterpillar treads; he widened the hole and mixed in a ton of earth. He knew his trade and he was quick. When the truck came back he was ready to load. It was a ten-ton dumper. There was room for everything. He watched the truck roll away. He knew where the stuff was going: to the ocean front at Partila, for fill. He lighted a cigarette and looked down at Reynosa. They were relieved and happy. They laughed.

THE MORNING AFTER

BY WADE MILLER

This story is the work of a writing team which signed itself collectively as Wade Miller or Whit Masterson and individually as Bob Wade and Bill Miller. The death of Miller in late 1961 brought to an end a partnership unique in literature. Collaboration between authors is nothing new, but few, if any, have begun so early, lasted so long and produced so many and varied works. In a 30-year association, Wade and Miller turned out dramas, screenplays, short stories, novelettes, music, radio and television scripts, newspaper columns, magazine articles and poetry, in addition to the 33 novels for which they are principally known. They were first thrown together at the age of 12 when they were assigned to write a one-act play for an English class. The play was a success, and the partnership was born. The stock question asked of them was: How do you work together? Their stock answer: "Wade writes the nouns and Miller the verbs." Nouns and verbs never had it so good as in this finely honed story of moral murder, "The Morning After."

DEE AND GERALD (in matching robes and pajamas) perched side by side at the breakfast bar in their kitchen, sipping coffee from monogrammed mugs. An average-looking young couple, except for an unused air about them. They were childless. They were healthy and gay. This morning Dee, her sun-streaked hair in a wanton tangle, had given it a lick and a promise with the brush, then capriciously tied it back with a large droopy bow of wrapping twine.

Gerald was just as careless. He had inherited the lumber companies which didn't need him at the head office, but he usually went anyway, simply to be with his neighbor husbands in the city and to drive home at the same cocktail hour. Not a friend in their community—one of the richer Southern California ones—hadn't envied the Porslins on occasion. And they had lots of friends.

"So much for the world of trivia." Dee dropped the last of the newspaper to the strewn floor, except Section A, which lay before her husband.

"I told you it was all on the first three pages. Most of the Sunday paper is canned stuff, put together last week or even before."

The headlines were tall and black, but not in mourning.

RUDY BROCK SLAIN!
The last of fabulous Gang Figure Rudy Brock's no-torious, "nine lives" ebbed from him last night as he lay in a pool of blood in his furniture store at . . .

The rest of the copy was as royally purple, as the newspaper rushed to dump what looked like its entire crime morgue into the first three pages. But there was little actual news except the circumstances of the death and that a great police dragnet was rounding up all of Brock's "alleged" enemies for questioning. Brock had more enemies than the Porslins had friends.

"Nine lives," said Dee. "Bunk!"

"Fabulous," muttered Gerald. "How irresponsible can you get?" Meaning the newspaper.

The Porslins took themselves far more seriously than anyone guessed. But they knew their capabilities; in private they had assayed themselves and each other, and recognized how much was going to waste. Dee had underscored it in her questioning way the other night. "It's as if we're not *accomplishing* anything, isn't it?" Dee was generally first to vocalize a mutual thought, if only to find out how far Gerald was ahead of her.

"Not accomplishing anything for the community," he said. "This 'Know Thyself' business only takes a person so far."

. . .

The night before—Saturday—had been heavy with fog. The freeways into the city were canals of flowing phosphorescent lights. As he drove, Gerald kept wiping the inside of the windshield with the back of his gloved hand. They were cheap driving gloves, imitation kid, that he had bought last week, but they would look decent enough for this one outing. Both he and Dee wore reversible raincoats, white side out. Everything about them was as neat as could be, except for their usually spotless Corvette. The rear license plate bore two careful daubs of mud that altered the numbers entirely.

Dee wore white lace gloves and, beneath her open raincoat, a party dress that was memorable only at the neckline. She was quite blonde tonight, thanks to wigs being in fashion recently, and she had done her mouth in a bright tangerine color. As Gerald wheeled into the parking lot alongside the furniture store, she checked herself in her mirror. "If we meet anyone I know, I'll die."

"Please don't, dear. You'd only embarrass us both." Even he was surprised to hear the razor edge to his bantering voice. He hadn't realized there would be any strain to this.

"Should you take a tranquilizer, Gerald?"

"I don't think so."

Casually, the Porslins sauntered to the plate-glass front of the store and entered. They stood looking around. There were two sorts of salesmen on the floor, the usual harried kind and some large husky men in tropic-weight suits. Of the big men, the Porslins recognized a few from the newspaper photographs that accompanied all of the "Underworld Suspects" stories—Flores, Gross, Picozzi . . .

Picozzi trudged toward them. "Can I help you?"

Gerald smiled amiably and nodded toward his wife. She said, "The little round man I spoke to last week? Oh, there he is!"

They deserted Picozzi, who was interested in the plunging front of Dee's dress, and made straight for Rudy Brock. He stood at the foot of the carpeted staircase, a balding man of medium height but stumpy-looking because of his fat. He too evinced a heavy-lidded concern with Dee's low neckline, which was its purpose.

She said, "I'm so glad you're here! I was in last week looking at highboys? Now if I could show my husband?"

Brock wiped back the few hairs on his damp scalp and did his best to remember. But when Dee scouted the store, she had looked quite different. "Why certainly, Mrs. . . ."

"Atropos," supplied Gerald.

"Mr. and Mrs. Atropos, pleased to make your acquaintance." Brock led the way up the stairs to the mezzanine. Dee had chosen the ideal spot. The highboys lined a balcony overlooking the street floor but stood tall enough to provide absolute seclusion.

She caressed one of Sheraton design. "What do you think of this, dear?"

Gerald nodded. "It seems to fit in."

"It's a beautiful piece," Brock offered. "Reasonable, too. Not that we're running any bargain basement here, folks, but——"

"Are you positive?" Dee asked her husband. "We'll both have to live with it for a long while."

"I'm positive."

"Very well, here goes nothing." She gasped. "Oh, for pity's sake—it's *scratched!*"

"Goddamn," growled Brock, shoving forward. "Where?" He bent over the spot where her white lace forefinger pointed.

His sports jacket stretched taut across the basin of his broad back. Gerald pulled the hunting knife from his raincoat pocket. Like the gloves, it was cheap, ordinary and serviceable. He hesitated, but not from lack of resolution. It was because Brock was too fat for his vertebrae to show, as Dee's had during rehearsals. He had to estimate.

"I don't see it," Brock complained.

"It's there," insisted Dee impatiently. "Right *there!*" Imploring, her eyes clung to her husband.

Gerald plunged the knife in up to its guard. Exactly, he hoped, between number six vertebra and number seven. When there was no more blade to sink, he released the hilt quickly.

Brock made no sound louder than a cough. He tried to straighten. Gerald caught him under the arms and lowered him to the floor on his side. Then he inspected his gloves. He couldn't see any flecks of blood. Even so, he gingerly peeled them off by the cuffs, turning them inside out in the process. He had practiced that, too.

"Luck," he murmured to Dee. Slapping the gloves jauntily against his left hand, he strolled out onto the main mezzanine. Nothing was new on the floor below. Except that Picozzi was starting up the stairs. Gerald started down on the same side, remembering not to touch the banister.

Dee knelt down by Brock and opened her purse. Then it was her turn to hesitate until she decided to get the worst out of the way first. She lifted Brock's hand and pressed her mouth to the back of it. When she dropped it again, there was a gaudy tangerine lip print. Brock had a very hairy hand and she nearly gagged.

Next she produced from her purse four Chinese yen and lined the coins neatly in front of his open mouth. She had clipped them off an antique sachet basket before throwing it into the trash. From her purse, too, came the strip of six postage stamps that she licked from one end to the other. She pasted the stamps to his forehead.

Gerald said, "Mister," to Picozzi.

Picozzi stopped, midway on the staircase. "What do you want?"

"I'm curious about the price on that sectional over there. The one near the wall. The queer-colored one."

Picozzi still couldn't tell which one he meant. He followed Gerald down the stairs again and through the maze of living-room suites. Gerald sat down on a sectional near the side door to the parking lot. "This one."

"Here's the tag," said Picozzi. "You must have been looking on the wrong end. $899.95."

"That's a stupid price," Gerald smiled at him.

"I don't get you."

"Why don't you people come right out and say $900?" He got to his feet with a sigh. "Well, let's hear my wife's opinion on the subject."

He waved to Dee who had appeared at the top of the stairs. She waved back and trotted down gracefully. Picozzi was pleased to see her. Gerald patted the sectional cushions. "I was wondering——"

"Dear," she said, "one thing at a time. Besides, it would never *go* without recovering."

Gerald shrugged. "Thanks, anyway," he told Picozzi. The Porslins went out the side door. Dee's gloved hand opened it.

Gerald drove out of the parking lot the back way, through the freight alley and onto a residential street. "Mailed to hell, I trust."

"With utmost dispatch." Between corner lights, she plucked his hat off his head and tossed it behind the seat, unpinned her gleaming wig and stuffed it in the dashboard compartment. Then, squirming about, she reversed her raincoat so that it was blue with a white lining. (Once home, she would replace her wig in its plastic case in the depths of her dressing-room wardrobe; he would hose off the raincoats, both sides, on the patio flagstones, shake them out and hang them in the entry closet where they served in emergencies for guests.) "Three minutes away," she announced.

He pulled into the curb. As he got out of the car, he left his raincoat behind on the seat. With the cleansing tissue Dee had handed him, he swiftly erased the mud daubs from the rear license plate. When he returned to the wheel, his coat was reversed for him, ready to slip into. They set off for home, by way of the coast route.

"You know, I practically threw up? I'm glad you're not all primitive and hairy." Dee's voice was a little garbled, for she was wiping her mouth clean of the last traces of tangerine shade. She rolled down the window and let the tissue fly out onto the fogbound highway.

"But you didn't."

"Of course not. We left enough meaningless motifs lying about, didn't we? I don't believe in excess. Poor police . . ."

"Kiss mark, coins and stamps. Well, if they can locate a female Chinese postal employee with hoodlum connections, more power to them."

"Please—I'll laugh in a moment." By compact and dashlight, Dee was redrawing her lips in their usual pale coral.

"Nine minutes away," warned Gerald.

She emptied her purse in her lap, magically reversed it, too, then replaced everything but two small round stones. She dropped one of these in each of Gerald's gloves to serve as weights. Peering out her window, she waited. When they came to the long bridge over the estuary, she sailed the gloves out into the sea water. "All done." She nestled against her husband.

"Nice pitching. Now will you tell me where on earth you got that vulgar dress?"

"You liked it well enough when I wore it to Rona's party. Of course, tonight I have it on backward . . ." She muffled her peals of overwrought laughter against his sleeve.

When the Porslins were 13 minutes away, a janitor discovered Rudy Brock's body, their gift to the community.

.   .   .

"The—exquisite?—part is," decided Dee, "who would ever come looking for *us?*"

"Actually no one," Gerald said. "I read somewhere that the best thing is to do good yet be evil spoken of. Epictetus." He nudged his coffee mug nearer to her. "Refill, please, or I'll go back to bed."

"Then I'll have to settle for second best. We did good, didn't we? A purely philanthropic boon to mankind? And we don't care to be spoken of at all, do we?"

"Scarcely."

Dee poured. The steam rose about their faces like the brightening Sunday-morning fog outside. "The uninvolved Porslins . . . Certainly those ridiculous clues we planted, pointing in all directions, will keep any innocent person from becoming involved?"

"Certainly. The police always maintain secrecy over a couple of items like that, when they can, just to weed out the crackpots who enjoy confessing. Of course, there's always the chance that they might invent their own case. Against someone like Mr. Picozzi, for example." He tested his coffee; the mug was too hot to handle.

"Then what would we do, dear?"

"I think that would come under the heading of Killing Two Birds."

"I see. I didn't care for him, either." Dee rested her tousled head against his shoulder. After a while, she murmured, "Quite a sensation, eliminating someone so totally depraved. Do you suppose we'll ever do it again?"

Gerald dared a sip of his coffee. Then he sucked his scalded tongue thoughtfully. "It's possible."

"I've been wondering, dear. I mean, what would be the sensation, what would it feel like, if next time it were someone totally *good*?"

He looked down at her. She rolled her eyes up to meet his. In them he saw a faint flicker of evil, a glitter like red tinsel. He didn't know whether it was born there or whether it might be the reflection of his own glance.

Dee took a deep sweet breath. There was no reason for him to reply. He had been wondering, too.

WITH ALL DUE RESPECT

BY FRED MCMORROW

Fred McMorrow's varied experience as a newspaperman (he is now News Editor of The New York Post*) has provided him with much of the raw material for his fiction. But it was his stretch of active service in army artillery (1944–1946), taking part in the North Appennine and Po Valley campaigns in Italy, that furnished the backdrop for the following story, in which a sure cure for cranky captains is prescribed.*

SERGEANT GAGLIANO stood between the trails of the howitzer, bellowing out the commands he was getting over the telephone headset from the executive officer.

"Shell H-E, V-T fuse thu-ree niner fo-wer!"

Number Six Man kneed the fat projectile upright and Number Five expertly screwed the variable time fuse on its nose to the setting of 394.

"Charge seven!"

Numbers Four and Three slapped seven bags of powder into the casing. Six, Five, Four and Three placed the loading tray under the gaping maw of the breech, put the shell on the tray and heaved it home with the rammer staff.

Corporal Billings swung the breech closed.

"Base deflection left two niner zee-ro!"

Number Two Man whirled his wheel and the snout of the howitzer turned gently toward the northwest where, over the lip of the rise, lay the German lines, only a thousand yards away.

"Ele-vay-shun, eight fy-ev!"

Billings spun the wheel on his side of the breech and Number Four Gun rose, like an anaconda spotting its prey. Billings locked the setting, turned to face the sergeant and picked up the firing pin lanyard.

"Fire!"

And Number Four Gun thundered and recoiled with the grace of a great snake, and the earth shivered under Gagliano's feet. He breathed deeply, his nostrils stung by the sweet, biting smoke.

The earth quivered again under him but much more gently, as Charlie Battery's shells went to earth in the German lines.

"That did it, men, that did it," came the executive officer's voice in his ear and those of the other three gun sergeants. "Infantry says it turned them back, what was left of them. Sixteen goddam Tiger Tanks, men. The colonel sends you his compliments. Mission accomplished."

Gagliano took off the headset and dropped it at his feet. The crew, all still in position for another round, was looking at him expectantly.

"The colonel says you couldn't hit an old lady crossing the street, men," Gagliano said. "He's coming down here and show you eight-balls how to handle a gun."

"What was it, anyway?" Corporal Billings said.

"Tiger Tanks again," Gagliano said. "Over across from Loiano. They were trying to bust up the 36th's heavy weapons. We stopped them. Relax, men. Rest. Smoke, if you like."

It was such a tired old joke, but they loved him and they laughed anyway. All but Billings set to work, opening the breech of their gigantic child and swabbing out its hot throat with the solvent liquid. The phone jangled. Billings picked up the headset.

"Number Four," Billings said. "Hi, Ray. Oh. OK. He'll be right down." He dropped the headset and stepped close to Gagliano.

"Burk said the captain wants you and the other section chiefs down the orderly room tent right away," he said. "I guess you know why."

Gagliano shrugged hopelessly. "Yeah, I know why," he said. "Nobody on the crew knows about it, do they? You didn't tell none of the men?"

"Oh, hell, no," Billings said. "I figured you'd tell them yourself if you wanted them to know."

"Yeah," Gagliano said. "Well, I guess it had to happen some time. Listen—make sure that breech is clean, will you? I don't want no more hangfires this week."

As he trudged away, he smiled at himself, reminding Billings about cleaning the gun when that wouldn't be his responsibility any longer.

The other section chiefs were already there. They were all big men, as Gagliano was. At his desk sat Ray Burk, the tough little lantern-jawed man who was their first sergeant.

"Hi, Gag," Burk said, toying with a pencil. "All right. You men form a line in front of me here. Dress on the right."

"What is this? Are we gonna pass in review or something?" Gagliano said.

Burk sighed. "You been in the Army long enough to know what this is," he said. "You know how he is. He wants it real red-hot, like the Fourth of July or—ten-SHUT!"

And the captain stumped in, his head passing under the section chiefs' chests, his crisply pressed ODs ballooning about his thin little legs, his mousy face hidden under the burnished, battered steel helmet. He put the helmet on the desk and faced them.

"I think all you men know what's gonna happen here," he said. He nodded at Gagliano. "All right, you. One step fo-wahd—HARCH."

The giant clopped one step out of the line and snapped his heels together.

The captain folded his arms and looked at each one of them, savoring every second of the moment.

Then he pointed at Gagliano.

"Gagliano," he announced in his high, squeaky voice, "as far as I'm concerned, your appointment as a sergeant has terminated."

You motherless little crud, Gagliano thought, you haven't called me sergeant since we got you and you wouldn't do it even when you're busting me. You must have sat up all night thinking just how to say it. Well, I never called you sir, either. Just captain.

"I hope the rest of you men realize what this means," the captain said. For effect, he put his hands behind him and strutted solemnly to the tent door and gazed out at the titanic upward sweep of Montecatini Alto and its neighboring peaks, which looked like an angry stone ocean when you were on top of one.

The captain whirled around.

"Now if there's a man here that don't like it let him tell me so right to my face."

They only returned his stare, each one expressionless.

"This damn man here has been a bone of contention in my craw since I took over this outfit," the captain said. "He don't want to toe the mark. He don't think I know how to handle soldiers. He wants to wipe their noses for them. He don't deserve to wear a gun sergeant's stripes. Sergeant Burk! I want you to read off the charges against this man here."

Burk cleared his throat. "Captain, sir," he said, "with all due respect, sir, I just posted all them charges on the bulletin board and I don't see——"

"I don't see, Sergeant Burk, where the first sergeant gets off putting no interpretations on my orders," the captain said.

"It's not that, sir," Burk said.

"Then what is it? Maybe you don't think I should bust a man if I think he should be busted. Maybe you think I ought to ask you first. Is that it, Sergeant?"

Burk gave in. "All right, sir," he said, and took one of the quadruplicates from his TO BATTALION box. "Dereliction of duty; insubordination; failure to observe military courtesy; appropriation of a military vehicle for unauthorized uses; fraternization with the enemy."

"What's that?" Gagliano said. "What's that last one?"

"You will remain at attention, soldier," the captain said.

"Captain, sir," Burk said, "the ARs say a man has a right to hear all the charges against him."

The captain glared at Burk, helpless rage all over his face. He couldn't bust Burk and he knew it. They all respected Burk too much and the captain knew they did not respect *him*.

"All right, Sergeant," the captain said. He stepped up to Gagliano and glared up at the big face above him.

"You know damn well what I mean by fraternizing with the enemy," he said. A flush crept up Gagliano's thick neck.

"If I might have permission to speak, Captain," he said.

"I told you to remain at attention."

"If I might have permission to speak, goddam it, what the ell do you mean by the enemy?"

"I mean them dago whores we caught you with last night vhen you took the weapons carrier out," the captain said. "Is hat so hard to understand?"

"Just because I was with some Italian girls I was fraternizing vith the enemy?"

"That's right," the captain said. "I never seen a dago yet I ould trust and I'm sure General Truscott don't either."

"That's a lie, Captain," Gagliano said.

"Go ahead," the captain said. "Speak your piece. It'll sound ood when I take this to a higher court martial."

"The Italian people been on our side a long time now, aptain," Gagliano said, "and if you call that fraternizing with he enemy, me spending a nice, sociable evening with a couple of irls and their mothers, Captain——"

"A bunch of whores," the captain said. "What decent girl vould go out with some bum soldier who just stole some overnment property?"

"I admit that, Captain," Gagliano said. "If you're busting ne for taking the weapons carrier, I admit I took it without no uthorization. But the goddam enemy is them jerries, not the talian people."

"Captain, sir," Burk said. "A word in private, sir?" They tepped outside into the blasting Italian sunlight.

"With all due respect, Captain," Burk said, "you can't make hat charge stick and it'll only look bad if you try, sir. I know he colonel won't like it."

"Sergeant Burk," the captain said, "if I didn't need you ike I need my two hands here, I'd rip the stripes right off our arm. Are you gonna stand in my way here too or are you onna help me do my job and make soldiers out of this bunch f eight-balls?"

"With all due respect, sir," Burk said, showing no reaction t all, "any punk second lieutenant could knock the props right

out from under a dumbbell charge like that if he wa
Gagliano's counsel, sir. If I might speak right out, sir?'

"Well?"

"Thank you, sir. With all due respect, sir, I'm just trying to
save you from looking like a horse's ass."

The captain looked as if Burk had slapped him.

"All right, Sergeant," he said. "Eliminate that charge
against him. But I want that whole busting order typed over
again, all five copies including the one on the bulletin board
there. Rip it off."

"Yes, sir," said Burk, ripping it off the board and crumpling
it. "It's all right. Battalion don't know anything about the case
yet, sir. I hope the Captain won't take what I say personally
sir. It's my job as the first sergeant to advise——"

"Don't you tell me the duties of a first sergeant!" the captain
snapped. "Don't you think I know what a first sergeant's
supposed to do?"

"Yes, sir," Burk said. "I know you got a tough job here. I
just want to help you win the confidence and respect of the
men, sir. You gotta remember, Captain, these men been
together since this was a National Guard outfit back in '39.
You don't want to create no more problems than you already
got, sir. I hope the Captain understands me."

"You just understand *me*," the captain said. "If I have to
I'll bust every damn non-com including the mess sergeant. I'm
going to make this a fighting, military outfit, Sergeant. Just
remember that."

"Yes, sir," Burk said. They stepped back inside.

"Captain," said Burk, at his desk again, "will Private
Gagliano stay on Number Four crew or do you want him on
one of the other guns?"

The captain smiled.

"I don't want that man on the guns at all," he said. "You
will assign him to the ammo detail. I see by his MOS he's a
truck driver as well as a cannoneer. All right. He can drive

ith the ammo detail and help with the loading. He's got a
ood, strong back, if he ain't got a brain in his dago head."

"Will that be permanent duty or battery punishment, sir?"

"No, that's permanent duty," the captain said. "The ammo
etail. The pinhead squad."

The phone buzzed and Burk picked it up. "Charlie Bat-
ery," he said. "Good afternoon, sir. Yes, he's here. For you,
aptain."

"Captain Barker here," the captain said. "Oh, yes, Colonel.
es, sir, everything's just fine around here, just fine. Getting
long? I'm getting along just fine, sir. Of course we're ready
or a new fire mission, sir. Oh. Oh, yes, sir. Yes, I've seen that
n the map. No, we won't need any extra time, sir. Sixteen
undred? That'll be fine, sir. Yes, sir. Yes indeed, sir." He
anded the phone back to Burk.

"There's a big fire mission starting at 16 hundred," he said.
The 36th is moving up and we're in support. The colonel said
e can expect to keep each gun firing steadily until 24
undred. You section chiefs"—he noted with satisfaction that
agliano became unconsciously attentive—"can you do it?"

"We'll do it," said Sergeant Eaves, section chief of Number
One Gun. "We been doing it since El Guettar, Captain." That
ent home to the captain, that mention of the North African
ampaign, of a time when he wasn't even in the Army.

"Well, now, I don't know," the captain said. "That's a lot of
ring. I don't know if we got enough ammo."

"There's plenty of reserve ammo," Burk said. "We brought
n three new loads from Bassano this morning."

"I'll make that decision, Sergeant Burk," the captain said.
And my decision is that we will go back with the trucks now,
nd I will go along. I want to see Gagliano in action."

"Yes, sir," Burk said. "I'll call battalion and have the
unner bring the jeep back."

"No, don't bother," the captain said. "I'll ride in the trucks.
n fact, I'll drive one of the trucks."

The section chiefs looked at each other.

"Captain, sir," said Sergeant Dudley, section chief of Number Two, "them prime movers are an awful handful of truck for anybody but an experienced driver. Especially out on Highway 65, sir. It's a lousy road. It's banked the wrong way on the turns. It's——"

"Now I'll be damned," the captain said. "Here's a man in this battery who's a little concerned about his captain. Well, ain't that nice. Don't you think I know how to handle an artillery truck, Sergeant?"

"Yes, sir," said Dudley.

"Then keep your goddam mouth shut," the captain said. "Before we get started, there's a little ceremony I been saving up for this moment."

He stepped up to Gagliano and ripped the sergeant's stripes off the giant's arms.

The captain peered at the dark patch on the faded left sleeve, where the stripes had been.

"My, my," he said. "They been there a long time."

"Yes, they have, Captain," Gagliano said. "Since '39."

"Well, you'll never wear them again as long as I'm around," the captain said. "All right. Now you sergeants go out and get your cannoneers ready for the ammo detail."

"Cannoneers?" Burk said. "Captain, them cannoneers done three fire missions already today and they're gonna be firing all night, too. They gonna need their strength, Captain."

"Are they men or little boys who gotta have their bottle, Sergeant?" the captain said.

"They're cannoneers, sir," Burk said. "And with all due respect, sir, them are the best damn cannoneers in the Army. But they ain't machines, sir."

"You know, Sergeant," the captain said, "this is a war we got on our hands here and sometimes we gotta expend a little extra effort. We gotta show the men they gotta respect us."

"Yes, sir," Burk said. "But when your guns are in position

you save the cannoneers for the firing and you use the other men for the ammo details, sir. The telephone linemen and the radio section and the machine gunners, sir. That's who you use on an ammo detail."

"What kind of fairies I got here, anyway?" the captain said. "You sergeants afraid to make your men do a little work?"

Burk sighed. "All right, sir," he said. "We'll use the cannoneers."

"You're damn right we'll use the cannoneers," the captain said. "I'll be down the motor pool waiting for you."

He left the tent and they watched him until he was out of sight, beyond the ruin of the old German antiaircraft position.

"I'm sorry, Gag," Burk said. The giant shrugged.

"It's all right," he said. "I can't soldier under a man like that anyway."

"No, I mean that stuff he was saying about Italians," Burk said. "He shouldn't talk that way to any man."

"I'll tell you something else he shouldn't," Dudley said. "He shouldn't be in charge of no men. I wouldn't have a monkey-lover like that in charge of a latrine detail. He'd make you salute it before you buried it."

"By damn," said Sergeant Hansen, section chief of Number Three Gun, "I've seen this man's Army do some pretty damn dumb things, but when they made that red-hot a captain they started from the beginning again. What's the matter with the colonel, anyway, giving us a dope like that?"

"Don't blame the colonel," Burk said. "He couldn't help himself. You remember how it was when Captain Garver got it, them 24-hour fire missions, with jerry busting out all over the 36th's lines like an old pair of pants splitting. Hell, the colonel couldn't shift none of his officers around. He did all he could do, he asked Naples for a replacement."

"So we get a rear echelon commando from the Repple Depple," Eaves said, and spat on the floor.

"I never forget that first day," Burk said. "He says to me in that squeaky little voice of his, 'Sargint, I want you to get me the beat-upest old steel helmet you can find around here.' So I got it for him, and you know what he done? He sat up in his tent, half the night, hitting that helmet with a hammer. It wasn't beat up enough for him. And then he polishes it! Boy, what a red-hot."

"Where was he before he come to us, Ray?" Hansen asked.

"Just in the officer's pool at the Repple Depple," Burk said. "He was there six months and before that he was cadre at Fort Bragg. That's why he's such a red-hot, I guess. Back in the States all he had to do was push dumb recruits around and they put him in an outfit like this, with real soldiers, he don't know how to handle them. He don't understand why we ain't out policing up the area every morning. He misses the bugles."

"Here's his bugle, right here," Gagliano said. "Listen, Ray who are you going to make?"

"For your section? Billings," Burk said.

"Good," Gagliano said. "He'll be a good sergeant. They're used to listening to him. I was afraid the captain'd try to put somebody on who wasn't in the crew."

"Not while I'm the first sergeant," Burk said. "I know what he's up to."

"Just what the hell *is* that crazy man up to?" Gagliano said.

"You got to be a first sergeant to spot it early," Burk said. "He figures that the way the battery is now, it's a bunch of little cliques, all working against him. What he wants to do is go right down the line, busting the non-coms and splitting up all the crews so they aren't with guys they been with for years. He figures that'll make it easier for him."

"He wants them stripes of yours awful bad, Ray," said Hansen. "I seen him looking at that first sergeant's diamond on your arm like it was a bare-ass woman."

"I know it," Burk said. "I know it better than any of you guys. I seen it that first day when he busted Johnson right in front of all the men and ripped the stripes off his arm."

"He'll never do that again," said Gagliano.

"He done it to you, didn't he?" Dudley said. "He done it right here, five minutes ago."

"Well, that was just among us sergeants," Gagliano said. "He would of done it in front of a formation if Johnson hadn't jumped him, that time. And me, big stupid me, I had to be Joe Noble and pull old Red off of him."

"And what if you let him kill the captain?" Burk said. "You would of been in command of a firing squad, the next morning. No, you done the right thing."

"Where's old Red now, Ray?" Eaves said.

"The last I heard he was in that Discipline Battalion near Naples," Burk said.

"I heard about that place," Eaves said.

"They sleep in shelter halves with one blanket, all year," Burk said. "They get one pair of fatigues and one razor blade and they gotta use that razor blade for a month and they got to shave twice a day."

"A guy in the 36th told me about it," Eaves said. "When he got out of there, he was glad to go back in the line. He said three guys died there last winter."

"Yeah," Burk said. "Well, let's get this over with. Go on, get the poor motherless cannoneers."

At the motor pool the captain was looking at his watch.

"Sergeant Burk, you know how long I been waiting here?" he bellowed.

"Sorry, sir," Burk said. "Some of the cannoneers was asleep."

"You just by damn better be sorry!" the captain said. The 40 men from the gun crews stood silent, watching Burk take it. The captain turned to them.

"Your sergeants, who been wiping your little noses all these years, they don't think you ought to go on no ammo details," he said. "Well, I think different. And I'm the captain. Anybody want to dispute that? Any son of a bitch want to differ with me?"

They just stood looking at him.

"I been your commanding officer three weeks, since Captain Garver was killed," he said. "Now I don't know how he held this outfit together, because when I took command, you were a bunch of Boy Scouts. You didn't know nothing about military courtesy and you didn't have no discipline and you still don't. Oh, I know what you think of me. I ain't a National Guard, so I stink. I ain't a member of the club. Well, gentlemen, you're gonna respect me or I'll die making you do it. It's gonna be one of us, gentlemen, you or me, and by damn, it's not gonna be me! Now let's mount up on these trucks here and get some work done."

"Captain, sir?" said one of the cannoneers.

The captain peered at him. "You're Private Zakian, ain't you?"

"Yes, sir," the cannoneer said. "Captain, sir, when you said son of a bitch, who did you mean?"

The captain smiled. He had had his outburst and he felt genial now.

"I meant myself, son," he said, "because I'm one."

"That's good, Captain," said the cannoneer, "because I'm not."

The laughter rolled over him like an ocean breaker.

"Put that damn man on report for seven days extra duty!" the captain shrieked at Burk.

After some coaxing the captain agreed to let one of the regular drivers sit with him in the cab. The trucks were tall, ugly seven-tonners, like buildings with wheels on them. They had the tremendous power necessary to jockey the great eight-inch guns around, and there was a lot the drivers had to know.

At the ammunition dump the captain perched himself on the fender of his truck, his shiny boots bouncing off the big, fat tire, shouting abuse at the silent, sweating cannoneers as they wrestled the shells up to the truck tail-gates. An eight-inch howitzer projectile weighs 200 pounds.

It was three hours before the trucks were loaded to capacity. Burk took the captain aside.

"With all due respect, sir," he said, "I think you'd better let the driver handle the truck on the way back."

"I'll drive," the captain said.

"Captain, sir," Burk said, "you don't know what it's like pushing one of these things over the mountains with a load of H-E."

"I said I'll drive," the captain said.

"But you'll have men riding with you, sir. Suppose there's an accident, sir. With all due respect, sir, I don't think you should take the responsibility."

"Is that the way you talked to Captain Garver?" the captain said. "Did you tell him his business, too? Did he need his nose wiped like the rest of these NGs here?"

Burk felt himself breathing hard.

"Listen, Sergeant Burk," the captain said. "I'm trying to set an example to these men here. I'm gonna drive that damn truck and what's more I'm gonna do it alone!"

"You mean you don't want the driver with you?" Burk said, controlling himself with a terrible effort.

"That's right. I'm gonna be up there in that little old cab all by myself."

"All right, you crazy bastard," Burk said. "But I'll tell you one thing you're not gonna do. If you take that wheel you're gonna have that truck all to yourself. I'm not gonna let any of my men ride with you."

"Your men, Sergeant?"

"Yeah, my men!" Burk said. "Listen, you: you're never gonna run this outfit because you don't deserve to be no officer. You can go to hell and I hope you do."

"I'm gonna enjoy this," the captain said. "I been waiting for you to hang yourself. You know what you just done, don't you? You just busted yourself."

"Yeah, I know," Burk said. "And if I look at that dumb bastard face of yours another second, I'm gonna bust *it*."

Burk stepped into the road and addressed the convoy.

"All you men riding on Captain Barker's truck," he called.

"You get off there and ride on the other trucks. The driver, too. Taylor, you go ride with Eaves. Captain, you want to lead the convoy?"

"Oh, no," said the captain. "Let Gagliano lead. I'll be right behind him. I want to keep my eye on that boy."

Burk waited until all the men were mounted up. Then he climbed up beside Gagliano, leaned out and waved his fist in a circle. The engines bellowed into life. Gagliano let out the clutch and led the lurching behemoths over the bumpy driveway of the ammo dump to Highway 65.

Burk sat and stared silently at the countryside going by. Gagliano sat back, relaxed, only one hand on the wheel, as if he were tooling a convertible down a parkway. His own great bulk matched the truck's perfectly.

He noticed that Burk was silent.

"What's the matter, Ray?"

"Move over," Burk said. "Make room for a private."

"What the hell are you talking about?"

"I mean I couldn't take it no more," Burk said. "I mean I blew my stack at the bastard and now I'm gonna get busted."

"Now what's the sense in that?"

"Who knows what's the sense," Burk said. "The hell with it."

"He can't do that to you," Gagliano said.

"Can't he?"

They were approaching the rise of Montecatini Alto. Gagliano's great paw grabbed the gearshift almost viciously and his big left foot thundered on the steel floor of the cab as he double-clutched the truck down into a more powerful gear for the climb.

"Listen, Ray," he said, "you mean he's really gonna bust the first sergeant?"

"Yeah, he's gonna bust the first sergeant," Burk said. "Doesn't matter. I can't soldier under that guy neither."

On a curve, Gagliano looked in his side mirror and saw the

captain hugging the wheel, his little head barely coming over the windshield.

"If he busts the first sergeant this outfit won't be worth a hill of crud any more," Gagliano said.

"I know."

"The men won't be no good."

"I know."

"You're the only guy who's holding us all together now."

"Sure."

They were near the top of the rise. Far to the west, Burk saw the British two-forty batteries firing, tiny puffs of white issuing from their mouths, and then, seconds later, in the German territory below them, the sudden bloom of the burst, the fat black smoke that seemed to sit on the earth like a tumbleweed.

Gagliano's eyes narrowed. He geared down to third, and the truck nearly crawled to a stop.

"He ain't gonna bust you, Ray."

"No, of course not," said Burk, "and there ain't going to be no all-night fire mission, and jerry ain't going to fight no more, he's gonna come in my orderly room and say Burk, I surrender, and we're all gonna go home. Sure."

The captain's horn honked irritably, right behind them.

"All right, you bitch," Gagliano said. He let out the clutch and the truck tilted its flat snout and began to descend the mountain.

"Burk," he said, "just suppose this captain had to have a replacement, who would we get?"

Burk thought a moment. "We'd get our old exec, Lieutenant Tumpane," he said. "From the colonel's staff. He's the S-3 now. Look, knock it off, will you, Gag? Bastards like this never get killed."

The truck was gathering speed, impelled by its tonnage of high explosive.

"You know," Gagliano said, "I done a lot of crazy jobs

when I was a civilian. I ever tell you about that?"

"How you was a wrestler, how you was a longshoreman, how you was a lumberjack, sure," Burk said.

"Well, back in '36 I was in the lumber camps," Gagliano said. "They give me a job driving a truck, hauling one of them big trailers, where the logs are held together with chains."

Burk noticed their speed but he did not mention it. He knew Gag was a hell of a driver and he trusted him.

"You think it's bad with jerry shooting at you." Gagliano said. "You should ride one of them log trucks. Man, you pucker up all over. The camp was up in the mountains and we hauled the logs down a road just like this, into town."

"Watch the speed, Gag," Burk said.

"I seen a couple of guys who got into accidents," Gagliano said. "You know what them logs did? The chains couldn't hold them. They just smashed right into the cab and squashed them guys as flat as a hamburger."

"Hey Gag, for Christ's sake take it easy," Burk said.

"One day there I told the boss my brakes was gone and you know what he said? He said fine, then you'll just get there all the faster. And he give me a 50-dollar bonus. Well, you remember what it was like in '36. You'd do a lot more than that for 50 bucks."

"Gag, goddam it! Slow down!"

In the side mirror Gagliano saw that the captain was right on his tail, but the other trucks were still far up the mountain, making a slow, cautious descent. Now their truck was lurching like a toy being flipped by a giant hand.

"You really learned to handle a truck on them mountains," Gagliano said. Burk gritted his teeth and braced his feet against the fire wall.

Ahead of them was a sharp turn at whose apex was nothing —nothing but the map of north Italy, the little farms making a crazy-quilt pattern of color.

"Now you take a turn like that down there," Gagliano said,

"with a load in back of you, a good driver, he'll know just how to handle it . . ." and swiftly, he geared the hurtling monster down to more power and gunned the truck for all it was worth as they entered the turn.

The engine snarled as if it were alive and the truck yawed sickeningly but the increased speed made the tires bite surely into the pavement and a hundred yards beyond the curve Gagliano's hands and feet flew again and the truck shuddered to a stop.

He sat back and listened, a dreamy smile on his face. Burk opened his eyes.

Seconds went by.

And then, far, far below them, they heard an explosion that sounded like all the guns on the front firing at once.

"Now a driver who don't know nothing," Gagliano said, "on a turn like that he loses his head and listens to his impulses, and his impulses say step on the brake, and when he does that, he just keeps going straight ahead. See?"

The other trucks pulled up behind them. The men swarmed off and ran to peer over the cliff.

"Like I said, Sergeant Burk," said Gagliano, "it really takes a hell of a driver to handle a mountain."

"Like you said, Sergeant Gagliano," Burk said. "With all due respect."

THE DEVIL
TO PAY

BY STEPHEN BARR

British-born Stephen Barr came to the United States at the age of 18, met a girl who got him interested in book jacket illustration, and made his living as a commercial artist for many years. It was only later that he turned his hand to writing, which he found he could do with ease and profit. In addition to multiple stories for PLAYBOY, *his writing has appeared in* The Atlantic, Vogue, Harper's Bazaar, Mademoiselle *and all the better science-fiction magazines. He is a winner of the Ellery Queen Award. As you begin to read "The Devil to Pay," you may wonder why the story is in this book instead of in "The Playboy Book of Science Fiction and Fantasy"—but before you finish reading, you will know why.*

SIR SWITHIN MONTROSS arrived at the door of his house in a mood of ultimate frustration. He had lost at cards and at the races, he had failed at love and he was about to fail at business if he didn't watch his step. His golf was shot to hell. He went in and walked heavily to his study and, approaching the decanter tray, resolutely picked up a bottle of whiskey.

"I shouldn't do that if I were you," a voice behind him said.

Sir Swithin put the bottle down automatically and, turning around, saw, sitting in his winged leather chair, a stranger with rather noticeable eyebrows set at different levels.

"Who the devil are you, sir?" he inquired, "and how did you get in?"

"Forgive me for not rising," said the stranger, "I am . . . tired beyond all comprehension. I came to see you, Sir Swithin."

"Well, you see me, and now get out!" said Sir Swithin Montross, "or I shall call the police!"

The stranger continued to look at him—not smiling, not frowning, but almost as though he were weighing him. The confounded blackguard had a little goatee. Some kind of foreigner? Evening clothes, though. Goodish cut. "Did Soames let you in?" said Sir Swithin. "Because if he did——"

"No one let me in," the stranger said. "However, I am here and you and I might talk business. You have something I want."

"The silver?" sneered Sir Swithin, "or are you here to blackmail me?"

"Now please don't think anything so vulgar," said the stranger, "and *please* don't drink any more whiskey," he added as Sir Swithin reached for a glass and picked up the whiskey again. "It's very bad for you. Not that it's your body I'm interested in. . . ."

Sir Swithin poured himself an enormous amount of straight whiskey, and sat down. "Then, sir," he said, "what is it of mine you *are* interested in?"

The stranger smiled for the first time. "I really don't know how to answer you," he said. "Some things defy accurate definition." He let his voice stop and it echoed in the distant spheres.

"Sounds like a touch," Sir Swithin said, and drained his glass.

"No, I am not asking you to lend me money," said the stranger. "I am talking about something far less mundane—something you don't even know you have."

"Hah," said Sir Swithin, refilling his glass, "then I probably shan't miss it, eh?" He stood up, taking another glass. "Will you join me?"

"A little brandy, if you please," said the stranger, "neat."

Sir Swithin filled a glass and handed it to him. It went down the stranger's throat as though it had been poured onto a cinder pathway. "I think," said Sir Swithin, "that I know who you are."

The stranger nodded but this time he did not smile—his face was as bleak and cold as the surface of the moon.

"But you see," went on Sir Swithin, "you've come to the wrong shop. I have no soul." It was a pleasing thought and Sir Swithin forgot his troubles. "But supposing I had—what have you to offer me for it?"

"The usual things," said the stranger. "Not what you want, but what you think you want. Three things."

"Quite," said Sir Swithin, and refilled their glasses. "But tell me," he asked, "why is it always three wishes?"

"You have three things that trouble you, haven't you?"

"Well . . . Hm." Sir Swithin thought this over. The horses—yes, no one could be as good a judge of horseflesh as he and have such bad luck; and the same with cards—bad hands and worse partners. And his golf—it really came under the same heading, play, but here the trouble was different. He was the second best player in his club, and no effort on his part or variation in luck had ever caused him to beat Pillsbury. When the club champion was off his game so was Sir Swithin, and if Sir Swithin, owing to some vagary of the wind, achieved a three for the seventh hole, Pillsbury did an incredible two. Then Millicent, with her damned, beseeching come-on look that meant nothing. And business—that was worst of all.

"I make this offer to you, Sir Swithin: free and with no strings I will give you your first wish. Will that convince you?"

Montross looked at him narrowly. "Very handsome of you, I'm sure," he said. "Have to think it over for a bit." The first wish . . . which would that be? The race track, or golf? No—ridiculous. Millicent? Again no—anyway, she must do the wishing.

"Business," said the stranger.

"Good heavens!" exclaimed Sir Swithin. "You read my mind!"

"Absurd; cupidity was written all over your face. Make your wish."

Sir Swithin's mind spiraled amidst the unpromising possibilities of the stock exchange. He didn't need a wish—he needed information.

"Sell your mining shares," the stranger said. "All of them. Tomorrow morning, the moment the exchange opens."

"Then what do I do?"

"Get it in cash and be ready for the afternoon."

"What do I do in the afternoon?"

"Tomorrow is Derby Day—or had you forgotten? Put the money on Fox Fire—to win," said the stranger, and his eyes seemed to glow.

"But—but Fox Fire is a rank outsider!"

"Precisely," said the stranger, "17 to one. If you're careful and spread it around you shouldn't hurt the odds too much. And now I really must be going. I shall see you tomorrow evening." The stranger disappeared through the French windows into Sir Swithin's garden, and the sound of some exotic night bird came in from the darkness with the petrol fumes. Sir Swithin went upstairs to bed.

. . .

When he awoke the next morning he looked at his watch and jumped out of bed. Where was Soames? Why had he not wakened him? Where was his early-morning cup of tea? The answer—pinned to the door of the valet's empty bedroom—was quite explicit. "I cannot work for a man like you, Sir Swithin Montross," it said in cold type, "if you call yourself a man. You are not a person of whom I should care to have a reference from."

"The man's mad," Sir Swithin muttered, and went down to cope with the kitchen. Cook was on her day off and he would have to make his own breakfast, but he gave it up when he found that every egg in the larder was addled. After a cup of black coffee—the cream had soured—he started for the city in his little Bentley, but his heart pounded like a triphammer and he went instead to Harley Street. Here he was examined and frowned over.

"Remember what I told you about the whiskey?" said the specialist.

"Shchah!" said Sir Swithin, and took the pill he was given. He drove to the city and his heart was calmer now—no doubt the pill. Selling his mining shares was rather fun, and so was getting the cash: everyone looked shocked. He was feeling pretty well and decided to ring up Millicent, the dear girl. He went to a telephone booth in Cornhill and called her number. She answered, herself—immediately.

"Hello, Millicent," he said to her, "this is Wuggy. . . ."

"Oh!" she replied, "*ugh!*"

"Why, what's the matter?"

"How *dare* you call me!" she said. "You're the most heartless man I ever *knew*! You're . . . you're *soulless*!"

"But, Millicent!" Sir Swithin said anxiously, "I only wanted to——"

"I won't talk to you!" she said. "I never want to see you again, ever! Don't call me—ever!" The phone went dead, and so did Sir Swithin's spirit. He staggered out of the phone booth and drove unsteadily to the golf links. When he got to the clubhouse he looked around for Pillsbury and saw a tall, thin figure standing at the bar. He went to him and slapped him on the shoulder.

"How about a game, old bean?" he said.

"Why," said the other, turning around, "I should be simply delighted!" It wasn't Pillsbury, though. It was the club dud. They looked rather alike from behind, actually.

It was too late to draw back and Sir Swithin got his clubs from the locker room and followed him out to the first tee. Well, if he couldn't have a game with Pillsbury at least he could give this fool a lesson. But from the first to the 18th hole every shot he made went wrong. In driving he sliced, in his approach shots he hooked—nothing went right except the putting, but by then it was too late and the club dud beat him.

Back in the clubhouse he had a whiskey and soda, and made one more try at calling Millicent, but as soon as she heard his voice she hung up.

Then it was time for the Derby.

He got into his Bentley and drove to the track. Within half an hour he had placed his bets and the odds had dropped to eight to one. Within another half hour the favorite had run out and Fox Fire had won by three lengths. Sir Swithin collected his unseemly winnings and drove back to London, but what good to him now was all this money? Without Millicent to share his good fortune? And *what* had happened to his golf?

He drove to the garage to park the car, and the owner on seeing him came out with a piece of paper in his hand. "Your bill, Sir Swithin," he said with repugnance.

"But it's not the first of the month yet!" said Sir Swithin.

"No, sir. But I want no more of your trade," replied the

owner, turning away. "Keep your car elsewhere," he added over his shoulder and slammed the door. Sir Swithin blinked and drove to a parking lot. Then he went to his club on foot—perhaps a game of bridge would soothe him.

As he walked into the noble Georgian hallway the porter looked at him with dismay and disappeared into the office. In a moment he reappeared, accompanied by the club secretary who glared at Sir Swithin as though he were a filterable virus.

"Why have you come here, Montross?" he said coldly.

"Why have I . . . But . . ." Sir Swithin felt dizzy.

"Since you are no longer a member of the club, I think you had better go," said the secretary, and turned away.

Sir Swithin found himself on the pavement outside. He felt crushed and abandoned and his heart was pounding again. Too unsure of himself to hail a cab, he walked miserably home. The cook was not yet back—instead he found a note for him on the kitchen table when he went in search of her, but he could not bring himself to read it. When he got to his study he made directly for the whiskey decanter.

"Only a short one," said a voice behind him.

He turned and saw the stranger, who looked at him with the compassion of a vivisectionist. "I see Fox Fire won," said the stranger. "Did you get your bets down all right?"

"Yes," said Sir Swithin Montross, "Fox Fire won—and so have you." He sat down and covered his face with his hands. "I won't go through with it," he said between his fingers. "You must let me off."

"My dear sir," said the stranger, "your first wish was granted, was it not? So let us proceed to business."

"No, no!" cried Sir Swithin, "I won't. You . . . you must cancel it! I don't want any more wishes, I want to go back to the way things were!"

"I think things have gone a little too far for that, don't you?" said the stranger. "Play the man, Master Montross; at least now you must be convinced you have a soul."

"I tell you I don't care whether I have or not!" Sir Swithin said. "You said there'd be no strings attached—take back the first wish, and set me free."

"The strings applied to your soul, you know," said the stranger, "and I shan't take that; but I can't very well cancel the past."

"You can, you must!" said Sir Swithin desperately, and, getting up, he drew his swollen wallet from his pocket and threw it on the table between them. "Take it—take back the money and give me back my life as it was! It was bad—it had its little defects, I grant you, but it wasn't as bad as this!"

"Well," the stranger said with reluctance.

"Take it, I beseech you!" Sir Swithin pushed the wallet toward him. The stranger stood up and shrugged, and his shoulders seemed like those of a bat. He took the wallet and shook his head, then without another word he walked out of the room. Sir Swithin heard the front door open and close, but there was no sound of footsteps from outside.

. . .

"Well, here's the cash," the stranger was saying a few minutes later to two friends. "If I'd only had the capital I'd have done it myself—but I hadn't. Anyway, this was safer: no risk. All right now—one share for you," he handed a packet of currency to one of the men. "That takes care of fixing his golf clubs. Have any trouble?"

"Nah. I opened the locker with a hairpin. Tilted the heads a little—that's all there was to it. Thanks."

"And one share for you, Joe. I must congratulate you on your ingenuity with the, er, servant problem."

"Thanks, boss. The cook's visiting her married sister in Brixton who's going to turn out to not be sick, and his valet's sleeping it off at a friend's."

"Poor fellow," said the stranger approvingly, "he'll be all right tomorrow morning. And the remaining three shares I will take. Now, gentlemen," he said, as the others looked up with resentment, "take it easy! Who thought up this scheme? Who wrote the notes from Soames and the cook? Who wrote the letter of insulting resignation to his club? Who had the idea of the indecent phone call to the garageman's wife—and in Sir Swithin's voice? Could either of you have imitated him well enough?" He looked at his friends, and it was plain they could not have.

"Could either of you have written so convincingly caddish a letter to his girl? Absurd! And the rotten eggs and the spoiled cream? Clever little touches, those. No, my friends, I am not grasping, but I think I have earned my three shares." He got up and looked at himself in the mirror appraisingly.

"When are you going to shave off that lousy beard?" one of his friends said. "You look like hell in it."

"D'you know, I think I'll keep it," the stranger said, turning this way and that. "I've rather grown to like it."

HARPY

BY T. K. BROWN III

Peripatetic T. K. Brown may be anywhere on the globe at this moment. In our last communiqué from him, he casually said, "Been traveling around (Oaxaca, Canary Islands, Spain, Germany) and writing stories. Plan to spend a month in Burgundy, helping to harvest the grapes; then probably to Kenya for the winter." Prior to this burst of wanderlust, he owned and operated a motel in the Florida keys, catering to the needs of other travelers, but 1960's Hurricane Donna swept his hostelry into the sea. He possesses degrees from four universities and has been a professor of English, French, Spanish and German. His stories have been honored in several award anthologies, including "O. Henry Prize Stories." Read now his beautifully wrought story of a man who owns and is owned by two varieties of "Harpy."

THE VAST AREA known as the great plains of the United States is a belt about six hundred miles wide between the Mississippi River and the mountains of Wyoming and Colorado. An ocean of land, mostly flat, sometimes with waves of hills, it rises in swells to the west, a dozen feet to the mile, league after league of earth becoming gradually more arid, until it is a mile above the sea. And then suddenly, west of Denver, it gives up its gradual climb. The escarpments of the Rocky Mountains burst from the plain and leap into the air, tier upon tier as far as the eye can reach, to snow and glacier.

The first row of these tremendous hills is known as the Rampart Range. Over the crest of this range, in the trough between it and the higher one beyond, lived a man who had got rid of his woman who was bad for him, had manned an eagle, and had found himself.

. . .

He was on the side lawn, by the hawk house, the peregrine on his glove and tearing the pigeon from his fingers, when he saw the convertible speeding up the valley toward the house, a plume of dust behind it. He knew immediately who was driving the convertible and that this was the difficult hour he had been expecting for almost a year. He eased the bird to the perch, where, with the food under her foot, she continued to pluck and rend. He limped down the slope to the driveway. As the car pulled around the circle he saw that she was wearing the green Alpine hat with the rakish white feather, his gift to her in Innsbruck. What had he said to her then, those three thousand years ago? *To Marian, maid, in everlasting; from Robin.* Well, it was typical of her to wear it now.

He was at the car when it stopped.

"Good afternoon, Marian," he said, without smiling. "Are you planning on a little visit? I see you have two bags in the back seat."

A little frown crossed her face and he knew he had disrupted the opening lines she had been rehearsing all the way from Denver.

He continued: "You would come back, you said, when I asked you to come back, and not before. But I have not asked you to come back. Why are you here?"

She got slowly from the car, with the ancient grace and easy command that now no longer commanded him; and when she was standing even with him on the lawn her huge eyes searched his face, trying to pierce him, and then dropped to his leg.

"You sent for me," she said, and raised her hand a little from her side, to point where she was looking. "That happened to you day-before-yesterday, about three. Oh Robin, it came to me that you'd been hurt, as clearly as if you'd sent me a wire. I thought at first a car had hit you, but then I knew it wasn't that. But something dark and heavy and dangerous hitting you in the leg."

What she said was true, to the very hour. A sort of terror struck him, that he would never be free of this incredible woman whose intuition could reach out from a distance and fiercely take possession of him.

It must have shown in his face. "That's why I'm here," she said. "I had to come. If we still have this thing—Robin, *no other two people have this thing*. We can't just throw it away after a stupid quarrel. Or anyway, it isn't so bad that we shouldn't talk about it a little, is it?"

"You put me in a difficult position, Marian," he answered. "There's nothing to talk about. We had a good thing for a while, and it blew up, and there's nothing left of it except a lot of memories, some very good, some not so good. And," he added, "apparently this crazy radar of yours."

" 'A good thing for a while,' " she quoted, letting her eyes go damp and tender. "Robin, how can you put it like that? For three years we were *one person*. One person in two bodies."

"Yes," he said. "You were the person, I was one of the bodies."

"You say there's nothing to talk about. But you see, we are talking already, and on a very essential level. Robin, let me stay for a few days."

He knew he had nothing to lose, and it was easier than being cruel. He turned and called, "John!"

John appeared at the door of the hawk house. He was a young man of 20 and a full-blooded Cheyenne. His grandfather, when a boy of 16, had helped cut down Custer on the Little Big Horn, and John's father, on the reservation in South Dakota, still had a pair of cavalry boots and some ancient dollar bills to prove it. John had gone to a white grammar school; later he had worked in a gas station outside Denver, where Robin had found him and made him his foreman. "John," Robin said, "come get Miss Marian's bags please, and ask Mrs. Emlen to take her to her old room. And tell Mrs. Emlen we'll have cocktails in about half an hour."

John came slowly down the slope, wiping his hands on a rag that he then put in his hip pocket. His eyes said nothing as he hoisted the bags from the back seat.

"Hello, John," Marian said. "How have you been?"

"The Cooper's is still bating," John said to Robin. "Been throwing itself off the perch all day. Nothing I can do will stop it."

"Don't worry about it," Robin said. "They get these spells."

Marian had started up the lawn toward the house.

"That woman's no good for you, boss," John said.

"She won't be here long," Robin said. "Now take those bags in while I finish feeding the peregrine, and we'll have a look at the Cooper's hawk. Maybe there's a scrap of meat in the mews that is setting her off."

.   .   .

In the living room with the two picture windows, one giving on the shadowed valley, one showing now the stark outline of the mountains against the sunset, she had taken up her old position on the couch, legs stretched out on it, back pillowed against the arm; and she was balancing her drink on her knee.

"Robin," she asked, "what was it that hurt your leg?"

He was at the bar stirring a martini. "An eagle," he said, without turning. "I have manned an eagle." Now he limped over and took the armchair. "Vicious creature—maybe you'll see her tomorrow. I was training her to the lure—a rabbit. She hit it fine. I let her take a few bites and then made in to her, to get her back on the glove. I guess she was feeling ornery. Anyway, one lunge and she had her talons in my thigh. Touch and go there for a minute. Lucky thing I had my leather apron on. But it'll be all right in a couple of days."

She was staring at him in amazement. "You?" she said. "You are training an eagle? But that's impossible!"

"Not at all," he replied. "Quite a few eagles have been manned for hunting. To be sure, very few of this particular brand of eagle."

"I don't mean that," she said. "I mean, *you*. You were always so shocked by violence and cruelty . . . so afraid of it," she stated.

"Yes," he said calmly. "Well, yes. Afraid is the word for a lot of things I was of. It feels very good to be out of that dismal swamp at last."

"Afraid of me, Robin?" she whispered.

"Of course I was afraid of you," he said strenuously. "Afraid of you most of all. You embodied everything that was wrong with my life. It was so easy to go along with the way you wanted things—so easy and so pleasant. The trouble was that it made me hate myself. Well, I've got away from that."

"I have never meant you any harm, Robin," she said. "You know that." She was looking not at him but at the drink balanced on her knee. Now she twitched her kneecap and caught the glass as it slid into her waiting hand. "We had something very wonderful. If I've come back, it's not to truss you up and carry you off. It's to find out, I guess, how tough a fight it will be to get that thing back. And maybe we'll never get it back —I've faced that, too."

She turned her head and stared at him and said strongly, "It wasn't easy for me to come back, Robin. Even when I got the message about your hurt my first reaction was, let him come to me. But I couldn't live with that. That was small, that was pride. So I came to you."

"Wearing that Tyrolean hat," he interjected, "with all its cargo of nostalgia and tender memory. Was that necessary? Wasn't that a bit phony?"

"No!" she cried. "That was to remind you of what we were in danger of losing!"

"Well, it reminded me," he said. "Marian, do you remember when my firm was invited to bid on that housing project in Colombo, Ceylon? And you talked me out of it—such a long way to go, such a small chance of getting the contract? So we went skiing in Austria. Do you remember the million-dollar shopping center in Atlanta we might have got? But it was such a filthy climate in August, you said. So we stayed in bed and had champagne for breakfast. And how many other times when you tempted me to make the less responsible choice. Well, that's what I'm in danger of losing. I've got the architect business back on a sound footing now. I give it my time and it gives me money and spiritual satisfaction. No green hat is going to change my mind about whether I am losing something or gaining something."

"Goodness, Robin," she said in a tiny voice. "You do sound determined. Will you call the constable and have me put out?"

"No," he said. "I'm not afraid of you any more."

. . .

She visited him that night.

He was lying awake, letting his mind stray up and down their last furious quarrel and parting, hearing again the final things he had said—weighing them in his emotions, to make sure that they still rang sound, and finding no regret, no wish to turn back. She opened his door softly, uninvited by any word or nuance, and came to his bed. She was naked.

"For auld lang syne, Robin, it would be sweet to lie with you again."

She took her place beside him; she simply took it. And—was it reflex? was it something stronger?—he put his arms around her.

"Ah, Robin!" she said. "I know you must have been thinking about us. Baby, let it simmer awhile on the back of the stove. It will smooth out and the answers will come."

"The answers have already come," he said.

She began to search his face with her mouth: his forehead, the verge of his hair, his eye, his nostril, his lips. "Yes," she whispered. "Maybe. Oh, Robin!"

And she did her best to put sand under all his foundations in that hour.

. . .

She was gay at breakfast. Apparently she felt that she had gained command. "What are we going to do today, darling?" she asked.

"I don't know what you may choose to do," he said, "but I have a day's hard work at the drawing board with two clients and shan't be back till dinner."

"Clients? In Denver?"

"Oh, I forgot, that happened after you left. I've moved the firm up here into the woods. We have quite a plant half a mile up the road—office building, guest house, and quarters for the staff. Very fine advertisement for the sort of buildings we can design. We still have a small liaison office in Denver, but now the customers come to us."

"I see," she said. She laughed nervously. "I guess it was stupid of me to think everything would be the same. After all, it's been nearly three years. I mean, you taking it easy in your eyrie up here, while the business went on by its own momentum. Somehow I got the idea from what you said yesterday that training this eagle was your life."

"It's my hobby, not my life," he said. "What ever gave you that crazy idea? Since you left I've become a working man."

He took the car up the road to the office. By noon he had sewed up the contract for the restaurant in Colorado Springs. The other client telephoned to say he would have to postpone his visit for a week. Robin had lunch with Alison in her apartment, one of the compound of units for the staff. She was a lean, blonde type, smart, hired as a draftsman but obviously destined for higher status. They had been to bed a few times— nothing serious, but she had attained the right to ask questions.

"The grapevine has it that your old flame is back," she said. This was a question.

"Just for a day or two," he answered. "Just a visit."

"Uh-huh," she said. "Sort of nostalgia for the scene of ancient conquest? Like Legionnaires going back in middle age to Château-Thierry to see all the crosses?"

"That's about it," he said. "Nothing to get excited about."

"I'll scratch her goddamn eyes out if I get close enough to," Alison said.

"Tut tut," he said. "Play it cool."

He took a look around after lunch: everything was moving smoothly and there was nothing urgent on his desk. He found his afternoon free. He drove back and found Marian sitting in a chaise longue in front of the house. She jumped up when she saw him. "You're early," she said.

"Yes. A client failed to show. That gives me time today to get some food for my birds with John. You don't have to come."

"But I'd love to come," she said. "On horse?"

"On horse," he said. "You won't like it."

"I'll get ready," she said.

Half an hour later they were walking toward the hawk house. She was again wearing the magic green hat. John had already saddled two of the three horses and was standing with them in the drive. The third horse had only bit and reins.

"Does he still show off with that bareback routine?" she asked. "I wish you'd get rid of that savage."

"He says a Plains Indian doesn't need a saddle and he's right. Call it showing off if you wish."

"Why are we going to the potting shed?" she asked.

"It's where I keep my birds now," he replied. "The magnificent peregrine you saw yesterday, a merlin, a Cooper's hawk, a prairie falcon, a little burrowing owl I threw a net over before he could get back into his hole; and my eagle."

He pushed open the door and they entered. The birds sat in a row on a long two-by-four with burlap wrapped around it and hanging to the floor. As they went in, the birds stirred; all but the burrowing owl, which stared at them stupidly, the way an owl should. The merlin, as they approached, moved his head in quick small swings, bright-eyed, and opened his beak wide to emit one thin weak cry, almost a squeak. The prairie falcon moved his feet about as if trying to find a comfortable stance, stepping on his swivel and the leash that tied it to the screen perch.

"Hello, girls and boys," Robin said, his face lighting up. He went to the prairie falcon and extended his forefinger. The falcon reached out and took the tip of his finger gently in his beak, and immediately let go. He smiled. "That's their greeting in the wild, beak to beak."

Marian was looking about with distaste. On the workbench and hanging on the walls were dozens of leather articles, strips of rawhide, hoods with gaudy pompons, leashes, cans of disinfectant, insecticide; the floor was littered with bits of pigeon feathers. In her nose was a smell of leather, blood, and something peppery. "What's that nasty odor?" she asked.

"Dried excrement, mainly."

Suddenly the Cooper's hawk bated, banging her wings against the perch. She lunged into the air to the full length of her jesses again and again, recoiling each time to the same balanced stance. As suddenly as she had begun she stopped; flicked a wing to compose a feather; sat quietly. Clouds of dust rose from the floor; the peppery smell got stronger.

"Exercise," he said. "John thought there was something wrong, but it's only that she hasn't been flown for a week."

"Is that why you keep it behind a wall from the others? Because of this insane flapping? God, what a madhouse!"

A piece of plywood astride the perch separated the Cooper's from the others.

"She's an Accipiter," he said. "The Accipiters are killers, all the time. If she could look down the perch and see four potential victims, and not be able to get to them when she got the urge, she would go crazy and kill herself in a frenzy."

"That would be perfectly OK by me," Marian said. "Filthy blood-thirsty creatures."

"You don't care for my birds?" he said. "Well, come have a look at the eagle." He led her into the back part of the shed, which was partitioned off. The eagle sat on a perch of her own like an enormous croquet wicket. She had been resting almost vertical; now she leaned forward, watching. She shifted on her perch with a faint plucking of talons on burlap and a larger sound of pinions rustling as she raised her wings and shook herself like a dog and seemed to settle herself more comfortably in her harsh feathers. The fearless blank keen soulless eyes observed each move they made. Marian looked at her with loathing.

"Robin!" she said. "You are training this monster? Have you lost your senses completely?"

He went up to the bird and knocked its beak with his knuckle. The eagle dodged and lifted one tremendous horned foot from the hoop. "Ah, none of that," he said. "You put those hooks into me last week and that's enough for a while." The eagle settled back on her perch, never for one instant letting her gaze leave his eyes.

"The harpy eagle of South America," he said proudly. "Larger than the golden, and more dangerous. It fears nothing, has never had to learn the value of fear. And I've trained the beast to obey my will and come to my glove and to hunt for me. We took five coyotes in the week before my accident."

"And to rip your leg open," she said, "and maybe your eyes or your throat next time." Her face was white. "Something has gone wrong inside you, Robin, to have dealings with this ugly creature. This is not you at all. This is insane!"

She looked at the harpy eagle with abhorrence. Its great hooked beak, with the nostril slits, pointed toward her; the cruel eyes watched her slightest move. A double crest of feathers crowned the head. Worst of all were the feet: monstrous, impossible killers, as big in themselves as the owl she had just seen, hooked and deadly, six inches across. This was what had caused her that terrible fright, that afternoon, when she knew Robin had been hurt. She looked at him now with horrid surmise.

"You have changed, Robin," she whispered, "since you let me go."

"Oh yes," he said. "I have changed, all right. Now let's get the peregrine and go out for the food."

Back in the main part of the shed he took the peregrine's hood from its hook. The bird dodged once or twice but made no serious effort to avoid having it placed on her head. He got his gauntlet from the workbench and put it on. He untied the leash from where it was tied under the beam, through a hole in the burlap screen, and nudged the falcon onto his glove, gripping the swivel between thumb and forefinger and wrapping the leash around his other three fingers. They left the hawk house and went to the horses. The bird balanced on the glove with ease, dipping and bowing, her enameled feet set wide apart.

"You have the bag and the tape, John?" he asked.

"You know I have, boss," the Indian answered. He looked without expression at the woman, and there was hostility in the very absence of expression and in the omission of any greeting.

They mounted—Robin from the wrong side because of the bird on his left arm, John in one leap to the bare back of his animal, only Marian in the orthodox way. They set off up the trail behind the house.

"Let's go up on the ridge and look around," Robin said, after they had passed the complex of office and dwellings. "See what activity we find near that patch of alders at the brook, maybe."

"Better we keep to the bushes," John said. "Otherwise the birds all hide in the trees and I gotta climb."

They trotted up the path until it got too steep; then the horses walked. Robin made conversation. "This bird is without much question the most perfect creature ever fashioned. *Falco peregrinus*, which no one below the rank of earl could own in olden times. When this bird is aloft, all other life falls still. They've clocked it at two hundred and seventy miles per hour. Nothing in the air can escape it."

"Not even that damnable eagle?" Marian asked.

Robin laughed. "We're going to find that out tomorrow. Oh, what a battle that will be." He dropped his reins and stroked the falcon's back. "Wanderer," he said gently, "shall you kill my eagle, or will my eagle kill you? One of you will die."

"It's a shame, boss," John said. "You shouldn't do it. They're both fine birds."

"I have to know about the eagle," Robin said. "I have to know how much she has in her."

"She's not built to fight falcons," the Indian said, "and no natural falcon would ever go after her. It's a waste and a shame."

"I have to know what that eagle has in her," Robin repeated with great vigor. "Don't you understand? If she wins against the falcon she is the mightiest creature in the world."

"And you are its master," Marian said. "Is that it?"

"Yes," he said. "I guess that's it."

"How wrong!" she exclaimed. "Oh, how *wrong*!"

They came up over the crest of the Rampart Range and reined in. The slope dropped off steeply before them, a scraggy talus of runty trees and sagebrush, down to the plain that spread itself in a great semicircle to the horizon. Far off, a patch of haze announced the existence of Denver. A highway strung itself through the middle distance. At their backs the hills rose, leap on leap, becoming mountains, lean and formidable.

John urged his horse past the others until he had the lead, and took them to the left. They rode for another half a mile, hardly speaking. "This is a good place," he said.

They dismounted in a loose thicket of scrub maple, where birds were seen flitting and passing by. Robin detached the swivel and the leash from the jesses, and lifted off the hood. The peregrine seemed to frown and stared sharply in all directions. Then, with great strokes of her wings, she lifted herself to the top of the air and circled, studying what was below her with head movements to the left and right. Now suddenly she stooped, sculling with her wings in a dive of unbelievable speed at a jay. The jay fled headlong into a bush —simply crashed into it at full throttle and disappeared. The falcon veered away at the last possible moment and rang up to pitch again.

"OK, John, let's get that one," Robin said.

"How do you know he can get that one?" Marian demanded angrily. "That bird isn't hurt."

"Watch," Robin said. John went to the bush. The bird was crouching under a branch. He reached in and picked it up: it made no effort to escape. He stripped off a length of masking tape and passed it once around the jay, trussing its wings, and dropped it into the sack.

"No bird will fly or even move," Robin said, "when a peregrine is on the hunt. These trees and bushes are full of frozen birds. And John here is the best frozen-bird-thawer west of the Denver supermarkets."

"And you feed these helpless creatures later to your predators?" she said. "You just take their lives away, like that? For shame! And your name is a bird's name, too."

"Oh, come off it, Marian," he said.

While she stayed with the horses the two men made their way back and forth through the underbrush, with the falcon wheeling overhead. Now and again they reached into the leaves and took out warm frightened life. Once a song sparrow made a dash for it and rose above the bushes. The peregrine stooped on it instantly and struck it in flight. There was a small explosion in the air: feathers burst from the stricken sparrow and it dropped dead to the ground. The falcon dropped also and stood on her quarry. While she was plucking, John made in to her with a scrap of red meat, got his hand between her and the sparrow, and palmed the sparrow when the falcon raised her head to swallow the meat. Then, seeing no more to eat, she went aloft again. After that no bird moved except one magpie that, seeing the falcon darting close, ran up John's pants leg. John took it out and taped it and put it in the bag.

When the area was clean of birds they went back to the horses and Robin tied the dead sparrow to a length of string. Giving a strong call, he swung it in circles about his head. The peregrine dived at once and hit it as it fell to the ground. After a leisurely proud gaze in all directions she bent her head between her hunched shoulders and began to feed.

"Lucky no bird took off down the slope," John said. "We'd be looking for the hawk the rest of the day."

"How many did we get?"

"Fifteen, twenty."

"That's a day's work," Robin said. He went to the falcon and got his gloved hand under the prey, and the bird on his fist. While she fed he attached the swivel and leash to the jesses. After a moment, when she lifted her head to gulp the meat, he removed what was left of the food and replaced the hood.

"I told you you wouldn't like it," he said as they rode back down the trail.

"*You*," she said. "You, taking pleasure in this. That's what sticks in the craw."

"We'll be having chicken for dinner," he said. "How do you like it? Fried? Broiled? Delicious either way. You killed that chicken, you know. You're a carnivore, a predator. What's so different about what you saw this morning? Some butcher feeds you; I feed my birds. What's so different?"

"Being the butcher is what is so different," she said. She reined her horse to a stop. "Robin, let those birds go."

He reined in also; and the Indian, who was leading, rode on a dozen paces and then drew up. He swung about and sat on his horse backwards, watching with a sort of impassive insolence for what the scene would unfold. He had the bag of birds over his shoulder.

"Let them go?" Robin said. "You are sentimental about birds? My hawks are birds too. Creatures of instinct. They can't help it if they need other birds to eat. You'll be eating a bird pretty soon."

"Robin," she cried, bursting into tears, "don't torment me! Let those poor creatures go!"

He saw her cringing in her saddle, hiding her weeping eyes, and he asked himself: is this the woman it cost me such pains to cast off?

"Oh, hell," he said. "John, turn them loose."

John, who could convey contempt without moving a muscle of his face, opened the sack and poured the birds to the ground. Trussed, they tumbled plop plop. She let out a small scream as they fell. Scattered on the ground they cocked their heads this way and that with desperate beady eyes.

"I let them loose, boss," John said.

"Wise guy. Take the tapes off."

John slid off his horse and knelt to the birds. He took the tape from a robin, not carelessly. The tape was covered with feathers and the bird was unable to fly. It fluttered to a bush, and to another: getting away from that hawk. John looked up, not at Robin but at the girl.

"You want the weasels to get these birds, is that it?" he asked.

With a sob she spurred her horse down the hill and out of sight. John began to put the birds back into the sack. "That woman is a damned fool, boss," he said.

"I know it," Robin said. "She'll go away pretty soon."

. . .

Marian stayed in her room the rest of the afternoon; but it was clearly no part of her plan to go away pretty soon: Robin saw her peering from an upstairs window while he gave the eagle a workout on the lawn. It was an exercise in training the harpy to come to the glove on the call, and to correct her habit of coming in low, with talons aimed at his belly. For working the eagle he had a special gauntlet, a lacrosse glove with two layers of horsehide up to the elbow and steel chain mail between them; and even so, when the eagle came in by the book and grasped his arm in those giant feet that completely circled it, it was always as if he were the prey. When the eagle shifted her stance, picked a foot up and set it down, even in this casual shuffling there was a shearing action that could snap his arm, he knew, if the eagle were the least bit careless about letting go with her foot before she picked it up. And the damned bird had tried to kill him less than a week ago. So it was a pretty tense operation, scooping the eagle up when she came in too low, as she mostly did, and knowing he could get a broken arm or a perforated gut on the next try. And it didn't help any to see Marian up at the window, hating him for whatever proficiency he had and hoping the worst, so that she would have an excuse to take over. What the hell was she doing here, anyway? Whatever tenderness she may have elicited from him last night, she must know she wasn't wanted. She had her intuition to tell her that. Well, one thing he was sure of: there would be no midnight visit tonight.

But in this he was wrong. She came again, as before, and dropped to her knees at the bedside; and this time she had assumed her penitent guise, the little-girl routine he knew so well.

"Robin," she said in her little voice. "I was wrong. I don't understand what you are doing, but I was wrong to take the attitude I did and I am sorry. And I will try to understand. May I come into your bed?" With astonishment he became aware that she thought that this morning's events were part of the old familiar fabric: she had "won" when he had told John to set the birds loose.

"And take the warm part again?" he asked. "No. Go around to the cold side."

This was precisely in the style she had chosen, and she rose and crept around the foot of the bed, the moonlight catching a glimpse of her breasts and flank; and crawled in on the cold side with a calculated shiver, and lay with her back toward him. She waited for his hand to slip over her side and up over the ridge of her ribs to her breast, but he had decided to let her carry the ball she had put into play, and did nothing whatsoever. After a moment she flipped over to face him and, as had always been her way, took over. Her technique was excellent. Later she lit two cigarettes at once, passed one to him, and made her play to nail him to her cross.

"Darling," she said, "do you remember? That used to be always the thing we did after our loving. One of us would light them both and give one to the other. Oh, I remember all the times! Once, on Lake Como, the moon was just coming up behind the hills across the water and we went out on the balcony to enjoy it. Do you remember?"

"I remember," he said. "It was very pretty."

"Robin," she said, "couldn't we go back to Como and Venice and Salzburg and Ravello and Villefranche and Toledo?"

"Toledo, Ohio?" he asked. "No springs?"

"Idiot," she said. She leaned over to kiss him and it was no accident that her breast grazed, and was then squashed down on, the hand he had laid on his chest. "Visit those places again; give ourselves a chance to discover each other again?"

"No," he said, "we couldn't do that."

He could feel a little stiffening in all her muscles.

"How can I leave here?" he went on. "Don't you realize that I have a profession to attend to? It's a big operation now, with eight full-time employees."

"You had the same profession three years ago," she said. "It didn't keep you from enjoying life."

"I'm enjoying life right here and now," he replied. "I like my job and the people I have around me and my surroundings and my hobby. I haven't got anything to run away from."

She got off his chest. "What you like most, I think, is feeding songbirds to your birds of prey."

"You are wrong," he said. "I do not enjoy that part of it at all. But I will say that it gives me satisfaction to have manned a harpy eagle." He paused a moment. "In the entire history of man not a dozen people have taught a harpy to obey them. It has been a tremendous experience to pull off that accomplishment. It has illuminated qualities I didn't even know I had in me."

"It is you who are wrong," she said. "Oh Robin, I know you so much better than you know yourself!"

"I think not," he said.

. . .

But the experiences of that night must have left her with the belief that she held the upper hand, because early the next morning she took it upon herself to fire the Indian, and even to call a cab from Denver to take him away. When the car arrived there was considerable confusion, with John contemptuous of the whole idea and the cabby wanting to know who was going to pay him for his trip. Robin came down from his bedroom into the midst of it and learned with surprise and anger what had happened.

"After his gross insolence yesterday," Marian tried to explain, "it seemed perfectly obvious that there was nothing else to do."

Robin paid the driver and sent him back down the valley. Then he turned on her with fury. "What in the name of God do you think you're doing?" he cried. "Do you suppose you can simply move in here and make dispositions over my household? I should have held that cab for you"—and he waved and shouted at the retreating vehicle, quite forgetting that her own car was in the garage. She had turned very pale and was watching him with great smouldering eyes. He said to John, "Come on, let's get the birds ready," and strode off toward the mews, barely limping now, and left her seething in the ruin of her enterprise. Inside the shed he looked at the Indian for the first time. "Forget it. Put it out of your mind. I'll handle that end of things. I'm sorry. OK?"

"OK, boss," John said. His eyes flickered with some Indian emotion.

Robin said, "I haven't had breakfast yet. Saddle my horse and tie the telescope on behind. Let the peregrine take a good look at the eagle; then put the hood on and take her down the hill. By the time you have her down on the plain, where I showed you, at the point of the spur, I'll have the eagle on the bluff. When I give the arm signal, strike the hood. Have you got your binoculars?"

The Indian pointed to the bench where they lay.

"Good," Robin said. "I'm going to mount the telescope on the bluff. It's up to you to follow them underneath if they move across country. If they move into the mountains, I'll ride up to some bald spot where the winner can see the lure when I swing it. What do you think?"

"I think you are wasting a good bird either way," the Indian said. "Maybe both. I give it to the falcon. Nothing can get out of the way of that falcon."

"I'll bet you your horse," Robin said, "against two months' wages, that the eagle wins."

The Indian's eyes flickered again. "You mean it would be my horse? My own horse?"

"And I'll keep on feeding it as long as you're here."

"You got a bet," John said. He almost smiled.

Robin went back to the house. Marian was on the terrace, where his breakfast was laid out. He expected to make the arrangements for her departure immediately but, as he might have known, she took the initiative.

"Robin!" she said, with no preliminary. "How could you do that to me? Oh Robin, how could you? I can't take that sort of treatment, you know. From you! I was doing what had to be done and you humiliated me in front of that—that negligible person."

"We will not even discuss it," he said; and his tone must have conveyed an authority that was new to her, for she seemed almost to shrink back. "You were as wrong as it is possible to be wrong. You do not understand the terms under which you are here, and I am sorry to be so inhospitable as to suggest that you make plans to return to Denver this afternoon or tomorrow morning."

"Robin!" she whispered.

"I'm sorry," he repeated, "but that's the way it's going to be."

He left his breakfast untouched and went to the kitchen, where he found a chunk of cheddar in the refrigerator and ignored Mrs. Emlen's plaintive cries. Chewing on it he went out the back door to the mews, gathered up his gear, and hooded the eagle. Every time he handled the great bird the excitement was like the first time, and now it was enhanced by his knowledge of what was to come.

"Old girl," he said, "mighty creature, will you leave the sky alive today, or dead?" The harpy shrugged her wings and turned her horrid beak this way and that in her blindness. Robin detached the leash from the perch, got the eagle on his arm, and went outside to his horse, which rolled its eyes toward the bird and trembled but had been trained also and did not bolt.

The saddle was rigged with a bar projecting upward and outward from near the stirrup and topped with a semicircular arm rest. After Robin had mounted he placed this bar in position and laid his arm across it. In this way he was able to sustain the eagle's twenty pounds while holding her at a distance. The alternative would have been to brace his elbow against his side, and no one who has had any dealings with eagles would wish to have those talons so close to his body.

He set off slowly up the trail, keeping a sharp eye on the eagle as she teetered with the motion of the horse. Their progress was slow; John would already be at the foot of the range, waiting with the falcon.

He heard a horse coming up behind; turning, he saw Marian trotting toward him. Incredible woman, she had put her magic green hat on her head again and was going to pretend that nothing had happened. She came up beside him and reined in to a walk.

"What a magnificent spectacle you make," she said, "riding with the eagle on your glove. Are you going to the battle of the giants?"

He could not recall another time when her behavior had been so transparent, and he felt shame for her.

"Of course you want the eagle to win," she went on. "That's why you're giving it the advantage of height. To dive down on the little bird."

It was not going to be possible to ignore her; he decided to make the best of it. "You will see. This mighty eagle, queen of the sky, when she sees that 'little bird' climbing toward her, will give up any thought of attack and will herself climb as fast as she is able. The head start is only to make the contest even. Up there in the thin air it will be the falcon that is above."

They came to the ridge; there was John, on his horse, far below, the bird on his wrist.

"The falcon has been trained to stoop on any bird in flight," Robin said, his voice thin with excitement. He dismounted carefully, undid the leash from the swivel, removed the hood, and cast the eagle to the air. She rose in two close spirals and rested, searching for prey. Robin signaled with his left arm; John loosed the peregrine and she rose powerfully up the slope. The eagle, which had tilted down to dive, seemed to recoil: she braked with her great wings, veered off to the right, and climbed steeply, circling in a wide sweep over the plain. The falcon too was spiraling upward, at an incredible rate, seemingly unaware of the eagle.

Robin unstrapped the telescope and mounted it on its tripod. It was a powerful Japanese instrument, binocular, giving an erect image at 120 diameters, with independent vertical and horizontal controls. He had also a pair of binoculars, with which he now followed the flight first of the eagle, then of the peregrine.

"Sometimes they pass quite close to each other," he reported. "They're ringing up over the plain, thank God. The eagle is a jungle bird and wouldn't naturally seek mountains. They're about a mile up and the falcon is gaining."

"This isn't what I expected at all," Marian said. "This seems a very tidy battle, with lots of fresh air between the combatants."

"Stop playing the fool," he said shortly. "One or both of these birds is about to die."

The birds were wheeling upward in wide circles, perhaps half a mile in diameter. Soon the range was too great for the seven-power binoculars and he ungallantly handed them to the girl. The telescope brought them close again. When they had risen about three miles, the falcon finally got on top.

"It must be a shocking experience for the eagle to be the prey," Robin said. "But that's what she is, and she knows it."

When her circle brought her back above the eagle, the falcon suddenly stooped, aiming herself like a bullet at the eagle's broad back. The eagle knew better than to try to evade the attack. Her beak parted in a scream as she rolled over and presented her talons to the diving peregrine and flew upside-down. The falcon veered aside at the last moment and began to ring up again in tight spirals. The eagle righted herself and climbed also.

The wind off the mountains carried them eastward as the falcon dived, and rang up, and stooped again and again. Each time the eagle turned upside-down; each time the falcon found no way to hit and tried again. They were losing altitude inexorably, and it was only a matter of time before the peregrine would force the eagle to the ground and be able to strike. But, while they were still a mile above the earth, the eagle seemed to lose its panic and start using its intelligence; and, when the birds had drifted almost too far to be closely observed and John had galloped several miles across the arid land under them, the eagle grabbed sideways at the peregrine as she shot by, and the peregrine did not zoom upward to renew the attack but dropped straight down, slowly turning, one wing outstretched above it like a rudder.

There were tears in Robin's eyes as he packed up the telescope and he could not tell what had caused them, sorrow for his dear falcon that was dead or pride for his eagle that had survived the deadliest creature of the air.

"The eagle probably has a broken leg and can't ride home," he said, trying to control his voice. "I'll have to go down with the station wagon right away."

"Robin," she said: and this was a real part of her, that the truth broke through, no matter how grievously it might hurt her cause: "you are a different person from the person I knew and loved. I do not know you and I do not want to know you."

"I may expect, then," he said coldly, "that you will be gone by the time I come back?"

She had mounted. "You can expect nothing from me," she

cried, "but what I choose to do." And she took off down the hill.

He followed; found her horse, still saddled, in the yard, but no sign of her; took the station wagon down the valley and met John on the plain coming back with the eagle on his arm: the leg was not broken after all and the eagle was quiet, wearing the alternate hood. John did not need any help.

"She was on the falcon when I came up," he said, "and when I made in to her she didn't drag or carry. I got the glove under her easy. That's a well-trained eagle, boss. I guess I lost myself two months' pay."

"I guess so," Robin said. "Too bad."

"That was some fight," the Indian said. For him this was loquacious enthusiasm.

"Yes. Some fight."

"I should have bet on the eagle," the Cheyenne said. "I don't know what got into me. Our tribe has always put its money on the eagle."

"Well, you were bedazzled by the peregrine," Robin said. "Damn, I hate to lose that beauty. Take the eagle back to the house and feed them all. I want to stay out of sight for a while, till that woman leaves."

"She won't leave," the Indian said. "Not till you call the police."

. . .

The Indian was right. She was still there, hidden in her room, when he returned several hours later. He had his supper with John in the room over the garage and they talked about the fight. That night he locked his bedroom door.

It was about three A.M. when he was awakened by the screams from the hawk house. All his birds were shrieking. He ran down the stairs in his pajamas and out the back door. The lights in the hawk house were on and through the open door he could see Marian methodically working her way along the perch, knocking down the birds with a knout she had made from several leashes. Even as he shouted she disappeared behind the partition and when he reached her she was flailing at the eagle with all her strength. The bird was on the floor by her bow perch, sitting back on her rump, screaming. She supported herself on her wings and held her feet open toward the girl. There was blood on Marian's wrists and breast.

Robin seized Marian from behind and threw her to the floor. She sat up at once and her eyes were blazing with a sort of possession. "I have freed you, Robin!" she shouted. "I have killed them all! Now you can return to yourself!"

John appeared. Robin dragged Marian to her feet, hauled her to the door, and literally threw her out, locking it behind her. Then he ran back to the eagle, which, after a moment, resumed a normal stance and hopped back to her perch.

"Hood her," Robin said. "See if any feathers are broken and if she's hurt. I'll see about the others." With the sick feeling one must have if one's child has been run down, he went to the other room. All the birds were hanging by their leashes. The Cooper's and the merlin, which had borne the brunt of her assault, were dead; so was the tiny burrowing owl, whose worst crime was the destruction of crickets and mice. The prairie falcon was beating its wings feebly and dripping blood. Robin got his gloves and the glue from the bench, lifted the bird to its perch, hooded it, and gently stopped its wounds with the glue. Then he removed the hood. One eye was swollen and closed, perhaps blind. So he had one hawk left, maybe, and the eagle. He went behind the partition, his heart raging with sorrow and anger, and saw that John had calmed the eagle and was examining her for broken feathers. Incredibly there were none.

"All dead but the prairie," he said. "That crazy, obsessed woman. We'll have to start all over."

"The eagle's all right," John said. "She's had quite a day. Shall I take off the hood?"

"Yes. Let's see how she feels now."

The eagle, when the hood was off, roused but did not bate. Her eyes were as unafraid and expressionless as ever; it was as if nothing had happened. Robin turned and went back to the main house.

He found Marian in the living room. She had poured herself a tumbler of straight bourbon and was in a state of exaltation, pacing up and down with long strides. She was disheveled and covered with dirt.

"How glad, how glad I am that it is done!" she exclaimed as soon as she saw him. "It was not easy for me, oh no. I hated it. Killing the eagle was the worst because you loved it most. But it was the only way to save you."

He stood speechless, his chest heaving.

"I could never understand why you were rejecting me until this afternoon when you made the two birds fight each other. Then I saw how you were making two parts of yourself, the big cruel part and the little tender part—of course, the falcon isn't tender, really, but only by comparison with the eagle— making these two parts of you fight each other and hoping for the cruel part to win. Oh, it was so clear! How could there be room in you for me while you were dominated by these violent forces? So I had to do away with them, Robin, to open up your path to me again."

He realized there was no hope of getting through to her.

"Oh, I know there will be a period of resentment," she went on, "when you will hate me and want to be rid of me. But that will pass, and I will see you coming back again to your old self, and to me. And I will be by your side to help you over the rough places."

"You will be here?" he asked. "In this house?"

"But of course I must be here. What good is it, however well I read your heart, if I am far away?"

"Good night, Marian," he said. "I am going back to bed now. We'll have more to say to each other in the morning."

Before he went to sleep, for the next hour, he heard her pacing.

. . .

Overnight his determination hardened and became rigid; with deliberate effort he held it over his rage like a lid. Hearing her voice downstairs before breakfast, he called the housekeeper up and had her pack Marian's things in her bag. He carried them down and put them in her car. Then he went around the house to where she was standing on the terrace.

"Marian," he said, "I have put your bags in your car. I want you to get in it now, and drive it away, and never come back. Last night you committed a crime for which I will have you arrested unless you get out of here in the next five minutes."

"But Robin," she said calmly, "*call* the sheriff and have me dragged out of here. Prefer your charges, put me in jail. I know you feel this way now—that's inevitable. I'll write you post cards from my cell every time you stub your toe or cut yourself shaving. And when I'm out of jail I'll come back to where I belong. You can't law me out of your life. There's no way you can get me out of your life."

He seized her arm and dragged her with deliberate roughness to the garage; opened the car door and shoved her in. She did not resist. "Now go!" he cried. She got out the other door and stood facing him, the car between them.

"Robin, you can force me to leave by calling the police, but that is the only way. I am prepared to withstand whatever you choose to do to me until you come back to your senses."

"Goddamn it!" he shouted, beside himself. "Have you completely lost your mind and your sensitivity? Can't you understand the impossible situation you're creating? Can't you get out of here like a civilized person?"

"No," she said. "You'll have to use force."

"The sheriff will be here as soon as I can get him here," Robin said, and went off toward the phone.

But he did not phone the sheriff, because he recognized the futility of doing so. He put the receiver back on its cradle and went out of the house, along the path to the office. Be calm, he thought, as he walked through the aspens; subdue your emotions for a time; look at this problem with your mind.

He knew this woman—ah, how well he knew her! She was like Beethoven's *Für Elise*, a spiderweb of steel. So gently she seemed to entangle; so relentlessly she held on. It was no use to call the police; she would come back, and back again. Her mind was made up and nothing could conceivably change it.

He was the first one in the building. He drew a cup of coffee from the coffee-break machine and took it to his office. The roughs for a subdivision in Florida were on his desk. All morning he worked on them with total absorption, divorcing his mind completely from the problem that Marian presented. And yet, though he had not given it a moment of conscious thought, it had been curing in his subconscious. By noon he knew its solution.

Back at his house he found Marian in the living room, quite at home, reading Baudelaire.

"I suppose you've unpacked again," he said.

"Yes," she said, "thank you."

"Well, I'm not going to call the cops just yet. We'll leave a little time for the dust to settle and see if we can't work something out."

"Splendid," she said. "I'm sure we can."

"You didn't kill the eagle, you know," he said. "Or the prairie falcon."

"I will," she said.

"Don't try it," he said, "or by God I'll disfigure you."

He went upstairs and rooted around in his closet until he found the other hat, the identical one she had given him in Austria, green felt and white plume. He found John in the stable. "Get a half dozen rabbits from the hutch and cut them up into pieces. We have an afternoon's work ahead of us with the eagle." He went to the mews and hooded the eagle and got her on his glove, the terrible incalculable creature, and wondered with fear whether her experience of the night before had turned her against humankind and whether she would really try to get him this time. But he hardly thought now that what he was doing took nerve and courage, and this was a measure of the great distance he had come since he had set off on his own.

The eagle behaved well and was carried with the jesses pulled tight to the small meadow above the house, while John followed with the bag of rabbit meat. Robin tied the hat to a long string and sent John thirty yards away with it; and when John was swinging the lure in slow circles around his head he unleashed the eagle and struck the hood, and John gave the shout that the bird associated with flying to the lure, and the eagle dived straight for the bait with mighty sweeps of her six-foot wings and hit it like an express train almost before John had let it drop to the ground, and clutched it under one great foot, looking imperiously about. Before she could find that the lure was not food, John tossed a chunk of rabbit to her and retrieved the lure undamaged. Then Robin got the feeding eagle up on his glove and grabbed the jesses and let her finish off the morsel. That was the most dangerous part, approaching the bird while she was feeding and had both feet free to strike with. But nothing had happened.

They repeated the exercise throughout the afternoon, gradually increasing the distance; rewarding the eagle each time for her recognition of the lure. At about three P.M. they stopped giving the shout signal and merely swung the hat on the string; at about four they stopped swinging the lure and simply hung it on a bush or stump at any point of the compass from the eagle, so that she had to ring up and search. She found it every time and attacked it; was not even distracted by a real live rabbit that blundered onto the scene and immediately fled. At about five Robin decided they were ready for a final test. He sent John to fetch a couple of horses and when he came back with them, on one and leading the other, he sent him a mile across the slope with the hat.

"Wear it on your head. Don't move. Throw it to the ground when the eagle approaches, and feed her a good big piece of rabbit. I'll be right behind."

John made his way across the slope, in and out among the pines, until he was in clear sight on the barren patch they had chosen; waiting; an almost invisible speck among the rocks and fireweed where a burn had been. But the eagle, once she saw him, would be able to count every eyelash. Robin prepared her and threw her to the air. She rang up and looked to where the lure had last been shown. Not finding it she rang up higher and stared all about. Suddenly all her forces gathered and she hurled herself aslant the slope, straight toward the tiny spot a mile away. Marveling, Robin set his horse after; some minutes later he reined up beside John and watched the bird as it plucked the food.

"I was scared," John said. "I saw that sonofabitch coming at me and I tossed the hat when she was still a quarter mile away. I dismounted and hid behind the horse. But she went straight for the hat."

"I guess we have her trained to the hat," Robin said.

The Indian put on his very special inscrutable Indian face. "You going through with this, boss?" he asked.

"I think I'll have to," Robin said.

The Indian looked across the mountains loping off to the south, his face immobile. "You'll need help," he said.

Robin understood what he was really saying: that he would do whatever was required of him, for this white man who had treated him as a human being and had allowed him to feel dignity, for the first time in his life. Obviously there was no way to express this. And there was no way for him, Robin, to show his gratitude. Anything he might do would not be enough. But he had to do something.

"That's your horse you're sitting on," he said. "You own it. I've been wanting to give it to you for a long while." He saw a flush spread over the Indian's features and he said strongly, "Damnit, John, stop being the Last of the Cheyennes for once, will you, for Christ's sake? You just gave me a great deal—can't I give you something without you getting insulted? Don't make things hard for me. Now let's get that eagle back to where she belongs."

"OK, boss," the Indian said; and, a most unusual thing, he smiled.

. . .

When Robin came down next morning he found Marian already at the breakfast table telling Mrs. Emlen that, yes, she would like a second poached egg but the toast a little darker this time, please. His heart was thudding so violently, and his spirit was in such agitation, that he was certain her intuition would warn her of her danger. But she perceived nothing.

"Good morning, darling," she said. "Did you sleep well?"

"No," he answered, "I did not. I had too much on my mind."

"Us?" she asked.

He sat down and poured himself some coffee. "Wasn't your radar working? Isn't it working right now?"

She laughed. "But you know it only works when something happens to you. I'm not a mind reader. When you're hurt, it's like an electric shock that goes through me and I get a sort of flash. It's what makes me so sure about us."

"We are so many miles apart," he said miserably. He ate his food in near silence after that, until she finally said, affectionately, "Old Grumblehead."

He summoned his strength and put on a casual voice. "Marian, this is a very difficult situation, as you must know. We have some serious talking to do. I think better in the open. Let's saddle a couple of horses and take a ride down to the plain. We can talk on the way, and there's something I want to show you."

"What a fine idea," she said. "I'll go get ready." And she flew up the stairs. He walked with heavy heart to the yard. I don't, I don't, he thought, I don't want to go through with this.

He found John and he picked up from what he had been thinking. "This may be just a dry run—God, I hope it is. I'll give her every chance to get out. But if it has to be—John, we're taking the horses down to the plain. As soon as we leave, you take the eagle up to the bluff, where you can see us. If I see any other way, you'll have the pleasure of watching us ride horseback. If not——"

For a while he could not bring himself to say it. "If not, I'll give a signal like this." He extended his arm to the side, raised it, lowered it. "Strike the hood and throw the eagle."

The Indian was, if possible, even more inscrutable than usual.

"John," Robin said intensely, "I hate to put you in this position. If any questions are asked, you are just a dumb Indian helping me to train a bird. The bird was supposed to fly down to me and something went wrong. There's no danger to you. I wouldn't expose you to any danger."

"I know, Robin," the Cheyenne said. "Don't worry."

Robin went to the stable and saddled the horses. He led them out and, holding them by the reins, waited for Marian to appear. Maybe she won't be wearing the hat, he said to himself. Maybe her intuition has told her after all. I could not conceivably send her back for the hat. He heard her voice in the house and then she appeared on the lawn, walking toward him in her jodhpurs with her stock under her arm, very chic. Instead of the proper derby she was wearing the green hat with the white plume.

They mounted and trotted down the road a few hundred yards to where the path down the slope took off through the woods. He slowed to a walk as they began the steep descent.

"Marian," he said carefully, "have you given any more

thought to what you said yesterday? About yielding only to the police?"

"Why no," she answered. "That's the way I feel."

"I mean, you haven't, in a calmer moment, come to realize that if you want to stay here and I don't want you to stay here there can be nothing but friction and bad times for both of us?"

"No," she said. "I think there will be one or two bad times at first, but then I think we can get back to what we used to have and what we both really want."

He was ahead of her on the path and he turned in his saddle to look at her, to reinforce with the eye communication what he was about to say. "Marian, believe me, what I want is not at all what you want. I have said it already, and I will say it again: the life I intend to lead has no place in it for you, and I most earnestly implore you to get out of it."

"I will not get out of it, Robin," she said firmly.

He turned his eyes ahead again and with a surge of confused emotions spurred his horse to a canter down the hundred yards to the bottom. He drew up and waited for her to catch up; and from then on they rode side by side toward the place where they would come into view past the end of the spur.

"Marian," he said fiercely, "I implore you to accept this fact! I simply do not need or want you in my life. You have to realize this or the consequences will be horrible."

"I do not realize this," she said clearly. "On the contrary, I realize that you are a person different from your real person. Ah, Robin, I have known you so well and so long, how can I be wrong?"

They had passed the spur and were in open country. "You are wrong!" he almost whispered. "Marian, for God's sake and your own sake and my sake, admit it! Get us out of this deadly thing!"

She rode calmly on. "I am stronger than you, Robin," she said, "where it really matters. I will wait you out. I will stay."

In anger, in anguish, in despair, he put his arm straight out to his side, raised it high, and lowered it. She did not see his gesture but something suddenly, at last, seized her attention: at last, too late, her intuition was working for her instead of for him.

"Robin!" she said sharply. "Something is really wrong, isn't it? *Really* wrong."

"Yes!" he said. "Oh God, yes!" For he knew, without looking, that John had struck the hood and had hurled the harpy from his arm, and the great bird had wheeled once, casting her eyes over all she could see, and had aimed herself like a projectile at Marian's neck and was thundering down the slope behind them, a hundred feet a second toward the prey.

"Over there!" he said in a strangled voice, pointing across the plain. "What I wanted to show you. Over there!"

So that the eagle, when she hit with all her weight and speed and dreadful talons thrust forward and opening at the last moment, would not mar the beautiful, once beloved face.

THE
HOBBYIST

BY FREDRIC BROWN

When Fredric Brown feels a novel coming on, he climbs aboard a Greyhound bus and takes a long cross-country ride. When he gets to the end of the line, he turns around and comes back. During the trip, he does not see his fellow passengers or the stunning scenery rolling by his window; he sees the characters of the novel-to-be and the shifting scenes against which their drama is played. Journey over, he sits down at the typewriter and transcribes the book that is already written in his mind. Author of more than 300 stories and over two dozen novels (some book titles: "The Lights in the Sky Are Stars," "What Mad Universe," and "The Fabulous Clipjoint," a winner of the Mystery Writers of America's Edgar Allan Poe Award), he is also a regular contributor of fiction to PLAYBOY. *"The Hobbyist" is the story of a man who devotes his whole life to murder—but not in the way you may think.*

"I HEARD A RUMOR," Sangstrom said, "to the effect that you—" He turned his head and looked about him to make absolutely sure that he and the druggist were alone in the tiny prescription pharmacy. The druggist was a gnome-like, gnarled little man who could have been any age from fifty to a hundred. They were alone, but Sangstrom dropped his voice just the same. "—to the effect that you have a completely undetectable poison."

The druggist nodded. He came around the counter and locked the front door of the shop, then walked toward a doorway behind the counter. "I was about to take a coffee break," he said. "Come with me and have a cup."

Sangstrom followed him around the counter and through the doorway to a back room ringed by shelves of bottles from floor to ceiling. The druggist plugged in an electric percolator, found two cups and put them on a table that had a chair on either side of it. He motioned Sangstrom to one of the chairs and took the other himself. "Now," he said. "Tell me. Whom do you want to kill, and why?"

"Does it matter?" Sangstrom asked. "Isn't it enough that I pay for——"

The druggist interrupted him with an upraised hand. "Yes, it matters. I must be convinced that you deserve what I can give you. Otherwise——" He shrugged.

"All right," Sangstrom said. "The *whom* is my wife. The *why*——" He started the long story. Before he had quite finished the percolator had completed its task and the druggist briefly interrupted to get the coffee for them. Sangstrom concluded his story.

The little druggist nodded. "Yes, I occasionally dispense an undetectable poison. I do so freely; I do not charge for it, if I think the case is deserving. I have helped many murderers."

"Fine," Sangstrom said. "Please give it to me, then."

The druggist smiled at him. "I already have. By the time the coffee was ready I had decided that you deserved it. It was, as I said, free. But there is a price for the antidote."

Sangstrom turned pale. But he had anticipated—not this, but the possibility of a double cross or some form of blackmail. He pulled a pistol from his pocket.

The little druggist chuckled. "You daren't use that. Can you find the antidote—" he waved at the shelves "—among those thousands of bottles? Or would you find a faster, more virulent poison? Or if you think I'm bluffing, that you are not really poisoned, go ahead and shoot. You'll know the answer within three hours when the poison starts to work."

"How much for the antidote?" Sangstrom growled.

"Quite reasonable, a thousand dollars. After all, a man must live; even if his hobby is preventing murders, there's no reason why he shouldn't make money at it, is there?"

Sangstrom growled and put the pistol down, but within reach, and took out his wallet. Maybe after he had the antidote, he'd still use that pistol. He counted out a thousand dollars in hundred-dollar bills and put them on the table.

The druggist made no immediate move to pick them up. He said, "And one other thing—for your wife's safety and mine. You will write a confession of your intention—your former intention, I trust—to murder your wife. Then you will wait till I go out and mail it to a friend of mine on the homicide detail. He'll keep it as evidence in case you ever *do* decide to kill your wife. Or me, for that matter.

"When that is in the mail it will be safe for me to return here and give you the antidote. I'll get you paper and pen. Oh, one other thing—although I do not absolutely insist on it. Please help spread the word about my undetectable poison, will you? One never knows, Mr. Sangstrom. The life you save, if you have any enemies, just might be your own."

THE SENDER OF LETTERS

BY HERBERT GOLD

Herbert Gold has been contributing to PLAYBOY *since the magazine's beginnings, and this has not interfered with his making a name for himself as a perceptive, poetic novelist with a special sensitivity toward the plight of the young urban man in this "age of happy problems" (the title piece of his book of essays). His novels include "The Man Who Was Not With It," "The Prospect Before Us," "The Optimist," "Salt" and his most recent, "Fathers." Some of his finest short stories were collected in "Love and Like." Granville Hicks says Gold dares "to look for heroes, and he finds them in unlikely places." He finds antiheroes in unlikely places, too, as in this tale which tells of the ardent, angry, dangerous tribute of a pickup on a beach.*

"ALL RIGHT!" SHE SAID. "Feel better tonight. I'll try to do the same.

"We'll both try," her husband said dryly, and she stood holding the door open for him. Within herself Sheila felt the quarrel reaching the point of fire again, anguish and hatred, then pure bright contempt, simply because his hasty unhappy breakfast had left a smudge of soft-boiled egg in the corner of his mouth; but of course she said nothing; she was sorry, he was sorry; and as the screen door fell to, she leaned, frowned, watched his sagging retreating shoulders out to the car, the cotton sack suit pulled shapeless at the pockets.

She wished that he would learn not to stuff things in his pockets—it gave him fat hips—but nevertheless she was sorry for him. He had arranged a transfer to the Miami laboratories of G. S. Perry, Inc., just because she loved the sun; now he suffered the daily rush-hour trip through heat into town from Fort Lauderdale, leaving her behind to consider how tropical clothes robbed his rapidly aging body of the dignity which bulky northern tweeds had allowed it. She was sorry they quarreled. She was sorry they had no children, sorry she looked so much younger than Fred, sorry they fed on a diet of senseless cruelty and quarrels whose origin she could often not even remember; sorry, sorry, sorry.

Most of all she was sorry for herself.

But she would do the best she could for both of them. The nights of tears and chill tense huddling on separate countries of their double bed usually ended with an abrupt desperate spasm of lovemaking, engorging and unsatisfying, and then perhaps they slept an hour or two, and then the alarm clock sounded—nothing settled, nothing changed, nothing helped. There would be the weary clop-clop bumping about, breakfast, and then—as on this morning—he left her in peace.

Peace and loneliness, not friends but her most intimate parents.

But abruptly Sheila smiled; her mood changed; luxuriously she stretched, shook her hair, and shed her clothes. She took a quick comfort, like an extra cup of coffee, in the reminder that she still looked young enough to wear her sun-lightened hair long to her shoulders, or in thick plaits, or any way she chose. Naked but for her hair, she walked about the house, strolling idly, enjoying her body alone as she never did under her husband's clasp. She felt the early heat of the Florida summer day seeping in under the roof and through the window against which the slats of Venetian blinds rustled in an occasional sea breeze. No living person could see her, but the white of sky and the flash of sun were eyes. And she could glimpse her own body in the mirror, although in her innermost northern heart she felt it immoral to stand and stare. She merely walked slowly, casually peeking, back and forth before the glass.

It was still fine, high, lithe. She stood stretching on the chill tiles. Yes, why should foolish childhood prohibitions deprive her of pleasure in her own body? There was a poet who said, "The lust of the goat is the bounty of God." In an unhappy world, Sheila argued, don't we all deserve what little joy we can find? And did not poor Sheila's flesh—her work of art— deserve the same rapt contemplation which the sculptor gives his statue?

Yes. She stopped and found new slopes and valleys, the marvelous shifting geography of a lovely woman's body. At 30, Sheila still possessed that faintly adolescent grace, gawky and unused, for which the pretty woman who will never bear children is sometimes the envy of her friends. Self-love seems to replace love of family, and at its highest skill molds an adorable creature barely betrayed by line at nose and dip at mouth. The tan too served Sheila well, and in the half-light of sunny yellows and browns, the marks of straps and the line of her swimsuit framed the delicious forbidden areas.

With an angry pout she turned from the mirror. She had come too close without realizing it. Dreams are no one's fault.

Hastily now she seized swimsuit, extravagant sail of towel, terrycloth robe, sunglasses and notebook. The notebook was in case she wanted to write a poem, although she never did. She thought thoughts, however, and it was nice to know that she could write them down if she only cared to. She put her beach equipment into the woven souvenir basket that Fred had bought her on their trip to Puerto Rico and set it on the back seat of her red Renault convertible in the carport, its top already folded down and ready. The little French runabout was an anniversary gift from Fred, paid for out of his bonus for solving a troublesome detail at the lab; it had brought a truce between them which lasted for weeks; it was a putt-putt darling and a marvel for her little trips to the beach. She loved the way she looked in it bouncing down the sand road, her long blonde hair flying (its color changed by the sun, not by anything artificial), her intense little chin lifted to the breeze and her eyes secretive behind sunglasses.

The move to Fort Lauderdale was justified by such fine moments. After their quarrels and furtive reconciliations, Fred could sometimes sleep a little, but Sheila got none of the good of these bitter nights. Insomnia had been a menace to her skin, her hair, her health itself up north. It would steal the gloss. Now, however, she could hurry off to the beach and lie quivering, easing under the sun in the gentle urging of sun. The salt smell of ocean and the everlasting fierce probing light burned her to sleep; she could return home later and make dinner for Fred and perhaps life would go on. He would be exhausted from his day at the laboratory after the terrible nights of unhappy marriage. Sometimes she returned from the beach rested, at peace, and willing to forgive. It was as if the occasional flies, like imperative lovers, headlong and undeterred by either slap or passivity, sucked the anger from her body which yielded only under the sun.

Fred was a nice guy, one of the world's slender store of nice guys, and also inward-looking, gifted, and pleased with his gift. This is not enough for happiness. Sandy, pale, thin chested, with softly folding pout of a middle-aged belly despite his boyish legs and arms, he had, it seemed, been born with a passion for chemistry; and when it turned out that Sheila could never have children, he directed all his creative lust into his work, except for that forever new, forever crushed adoration of Sheila that made each argument a torment and made him then go touching her at night, tentatively, imploringly, like that first time years before when they parked in his father's prewar Hudson. He wore glasses and held the newspaper nearly at arm's length; he needed bifocals, but would not get them because he did not want Sheila to be reminded that age catches up with everyone, even those who love their youth too much, as she did. Despite his sandy receding hair and narrow, peaked face, he had a firm, determined and realistic mouth. He was a good organic chemist and an intelligent man. If his choice of Sheila to love was foolish, he did not fool himself about her. The most logical minds have the most irrational ambitions. He accepted the fact that he loved her and he could not bear the thought of losing her. He would fight, he would plead, he would wait patiently through all her moods of childish petulance.

Both weak men and strong men would long since have given her up—the weak because of weakness, the strong because of strength. The weak man would despair of her; the strong one would learn to go his way without her. Fred knew himself to be neither of these final cases. He simply loved her and was determined not to be broken by her. And not to lose her.

He had a rare consolation and nourishment—a deep love of his research—and this absorption in work helped him to survive and even to grow while in thrall to an angry woman. He could turn outside himself; Sheila could only turn within to that girlish dream of the cavalier lover, her first and last recourse.

She knew it of herself.

Why now did the dream return with such stifling intensity? Sun-battered flecks of green and yellow spun slowly, revolved to a stop behind her eyelids. The deserted weekday beach had altered. Someone was watching. She could not see him, but her body responded, yearning toward admiration. It was odd how this happened; the black dead fall of the beach nap which remedied her nighttime insomnia depended on the study of strolling men—*they* were her silent protecting chamber—and usually she awoke suddenly, with a lively pleasure, when a man stopped and stared and she felt his desire penetrate her dreamless sun-drenched dozing.

She opened her eyes. "What—what?"

"I'm sorry, Miss—ah, Ma'm," he said, elaborately taking notice of her wedding ring when she moved. "I thought maybe you were asleep and maybe I should wake you up." He grinned and showed a coarse, healthy row of thickly tobacco-stained teeth. "Reason is, Ma'm, I once had a friend fell asleep face up like that in the sun, and she—I mean *he*—was wearing sunglasses but she really burned her eyes bad. Dangerous business. Maybe you're not used to the sun down here."

She stretched, pushing sand, and then sat up and held her knees. "No, I'm from up north until this year, but you get the tan fast."

"Yes, yes," he said, eying her deliberately, all over, his excuse a scholarly concern with her color. "Yes, Ma'm, but eyelids are another story, and the tender eye . . . Well, my friend, she, I mean *he*. . . ."

While he talked to her, standing with his shadow stretched out in the morning sun on the deserted beach, she studied the stranger. He was wearing a tee-shirt and denim pants and white tennis shoes without socks, almost a college-boy carwashing uniform; the tee-shirt was cut at the neck, and then drawn together with a shoelace in an odd affectation; he was no college boy—he was at an indeterminate slender healthy age, with a salt-weathered, deeply tanned face, small, prying black

eyes, and a graceful, very youthful stance as he grinned and
chattered at her so fast that it took her a time to understand
that what he said made no difference to him or to her; it was
just his clever and experienced way of putting them at their
ease with each other.

"Engineer on Captain Sam Olliver's boat . . . The engineer gets a share and a quarter on shrimp, you know, and we
had ourselves a real good trip—thirty-five days and twenty-
eight hundred dollars was my share . . . Happens sometimes, Ma'm."

She was interested and, still standing, he grinned and told
her. "The captain gets a share and a half, plus two percent—oh
it's complicated. The cook and me, we get a share and a
quarter. Mess time is important to men out like that. The
crew, well, a share each. When you have a good catch, you're
rich for a while. Then you wait till it's time to go out again."

"Sounds like a good life."

He did not answer. Instead he stretched, still grinning, and
finally said, "Yes, but out on a small ship like that, just pulling
in nets and seeing to the engine for thirty, thirty-five days
. . . Well, Ma'm, you get to missing things."

Sheila gasped. Abruptly he had reached for his belt and was
unloosening it and unsnapping the pants and down they fell.

"My Lord, honey, I mean Ma'm, you're jumpy, aren't you?
What do you think a sailor is made of?"

Of course he was wearing something underneath, a black
bikini swimsuit which did not at all match the rough beach-
strolling clothes. He was an engineer, not a mere sailor. "I'm
sorry," Sheila said, feeling the flush rise to her face and
relieved that the glare of sun would hide her embarrassed
color. Involuntarily, instinctively, like the flies which sometimes attacked her in the high grass between her car and the
beach, she gazed at his body, an agile, wiry and powerful one
of middle height, with just slightly bowed legs as he stood in

he sand, his pants dropped to his ankles and the tee-shirt now ulled over his head. During that quick moment when he ould not see her, her eyes fled to the brief clothed part of his ody. He looked much stronger, more wiry, bunched and hicker than Fred . . . And the hectic flush rose again to her ace. She wanted to jump up, kicking sand, and run for the urf.

"Reason we do this to our tee-shirts, Ma'm, it's a mariner rick, is you know it gets hot, sticky, and you get that salt pray. Hard to get them off unless you can loosen at the neck."

He handed her the tee-shirt to let her admire his sailor's kill at piercing the cloth and threading in a shoelace. It was as f he had read her mind at wondering about it. She could smell im in the cloth as she held it. She let it fall near his pants and he tennis shoes. Abruptly, without warning, just as he had lropped his pants, he now dropped himself in the sand beside ier, again talking rapidly to get over the moment of shyness at new step in this pickup dance which must have been ritual vith him. He was too good at it. Sheila resented and admired iis boldness, his skill, and especially the way he would nention his friends, saying, "She—I mean *he*," in a cunning orrection which somehow made the whole question of sex ery important.

With this recognition of jealousy—she did not even know iis name!—she became angry. "I'm going in," she said, umping up in an imitation of his brusqueness and running oward the sea.

"Me too! Wait up!"

Of course! But she ran, laughing, to be first in the boiling vhite and blue surf, and for an instant felt his hand pursuing ier as she slipped away, diving into a rolling wave and grateful for its cooling touch to her fever. It did not count in he water, she decided. She could not be expected to know his ouch from that of the sea.

They came out together, ostentatiously separated. But ha
they really touched? Why this shyness? she thought. Wh
guilt already for nothing at all?

Perhaps because she did not like his laughter. It had a shril
almost feminine note in it. It was unlike him.

"What's your name?"

"Larry, didn't I tell you? Engineer Larry Fortiner, th
shrimper's friend, changes kerosine to Cuba rum!" And agai
that shrill insistent laughter.

She lay back, closed her eyes, and drowsily they talked. Th
morning sun rose; the stretch of beach was deserted except fc
an occasional stroller, picking shells—most people went to th
guarded beaches. Perhaps she slept for a time; perhaps h
slept, too. At least there was a silence of deep consideratio
between them. She could never recall the act of falling aslee
on the beach, but she slept often, because she would retur
home refreshed, the tumult within stilled for a time, an
perhaps ready to help poor Fred feel better after the hu
night and the long hurt exhausted day at the laboratory. Lik
the days without Larry, this morning passed mostly in drean
and she might then go home to admire the fresh reddish glo
of her skin and the newly lightened hair. She would brush an
brush her hair until all the sand was out, but she knew it sti
smelled of sun. The thought made her feel desired; she kne
she was. While she dozed, she sensed through her pores th
stares of other strange men passing by. Without opening he
eyes, she raised one knee, slowly, languidly, giving them th
sight in motion of the inside of her thigh against the inside c
her thigh. She always wore her black swimsuit for these siler
lonely outings.

Silent and lonely! And yet when she moved her legs no
she knew the name of an important watcher: Larry. An
Larry loved watching. Sheila felt the sun and his hot blac
gaze pouring over her, probing and pleasing her, so that sh

y for a moment spreading in the golden light, and it seemed
her that the invisible secret organs of pleasure were
elling, replying; and then with abrupt shame she thrust her
nd between her legs, just as if she were a man, to hide
rself; and then remembered that she was a woman and
thing could be seen and the hand fluttered away.

She opened her eyes, smiled, shook her head, sat up, and
d, "My Lord. The sun must be . . . I've got to get home,
arry."

And burned fiercely inside.

And went on, staring at him with a sun-dazzled boldness.
ou must be, on that shrimp boat of yours—you seem to be
n all over—do you——?"

"Say it. Spit it out, Sheila."

When had she told him her name? When had he begun
ing her name so casually?

"Do you work on shipboard without clothes? Without
thes at all?"

He threw back his head to laugh, the sun glinting on the
ly black hair, his thick eyebrows gleaming, and the hair of his
dy and the slightly bowed legs glittering with salt slick; and
mehow now she did not mind the high note of his laughter.

The rest happened very rapidly, but Sheila did not object
her to being a classic case. He asked her to go with him now
his hotel in town. She lowered her eyes and shook her head.
e seemed to expect this, and was willing to allow her to
ower, to make preparations. He paused a moment. He asked
r to meet him later in the afternoon, in about three hours—
his hotel, in room 318, just go straight up. She did not need
run the risk of being seen with him.

"*No,*" she whispered.

"Let's say two o'clock. I'm an impatient man."

"Oh no, please Larry, don't!" she said, shaking her head
olently.

"Why not? We understand each other pretty well alrea in fact we agree." He showed his teeth in a smile witho humor. "I *know* we agree. So why not, Sheila?"

"Well . . . Well . . ." Head lowered, face hot. "I ha a jealous husband."

And again his high infuriating laughter. Sheila, who w mobilized for communication with him, knew the reason his amusement. Her words were a seal to the agreement, a they both knew it, for she had said, "I have a jeal husband"; not *I'm married, I won't*, but simply, "I have jealous husband . . ."

But if I could!

And so quickly he made plans for her. She was to take t Renault in for a change of oil, leave it, go down Front Str to the Tides Hotel; he lived on the third floor, she could w up the alley stairway—"Agreed?"

Swept along, it seemed inevitable. She nodded yes. She g up and gathered her towel, sunglasses, slippers. She felt congested adrenaline pout filling her lips. Larry's nasal vo and angry eyes altered her blood as the weight of Fred's bo could only rarely do.

"One thing more before you go," he said. He was looking her solemnly, standing with his hands on his hips, rocki slightly in the sand on those dark, strong, slightly bowed le "I've been at sea a long time, Sheila. I'm rough, but that's O You want that. But it means something, honey: Do disappoint me, hear?"

"I'll be there, Larry."

"Hear me now?"

"I said so, Larry."

"Don't change heads on me when you're safe at home."

"Don't threaten me!" she cried, shaken and near tears w excitement, and turned toward the high grass where her was parked. Then she faced around to where Larry stoo watching her thoughtfully and pulling his jeans back on. "I hat I want," she said quietly. "I haven't wanted this before, ut now I do. So I'll do exactly what I want."

The last thing she saw was his casual grin and wave as she lipped onto the scorched seat of the little 4-CV. The motor arked as she spun in a half-circle and fled up the dirt road to he highway. While in town she could also have the tailpipe eplaced.

. . .

Home after this long morning in the sun, Sheila found it ast lunchtime already. She had a headache compounded of un, hunger, excitement. She made herself a salad with bits of heese and long slices of cucumber, and ate even the rye acker with relish (a gesture toward protecting her weight), nd then, for pure high spirits, allowed herself a slice of the mon pie she had bought for Fred the day before. As if a urtain had been dropped, her headache was blocked away. She lt merely drowsy and satiated in the pleasure of return to the miliar rooms, filled with the comforts of her ten-year arriage, after a tricky and dangerous adventure. The best art of this strange morning was that nothing had been ltered.

Not yet.

She showered, considering this *yet*. With the relief of lunch nd a shower, she thought back on the morning as if it were leasant ancient history. It seemed complete already. After-ards, wrapped in a robe and ready for a nap, she took an spirin, not because she had the headache again, but just in se.

No, she thought, of course she would not meet him. What nonsense!

What foolishness!

No, she did not like his laughter. And though his legs were owerful and rippled tautly, she found the slight bow obscene o contemplate now in her cool shaded cottage. And the hairs ll over his body. And his nasty yellow teeth. And that laugh

again! Deliciously she shivered with the fright of what s]
almost did, might have done, perhaps even someday would d

And with this renewal of her sense of daring pride, her hea
turned on the pillow and she slept.

A long time she slept. She slept right through the tin
when she was supposed to meet Larry. Well, too ba
Awakening, she lay slugabed, rubbing her scalp with the pa
of fingers, as you are supposed to do, especially when you'v
had too much sun. Too bad about Larry. Too bad about h
waiting for her. Men are such pigs, so eager and greedy for tl
great struggle, and then so sure of themselves, complete, sile
and insufferable afterwards. Let him be sorry! It would be
lesson for his huge male conceit. Next time he would b
careful when he preyed on a woman's loneliness.

So she got up to prepare dinner, making the small hous
wifely gestures of straightening the house, pulling the blin
against the late afternoon sun, emptying the ashtrays, settin
the table. Then she put a stack of Frank Sinatra records on tl
machine and sat down to do her nails. She used colorle
polish; she was proud of her taste. (She also preferred la
Sinatra and early Anita O'Day.) Just as she heard Fred's ca
pulling onto the gravel—she kept her Renault in the carpor
he left the other car outside—the telephone rang. She knev
she knew, and she ran to get it.

"Please, you're late. What happened? I've been waiting an
waiting." His voice had a hurt urgency that made it ver
different from the drawling nasal one on the beach.

"No," she hissed, watching the door for Fred, "no, no, I'v
decided no—don't call here again."

"Please, honey."

"No!"

"You promised me, Sheila."

"It was a mistake. Now don't bother me again, it was just
terrible mistake. I'm sorry if I—oh, why should I have t
apologize to you? Just don't bother me again."

There was an instant of silence. In this silence she could feel his arrogance flowing back, and now abruptly she saw him again on the beach, shocking her by ripping at the snaps and dropping his pants. And over the telephone came that shrill laughter, almost like a woman's, and she was abruptly grateful for her narrow escape, that prudence which had protected her from the sun-twisted, fleeting desires of the beach. A bow-legged sailor with oily hair all over his body and a womanish giggle! She hung up on him while he was still laughing.

Putting away the garden tools, puttering outside, admiring his little property before going in to the risks of troubled marriage, Fred gave her a moment to gather her calm like black netting about her, revealing and not revealing, ready. She was impatient to see him, and finally ran outside. "Darling, whatever are you doing? Don't worry about the plants, I'm waiting for you!" She wrapped her arms lightly about his shoulders and kissed him, mouth and tongue, and then, smiling, pulled away the upper part of her body. "Why don't you take a shower, darling? Of course I like your big bad male smell, but it's been a long day. While you wash up I'll have a drink out for the both of us, OK?"

"What a rush!" He grinned, rising at once to the unexpected boon of her good spirits. "What have *you* been doing? I see a fresh sunburn under your tan——"

"Just waiting for you, darling. Hurry now," and she got behind him and put both hands on his rump and playfully pushed him, talking train, "Choo! choo! choo! We're heading to clean up the great scientist!"

Fred's wanness passed over to good cheer and gratitude under her happy welcoming mood. Oddly enough, his jacket pockets did not seem to sag when he smiled, was joshing and gallant, clinked glasses. She did not resent his pale, untanned face, because when he took off his glasses she could see that he had managed to get some sun anyway: the browned cheeks contrasted with the pale, bluish pouches under his eyes.

"Honey," he said, "you're full of vinegar, you even spille
your bottle of nail polish. Want to go into town for a movie?

"Let's just stay home," she murmured, "and . .
and. . . ."

"I'll help you clean up the polish," he said.

And she was touching, touching, touching him, and the
were slipping down. They made love on the cold tiles of th
inside patio floor in the heat of the Florida summer evening
With fierce gratitude Sheila clutched the dear straining fac
looming over her, and feeling the icy smoothness of til
against her sunburned back and against the flesh of he
buttocks, an unprecedented marvel of desire came to dwell i
her; she believed that she loved Fred, had always loved Fred
only only Fred. Breathless and gasping, she asked him to carr
her to bed afterwards. He smiled and was strong enough to d
it. Dreamily she kissed him, many light sleepy kisses now
grateful and dreaming, and then turned to sleep.

Lucky Fred, lucky Sheila.

Poor Larry, poor boy, she thought. Hunting on the endle
beach. Tanned sailor with sly tobacco smile and powerfu
bowlegs. No, engineer on the shrimper, not sailor, and h
jeans full of lazy money. Tribute of his hurt voice on th
telephone. A history of hurt desire in that hard calculatin
face. He couldn't take his eyes from the inside of he
thighs. That black suit looked swell on her—no, charming, no
swell. Vulgar word. Piquant. Pee-kwunt. Adorable. Those ar
words for thighs rising to grip Fred's shoulders. Larry's mea
laughter. Oily hair all over him. Why, he even dared to touc
her in the boiling surf.

Maybe that's what a wife needs to be loyal to her husban
and content with him—the ardent, angry, dangerous tribute
a pickup on the beach.

Foreplay, she believed it was called.

. . .

They, Sheila thought bitterly, They won't let you be happ

You have to pay and pay and pay in this hard life. It was as if the decision had been made on some fiery beach in the underworld.

But the Devil was not They. It was simply He.

The next morning, shortly after a tender silent breakfast—Sheila had got up to squeeze the juice for Fred—just a few minutes after Fred left for work, the first special delivery letter came.

> . . . *For God's sake, after what we have meant to each other, you can't just break it off now. You came into my life like a gift I did not deserve, but you just tear yourself away. You can't. I know you don't really want to break with me. . . .*

And on like that. Ever yours as always, Larry. She recognized the game at once. Blackmail. But the question was: when would he stop? Was he crazy or merely malicious? Did it make any difference which?

Impulsively she ran to the telephone and dialed his hotel. Breathlessly she shouted at him over the telephone, "I know your trick! Don't! You have no rights on me! How can you take advantage of a woman without defense?" And then, struggling to master herself, "Please, Larry, I beg you. It was fine to meet you like that, you were handsome——" She tried purring to match his. She purred in a voice she recognized as her last-night's voice on the tile. "You were so attractive I didn't know what I was saying. I was tempted. You're so—but please now, Larry, my self-respect . . . You know I'm a married woman."

He answered, "I'm waiting for you. I'll stay in this hotel. I want you, I must have you, Sheila. You promised. For God's sake, for my sake and your sake——"

"Oh please!"

"Even for your husband's sake——" And the steady ardent courting voice suddenly broke to shrill laughter. It was no use. She hung up.

Was it her imagination, or did the postman have a nasty little grin on his face when he came with the second special delivery letter? It was very short this time.

Deep within my loneliness I kiss again in memory the little mole on the highest tender part of your left thigh. Darling I need you.

She did not go out all day. She locked the doors and pulled the blinds, though she believed that he would not approach the house. She stared into space and jumped at each creak, and she pulled the plug of the electric clock because she could not stand to watch the second hand turning, turning, going no place, and finally Fred came home, and then it was worse because she had to pretend for Fred while she felt the black bile of anxiety welling up within her at every sound. Was it the postman again? Would the telephone ring? How could she explain to Fred if Larry took it into his head to report about the mole which must have showed just at the elastic line of her swimsuit?

Shouldn't she just tell Fred the truth? The truth wasn't so bad. He should be able to forgive a momentary weakness that came to nothing. But after their quarrels, his suspicions, her habit of running to the beach when there was trouble between them . . .

In his dry way Fred would ask for an explanation of her passionate demand for him yesterday evening. It would spoil everything; it would sink them.

She was not a brave woman, she would admit it to anyone. She was a coward. All right. Perhaps she should tell Fred, and maybe Larry would tire of his tormenting of her and just go back to his shrimp boat. Eventually he would have to go. Perhaps he would have mercy. At least the early evening passed without another letter, without a telephone call.

Before ten o'clock, before Fred had even finished his newspaper, Sheila could stand it no longer and threw herself into his arms. "Oh love me, love me, love me," she wept.

"I do, darling. But what's the matter?"

"Nothing."

"What is it?"

She could not speak. She would protect Fred: *He* would go away. "Nothing," she said, "just love me and take care of me, darling, hurry, please——"

When she awakened next morning, she was convinced that she had done the right thing. Larry wanted to frighten her, but not to destroy her. He knew very well how to send a letter so that it would arrive in the evening, or to telephone in the evening and arouse Fred's suspicions . . . She felt almost grateful to Larry, as the prisoner is said to be flooded with love when his tormentor stops hurting him. Oh she would be good to Fred now! Oh she would be kind! He deserved it; he had been sweet, loving, understanding during these last terrible days.

Understanding. She smiled wryly. Men don't need to understand very much to be ardent, understanding.

And then the postman rang again. And the day passed. And the evening.

And the next day again. Another letter. Sheila thought that she would break, but she found strength in herself that she did not suspect. She did not crack. She spent the entire day indoors, waiting, wondering if Larry would go to the trouble of getting Fred's address at the laboratories and writing directly to him. She wondered if he would dare to call Fred there. She figured out things to say to Fred, speeches of justification; she imagined scenes of confession and reconciliation. But she did not dare.

She had come to need Fred's love and trust as she never suspected she could. Her self-love, her control of Fred, her dreams of better men and better fates for pretty little Sheila had disappeared under this threat to the entire structure of her life. One morning she labored and panted and struggled to turn the big mirror to the wall. She did not want to look at herself. She had strange belly weaknesses and pains. Perhaps it had really happened at last and she was pregnant. She ran to the mirror to see if her silhouette had altered, but someone had turned the big mirror to the wall.

And still the letters kept coming.

Each night she studied Fred's face. It was bland and peaceful. Surely he knew nothing. But he was deep, he had quietnesses within him that she only now suspected. It seemed curious to her that he never discussed his work at the laboratory. When she asked him, he said, "Why, I just didn't know you were interested. You haven't asked me in years."

"Tell me! Tell me everything that's on your mind!"

He smiled and stroked her hair. "Kitten," he said, "you're a ruffled little kitten these days. What's on *your* mind?"

If she were only pregnant, that might explain everything— or it might make it horribly worse.

And still the letters kept coming.

When the resolution to her problem occurred to her, it seemed so easy and inevitable that she could not understand why she had balked at it for so long. She telephoned the hotel. "All right, you win," she said. "I'll be there at two this afternoon."

"Thank you, thank you, darling," said his now grave voice, and then with the nasal imperative note that was the next thing to his fierce laughter: "For God's sake don't disappoint me this time. And then the hilarity: "You are overdue!" And finally the churning high laughter.

She went. She remembered that oddly pleasant, oddly unpleasant kiss of adrenaline at her lips, and with her anticipation both the swelling pout returned and her bewilderment at it. She was ten minutes early, but he was waiting. She parked her red Renault down the street and walked a block in the heavy midday heat, dazzled, blinking back tears behind her dark glasses. With a little shock she discovered that it was easy to blink back the tears. There was relief. There was a purpose and hope. Anything to drain him, diminish him, shut him up!

His room was unlocked. She opened the door, closed it behind her, turned, and said calmly, "All right, Larry." It was as if the events of the last week had made them old friends.

He was lying on the bed in the same clothes he had worn when they first met on the beach. He turned on his side without getting up. "Take off your clothes slowly," he said, "and then come here and help me undress."

With an unwinding shiver of release and gratification, she understood that she would now do anything, anything he wanted, and that this passive and brutal control of her was something that, deep within her angry heart, she had always sought and no man had given her before Larry. That night on the tiles with Fred, she had been in fear of herself and what she might do; now she was in fear of Larry, but this dread was a strange sweet excitement that said, Fear nothing, obey!

Silent urging, clenched teeth, throbbing heat, very hot . . . It was over very quickly. He rolled away from her without a word. He got up, dressed, and went out. She understood that he wanted her to be gone when he returned.

She hurried, feeling soiled, and left without washing. But now at last she could return to the beach. She would swim in the salt and cleanse herself. She would take the sun again.

Downstairs in the lobby, she found to her surprise that she could look in the mirror. No, she was not soiled. No, she was not pregnant either; that had been morbid fantasy. In the mirror on the elevator door stood a lovely young woman with a hectic flush on her face and her shoulder-bobbed blonde hair tousled. The way a light cotton dress clings to the hips is significantly different among women, and Sheila could see even in this rumpled state that hers clung nicely, sweetly, clingingly. It has something to do with the hips. It even has something to do with the quality of the dress. But mostly, Sheila decided, it is the walk, the way a girl carries herself, her pride in her ability to seize and draw a man so that he can never never never forget her or make do with anyone else, never, no matter where he goes after they pay him his share of the load of shrimp.

She listened to the clack of her heels smarting down the pavement toward the little red Renault. She swam that afternoon; she came home tired and content and at peace. At last it was over, and Fred did not know.

Such innocence! While they were having dinner, the telephone rang and Sheila seized it and heard a tumult of compliments, of wonderful flattery and recollections of the afternoon. "I don't want any! Leave me alone!" she shouted, and hung up.

"What is it, Sheila?" Fred asked.

"Oh nothing, nothing. Telephone salesman wants to know. . . ."

"What, Sheila?"

"If we want to buy something! What difference does it make?" she almost screamed. "I'm sorry, Fred, I have the jitters and when you pester me with questions——"

A long slow puzzled look was passed across the table from Fred to her. She felt it like an almost physical transaction. "I wasn't pestering you," he said mildly, and bent to his plate.

Sheila tried to eat, but the diced carrots kept falling off her fork. She had to pierce them like little hearts, and still they fumbled, fell. She looked up and caught Fred staring at her, but he said nothing and she was afraid to ask what he was thinking.

The next day there were no telephone calls or letters, but that evening, after dinner, the postman came with a special delivery letter. She managed to intercept it and tell Fred it was the drugstore with some pills she had ordered. He seemed to accept this.

"But why don't you let me bring them home from the laboratories?" he asked. "If it's sleeping pills, well, I know the fellows working on that project—it's big business, you know. They're constantly being improved. New compounds. I know one of the boys on——"

She believed that Larry would never finish with her. One letter came the next morning. And then the next evening. And the next. And they kept coming in the evening. Sheila tried getting Fred to go out every night, and then while he parked in the carport—she now gave up the space to his sedan—she would run to the front door and intercept the notice at the mailbox, "A Special Delivery Letter has been placed under your door," and open the door and get the letter before Fred caught up with her.

. . . You can't change your mind like this. We mean too much to each other. You must not stop now. You must make arrangements, you must. . . .

Must, must, must! She wanted to scream. He was torturing her, and although she was always on the edge of confessing to Fred and pleading for his mercy, she never could. She would plan, resolve, make a little speech, weep . . . But she never delivered the speech. Once in the middle of the night she woke up with a suspicion. The reason she had gone to Larry, the reason she could not ever tell Fred, was that she *wanted* to go. Her new dependence on Fred was a gift from Larry, and this was why she could never confess it to Fred and ask his forgiveness. It was Larry who had moved her to Fred with love at last.

. . . Dearest darling, it won't hurt if once more, once more in a lifetime of missing each other, we feel again what we mean for each other, what we do for each other. I've never known a woman like you, and you know you told me (I hear your voice again and again through the sleepless nights) how no other man has been able to stir you as I have. What is the right of a husband compared with the rights of desire?

Oh he was clever! He must have spent his days with pen and paper, writing and rewriting and copying these crazy love-notes. She called him once more. She tried pleading, sarcasm, threats. "It's filthy of you! I could tell the police——" All she received in answer was his wild gift of laughter. But she would not go to him now, no more! She knew him. Merciless he was.

Exactly when Fred began to suspect, she was not certain. Perhaps it happened when she had looked up to find him staring at her after the first evening telephone call. (Now, when the calls came, she would say, "Wrong number. This is the Frederick Wayne residence.") Perhaps he had intercepted one of the letters and simply lacked the courage to say anything. That would be like Fred, she thought. Maybe it was just his dour, depressed suspiciousness in operation. An odd change had taken place. He began to make love more frequently. She never thought that Fred would react this way to jealousy. He insisted greedily, pursued, rose over her with a fevered will. But she knew it was sick. His lovemaking had a quality, enraged and furtive, that she had never felt in him—not love, but a thin sick fury.

"Are you all right? Do you feel well?" she asked.

"Yes, yes," he muttered, and turned over. He admitted nothing, no matter how she probed. She would almost have welcomed an accusation, and then perhaps she could confess. He turned back and peered into her face in the darkness. "Yes, I feel fine. You, darling? You? Something on your mind?"

She said nothing. The unbearable suspense somehow was borne. The telephone calls kept coming. The letters. At different times. Sometimes a day would pass without a letter or a call, and then she had to wonder if Fred had received it instead.

One evening she lay sleepless, panting and crushed beneath Fred's now ferocious insistence. He had exhausted himself in a sick transport of sex, rising again and again, like a tormented boy, and now he lay breathing shallowly by her side. Then he got up. He put on the lamp. "Ohh!" he said, and touched himself with both hands.

"What's the matter, Fred?"

"Just an ache." He had a wry, wan smile on his face. "Very frequent phenomenon. A pain from excess of . . . too much of . . . Happens very often."

"Are you getting an aspirin?"

"No, no, it's the best kind of pain. Goes away with rest. Many men would be proud . . . No, I feel fine, darling, I'm just getting up to find you a sleeping tablet. I notice you have trouble sleeping these days, and we've been working on this new compound——"

"I don't want it!"

He took two pale green pills, wrapped in tissue paper, out of his briefcase. He said, "It's not habit-forming. It hasn't been released to the general public yet."

"No, no, I don't want any!"

"Take them!" he commanded.

"There's something I've got to tell you first, Fred. I can explain it if you'll only let me——"

"Tomorrow, tomorrow. There's all the time in the world for explaining. Here, open your mouth now."

And in some deep dim way she knew that Fred had become strong enough to take control of her life. She accepted the tablets from his fingers. Yes, at last she was willing. He had a glass of water ready by the bed. Yes, let Fred decide. She was tired. Yes, willingly she now gave Fred the right. She felt his fingers place the capsules on her tongue, caress her lips, and then, as if to press the wakefulness away, brush across her eyes to close them. She knew how lovely she would look to him, stretched out at peace on their bed.

The letters kept coming; the telephone jangled. The last note said:

I haven't heard from you in a week now, darling. What has happened? Why don't you answer the telephone? Where have you been?

This letter was sent back to Larry Fortiner at the Tides Hotel with a routine stamp on the envelope: RETURN TO SENDER. ADDRESSEE DECEASED.

BALANCE SHEET

BY MORTON FINEMAN

Morton Fineman is a short-story writer—and that makes him a rare bird in a time when too many writers turn to the short-story form only as a stop-gap between elephantine novels or lucrative but ephemeral film jobs. His work has appeared literally everywhere: in the slicks (PLAYBOY, Harper's Bazaar, Cosmopolitan, Mademoiselle), *in the pulps* (Alfred Hitchcock's Mystery Magazine) *and in the loftiest literary anthologies* ("The Antioch Review Reader," Martha Foley's "Best American Short Stories," and "O. Henry Prize Stories"). *As for novels, Mr. Fineman's attitude can best be assessed by something he recently told us: "I'm working on a group of stories—and some longer material which may jell into a novel, though I can't be sure about that." In the eccentric arithmetic of his "Balance Sheet," one plus two equals zero. If that puzzles you, read on and be enlightened.*

"Best damn beat in town," Mundy reaffirmed fondly, remembering. "All the girls in them stores, the bank. Man, when I walked that beat I was busy all day. I had coffee with five hundred different women on the city's time. And then on *my* time——" He laughed fatly, then went on to tell some highly unlikely sexual adventures.

Bored, Redmond let his mind wander. But it was true what Mundy said about the downtown beat. There were women all over the place, and most of them happy to talk to you. He wondered why. The uniform, yes, but it was more. The gun. Authority. He stared thoughtfully up at the moon. He remembered vague tales some of the men told about the way women acted around the gun. How one of them had even wanted the man to wear it to bed. The gun, yes. And all the power it represented. Authority. The Law.

The Law, Redmond thought. This is the Law.

Mundy was sighing reflectively. "But that was a good beat. Yes *sir*. Few good months of that could kill a man." He chortled, then broke it off. "Crap," he said with feeling. "I could sure use a little of that. They ain't had me on that beat in three years."

"Wonder why," Redmond said wryly.

"Ah, they don't know what they're doin'." Mundy brooded. He said some very brutal things about the brass upstairs. He told Redmond to stick with him; he'd learn something.

"Too bad you only ride with me one night a week," he said. "You'd learn fast, boy. But ridin' relief is all right. Who else you ride with?"

"I only ride two nights a week. Other nights I walk, four to midnight."

"Walk? Ninth and Central?"

"Yep. I walk that tomorrow."

"Jesus," Mundy breathed heavily and wagged his head. "You must know somebody."

They rode on for a while in silence, Mundy brooding about

the injustice of it, Redmond hoping there weren't many more cops like this. Mundy took it out on the next couple they flushed.

The girl was badly flustered. She had buttoned her blouse before they got there but she had done it too quickly and when Mundy's light shone in, her two middle buttons had come back open. Mundy gave the two kids a vicious lecture. Redmond turned away from it and went back to the cruiser.

"Listen," he said, when Mundy was done, "you keep at this long enough, and one of these days you're gonna run across somebody you know."

"Nah," Mundy said, grinning. "Only the kids come out here. Only the amateurs. The smart money finds a motel or stays home. The old pros got their own places. All you get out here is the ones that don't know their way around. Sometimes you get *old* couples. Jesus. And I got a doctor once, *him* I knew. He and his nurse, goin' at it hot and heavy. And him married with four kids. You should've heard the way I give it to *him*."

Mundy glowed with satisfaction. Redmond looked away.

"There's one more good spot up ahead," Mundy said. "I've been savin' it 'til it got late. We check that out and then we go home. Best place I've got. Always get somebody there."

He turned off down another dirt road. He cut the lights again and when he could see the ocean gleaming beyond the trees he stopped the car. He grinned excitedly at Redmond.

"From here we walk. Take no chances this time. Keep damned quiet."

"I'll stay here," Redmond said.

"The hell you will." Mundy's voice was quietly ugly. "Suppose that son of a bitch decides to get rough? You're my partner, boy. Where I go, you go."

"All right," Redmond said. He got out of the car.

"Keep good and goddam quiet," Mundy whispered.

They walked off down the road. Redmond breathed deeply

in the cool night air. "Watch your senior man," he thought. He remembered the captain saying it: "Watch your senior man, boys, *learn* from him! Watch him in action!" Redmond grunted in disgust. Mundy in action!

He looked up ahead and watched Mundy in action. The older man was stepping lightly down the ruts in the road, lightly and ridiculously, walking on eggs. Redmond could not bring himself to be careful. He couldn't help it. He told himself that Mundy up there was the Law, old John Law, and he giggled aloud. A twig snapped. He saw Mundy's angry turn. He grinned back, knowing his face couldn't be seen. Then he saw the car.

It was parked out in the open, on the beach. Real amateurs, Redmond thought. It was facing the ocean and Mundy was going in on it from behind. The moonlight was very strong and Redmond could see straight through the car and see the ocean through the windshield, but he could see nobody in it.

Mundy went in very close, beginning to crouch. Redmond walked more silently without realizing it. He watched Mundy go up to the car. He knew this one was it, that Mundy had them this time, cleanly and without hope, and a shiver went through him. He thought of shouting. He didn't. He walked in close and waited.

He saw Mundy waving him down. Obediently, he knelt. He waited for Mundy to shine the light, but the older man didn't; he rose slowly and looked in the rear window. Redmond could not see his face. But he was in close enough now and he could hear the car moving, hear the people moving inside it. Jesus, he thought, chilled. He did not go up to look. He waited by the rear of the shaking car.

After a very long while Mundy exploded the light. It blasted into the car and the couple inside jumped frantically. Redmond felt his face grow hot; he had to look down at the ground with shame. He heard Mundy begin to speak.

"All right now," Mundy was saying happily, "come on out

of there. *Now.*" He pulled the door open wide. "I said *now.* Or do you want me to run you in?"

The commotion inside the car stopped. A man got out the front door. He had his pants on but nothing else. Redmond felt himself irresistibly drawn to the other side of the car.

He watched the girl get out in the glare of Mundy's light. She was clutching her clothes desperately to the front of her, her face an agony of shock. She was completely nude.

"All right, sister," Mundy said, "you can put your dress on."

The girl turned to face the car. They all watched, all three men. She dropped all her clothes, her fingers horribly nervous, and bent to separate her dress from the rest. She raised her arms and put the dress on over her head and for an instant her whole body was gleaming and bare in the light of Mundy's flash. Nobody said anything while she put the dress on. When she was done she turned and the light fell again in her face, and Redmond realized dumbly that he knew her.

Mundy let the man put his shirt on, beginning to question him. When the man told who he was and who the girl was and showed his driver's license, Mundy asked him for one good reason why he shouldn't run him in. The man asked for a break. Redmond watched the girl.

She worked in the insurance office on the corner of Ninth and Central. She was about 20 years old and so pretty she made him shy. He had seen her every day when he was walking the downtown beat, seen her coming to work and going home and stepping out now and then for coffee, but he had never spoken to her. He knew all the girls in her office, he had had coffee dates with most of them and dated some of them, but never her. She was too pretty. He remembered that the other girls had not liked her for it, but they had never said anything against her. She was too remote. Cold and remote, and beautiful. He continued to stare at her, unable to move.

Once she had her dress on, Mundy took the light away from her. She had her head down, she did not see him. The dress was still open at the neck; she began to button it slowly, fumbling with the buttons. Her hair was wild and hung down in black streaks across her face. Without shoes she looked smaller than he remembered her. He wanted suddenly very much to help her. But he did not move.

He went on watching her, looked down once at the soft white pile of underclothes around her bare feet. He could feel his heart beat violently under his badge. She knelt in the sand and began to gather her clothes, lifting one hand to brush the black hair from her eyes, and then looked up and saw him.

She recognized him. She froze with her hand in her hair, on her knees, staring at him. It was the first time in his life Redmond had ever seen anyone look at him with terror.

He turned his eyes away. He heard the man trying painfully to be friendly with Mundy, asking him please to be a regular guy. Redmond began to want badly to kill Mundy. After a while Mundy turned toward him.

"Well," he said slowly, drawing it out, sucking it, feeding on it, "well, Red, what do you think? Should we give 'em a break? Hah?"

You son of a bitch, Redmond thought, oh, you lousy son of a dirty bitch. Because Mundy knew already he would let them go—he always let them go. Because then afterward, when he thought back on it and saw the girl naked and in agony and felt the thrill of it, he could still be virtuous, still be clean, because he had been a good joe, he had let them go. And I ought to take you, Redmond thought, I ought to open you up right here and now, you son of a bitch. But there was a kind of sick paralysis in his belly, and he could not move. He had to stand looking at the girl and he said finally, huskily, "Yes, let them go."

He listened while Mundy turned back to the man and told him how rough it would be if he got pulled in on a charge like this. He might lose his job. And how about the girl's reputation? He ought to think before he did a thing like this again. The man waited, smiled sickly, sweating. Redmond looked again at the girl's face.

She was standing now, her underclothes held crumpled in her hands, against her breast. He could not see her face clearly, but her eyes were wide and dark in the moonlight, and he understood. She thought he would talk about it. She thought he would tell it all over Ninth and Central. The paralysis was going away, he began to feel ugly. He thought this business better end quickly. She waited in front of him, unbearably tense, the white silk shining in her hands, like an offering. Something broke in him and he turned to Mundy.

"All right," he said. "That's enough." He spun and walked away, his feet thick and heavy in the sand.

Mundy was left alone. He did not like it but he had to break off. He told them both to get the hell out of there and came stalking back down the road. Redmond watched him come and behind him watched the soft light flowing down the girl's body.

"Now just what the hell——"

"You," Redmond said. "You. Listen. Nothing, you son of a bitch, nothing. Don't say anything. I'm telling you, I'm telling you this one time, don't say anything. Not a word. Not a goddam other word."

There was this thing in his voice, this cold and enormous thing, that Mundy had heard before. He was an old cop and patient and not a fool. He said nothing. They checked off duty and Redmond went home and thought about the girl standing with her underwear in her hands.

. . .

The next day was his day at Ninth and Central. He checked on at four and went over to the corner by the bank and waited. He had thought about it all day and the more he thought the worse it got. Because no matter which way you looked at it, it had been sexy. It was a damn dirty thing to do but he had felt the thrill and it shook him to admit it. Now it was necessary for him to make it right. He had to talk to her, to apologize, to make her see that he would never tell anybody.

She came out of the bank. She looked up to the corner and saw him and stopped, staring at him.

She was neat and small and shockingly pretty. She wore a light pink dress which swirled around her legs as she moved. She looked toward him for a long moment and he could see no expression on her face, no expression at all. She came and walked straight to him and stopped.

"Got time for a cup of coffee?" he said.

She gazed at him blankly, her eyes cold and clear. After a moment she nodded. They went silently across the street into Sam's and sat down in a booth. He had trouble beginning it. She was older than he had thought, more woman than girl. It startled him to see that she was more composed than he was.

"I just wanted to tell you," he began, "about last night . . ."

She watched him calmly, still without expression, lighting a cigarette as he talked. A cool customer, he thought admiringly, a cool, cool customer. He saw her eyes go down to his badge and then back up to his face and an odd, thoughtful look came into her eyes. He became suddenly and joltingly aware of her body. He could not help thinking of how she had looked last night.

But he went on with it. When he was done he told her he would feel a damn sight better if she would say something. A slight smile came over her face, along with the odd look still in her wide, dark eyes. She said simply that she believed him.

He relaxed and was able to grin. The coffee came and they sat making conversation and it was gradually and surprisingly very pleasant. She chatted briefly about nothing, but her voice was low and warm and her smile delightful and he began to wonder just what in hell was behind that puzzling look in her eyes. The vision of her in the night kept coming back. He passed through one of those moments when it was absolutely necessary to reach out and touch her. But he didn't move. And you can't ask her out, he thought. How the hell could he ask her? She'd think it was blackmail.

"It must be very interesting," she was saying, "being a cop."

"Yep," Redmond said. He started to rise. "Well, I better get back to the beat."

She made no move to go. She sat looking up at him, smiling, something rare and delightful dancing in her eyes.

"I feel very peculiar about you," she said. "You know all about me."

"Not all," Redmond said.

"You know what I mean. I . . . don't have to hide anything from you. We're not trying to . . . well, *kid* each other. You see? It's odd."

He didn't quite understand. His eyes went automatically down the front of her dress and she leaned back suddenly and moved her arms away from in front of her and smiled at him softly, lazily.

"I know what you're thinking," she said.

"I'll bet you do."

"Why don't you ask?"

"You know damn well why."

"Why?"

"You'd think it was only——"

"And it wouldn't be?"

Redmond took a deep breath.

"So you won't even ask?" the girl said. She was still smiling but her eyes had closed slightly and there was no mistaking the look in her face, and it came to him in that moment with an enormous shock how little he knew about women.

"All right," she said softly, "if *you* won't ask. When you get off duty tonight, Mr. Policeman, why don't you come on by and pick me up?"

THE ROOM
OF DARK

BY GILBERT WRIGHT

Gilbert Wright began his writing in 1928, and worked at it consistently and inventively until his death in 1966. Wright also turned much of his energy to a different kind of invention: that of electronic devices, for which he held upward of 40 patents. One of his inventions is an artificial larynx which has restored speech to over 5000 persons who had been deprived of that faculty. "Writing a story and inventing something," said Wright, "are exactly the same routine—in one you use words, in the other a coil; but both express an original idea." A highly original idea is expressed by Mr. Wright in this tale of a primitive contest that puts a good fellow in one corner, a bad fellow in the other, and a rattlesnake in between—all of which happens in an ominous place called "The Room of Dark."

IN MY COUNTRY when two fellows become angry enough to kill the other because of a lady, or some matter, it is the custom to arrange a duel. From such a duel as we arrange, the trouble between these two fellows will be settled, believe me.

The committee for duels prepares a house of one room so that, on the closing of the door, the room is dark. Fine sand, without little stones, is spread over the floor to the depth of a span. The bare feet of a man make not the smallest sound walking on such a floor.

The two fellows are made naked. Each has his knife, nothing more. The committee puts one fellow in a corner of the room and across from him, in that corner, the other fellow. And in one of the other two corners the committee puts a live rattlesnake of good size. The committee retires, the door is shut quickly, the duel now begins.

Outside, the people wait for the half of one minute. If the winner has not come out by that time, the committee piles empty oil cans against the door completely over the top. The people now go about their affairs because it may be many hours, even two or three days, before the winner opens the door and makes the cans crash down. The crashing down of the cans will be heard, day or night, all over the village and the people may now go to see which fellow has come out.

If it should happen that the duel is over in the half of one minute it will be because one of the fellows rushed. You see, on the closing of the door there will be a very short time when you still have the image of your enemy in the mind's eye. You can rush straight across the room to his position and perhaps finish him. But you must act very fast before the image goes. Both fellows could rush, but I have not heard of it.

Most often the rush is not made and so the cans are piled up. The duel is now an affair of patience, great care and much thought. Each fellow seeks to find the other without making his own presence known. One smart fellow may think of a method to work a trick on the other, but if the trick is not completely successful it will be the smart fellow who remains behind in the Room of Dark. Much will depend upon the control of the mind because, after some hours in complete dark, the mind can grow unreliable and a fellow may do something foolish and so inform his enemy of his position. Because of the thirst and the growing bad air, after three days one of the fellows is pretty sure to lose control. He may talk to himself, or even sing. And, should this happen, it will not be that fellow who crashes down the cans.

There are reasons for putting the rattlesnake into the Room of Dark. It is of great danger to both men equally, not caring who it might bite. We also believe that the snake will make the fellow who is most afraid even more fearful, so that the braver fellow has a better chance to win. Many times, we believe, the snake will prevent a duel. Fellows quick to fight if the snake were not to be with them, may think of a way to settle their quarrel without the duel.

But if the anger of two fellows to kill the other is strong enough they will duel, even if more than one snake would be put into the room.

Such an anger was between Damundo and Pito. Both these fellows were my cousins because, in our village, if a fellow is not your brother he is certain to be your cousin.

Damundo is a cousin not liked by me and others. He is more than 30, dark, strong and rough, much hair, and a mustache that he trims like a lady's little eyebrow. Damundo has the strong belief that he is a great victor over men and girls. In this, there is truth. Five times in not two years he has dueled and each time it was he who crashed down the cans. Never did he receive even a small wound and the times of his winnings were never more than an hour, often less. A thing unheard of in history! He brags that only cowards take the time of two or three days. Ridiculous! Damundo gets hungry! Damundo misses his girl! Every year he goes working on a ship for two months and on his return from foreign places he brings presents of bracelets, necklaces, shining chains to hang from the waist, ribbons, combs, candies, lipsticks, perfumes and other delights.

Pito is a cousin much liked by me and others. He is slim and has a mustache of first growth which he does not yet trim or it would be gone. Pito is three years older than me and the feeling has come upon him that he is no longer a boy. His voice has become deep, but is not yet dependable to remain so. Several girls of our village notice him, but when we all go out upon the beach at low tide to gather the harvest of the shore, Pito digs with Angia and their hands meet together under the sand. Angia is some younger than Pito and has much charm. She smiles softly and does not scream and produce silly laughing like these young girls who want only to bring you embarrassment.

This day Pito and Angia and I dug together. Damundo came up to stand, looking down at Angia. We did not show we knew that he was there, but dug, putting the small clams into our one basket.

Damundo dropped a little bottle of shining glass and gold into the sand before Angia's hands. She looked at it, but did not look up. She then dug to one side of the little bottle. We dug, putting the clams into our one basket.

Damundo squatted. He took up the bottle and twisted out the stopper. There was a strong, sweet smell; the smell of some foreign flower. Damundo held the little bottle close to Angia.

We stopped digging and sat back from our knees because something would now happen. Angia took the bottle and put back the stopper. Then she gave it to Pito.

Pito stood. Damundo stood. Pito offered him back the little bottle and Damundo struck it from his hand. He said, "I, Damundo, gave that foreign perfume to Angia for a present, little boy."

"I give the presents to Angia," said Pito. "I, only." His

voice began very deep, but went suddenly like a young boy's. Pito's face was red with shame, but he stood looking Damundo hard in the eyes.

Damundo laughed and laughed at Pito. He laughed loud and others around us who were digging, looked. Soon, many stood.

Damundo stopped laughing, his face was now strong with anger. "So," he said, "so you think to give the presents to Angia. Only you! Listen, little boy, I will tell you something. Angia has come to the notice of a *man*!"

"I am that man," said Pito, and his voice remained deep.

Pito's mother came hurrying and scolding as if she did not know of the growing trouble. She ordered us home. We had enough clams. It was late. Pito should go to hunt the cow. She took his arm and pulled, "Make haste, my child."

Pito shook away her hand, looking straight at Damundo.

Damundo stepped close to Pito and placed his hand on Angia's shoulder. "So," he said to Pito, "so you are that man?"

And Pito was. He spat into Damundo's face.

Then, as was the custom, a friend of Damundo's led him one way and I, being Pito's friend, led him another way. Angia stood where we had dug, looking down at the little bottle shining in the sand. She put down her hand for it.

I and some of my family were at the house of Pito. I began to sharpen his knife, a thing at which I am good.

Not much was said and the duel, which would begin next day at noon, was not talked of. We had come to be with Pito and his people to show friendship.

Then came Pito's father with three old uncles. Each, long ago, had been winner in a duel and it was hoped that Pito might learn a little from them. You see, it is not right to ask a young man who has crashed down the cans how he did his winning. He may have to fight again and so does not want his method known. But with old men, they will not fight again. They do not mind to talk of their winning.

"When the door is shut, Pito," said old Uncle Chaco, who is thin and trembles, "squat down quickly in your corner. Hold you knife point up, thus. If Damundo rushes, the image in his mind will see you standing. He will strike too high. Then you may rise into him."

Old Uncle Cantu, who is blind, said strongly, "No, Pito, you must leave an image of more deception. As the door closes, move the left foot. Damundo will think you are stepping out of your corner. He will rush to the left of it, but you will remain in your corner. You can get him when he arrives."

"Damundo will not rush," said old Uncle Juan who speaks thick because the right side of his mouth does not move. "Damundo has never rushed."

"But he will do something very soon," said old Uncle Chaco. "He is known for the short times of his winnings. He will not lessen his reputation by delay. Not Damundo."

"Then, if he does not rush," said old Uncle Cantu, "he will come along the wall. He will count his steps by placing the heel and toe together. There are 15 of such steps to each wall of the room. He will come quickly and without sound. When the count of his steps brings him to where he thinks you to be, Pito, he will strike."

"But because Pito moved his left foot," said old Uncle Chaco, "Damundo will expect him to be a little out of his corner to the left. He will strike at that count. You, Pito, will hear nothing but you may feel the little fan of air stirred up by his empty blow. Strike in the direction of the air. To the right of it, my boy."

"Do not forget the snake," said old Uncle Juan. "Damundo will not come by way of the corner where the snake was put down."

"You may be sure of that, Pito," said old Uncle Cantu. "If Damundo comes measuring steps along the wall, he will come by way of the corner across from the snake. You will then know the direction of his approach to you."

"Never delude yourself, Pito," said old Uncle Juan, "that you know what Damundo will do. It is good to leave an image of deception, but how can you know you have left it? The door might close so quickly that the movement of your foot will not be seen by Damundo. My advice to you is to stay close to the wall at all times. Then you will at least know where something is. That will be a comfort."

"What!" said old Uncle Chaco, trembling greatly. "Stay close to the wall? Oh, no! The snake will come along the wall. He will go all the way around the room keeping close to the wall. He seeks a hole through which he may escape. The snake will meet you if you stay close to the wall, Pito. Then he will rattle and Damundo will know your position."

"To see, any eye must have some light," said old Uncle Cantu. "The snake will rattle, not because he sees you, Pito; but because he feels the heat from your naked body. This frightens him and the trembling of his tail sends forth the rattle. At any time you hear the rattle you will know that either you or Damundo is close to the snake."

"This need not be so," said old Uncle Juan. "Lie down, Pito, your feet against the wall and your body into the room. You will know where you are, with your feet against the wall. Now cover your feet, legs and all but the chest and arms with sand. When the snake comes along the wall he will crawl over you without rattling. The heat of your body will not come through the sand. And, should Damundo be close by, the snake will rattle at him."

"More can be done with sand," said old Uncle Chaco. "Mound the sand against one ear. It will happen that if Damundo moves by stepping, crawling or in any manner, he will disturb the grains of sand under his weight. These grains will pass on the disturbance to other grains and they to still other grains so that the disturbance will come to the grains mounded over your ear. You will know that Damundo moves."

"But not *where* he moves," said old Uncle Cantu. "To discover Damundo's direction both ears must be mounded over with sand."

"With both ears in the sand," said old Uncle Juan, "you will not hear the rattle of the snake. His tail is in the air and does not disturb grains of sand. The rattle may bring you information of importance, Pito. Surely, do not cover both ears with sand."

"It is important, Pito," said old Uncle Chaco, "to keep account of the time. This may be done by the sound of the village, cows asking to be milked at sundown, dogs howling at moonrise, roosters calling at dawn. In this way, my winning was helped. After the second calling of the cows I thought it reasonable to try to deceive my enemy by sounds of sleep. I came back along the wall a little way from my corner and, facing the corner, cupped my hand around my mouth and against the wall leaving a small opening to direct the sound. I made sounds of sleep, not too often, not too loud. The sounds echoed from the opposite wall of my corner. My enemy came to stab there, his knee brushed me. I had no confusion in placing my knife."

"On the second day," said old Uncle Juan, "my enemy began to talk to me in whispers. He said that we were fools. That the trouble between us was not of the importance to cost the life of either. He proposed that we go along the walls, find the door and crash down the cans together. I did not accept his proposal, neither did I altogether reject it. In this way we came to the door and I had my success. I have often wondered if he made his proposal with honest intent."

"Never believe," said old Uncle Cantu, "that the snake must rattle before he strikes. Always, if you move, keep the body low. More heat will go to the snake and he will rattle the sooner. If you move standing, the snake may feel the small, quick heat of your stepping foot and strike before he has time to grow fearful and rattle. I believe it was thus that I came to crash down the cans. Never did I hear the snake rattle, but at the first calling of the roosters I began to hear the dying of my enemy. After some hours these sounds ceased. I came out of the Room of Dark because I no longer had an enemy."

The old uncles thought for a time, thinking if more could be said. By now I had made Pito's knife very sharp with the stone and with the leather. I honed it upon my palm. I looked to see if Pito had received confidence from the wisdom of the uncles. I could not see that he had.

"If the duel should continue to the time of the bad air," said old Uncle Cantu, "stand tall and lift the face. There will be better air above than below."

"You are young, Pito, and therefore supple," said old Uncle Chaco, "still, do not remain long without some small movement of the limbs. The knee joints give snaps of sound if allowed to become set."

"If it happens that you make some such sound," said old Uncle Juan, "move quickly from the place where you made it."

"The boy is young," said old Uncle Cantu. "He has not defiled his body by smoke and drink and the numberless dissipations of Damundo. Pito's senses are alert and clear. In this he has great advantage."

After a long thinking old Uncle Chaco said, "Five times has this Damundo won. Never with a wound. Never with more time than an hour."

"Damundo," said old Uncle Cantu, "is a foolish and reckless man. Too much confidence. In addition, he has had much luck."

"To have had such luck," said old Uncle Juan, "seems beyond the possible."

"But if not luck, what then?" said old Uncle Cantu.

"A method," said old Uncle Juan. "Damundo has a method of perfection."

After this, the old uncles said nothing, not thinking of more to say. Old Uncle Juan went to sleep a little.

Pito looked to me and we stood and walked away together.

I gave him his knife and he whistled at its sharpness. Indeed, I can sharpen a knife. I had twice seen the knife of Damundo, an evil foreign thing with a jeweled handle and a hooked blade. I told Pito I believed that Damundo would not strike down with such a knife, but rip up with the hook. Also, to cheer Pito —and this was true—I said that his knife was longer than Damundo's. By a finger's breadth at least. I was certain of it.

Pito smiled a little. "Of one thing we may be sure, good friend of mine, you have made my knife sharper than any knife in the world. There can be no doubt of it."

We came to the tall tree by the village well. Many times I have climbed this tree with Pito. From the high branches one can see the tops of the distant mountains that rise from the far edge of the sea.

"Pito," I said, "do you truly feel yourself to be a man?"

He was angry. "Did I not show it upon the beach?" On the last word his voice changed into the voice of a young boy. Ashamed, Pito ran off.

By noon the committee had prepared the room. The sun was bright and shone fully on the house and all who desired went in and closed the door to inspect if the room was truly dark. Two sparks of sun were seen in the roof and a boy was sent with soft mud to the top of the house. Those inside tapped with a cane at the places where there was light and the boy stopped them with mud.

All came out, saying that the room was now truly dark. A fellow had come with a rattlesnake of good size in a sack. A member of the committee shook the sack roughly. The snake rattled well.

Damundo stood with two friends at the north of the door. He was laughing and talking, not so all must hear, but so all could hear. He said that he would be glad to go into the Room of Dark. It was cool there, away from the sun. He would take a nap, because he had drunk much the night before. After awakening, he would take a moment for the business of the day, and then crash down the cans. Damundo had plans for the evening.

Pito and his friends stood to the south of the door, as was the custom. None of us talked one word.

Angia came, beautiful in her best dress. Naturally, she had not been seen by anyone since Pito had insulted Damundo on the beach. She had remained in her house, as was the custom. But now, it was also the custom that she must come and look long at Pito and then go and look long at Damundo also.

When she came to Pito she did not come very close. She stood looking at him. And it was as though she had put something in her face for him to understand. There was something there to see, if one knew. I did not. She did not smile. Then she went to Damundo.

Her back was toward us and her face could not be seen as she looked at him. Damundo suddenly smiled big and put both his hands on her shoulders. And she put both her hands on his head. Then she turned and went back to her house.

Damundo called, "Tonight, little one! Do not change your clothes; I like that dress."

We, with Pito, were most sick to the heart. We could not believe what we had seen. On Pito's face was a very strange look. A look of anger, of not believing, of thinking.

For with us, when the man puts his hands on the girl's shoulders and she smooths her hands on his head, it is a greeting of lovers. It means, "I am glad you are here." It can also mean farewell, as when lovers part for a time.

For her to make such a greeting with Pito was expected by all. It was because of his love for her that he was now to fight Damundo. But she had stood back from Pito, then gone to Damundo and made the greeting with him. Unthinkable! What thing is a woman! It was bitter to believe what must be believed. Angia, like all of us, thought that Pito would be killed soon. So now, she chose Damundo because it would be he who would come out of the Room of Dark. But what cruelty to let Pito see! Now he must go in with no hope of her, no strength of love to fight with. Pito would be killed for nothing.

Damundo, waving and kissing his hand, went into the room with the committee. Then they came out and put his clothes to the north of the door.

Pito went in, with one smile for his mother and for us. The committee came out and put his clothes to the south of the door.

One man, the head of the committee, now went inside with the snake. Soon he came out and tossed the empty sack aside. He put his hand on the door and called in, "Farewell to one of you." He shut the door.

All waited for the half of one minute. Nothing happened. Then began the piling of the empty cans against the door. But before the cans were halfway, a scream came from the Room of Dark. It was the voice of Pito.

I went away and came to the tree Pito and I had climbed so many times. I looked into the high branches and I swore to the tree that I would kill Damundo. I could kill him when he slept. I could kill him when he lay drunk. I could kill him on a dark path at night. Oh, I would find a way to kill him. And soon. And I also swore that the day I had a son, that day my son would be called Pito.

After a time I went back. Damundo had not come out. No one had come out. There had been no more sounds. The cans were now piled fully over the top of the door.

People talked of Pito's scream. Some said that it was a scream of pain. Others were not sure of this. Another boy and I thought that Pito had given more of a yell. A cry of angry hate. Our talk decided nothing.

Many people beside Pito's family stayed all night before the door. Angia watched too, but apart from everyone and no one spoke to her or took notice of her presence.

When morning came, I went with my mother to our house,

she to get us something to eat, I to put our cow into the field.

Our house is a little distance from the village, but as I was fastening the wire of the gate I heard the crashing down of the cans.

I ran with all my power, but when I got to the Room of Dark, Pito was already dressed and the committee was examining the method of Damundo.

The handle of his knife was hollow and the jeweled plate at the butt unscrewed. It was in the handle that Damundo kept a light of electricity. The light was no bigger than a thumb but, in the Room of Dark, strong and blinding. There is no trouble to kill a man if you are behind such a light.

The flashing on of the light had caused Pito to scream out in anger. Then he had reached down quickly and thrown a handful of sand at the light. The sand went into Damundo's eyes. He turned off the light because, being now blinded, the light was of danger to him.

Also it was believed that he dropped the light. It was found in another part of the room from where Pito and Damundo at last met.

Of the meeting, Pito had not much to say. The snake had rattled for him, as he thought. He had not moved. The snake went away, not rattling hard. Then suddenly it had rattled loud again. The snake must now be rattling at Damundo. This was all that Pito would say.

"But you were close to the wall, Pito," said old Uncle Juan.

"Your senses were alert and clear," said old Uncle Cantu. "Damundo was close. He moved because of the snake. You heard him."

"It is plain that you were close together and that you knew his direction because of the snake," said old Uncle Chaco. "But how, Pito, could you know just *when* to strike? Just *where* to strike?"

"When I am old, my Uncles," said Pito, "I may speak of

how I came to crash down the cans if the occasion is of importance. But that will be many years."

He went to where Angia stood, beautiful with smiles, and only I heard what they said.

"It was long, Angia," said Pito, "before it came to my mind why you made the greeting with him." He brought her hands to his face, then smiled, "You have washed them well."

"Very well, man of this heart."

"Good," said Pito. "The perfume of that foreign flower I never want to smell again."

And they walked away toward the sea.

THE DISTRIBUTOR

BY RICHARD MATHESON

Richard Matheson began writing at the age of seven, and had some early poems published in The Brooklyn Eagle, *the same journal which published Walt Whitman's fledgling works. Now, he numbers his stories in the 80s and his books at an even dozen. His novels include "The Beardless Warriors," "I Am Legend" and "The Shrinking Man" (they all became movies) and his collections are "Born of Man and Woman," "The Shores of Space" and a trio of shockers appropriately entitled "Shock," "Shock II" and "Shock III." He has done extensive work in films, notably most of the screenplays for the Poe adaptations starring Vincent Price. Deeply interested in psychic phenomena, he is at present writing a serious novel on that theme. "The Distributor," which won him the* PLAYBOY *Best Fiction Award, may well be one of the most controversial works of fiction ever published in a popular magazine, for it has as its tacit target the exploitation of prejudice and unreason, and drew bales of letters, both pro-and-con, when it first appeared.*

July 20

TIME to move. The real estate office had found him a small, furnished house on Sylmar Street. The Saturday morning he moved in he went around the neighborhood introducing himself.

"Good morning," he said to the old man pruning ivy next door. "My name is Theodore Gordon. I just moved in."

The old man straightened up and shook Theodore's hand. "How do," he said. His name was Joseph Alston.

A dog came shuffling from the porch to sniff Theodore's cuffs. "He's making up his mind about you," said the old man.

"Isn't that cute?" said Theodore.

Across the street lived Inez Ferrel. She answered the door in a housecoat, a thin woman in her late thirties. Theodore apologized for disturbing her.

"Oh, that's all right," she said. She had lots of time to herself when her husband was selling on the road.

"I hope we'll be good neighbors," said Theodore.

"I'm sure we will," said Inez Ferrel. She watched him through the window as he left.

Next door, directly across from his own house, he knocked quietly because there was a NIGHTWORKER SLEEPING sign. Dorothy Backus opened the door, a tiny, withdrawn woman in her middle thirties.

"I'm so glad to meet you," said Theodore.

Next door lived the Walter Mortons. As Theodore came up the walk, he heard Bianca Morton talking loudly to her son, Walter, Jr.

"You are not old enough to stay out till three o'clock in the morning!" she was saying. "Especially with a girl as young as Katherine McCann!"

Theodore knocked and Mr. Morton, 52 and bald, opened the door.

"I just moved in across the street," said Theodore, smiling at them.

Patty Jefferson let him in next door. As he talked to her Theodore could see, through the back window, her husband, Arthur, filling a rubber pool for their son and daughter.

"They just love that pool," said Patty, smiling.

"I bet they do," said Theodore. As he left, he noticed the vacant house next door.

Across the street from the Jeffersons lived the McCanns and their 14-year-old daughter Katherine. As Theodore approached the door he heard the voice of James McCann saying, "Aah, he's nuts. Why should I take his lawn edger? Just because I borrowed his lousy mower a couple of times."

"Darling, *please*," said Faye McCann, "I've got to finish these notes in time for the Council's next meeting."

"Just because Kathy goes out with his lousy son . . ." grumbled her husband.

Theodore knocked on the door and introduced himself. He chatted briefly with them, informing Mrs. McCann that he certainly *would* like to join the National Council of Christians and Jews. It was a worthy organization.

"What's your business, Gordon?" asked McCann.

"I'm in distribution," said Theodore.

Next door, two boys mowed and raked while their dog gamboled around them.

"Hello there," said Theodore. They grunted and watched him as he headed for the porch. The dog ignored him.

"I just *told* him," Henry Putnam's voice came through the living room window. "Put a coon in my department and I'm through. That's all."

"Yes, dear," said Mrs. Irma Putnam.

Theodore's knock was answered by the undershirted Mr. Putnam. His wife was lying on the sofa. Her heart, explained Mr. Putnam.

"Oh, I'm sorry," Theodore said.

In the last house lived the Gorses.

"I just moved in next door," said Theodore. He shook Eleanor Gorse's lean hand and she told him that her father was at work.

"Is that him?" asked Theodore, pointing at the portrait of a stony-faced old man that hung above a mantel crowded with religious objects.

"Yes," said Eleanor, 34 and ugly.

"Well, I hope we'll be good neighbors," Theodore said.

That afternoon, he went to his new office and set up the darkroom.

July 23

That morning, before he left for the office, he checked the telephone directory and jotted down four numbers. He dialed the first.

"Would you please send a cab to 12057 Sylmar Street?" he said. "Thank you."

He dialed the second number. "Would you please send a repairman to my house?" he said. "I don't get any picture. I live at 12070 Sylmar Street."

He dialed the third number. "I'd like to run this ad in Sunday's edition," he said. "1957 Ford. Perfect condition. Seven hundred and eighty-nine dollars. That's right, 789. The number is DA 4-7408."

Then he stood by the living room window until the taxicab stopped in front of the Backus house.

As he was driving off, a television repair truck passed him. He looked back and saw it stop in front of Henry Putnam's house.

Dear Sirs, he typed in the office later, *Please send me ten booklets for which I enclose $20.00 in payment.* He put down the name and address.

The envelope dropped into the OUT box.

July 27

When Inez Ferrel, the salesman's wife, left her house that evening, Theodore followed in his car. Downtown, Mrs. Ferrel got off the bus and went into a bar called The Irish Lantern. Parking, Theodore entered the bar cautiously and slipped into a shadowy booth.

Inez Ferrel was at the back of the room perched on a bar stool. She'd taken off her jacket to reveal a clinging yellow sweater. Theodore ran his gaze across the studied exposition of her bust.

At length, a man accosted her and spoke and laughed and spent a modicum of time with her. Theodore watched them exit, arm in arm. Paying for his coffee, he followed. It was a short walk; Mrs. Ferrel and the man entered a hotel on the next block.

Theodore drove home, whistling.

The next morning, when Eleanor Gorse and her father had left for church with Mrs. Backus, Theodore followed.

He met them in the church vestibule when the service was over. Wasn't it a wonderful coincidence, he said, that he, too, was a Baptist? And he shook the indurate hand of Donald Gorse.

As they walked into the sunshine, Theodore asked them if they wouldn't share his Sunday dinner with him. Mrs. Backus smiled faintly and murmured something about her husband. Donald Gorse looked doubtful.

"Oh, please," begged Theodore. "Make a lonely widower happy."

"Widower," tasted Mr. Gorse.

Theodore hung his head. "These many years," he said. "Pneumonia."

"Been a Baptist long?" asked Mr. Gorse.

"Since birth," said Theodore with fervor. "It's been my only solace."

For dinner he served lamb chops, peas and mashed potatoes. For dessert, apple cobbler and coffee.

"I'm so pleased you'd share my humble food," he said. "This is, truly, loving thy neighbor as thyself." He smiled at Eleanor who returned it stiffly.

That evening, as darkness fell, Theodore took a stroll. As he passed the McCann house, he heard the telephone ringing, then James McCann shouting, "It's a *mistake*, damn it! Why in the lousy hell should I sell a '57 Ford for seven hundred and eighty-nine bucks?"

The phone slammed down. "God *damn*!" howled James McCann. "Darling, please be *tolerant*!" begged his wife. The telephone rang again.

Theodore moved on.

August 1

At exactly 2:15 A.M. Theodore slipped outside, pulled up one of Joseph Alston's longest ivy plants and left it on the sidewalk.

In the morning, as he left the house, he saw Walter Morton, Jr., heading for the McCann house with a blanket, a towel and a portable radio. The old man was replanting the ivy.

"Was it pulled up?" asked Theodore.

Joseph Alston grunted.

"So *that* was it," said Theodore.

"*What?*" The old man looked up.

"Last night," said Theodore, "I heard some noise out here. I looked out and saw a couple of boys."

"You seen their faces?" asked Alston, his face hardening.

"No, it was too dark," said Theodore, "but I'd say they were—oh, about the age of the Putnam boys. Not that it was them, of course."

Joe Alston nodded slowly, looking up the street.

Theodore drove up to the boulevard and parked. Twenty minutes later, Walter Morton, Jr., and Katherine McCann boarded a bus.

At the beach, Theodore sat a few yards behind them.

"That Mack is a character," he heard Walter Morton say. "He gets the urge, he drives to Tijuana; just for kicks."

In a while Morton and the girl ran into the ocean, laughing. Theodore stood and walked to a telephone booth.

"I'd like to have a swimming pool installed in my back yard next week," he said, "my name is Backus."

Back on the beach he sat patiently until Walter Morton and the girl were lying in each other's arms. Then, at specific moments, he pressed a shutter hidden in his palm. This done, he returned to his car, buttoning his shirt front over the tiny lens. On his way to the office, he stopped at a hardware store to buy a brush and a can of black paint.

He spent the afternoon printing the pictures. He made them appear as if they had been taken at night and as if the young couple had been engaged in something else.

The envelope dropped softly into the OUT box.

August 5

The street was silent and deserted. Tennis shoes soundless on the paving, Theodore moved across the street.

He found the Mortons' lawn mower in the back yard. Lifting it quietly, he carried it back across the street to the McCann garage. After carefully raising the door, he slid the mower behind the workbench. The envelope of photographs he put in a drawer behind a box of nails.

Returning to his house then, he phoned James McCann and, muffledly, asked if the Ford was still for sale.

In the morning, the mailman placed a bulky envelope on the Gorses' porch. Gorse's daughter Eleanor emerged and opened it, sliding out one of the booklets. Theodore watched the furtive look she cast about, the rising of dark color in her cheeks.

As he was mowing the lawn that evening he saw Walter Morton, Sr., march across the street to where James McCann was trimming bushes. He heard them talking loudly. Finally, they went into McCann's garage from which Morton emerged pushing his lawn mower and making no reply to McCann's angry protests.

Across the street from McCann, Arthur Jefferson was just getting home from work. The two Putnam boys were riding their bicycles, their dog racing around them.

Now, across from where Theodore stood, a door slammed. He turned his head and watched Mr. Backus, in work clothes, storming to his car, muttering disgustedly, *"A swimming pool!"* Theodore looked to the next house and saw Inez Ferrel moving in her living room.

He smiled and mowed along the side of his house, glancing into Eleanor Gorse's bedroom. She was sitting with her back to him, reading something. When she heard the clatter of his mower she stood and left the bedroom, pushing the bulky envelope into a bureau drawer.

August 15

Henry Putnam answered the door.

"Good evening," said Theodore, "I hope I'm not intruding on you . . . ?"

"Just chatting in the den with Irma's folks," said Putnam. "They're drivin' to New York in the mornin'."

"Oh? Well, I'll only be a moment." Theodore held out a pair of BB guns. "A plant I distribute for was getting rid of these," he said. "I thought your two boys might like them."

"Well, *sure*," said Putnam. He started for the den to get his sons.

While Putnam was gone, Theodore picked up a couple of

matchbooks whose covers read *Putnam's Wines and Liquors.* He'd slipped them into his pocket before the boys were led in to thank him.

"Mighty nice of you, Gordon," said Putnam at the door. "Sure appreciate it."

"My pleasure," said Theodore.

Walking home, he set the clock-radio for 3:15 and lay down. When the music began, he moved outside on silent feet and tore up 47 ivy plants, strewing them over Alston's sidewalk.

"Oh, *no*," he said to Alston in the morning. He shook his head, appalled.

Joseph Alston didn't speak. He glanced down the block with hating eyes.

"Here, let me help you," Theodore said. The old man shook his head but Theodore insisted. Driving to the nearest nursery he brought back two sacks of peat moss, then squatted by Alston's side to help him replant.

"You hear anything last night?" the old man asked.

"You think it was those boys again?" asked Theodore, open-mouthed.

"Ain't sayin'," Alston said.

Later, Theodore drove downtown and bought a dozen postcard photographs. He took them to the office.

Dear Walt, he printed crudely on the back of one, *Got these here in Tijuana. Hot enough for you?* In addressing the envelope, he failed to add *Jr. to Mr. Walter Morton.*

Into the OUT box.

August 23

"Mrs. Ferrel!"

She shuddered on the bar stool. "Why, Mister——"

"Gordon," he provided, smiling. "How nice to see you again."

"Yes." She pressed together lips that trembled.

"You come here often?" Theodore asked.

"Oh, no, *never*," Inez Ferrel blurted, "I'm—just supposed to meet a friend here tonight. A *girl* friend."

"Oh I see," said Theodore. "Well, may a lonely widower keep you company until she comes?"

"Why . . ." Mrs. Ferrel shrugged. "I guess." Her lips were painted brightly red against the alabaster of her skin. The sweater clung adhesively to the hoisted jut of her breasts.

After a while, when Mrs. Ferrel's friend didn't show up, they slid into a darkened booth. There, Theodore used Mrs. Ferrel's powder room retreat to slip a pale and tasteless powder into her drink. On her return she swallowed this and, in minutes, grew stupefied. She smiled at Theodore.

"I like you Misser Gor'n," she confessed. The words crawled viscidly across her lolling tongue.

Shortly thereafter, he led her, stumbling and giggling, to his car and drove her to a motel. Inside the room, he helped her strip to stockings, garter belt and shoes, and, while she posed with drugged complacency, Theodore took flashbulb pictures.

After she'd collapsed at two A.M., Theodore dressed her and drove her home. He stretched her fully dressed across her bed. After that he went outside and poured concentrated weed killer on Alston's replanted ivy.

Back in the house he dialed the Jefferson's number.

"Yes?" said Arthur Jefferson, irritably.

"Get out of this neighborhood or you'll be sorry," whispered Theodore, then hung up.

In the morning he walked to Mrs. Ferrel's house and rang the bell.

"Hello," he said politely. "Are you feeling better?"

She stared at him blankly while he explained how she'd gotten violently ill the night before and he'd taken her home from the bar. "I do hope you're feeling better," he concluded.

"Yes," she said, confusedly, "I'm—all right."

As he left her house he saw a red-faced James McCann approaching the Morton house, the envelope of photographs in his hand. Beside him walked a distraught Mrs. McCann.

"We must be *tolerant*, Jim," Theodore heard her say.

August 31

At 2:15 A.M. Theodore took the brush and the can of paint and went outside.

Walking to the Jefferson house he set the can down and painted, jaggedly, across the door—NIGGER!

Then he moved across the street allowing an occasional drip of paint. He left the can under Henry Putnam's back porch, accidentally upsetting the dog's plate. Fortunately, the Putnam's dog slept indoors.

Later, he put more weed killer on Joseph Alston's ivy.

In the morning, when Donald Gorse had gone to work, he took a heavy envelope and went to see Eleanor Gorse. "Look at this," he said, sliding a pornographic booklet from the envelope. "I received this in the mail today. *Look* at it." He thrust it into her hands.

She held the booklet as if it were a spider.

"Isn't it hideous?" he said.

She made a face. "*Revolting*," she said.

"I thought I'd check with you and several others before I phoned the police," said Theodore. "Have *you* received any of this filth?"

Eleanor Gorse bristled. "Why should *I* receive them?" she demanded.

Outside, Theodore found the old man squatting by his ivy. "How are they coming?" he asked.

"They're dyin'."

Theodore looked stricken. "How can this be?" he asked.

Alston shook his head.

"Oh, this is *horrible*." Theodore turned away, clucking. As he walked to his house he saw, up the street, Arthur Jefferson cleaning off his door and, across the way, Henry Putnam watching carefully.

Mrs. McCann was waiting on his porch.

"Well," said Theodore, surprised, "I'm so glad to see you."

"What I came to say may not make you so glad," she said unhappily.

"Oh?" said Theodore. They went into his house.

"There have been a lot of . . . *things* happening in this neighborhood since you moved in," said Mrs. McCann after they were seated in the living room.

"Things?" asked Theodore.

"I think you know what I mean," said Mrs. McCann. "However, this—this *bigotry* on Mr. Jefferson's door is too much, Mr. Gordon, too much."

Theodore gestured helplessly. "I don't understand."

"Please don't make it difficult," she said. "I may have to call the authorities if these things don't stop, Mr. Gordon. I hate to think of doing such a thing but——"

"*Authorities?*" Theodore looked terrified.

"None of these things happened until you moved in, Mr. Gordon," she said. "Believe me, I hate what I'm saying, but I simply have no choice. The fact that none of these things have happened to you——"

She broke off startledly as a sob wracked Theodore's chest. She stared at him. "Mr. Gordon——" she began, uncertainly.

"I don't know what these things are you speak of," said Theodore in a shaking voice, "but I'd *kill* myself before I harmed a fellow human being, Mrs. McCann."

He looked around as if to make sure they were alone.

"I'm going to tell you something I've never told a single

soul," he said. He wiped away a tear. "My name isn't Gordon," he said. "It's Gottlieb. I'm a Jew. I spent a year at Dachau."

Mrs. McCann's lips moved but she said nothing. Her face was getting red.

"I came from there a broken man," said Theodore. "I haven't long to live, Mrs. McCann. My wife is dead, my three children are dead. I'm all alone. I only want to live in peace—in a little place like this—among people like you. To be a neighbor, a friend . . ."

"Mr.—*Gottlieb*," she said, brokenly.

After she was gone, Theodore stood silent in the living room, hands clenched whitely at his sides. Then he went into the kitchen to discipline himself.

"Good morning, Mrs. Backus," he said an hour later when the mousy little woman answered the door, "I wonder if I might ask you some questions about our church?"

"Oh. Oh, yes." She stepped back feebly. "Won't you—come in?"

"I'll be very still so as not to wake your husband," Theodore whispered. He saw her looking at his bandaged hand. "I burned myself," he said. "Now, about the church. Oh, there's someone knocking at your back door."

"There is?"

When she'd gone into the kitchen, Theodore pulled open the hall closet door and dropped the photographs of Inez Ferrel behind a pile of overshoes and garden tools. The door was shut when she returned.

"There wasn't anyone," she said.

"I could have sworn . . ." He smiled depreciatingly. He looked down at a circular bag on the floor. "Oh, does Mr. Backus bowl?"

"Wednesdays and Fridays when his shift is over," she said. "There's an all-night alley over on Western Avenue."

"I love to bowl," said Theodore.

He asked his questions about the church, then left. As he started down the path he heard loud voices from the Morton house.

"It wasn't bad enough about Katherine McCann and *those* awful pictures," shrieked Mrs. Morton. "Now these . . . filthy postcards!"

"But Mom!" cried Walter, Jr.

September 14

Theodore awoke and turned the radio off. Standing, he put a small bottle of grayish powder in his pocket and slipped from the house. Reaching his destination, he sprinkled powder into the dog's water bowl and stirred it with a finger until it dissolved.

Back in the house he scrawled four letters reading: *Arthur Jefferson is trying to pass the color line. He is my cousin and should admit he is a Negro like the rest of us. I am doing this for his own good.*

He signed the letter *John Thomas Jefferson* and addressed three of the envelopes to Donald Gorse, the Mortons and Mr. Henry Putnam. The fourth he addressed to himself.

In the morning, he saw Mrs. Backus walking toward the boulevard and followed. "May I walk with you?" he asked.

"Oh," she said. "All right."

"I missed your husband last night," he told her.

She glanced at him.

"I thought I'd join him bowling," Theodore said, "but I guess he was sick again."

"Sick?"

"I asked the man behind the counter at the alley and he said that Mr. Backus hadn't been coming in because he was sick."

"Oh?" Mrs. Backus' voice was thinly stricken.

"Well, maybe next Friday," said Theodore.

Later, when he came back, he saw the animal shelter truck in front of Henry Putnam's house. A man came out of the alley carrying the blanket-wrapped dog which he laid in the truck. The Putnam boys were crying as they watched.

Arthur Jefferson answered the door. Theodore showed the letter to Jefferson and his wife. "It came this morning," he said.

"This is *monstrous*!" said Jefferson, reading it.

"Of *course* it is," said Theodore. "Negroes *indeed*."

While they were talking, Jefferson looked through the window at the Putnam house across the street.

September 15

Pale morning mist engulfed Sylmar Street. Theodore moved through it silently. Under the back porch of the Jefferson's house he set fire to a box of damp papers. As it began to smolder he walked across the yard, and, with a single knife stroke, slashed apart the rubber pool. He heard it pulsing water on the grass as he left. In the alley, he dropped a book of matches that read *Putnam's Wines and Liquors*.

A little after six that morning he woke to the howl of sirens and felt the small house tremble at the heavy trucks passing by. Turning on his side, he yawned and mumbled "Goody."

September 17

It was a trembling Mrs. Backus who answered Theodore's knock that Sunday morning.

"May I drive you to church?" asked Theodore.

"I—I don't believe I—I'm not . . . feeling too well," stumbled Mrs. Backus.

"Oh, I'm sorry," Theodore said. He saw the photographs of Inez Ferrel protruding from her apron pocket.

Theodore went to church with Donald Gorse who said that his daughter Eleanor was feeling ill.

"I'm so sorry," Theodore said.

That afternoon, he spent a while at the Jefferson house helping clear away the charred debris of their back porch. When he saw the slashed rubber pool he drove immediately to a drug store and bought another one.

"But they love that pool," said Theodore, when Patty Jefferson protested. "You told me so yourself."

He winked at Arthur Jefferson but Jefferson was not communicative that afternoon.

September 23

Early in the evening Theodore saw Alston's dog walking in the street. He got his BB gun and, from the bedroom window, soundlessly, fired. The dog nipped fiercely at its side and spun around. Then, whimpering, it started home.

Several minutes later, Theodore went outside and started pulling up the door to the garage. He saw the old man hurrying down his alley, the dog in his arms.

"What's wrong?" asked Theodore.

"Don't know," said Alston in a breathless, frightened voice. "He's hurt."

"Quickly!" said Theodore. "Into my car!"

He rushed Alston and the dog to the nearest veterinary, passing three stop signs and groaning when the old man held his hand up, palsiedly, and whimpered, "*Blood*."

For three hours Theodore sat in the veterinary's waiting room until the old man staggered forth, his face a grayish white.

"*No*," said Theodore, jumping to his feet.

He led the old man, weeping, to the car and drove him home. There, Alston said he'd rather be alone so Theodore left. Shortly afterward, the black and white police car rolled to a stop in front of Alston's house and the old man led the two officers down the street, telling them that the Putnam boys had shot his dog.

September 27

"Good evening," said Theodore. He bowed.

Eleanor Gorse nodded stiffly.

"I've brought you and your father a casserole," said Theodore, smiling, holding up a towel-wrapped dish. When she told him that her father was gone for the night Theodore clucked and sighed as if he hadn't seen the old man drive away that afternoon.

"Well then," he said, proffering the dish, "for *you*. With my sincerest compliments."

Stepping off the porch he saw Arthur Jefferson and Henry Putnam standing under a street lamp down the block. While he watched, Arthur Jefferson struck the other man and, suddenly, they were brawling in the gutter. Theodore broke into a hurried run.

"But this is *terrible!*" he gasped, pulling the men apart.

"Stay out of this!" warned Jefferson, then, to Putnam, challenged, "You better tell me how that paint can got under your porch! The police may believe it was an accident I found that matchbook in my alley but I don't!"

"I'll tell you nothing," Putnam said, contemptuously, "*coon.*"

"Coon! Oh, of course! You'd be the first to believe that, you stupid——!"

Five times Theodore stood between them. It wasn't until Jefferson had, accidentally, struck him on the nose that tension faded. Curtly, Jefferson apologized; then, with a murderous look at Putnam, left.

"Sorry he hit you," Putnam sympathized. "Damned boogie."

"Oh, surely you're mistaken," Theodore said, daubing at his nostrils. "Mr. Jefferson told me how afraid he was of people believing this talk. Because of the value of his two houses, you know."

"Two?" asked Putnam.

"Yes, he owns the vacant house next door to his," said Theodore. "I assumed you knew."

"*No*," said Putnam, warily.

"Well, you see," said Theodore, "if people think Mr. Jefferson is a Negro, the value of his houses will go down."

"So will the values of all of them," said Putnam, glaring across the street. "That dirty son-of-a——"

Theodore patted his shoulder. "How are your wife's parents enjoying their stay in New York?" he asked as if changing the subject.

"They're on their way back," said Putnam.

"Good," said Theodore. "And how is Mrs. Putnam's heart?"

Putnam shrugged. "About the same, I guess," he said.

Theodore went home and read the funny papers for an hour. Then he went out.

A florid-faced Eleanor Gorse opened to his knock. Her bathrobe was disarrayed, her dark eyes feverish.

"May I get my dish?" asked Theodore politely.

She grunted, stepping back jerkily. His hand, in passing, brushed on hers. She twitched away as if he'd stabbed her.

"Ah, you've eaten it all," said Theodore, noticing the tiny residue of powder on the bottom of the dish. He turned. "When will your father return?" he asked.

Her body seemed to tense. "After midnight," she muttered.

Theodore stepped to the wall switch and cut off the light. He heard her gasp in the darkness. "No," she muttered.

"Is this what you want, Eleanor?" he asked, grabbing harshly.

Her embrace was a mindless, fiery swallow. There was nothing but burning flesh beneath her robe.

Later, when she lay snoring satedly on the kitchen floor, Theodore retrieved the camera he'd left outside the door. Drawing down the shades, he arranged Eleanor's limbs and took 12 exposures. Then he retrieved the dish, went home and washed it.

Before retiring, he phoned the Putnams.

"Western Union," he said. "I have a message for Mrs. Irma Putnam of 12070 Sylmar Street."

"That's me," she said.

"Both parents killed in auto collision this afternoon," said Theodore. "Await word regarding disposition of bodies. Chief of Police, Tulsa, Okla——"

At the other end of the line there was a strangled gasp, a thud; then Henry Putnam's cry of "Irma!" Theodore hung up.

After the ambulance had come and gone, he went outside and tore up 35 of Joseph Alston's ivy plants. He left, in the debris, another matchbook reading *Putnam's Wines and Liquors*.

September 28

In the morning, when Donald Gorse had gone to work, Theodore went over. Eleanor tried to shut the door on him but he pushed in.

"I want money," he said. "These are my collateral." He threw down copies of the photographs and Eleanor recoiled, gagging. "Your father will receive a set of these tonight," he said, "unless I get two hundred dollars."

"But I——!"

"*Tonight*." He left and drove downtown to the real estate office where he signed some papers and sold his house.

When he returned home, there was a police car in front of the Backus house.

"What happened?" he asked Joseph Alston who was sitting quietly on his porch.

"Mrs. Backus," said the old man, lifelessly. "She tried to kill Mrs. Ferrel."

"But *why?*" asked Theodore.

"Dunno," said Alston. "Something about pictures."

That night, in his office, Theodore made his entries on page 700 of the book.

Mrs. Ferrel dying of knife wounds in local hospital. Mrs. Backus in jail; suspects husband of adultery. J. Alston accused of dog poisoning, probably more. Putnam boys accused of shooting Alston's dog, ruining his lawn. Mrs. Putnam dead of heart attack. Mr. Putnam being sued for property destruction. Jeffersons thought to be Negroes. McCanns and Mortons deadly enemies. Katherine McCann believed to have had relations with Walter Morton, Jr. Morton, Jr. being sent to school in Washington. Eleanor Gorse has hanged herself. Job completed.

Time to move.

LAST WILL AND TESTAMENT

BY RAY RUSSELL

We close this book with a little piece that, being plotless, is hardly a story at all; and yet, in well under a thousand words, it proffers sardonic wit, irony, wisdom, a couple of original poems, a catalog of crimes that includes incest, fratricide, matricide, uxoricide and suicide—plus something of a surprise at the end.

EVENTS HAVING TAKEN an unexpected and intolerable turn, I, the undersigned, sound of mind and body, having this day resolved to die by my own hand, do acknowledge the following articles as my final words and solemn legacy:

To my lovely and loving wife, were she alive, I should have left that which is now without value to me, my worldly goods. Esteeming, as she did, material things above all else, she would have been welcome to all of my estates and possessions. I do not expect to meet her spirit in the other world: she was so much of the flesh that I am certain she ceased to be the moment I killed her.

To my advisors, I leave the guidance and comfort of their own advice.

To the shades of my mother, my half-brother, and my first wife, I send my greetings before me and my heartfelt apologies for having murdered their fleshly counterparts. Also these messages:

To my first wife: my dear, I look forward to your company. In this life, I never appreciated you. Your gentle wit, your graciousness, your nobility and charm of person were wasted upon me. In the fever of my youth, I preferred the hot limbs of your successor to the cool wisdom of your conversation. Forgive me, my dear. My erring flesh I leave behind me. Welcome my flawless spirit, I entreat you.

Brother, I know you were angry with me after I fed you that poison. I felt your spirit haunting me for months. Gradually, you stopped, so I assume that you have forgiven me and have reflected that, after all, one of us had to go. If you had thought of it first, *I* would have been the haunting spirit. See how time brings equality to everything. Soon I, too, will be a spirit and there will be no jealousy between us. I look forward to meeting you again.

Mother, between us there need be no apologies. In this life you became an obstruction. In the realm of the spirit you will be a constant joy. Let me assure you that I have never felt shame about our intimacy, that the criticism levelled at us by moralists has neither brought a blush to my face nor regret to my heart. Man is born out of Woman. What could be more fitting, more poetic, than that she should introduce him to the mysteries of Aphrodite? I have always considered *King Oedipus* an exciting, but silly, play.

It is well known that I am gifted with a poetic turn-of-mind. Perhaps, then, I may be forgiven for lapsing into verse for a brief space here. It is not, perhaps, my best, but be charitable— it is my last. To the common man, I leave these lines:

> *I stand apart from the ugly folk.*
> *The ugly folk with unbeautiful voices*
> *Choke the streets and arbors that I*
> *   love,*
> *Obstructing beauty, filtering it*
> *Through literal minds and tiny souls*
> *And unenthusiastic appetites.*
>
> *I stand apart. I may not be*
> *A lovely thing to hear nor yet to see;*
> *My soul is maybe puny, and my mind*
> *Is often narrower than humankind;*
> *My lusts, off-hand sometimes, and*
> *   lacking heart.*
> *No matter. I am I. I stand apart.*

To my venerable tutors, both living and dead: to all philosophers and logicians in general, I leave this little jingle:

> *A traitor serpent sleeps below*
> *Who rises at a glance, a play*

Of light upon a curve, a sway
Of flesh, deliberate and slow.

Come off it, then. Cast off your load
Of logic, for it's all a whim
That can be swept away by him
Each time he hankers to explode.

Enough of that. My muse is satisfied.

To Posterity; to the bloodhounds and scavengers of history; to that breed of men who presume to judge other men; to the shaking heads and clucking tongues and the hands thrown high in horror, I send greetings and some wisdom garnered during a relatively short but immeasurably full life:

Turn your eyes inward. Examine mercilessly your weaknesses, your prejudices, your passions. Peer deep, deep down into the dark and airless labyrinth of unvoiced, unsated, sometimes unheard-of, almost unthought-of desires. Bring out each black lust and vengeful feeling; root out all selfish thoughts; line them up and scrutinize them in the clear unwavering light of Total Honesty. Reflect how opportunity combined with authority might have made Acts out of those hideous Caprices cowering there in the light. And then—then only—in the words of that renegade Jew of Nazareth, "He that is without sin among you, let him first cast a stone."

These articles I do most earnestly pledge to be my legacy, to which I affix my signature below, calling as witness the spirit of my foster father, Claudius, now enthroned among the gods in timeless glory.

—*Nero, Emperor of Rome.*

INDEX OF AUTHORS